Alice Through the Zombie Glass

GENA SHOWALTER

The White Rabbit Chronicles

Book 2

MIRA Ink is a registered trademark of Harlequin Enterprises Limited, used under licence.

This Edition Published in Great Britain 2016
by MIRA Ink, an imprint of Harlequin (UK) Limited,
Eton House, 18-24 Paradise Road,
Richmond, Surrey, TW9 1SR

© 2013 Gena Showalter
(Originally published as *Through The Zombie Glass*)

ISBN 978 1 848 45253 4

47-0214

Harlequin (UK) Limited's policy is to use papers that are natural, renewable and recyclable products and made from wood grown in sustainable forests. The logging and manufacturing processes conform to the legal environmental regulations of the country of origin.

Printed and bound in Great Britain

To three bright lights in my life—
Shane, Shonna and Michelle

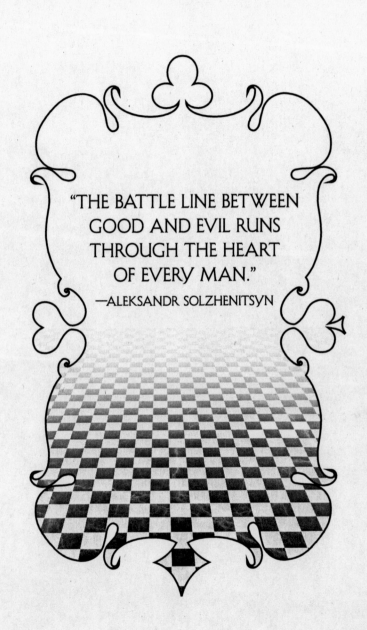

"THE BATTLE LINE BETWEEN GOOD AND EVIL RUNS THROUGH THE HEART OF EVERY MAN."

—ALEKSANDR SOLZHENITSYN

A NOTE FROM ALI

Where should I begin?

With travesty? Heartache?

No. I don't want to begin with where I am now.

I don't want to end that way, either.

We'll start with this. A truth. Everything around us is subject to change. Today is cold. Tomorrow, heat will come. Flowers bloom, then wither. Those we love, we can grow to hate. And life...life can be perfect one minute and in shambles the next. I learned that lesson the hard way when my parents and beloved little sister died in a car crash, shattering every corridor of my heart.

I've done my best to weld the pieces back together, but—*tick, tock.* Another change.

A change that cost me everything.

The respect of my friends. My new home. My purpose. My pride.

My boyfriend.

And it's my fault. I can blame no one else.

One mistake gave birth to a thousand others.

I knew there were monsters out there. Zombies. I knew they weren't the mindless beings movies and books portrayed them to be. They exist in spirit form, unseen to the ungifted eye. They're fast, determined and, at times, smart. They hunger for the source of life. *Our* spirits.

I know, I know. That's laughable, right? Invisible creatures determined to feast on humans from the inside out? Please. But it's true. I know, because I became an all-you-can-eat buffet—and offered my friends as dessert.

Now I'm not just fighting the zombies. I'm fighting to save the life I've grown to love.

I will succeed.

Tick, tock.

It's time.

BEGIN AT THE BEGINNING

A few months earlier

More and more I'd been dreaming about the crash that killed my parents and younger sister. I relived the moments as our car flipped end over end. The sounds of metal crunching into pavement. The stillness when everything was over, and I was the only one awake…maybe the only one alive.

I'd struggled to free myself from the seat belt, desperate to help little Emma. Her head had been twisted at such an odd angle. My mother's cheek had been slashed open like a Christmas ham, and my father's body had been thrown out of the car. Panic had made me stupid, and I'd hit my head on a sharp piece of metal. Darkness had swallowed me whole.

But in my dreams, I watched my mother blink open her eyes. She was disoriented at first, moaning in pain and trying to make sense of the chaos around her.

Unlike me, she had no problem with her seat belt, freeing herself and turning, her gaze landing on Emma. Tears began to rain down her cheeks.

She looked at me and gasped, reaching out to place a trembling hand on my leg. A river of warmth seemed to rush through me, strengthening me.

"Alice," she shouted, shaking me. "Wake up—"

I jolted upright.

Panting, my body dotted with perspiration, I scanned my surroundings. I saw walls of ivory and gold, painted in swirling patterns. An antique dresser. A furry white rug on the floor. A mahogany nightstand, with a Tiffany lamp perched next to a photo of my boyfriend, Cole.

I was in my new bedroom, safe.

Alone.

My heart slammed against my ribs as though trying to burst free. I forced the dream to the back of my mind and moved to the edge of the bed to peer out the large bay window and find a sense of calm. Despite the gorgeousness of the view—a garden teeming with bright, lush flowers that somehow thrived in the cool October weather—my stomach twisted. Night was in full bloom, and so were the creepies.

Fog that had brewed on the horizon for hours had finally spilled over, gliding closer and closer to my window. The moon was round and full, set ablaze with orange and red, as if the surface had been wounded and was bleeding.

Anything was possible.

Zombies were out tonight.

My friends were out there, too, fighting the creatures

without me. I hated myself for falling asleep at such a critical time. What if a slayer needed my help? Called me?

Who was I kidding? No one would call, no matter how badly I was needed.

I stood and paced the room, cursing the injuries that kept me tucked inside. So I'd been sliced from hip to hip a few weeks ago. So what? My stitches had been removed and the flesh was already scarring.

Maybe I should just arm up and head out. I'd rather save someone I love and risk another life-threatening injury than do nothing and stay out of harm's way. But…I didn't know where the group had gone, and more than that, if I did manage to track them down, Cole would freak. He would be distracted.

Distraction killed.

Dang it. I would do as I'd been told and wait.

Minutes stretched into hours as I continued to pace, a sense of unease growing sharper with every second that passed. Would everyone come back alive? We'd lost two slayers in the past month alone. None of us were prepared to lose another.

The hinges on my door squeaked.

Cole slipped inside the room and threw the lock, ensuring that no one would bust in on us. Relief plucked the claws right out of the unease, and I thrilled.

He was here. He was okay.

He was mine.

His gaze landed on me, and I shivered, waiting for a vision…hoping for one.

Since the day we'd met, we'd experienced a small glimpse

of the future the first time our eyes locked on any given day. We'd seen ourselves making out, fighting zombies and even relaxing in a swing. Today, like almost every day since my stabbing, I experienced nothing but crushing disappointment.

Why had the visions stopped?

Deep down, I suspected one of us had built up some sort of emotional wall—and I knew it hadn't been me.

I was too entranced by him.

Always he threw off enough testosterone to draw the notice of every girl within a ten-mile radius. Though he was only seventeen years old, he seemed far older. He had major experience on the battlefield, had fought in the human/ zombie war since he could walk. He had experience with girls, too. Maybe *too* much experience. He knew just what to say…how to touch…and we melted. I'd never met anyone like him. I doubted I ever would again.

He wore all black, like a phantom of the night. Inky hair stuck out in spikes, with leaves and twigs intertwined in the strands. He hadn't bothered to clean his face, so his cheeks were streaked with black paint, dirt and blood.

So. Danged. Hot.

Violet eyes almost otherworldly in their purity shuttered, becoming unreadable, even as his lips compressed into a hard, anguished line. I knew him, and knew this was his let's-just-burn-the-world-to-the-ground-and-call-it-good face.

"What are you doing out of bed, Ali?"

I ignored the question as well as the harshness of his tone, understanding that both sprang from a place of deep concern for me. "What's wrong?" I asked. "What happened out there?"

Silent, he disarmed, dropping daggers, guns, magazines of ammo and his personal favorite, a crossbow. He'd come to me first, I realized, not even bothering to stop at his house.

"Were you bitten?" I asked. Suffering? Zombie bites left a burning toxin behind. Yes, we had an antidote, but the human body could take only so much before it broke down.

"I saw Haun," he finally responded.

Oh, no. "Cole, I'm so sorry." A while back, Haun had been killed by zombies. The fact that Cole had seen him again meant only one thing. Haun had risen from his grave as the enemy.

"I suspected it would happen, but I wasn't ready for the reality of it." Cole's shirt was the next to go.

The blade-sharp cut of his body always stole my breath, and now was no exception, regardless of the horror of our conversation. I drank him in—the delightfully wicked nipple ring, the sinewy chest and washboard abs covered with a plethora of tattoos. Every design, every word, meant something to him, from the names of the friends he'd lost in the war to the depiction of the grim reaper's scythe. Because that was what he was. A zombie killer.

He was total bad boy—the dangerous guy monsters feared finding in *their* closets.

And he was closing the distance between us. I buzzed with anticipation, expecting him to draw me into his arms. Instead, he bypassed me to fall onto the bed and cover his face with scabbed hands.

"I ashed him tonight. Ended him forever."

"I'm so sorry." I eased beside him and brushed my fingers over his thigh, offering what comfort I could. I knew he understood that he hadn't actually ashed Haun, or even the ghost of Haun. The creature he'd fought hadn't had Haun's memories or his personality. It had had his face and nothing more. His body had simply been a shell for unending hunger and malevolence.

"You had to do it," I added. "If you'd let him go, he would have come back for you and our friends, and he would have done his best to destroy us."

"I know, but that doesn't make it any easier." He released a shuddering sigh.

I looked him over more intently. He had angry cuts on his arms, chest and stomach. Zombies were spirits, the source of life—or afterlife in their case—and had to be fought by other spirits. That was why, to engage, we had to force ours out of our bodies, like a hand being pulled out of glove. And yet, even though we left our bodies behind, frozen in place, the two were still connected. Whatever injury one received, the other received, as well.

I padded to the bathroom, wet several washrags and grabbed a tube of antibiotic cream.

"Tomorrow I start training again," I said as I tended him, distracting us both.

He glared up at me through lashes so thick and black he looked as if he wore eyeliner. "Tomorrow's Halloween. All of us have the day and night off. And by the way, I'm taking you to a costume party at the club. I'm thinking we'll stick with the whole battered and bruised theme and go as a naughty nurse and even naughtier patient."

My first outing in weeks would be a date with Cole. *Yes, please.* "I think you'll make a very sexy naughty nurse."

"I know," he said without missing a beat. "Just wait till you see my dress. Slutty doesn't even begin to describe. And you will, of course, require a sponge bath."

Don't laugh. "Promises, promises." I tsked, then tried to continue more seriously. "But I never mentioned hunting." Too many people would be out, and some would be dressed as zombies. At first glance, we might not be able to tell the real deal from the fake. "I only mentioned training. You *are* working out tomorrow morning, aren't you?" He always did.

He ignored my question, saying, "You're not ready."

"No, *you're* not ready for me to be ready, but it's happening whether you like it or not."

He scowled at me, dark and dangerous. "Is that so?"

"Yes." Not many people stood up to Cole Holland. Everyone at our school considered him a full-blown predator, more animal than human. Feral. Dangerous.

They weren't wrong.

Cole wouldn't hesitate to tear into someone—anyone—for the slightest offense. Except me. I could do what I wanted, say what I wanted, and he was charmed. Even when he was scowling. And it was strange, definitely something I wasn't used to—having power over someone else—but I'd be lying if I claimed not to like it.

"Two problems with your plan," he said. "One, you don't have a key to the gym. And two, there's a good chance your instructor will suddenly become unreachable."

Since *he* was my instructor, I took his words as the gentle threat they were and sighed.

When I'd first joined his group, he'd thrown me into the thick of battle without hesitation. I think he'd trusted his ability to protect me from any kind of threat more than he'd trusted my skills.

Then I'd proved myself and he'd backed off.

Then he'd accidentally stabbed me.

Yep. Him. He'd aimed for the zombie snarling and biting at him; I'd stepped in to help, and, with a single touch, ashed the only thing shielding my body from his strike. Cole had yet to forgive himself.

Maybe that was why he'd built a wall.

Maybe he needed a reminder of just how wily I could be.

"Cole," I said huskily, and his eyelids lowered to half-mast.

"Yes, Ali."

"This." A slow smile spread as I circled my hands around his ankles—and jerked. He slid off the bed and thumped to the floor.

"What the hell?"

I leaped on top of him, pinning his shoulders with my knees. The action caused the scar on my stomach to throb, but I masked my wince with another smile. "What are you going to do now, Mr. Holland?"

He watched me intently, amusement darkening his irises. "I think I'll just enjoy the view." He gripped me by the waist, squeezed just enough to make sure he had my full attention. "From this angle, I can see your—"

Choking back a laugh, I took a swing at him.

"Shorts," he finished, catching my hand just before impact. I wasn't given the chance to tug free. He rolled me over, stretched my arms over my head and held me down.

Tricky slayer.

"What are you going to do now, Miss Bell?"

Stay just like this and enjoy? I could smell the pine and soap of his scent. Could hear the rasp of our breath intermingling. Could feel the heat and hardness of his body pressing against me.

"What would you like me to do?" I met his gaze, and the air around us thickened, charged with electricity.

Would he touch me?

I wanted him to touch me.

"You're not ready for what I'd like you to do." He searched my face as he reached between us, his actions belying his words...*please, please*...until he slowly pushed the hem of my tee over my navel, revealing every inch of damaged flesh.

He looked me over, and my stomach quivered. Heck, all of me quivered. He crawled down, down, and kissed one edge of the wound, then the other, and a moan left me.

Please. More.

But a moment passed, then another, and he merely returned to his former position, driving me crazy with his nearness but never doing anything to relieve the tension spiraling inside me.

"One more week of rest," he said, his jaw clenched as if he'd had to force the words to leave his mouth. "Doctor's orders."

I shook my head. "I'll ask Bronx and Frosty to train me."

His eyes narrowed to tiny slits. "They'll say no. I'll make sure of it."

"At first, maybe." Definitely. Everyone always followed

Cole's rules. Even other alpha males recognized a bigger, badder predator. "However, I have a secret weapon."

He arched a brow. "And what's that?"

"Sure you want to know?" I asked, rubbing my knees along his hips.

"Yes. Tell me." His tone had gone low, gruff.

My knees slid higher, higher still, and he went utterly motionless, waiting to see what I would do next. I had two options. Try to seduce him into making out with me—*the way he's looking at me...I might actually succeed this time*—or prove I wasn't out for the count.

Sometimes I hated my priorities.

I planted my feet against his shoulders and pushed with all my might. He propelled backward, catching himself on his knees.

"With you? Distraction," I purred.

Laughing, he stayed where he was and lifted my leg to place a soft kiss on my ankle. "I must be seriously disturbed, because I like when you rough me up."

Heat spilled into my cheeks. "You make me sound like some kind of he-woman."

He laughed again, and oh, it was a beautiful sound. Lately, he'd been so somber. "I also like when you blush."

"Yes, well, I'll bug Frosty and Bronx until they say yes." Apparently my inquisitive personality was *not* charming to everyone. Go figure. "They'll be so irritated by their lack of fortitude, they'll throw me around like I'm a meat bag."

"So? You'll get a boo-boo I'll have to kiss and make better. Problem, meet solution."

I swallowed a laugh of my own and had to concentrate to

adopt a stern expression. "I'll let you kiss me better—if the boo-boo is on my butt."

"Hmm. Kinky. This is a plan I can get behind... It's a very nice behind."

Tease! "Cole," I said with a pout. "You can't flirt with me like this and then do nothing about it."

"Oh, I'll do something about it." The gruff, wanting tone was back. His gaze locked on my mouth, heating with awareness. "Once you've been cleared."

So, seven more days of Cole's china-doll treatment? *Don't whimper.* "Mr. Ankh would have cleared me already if not for you and your protests." I sat up and shifted my fingers through the silk of his hair. "I'm better now. I swear!"

"No, you're finally on the road to better. But if you start training, that could slow your progress. Besides, you're mine, Ali-gator, and you're precious to me. I want you better. I *need* you better. And okay, yeah, I don't like the thought of my friends putting their hands on you."

Ali-gator? Really? I think I would have preferred something like, I don't know, cuddlecakes. Anything was better than a comparison to an overgrown lizard, right?

And had he just called me *his?*

See? Melting...

"Bronx is secretly into Reeve and Frosty is bat-crap crazy for Kat. They wouldn't try anything." And really, before Cole, no boy had *ever* tried anything with me. I had no idea what made me so irresistible to him.

"Don't care," he said, leaning forward to nuzzle my neck. "I will put my boys in the hospital if they come near you. I don't share my toys."

I had to swallow a snort. "If anyone else called me their toy, internal organs would spill."

"Agreed. Like I said, you're mine. And, Ali, I'd love to be called your anything, especially your toy. I *reeeally* want you to play with me."

Okay, I did snort. Hello, mixed signals. "I'd really like you to prove that, Cole Holland."

His response? A groan.

I sighed. There was nothing mixed about that, was there? "Back to the pimp hand you're planning to throw around." I had no doubt he could put people in the hospital—he had before—but his friends? Never. I opened my mouth to tell him so, only to gasp. He'd just bitten the cord of my shoulder, and the most delicious lance of pleasure had shot through me. *"Cole."*

"Sorry. Couldn't help myself. Had to do a little proving."

"Don't stop," I breathed. "Not this time."

"Ali," he said with another groan. "You're killing me." He stood with me in his arms and gently laid me on the bed. He stretched out next to me but didn't pull me into his side.

I swallowed a shriek of frustration. I wasn't sure if he was punishing himself for what he'd done to me or if he really was afraid he would break me. All I knew was that I missed the feel and taste of him.

I rolled toward him and rested my head on his shoulder. His skin was warm and surprisingly soft as I traced a circle around the piercing in his nipple. *Bad Ali.*

Smart Ali. His heart kicked into a faster rhythm, delighting me.

Disappointed Ali. He remained just as he was, here but set apart from me.

"When you're better," he finally said.

His ability to resist me was *so* not flattering.

"I wouldn't be able to forgive myself if I caused you any more harm," he added, and I lost my ire.

His concern for me was *beyond* flattering.

"Look, I have to help you guys in some way, King Cole." The moment the nickname left my lips, I knew I'd made a mistake. He'd embrace that one a little too tightly. "Doing nothing is *destroying* me."

He pushed out a heavy breath. "All right. Okay. You can come to the gym tomorrow morning. We'll see how you handle things."

I kissed his jaw, the shadow-beard he sported tickling my lips. "I think it's cute that you thought I was asking for permission."

"Thank you, Cole," he grumbled. He cupped the back of my neck, tilting my head. My gaze met his. "I just want to take care of you."

"You will…just as long as you keep your swords to your-self."

His eyes darkened. "That's not funny."

"What? Too soon? My near-death experience and your part in it aren't something we can joke about yet?"

"Probably not ever."

I nipped playfully at his chin. "Okay." Taking mercy on him, I changed the subject. "Will you finally tell me what's been going on these past few weeks?" Boss's orders. Business wasn't to be discussed. "As you can see, if it's bad news, I can take it."

"Yeah. All right," he replied, his relief obvious. "To start, Kat and Frosty broke up again."

I made a mental note to contact her first thing in the morning.

"Also, Justin's sister is missing."

Justin Silverstone used to be a slayer. Then his twin sister, Jaclyn, had convinced him to switch sides and join Anima Industries; the Hazmats, we called them. They wanted to preserve the zombies for testing and studying and planned to one day use them as weapons, uncaring about the inno-cent lives that were lost along the way.

"She probably ran off, afraid we'd come after her," I said. She and her crew had helped bomb my grandparents' home. I owed her.

Cole nodded. "Then there's my search. We need more slayers. I know there are kids out there as confused as you used to be, unsure why they see monsters no one else can see, and they have no idea what to do about it."

"Any possibles?"

"Not yet. But two slayers from Georgia came to help us out until we've rebuilt our team."

For a while, I'd thought the zombie problem existed only in my home state of Alabama. I'd since learned differently. There were zombies all over the world. Slayers, too.

"You should have shared this info long before now. You are such a pain, Coleslaw," I said. Better, but that nickname wasn't the winner, either.

"I know, but I'm *your* pain."

And just like that, my irritation drained away. How did he do it?

"Does Mr. Ankh know you're here?" Since my grandfather had died and my grandparents' house had been torched, Nana and I had moved in with Mr. Ankh and his daughter, Reeve.

Mr. Ankh—Dr. Ankh to everyone outside his circle of trust—knew about the zombies and did all the medical work on the slayers. Reeve had no idea what was going on, and we were supposed to keep her in the dark. Or else. Her father wanted her to have as normal a life as possible.

What was normal, exactly?

"I gave Ankh's security the finger," Cole said with a twinge of pride. "He would feel the need to tell your grandmother, and I don't want to be kicked out and have to sneak back in. I just want to be with you."

"So you're planning to stay here all night and hold me, Coley Guacamole?" Ugh. I shouldn't have gone there. That one reeked.

He barked out a laugh. "I liked King Cole better."

"That's not actually a surprise."

"It just fits me so well."

"I'm sure you think so." I gave a gentle tug on his nipple ring.

"I doubt I'm the only one. And yes, I'm staying." He curled his fingers over mine, pried my grip loose and brought my knuckles to his mouth for a kiss. A second later, there was a flash of panic in his eyes. One I didn't understand

and must have misread. Because he said, "Just so you know, you can call me anything you want—just as long as you always call me."

ON YOUR MARK, GET SET—STOP!

I woke up alone, drenched in sweat and gasping for breath, another dream of the accident hovering at the back of my mind. I'd seen my mother reaching for me. Felt the unusual heat of her touch. Heard her yell at me. Then I'd watched as the zombies finished eating my dad, glided to our car and jerked her out, ready for dessert.

She'd fought against their hold, her expression panicked. She'd called my name again. "Alice! Alice!"

I'd struggled to reach her, begging the creatures not to hurt her.

Then nothing.

Now I wanted to cry.

Why was I seeing this? It hadn't happened. Not really.

Had it?

Had I woken up in the car and just didn't remember? Could this be my mind's way of reminding me?

Mom *had* ended up outside, next to my dad, even though she'd been in the car when I'd lost consciousness.

"Cole," I said, patting the space next to me. I needed his arms around me, strong and sure. He would comfort me, whatever the answers.

The mattress was disappointingly cold. He was gone.

I thought…yeah, I remembered hearing him speak to me before he'd taken off.

"I'm supposed to believe you? Just like that," he'd said, his tone angry.

No, he hadn't been speaking to me. There'd been a tense pause before he'd snapped, "Stop calling me, Justin. I told you a long time ago I'm done with you. There's nothing you can do or say to change that." Another crackling pause. "No, I don't want to hear the info you've got."

I knew of only one Justin. Either Cole had been on the phone with a boy he'd sworn never to speak with again, or my mind had played tricks on me. Right now I wasn't exactly in a mind-trusting mood.

Gingerly I sat up to gaze around the room. Bright sunlight slanted through the window. The ice-blue comforter draping the four-poster bed was wrinkled, and one of the pillows was stained with flecks of black from Cole's face paint. Oops. I'd have to clean that off before I left.

His weapons were no longer piled on the floor, and neither were his clothes. In fact, the only other sign that he'd been here was the note on my nightstand.

I'm at the gym. Call me and I'll come for you. X C

Humming with sudden happiness, I brushed my teeth, showered and dressed in my winter workout clothes. I dialed his cell, and…went straight to voice mail.

"I'm awake and ready," I said. "You can come get me anytime." I didn't have a car. Or a license. Only a permit. If I didn't hear from him soon, I'd walk. The gym was at a barn a few miles away. "I hope you're prepared to have your butt handed to you."

When I hung up, I noticed there were eleven texts waiting for me. All from my best friend, Kat. I grinned as I read.

One: Frosty SUCKS!

Two: Have I mentioned Frosty sucks it raw??

Three: How do U feel about murder? 4 or against?? Before U answer, know that I have good reason!

Four: If 4, do U know good place 2 hide body??

The rest described the many ways she'd like to kill him. My favorite involved a bag of Skittles and a silk scarf.

Mmm. Skittles.

My stomach rumbled, and I set my phone on the night-stand. I'd call Kat after breakfast, when she was more likely to be awake and I was more likely to be lucid, and find out what happened. There was a good chance Frosty had simply failed to call her after the fight last night, and she'd worried. I wasn't sure how to comfort her about that. She'd made it clear the zombies weren't a topic of conversation she welcomed.

First, though, I cleaned every inch of my room. I refused to let Mr. Ankh's housekeeper do it for me. I wasn't a sponge and wasn't going to take anything for granted. I was determined to give back, somehow. Thankfully, water and hand soap removed the paint from the pillow.

"Alice."

Emma's voice.

I turned, and oh, glory, there she was. My eight-year-old sister. Her spirit anyway. What she'd taught me: death is never the end. "You're here," I said, my heart soaring. She'd visited me before, but every time felt like the first time—shocking and unreal.

She smiled at me, and I wanted so badly to hug her close and never let go. "I only have a moment."

She wore the clothes she'd died in: a pink leotard and tutu. The dark hair she'd inherited from our mother was pulled into two pigtails, swinging over her delicate shoulders. Golden eyes that had always watched me with adoration were bright.

She'd once told me she wasn't a ghost, but a witness. Ghosts—not that they existed—were spirits of the dead that retained their memories and haunted. A myth probably born from zombie sightings. Witnesses were spirits that aided.

"I wanted to warn you that you'll be seeing less of me," she said, the smile slipping. "Visiting you is becoming more difficult. *But.* If you call for me, I will find a way to reach you."

"More difficult how?" I asked, concerned for her.

"My tie to this world is fading."

Oh.

I knew what that meant. One day I was going to lose her for good.

"Don't be sad," she said. "I hate when you're sad."

I forced my features to brighten. "No matter what, I'll

know you're out there, watching over me. There's no reason to be sad."

"Exactly." Beaming, she blew me a kiss. "I love you. And seriously, don't forget to call for me if you need me." Then she was gone.

My features fell and, I was sure, dimmed. I could have curled into a ball and cried, but I refused to let myself worry about any tomorrows without her. I'd deal with her loss when it came.

Pulling my hair into a ponytail, I headed to the kitchen. I expected to find the housekeeper. Instead I found Reeve, Nana and Kat seated at the table, sipping from steaming mugs of coffee.

"—something's going on," Reeve was saying, twining a lock of dark hair around her finger. "Dad put more security cameras in both the front and backyard—and we already had a thousand to begin with! Worse, he's put up so many lamps, my blackout curtains are no longer able to do their job."

Nana and Kat shifted uncomfortably.

"Has he said anything to either of you?"

"Well…" Nana hedged. She moved her gaze through the room, as if hoping a distraction would present itself.

One did.

"Ali! You're out of bed a week early." Her chair skidded behind her as she stood. She closed the distance between us and drew me in for a hug. "I'm not sure I approve."

Kat buffed her nails and smiled, not looking at all like a girl on the verge of committing a violent crime. She did look tired, though. There were dark circles under her eyes, and her cheeks were hollowed, as if she hadn't eaten in days. "I would have been up *two* weeks early, but we can't all have my amazing bounce-back, can we?"

I kissed Nana's cheek and returned Kat's smile. The girl had a healthy (and justifiable) ego and wasn't afraid to show it. Me? I'd always been the girl with her head ducked as she questioned her worth.

I'd faced death and won, I reminded myself—I should probably get over that.

But…just then, I kind of thought Kat was using her ego as a shield to hide her physical weakness. She suffered from degenerative kidney disease.

"What are you doing here?" I asked her. "Not that I'm not thrilled to see you. I so am." More than thrilled, actually. From the very beginning, she'd never cared what I looked like or how socially awkward I could be. She'd just accepted me and rolled. "I thought you preferred to sleep till two on weekends."

"I came to see you, naughty girl that you are. You never answer your phone or respond to my mind-blowing texts anymore. My plan was to lecture you until you promised to have your phone surgically attached to your hand, but I decided to have some coffee first."

Speaking of coffee… "I'll take that." I confiscated her mug as I eased into the seat beside her. I wouldn't allow myself to eat or drink anything from the Ankhs, which made coffee a luxury. But I didn't mind taking from my best friend.

"Hey!" A second later, she confiscated Reeve's.

"Hey," Reeve said, then confiscated Nana's.

Musical coffees.

Nana shook her head, but I could see the gleam of amusement in her eyes.

"No need for a lecture," I said to Kat, flattening my hand on my side. "There'll be no more surgeries for me."

Her features softened. "My poor, sweet Ali."

"I don't understand how you fell down our stairs and received such a life-threatening injury," Reeve said. "You're not the clumsy type, and there's nothing sharp on the railing or the floor."

"Of course she's clumsy," Kat exclaimed, covering for me as I stuttered for some type of response. "Ali could get tangled up in a cordless phone."

I nodded and tried not to look miserable—the claim was only a lie if I failed to believe it. Maybe I *was* clumsy. Once, I'd stepped into Cole's ankle trap and dangled upside down from a tree. Another time, he'd been teaching me how to work a sword and I'd nearly removed his head.

So...yeah.

"Anyway," Kat said, quickly changing the subject, "I'm sure everyone will be pleased to know we won the football game last night."

"Go, Tigers!" we said in unison, and burst into peals of laughter.

An alarm sounded from Reeve's phone. "Crap!" She jumped up. "Sorry, guys, but I've got plans for Halloween and they actually start this morning. See ya!" She raced out of the kitchen.

Nana stood. "I've got to go, too. I want to lecture that girl's father about the importance of being well informed. Oh, and, Ali, Cole called me a little while ago and told me you were in need of a costume, but that you'd be too busy training to shop. I thought he was kidding, like some kind of Halloween joke I just didn't understand, since only yesterday he'd been so adamant about you staying in bed. But if he thinks you're ready, you're ready—and I won't ask how he reached that conclusion."

Please don't!

And Cole had actually called *Nana?* "That's sweet of you, but I don't want us to spend money on an article of clothing I'll only wear once. I can make something I already own work."

Smiling, she patted my hand. "Darling, we're not destitute. We have the insurance settlement."

"But we *are* saving for a house of our own." There were conditions for living here, and with conditions came an expiration date. I wanted Nana taken care of for the rest of her life, no surprises. In fact, I should probably find a job… though that might prove impossible, considering I would need to take time off for school and slaying.

No. There had to be a way.

"I'm getting you a costume, young lady, and that's final. I'm looking forward to this."

I sighed. "All right, but something from the thrift store will work just fine."

She kissed the top of my head and followed the same path Reeve had taken. Without agreeing, I realized too late.

My phone vibrated, and I checked the screen.

Cole McHottie (as Kat had dubbed him): I can't leave the gym 2 get U, Ali-gator, I'm sorry. But we R still on 4 2nite. I miss U

I wondered what had happened to keep him trapped at the gym.

Disappointed, I looked to Kat.

"So, where are you and Cole going?" she asked.

"Hearts, I'm sure." It was the only nightclub the slayers frequented. "Now, about your phone calls and texts. I wasn't ignoring you, I promise. It's just strange, knowing you now know what I know, yet trying to buffer you from the worst of the details."

"It's not strange. It's terrible! I hate knowing, but I've decided to girl up and finally discuss the...you-knows from now on. And just so we're clear, girling up is far better than manning up."

"Good. About the you-knows." Knowledge was power, and I wanted her safe. Always.

The housekeeper bustled into the kitchen, spotted me, and asked if she could fix me something to eat. I declined, and she loaded a tray with croissants and cappuccino to take to Mr. Ankh. The fragrance of yeast and sugar mingled, filling the room and making my mouth water.

The moment she was gone, I hopped up to wipe the crumbs from the counter. Then I grabbed the bag of bagels I'd bought with my allowance and offered one to Kat.

She shook her head. "So...I'm sure you surmised from my oh so subtle texts that Frosty and I are over. Or is it Frosty and me? I always forget. Anyway, it's for reals this time."

"What happened?" I devoured the bagel in record time, and though I craved a second one *so* bad, I resisted. The longer these lasted, the fewer I would have to buy, and the less I'd have to spend.

"Last night," she said, looking miserable, "I wasn't feeling well—not that Frosty knew that part. I asked him to stay with me, and he refused."

"When the you-knows are out, he has to fight. We all do, if we're well. It's our duty." Our privilege.

"A night off wouldn't have killed him," she grumbled.

"But it might have killed his friends. They need all the backup they can get."

She frowned at me. "Do you have to be so reasonable, tossing out such intelligent responses?"

"I'm sorry. I'll try to do better."

"Thank you."

I studied her. She was such a beautiful girl. Petite, but curvy. Fragile, yet resilient. Her mom had suffered with the same kidney disease most of her too-short life. Kat was militant about keeping her declining health from Frosty and the boys, and so far she'd succeeded.

She lived for the moment. She never held back—in words or in action. She had no desire to fade from the world, but wanted to make an impact, a difference, and go out swinging. I could help her with that.

"How would you feel about learning to defend yourself against the you-knows?" I asked. My dad had trained me to fight them before I'd possessed the ability to see them, and that training had been invaluable when my circumstances changed. Maybe Kat would see the zombies one day. Maybe she wouldn't. Either way, I could equip her to make smarter choices.

"I'd feel…great. I think."

"That's good enough for me. Cole has a gym, and it's

loaded with all the equipment we'll need. I can show you how to shoot a gun and use a bow and arrow."

She waved a hand through the air, probably trying for dismissive, but I saw the gleam of fear behind the action. "No need for that part of the training."

"You've used both weapons before?"

"No, but the unaimed weapon never misses. I'd rather stick with that method."

I rolled my eyes.

"Will Frosty be there?" She nibbled on her bottom lip as she waited for my answer.

"Maybe."

I couldn't tell whether that pleased her or upset her; the chewing never stopped. "Well, today's, like, the biggest holiday of the year, so I'll pencil you in for noon sharp tomorrow. Or maybe sometime next week would be best. Yes. Definitely next week."

"Nope. You'll pencil me in for now *and* tomorrow *and* next week. I'm not letting you put this off. We're going to turn you into a rabid, frothing-at-the-mouth fighting machine. You'll be so hard-core, you'll be able to knock Frosty on his butt as easily as breathing."

A scary kind of anticipation lit her features. "Okay, I'm in. But only because I know I'll look good with biceps. True story." She drained what remained of her coffee and slammed the mug onto the table. "Let's go before I change my mind."

I left my grandmother a note, telling her not to expect me back until after lunch and that I loved her. I thought about texting Cole, but quickly discarded the idea. I'd surprise him.

"You want to drive?" Kat asked as I made a beeline for the passenger side of her Mustang. "You have a permit."

Acid burned a path up my throat. "No thanks. You're not old enough to be my escort or whatever."

"But you need the practice."

"Another day," I hedged.

"That's what I said about training, and you shot me down."

"Do you want to reach the gym in fifteen minutes or fifteen hours?" I asked. If I had to pick between driving and bathing in manure, I'd pick the manure. Every time. "You know how slow I go."

"True." She settled behind the wheel.

"Did Frosty ever take you to Cole's gym? Not the one in his garage, but the gym several miles from his house?" The seat belt rubbed against my wound, and I shifted uncomfortably.

"Nope. According to Frosty, the high and mighty workout station for stallions—his words, not mine—is off-limits to nonslayers."

Not any longer. I gave her the address without a qualm. The boys had brought Kat into this treacherous world of secrets, and they could deal with the consequences.

As we soared down the highway, I checked the sky for the rabbit-shaped cloud Emma used to warn me about coming zombie attacks. Today, there wasn't one, and I breathed a sigh of relief.

Kat swerved to avoid hitting another car, and I yelped.

"Is my driving making you nervous?" she asked. "I mean, you're supertense. Which is silly, considering the fact that I've only been in, like, three wrecks since you were confined to a bed, and, when you think about it, none of them were my fault. I mean, sure, I was in the wrong lane, texting, but the other drivers had plenty of time to move out of my way."

How was she still alive? "Mad Dog, you are the best worst driver I know."

She preened. "That might be the sweetest compliment anyone's ever given me. Thank you."

A car honked as she swerved across four lanes to exit the highway, and she seemed utterly oblivious. "So, you and Cole are at the stage where he's comfortable enough to call your Nana, huh?"

"I know. It's kind of weird, right, and..." Wait. I knew Cole. He'd always been a guy with a plan. A purpose. He never did anything without a rock-solid reason. But what reason could he possibly have had to—

The answer slammed into me, and I nearly liquefied in my seat. I'd lost my family, and this was my first Halloween without them. He was trying to reduce the number of memories I'd have to battle.

He didn't know that I'd never before celebrated Halloween. My dad hadn't allowed us to leave the house at night, so there had been no reason to buy a costume, and opening the door to strangers to pass out candy had been just as big a no-no.

"Yeah," I said to Kat, wishing I could crawl into Cole's arms and never leave. "We are."

"You're so lucky. My dad has never been a Frosty fan. I'm pretty sure he's only ever threatened to castrate the boy."

Had to be those serial-killer eyes. Sometimes, when Frosty looked at you, you just expected to die horribly. "Your dad still lets you guys date, though."

"Yeah, and he always will. When I was first diagnosed with defunct kidneys, he promised to let me make my own decisions and live my life the way I wanted."

Good man. "So, what have you decided to do tonight?"

"The same thing you are. And I didn't mention it before now because I didn't want you drowning in jealousy knowing I was out having the best time ever while you were still languishing in your sickbed." She gripped the steering wheel so tightly her knuckles bleached of color. "I'm trying not to be nervous. I mean, I know all the slayers will be there, but the night will be filled with all kinds of creepers, so how will I know who's dangerous and who's not?"

"You aren't able to see real zombies," I reminded her.

"That doesn't mean they aren't there. First, I told Frosty no, but then he said, 'Would I ever put you at risk, woman?' And I said, 'How would I know? You've been living a double life since we started dating.' And he said, 'You want me to apologize again, don't you?' And I said, 'Every day for the rest of your life.' He had the nerve to laugh as if I was joking."

I smothered a laugh of my own. "So…what's your costume?"

"A too-sexy-to-handle Little Red Riding Hood."

"Let me guess. Frosty's going as the Big Bad Wolf."

"What else? I have a feeling he thinks it'll be hilarious to snap his teeth at me and say, 'I'm going to eat you up, my dear.'"

Picturing it, I shook my head. "You're going to tell him to prove it. Aren't you?"

"I like that you know me so well."

She turned onto a winding gravel road nestled between rows of trees in the process of shedding their fall coats. When the trees finally gave way to fields of wheat, Cole's "work-out station for stallions" became visible—a big red barn that looked ready to topple over. Actually, the thing could withstand a military invasion.

"This place is in the middle of nowhere," Kat remarked as she eased to a stop.

"For many reasons." Slayers coming at all hours of the day and night. The sheer number of weapons kept here. The condition we sometimes left in.

There were more cars than usual in the driveway. I frowned as I stepped into the coolness of the day. Grunts, groans and even cheers seeped from the crack in the door. "Come on." I quickened my pace.

I stopped just inside the entrance and could only gape. I'd assumed Cole, and maybe the überdedicated Frosty and Bronx would be the only guys willing to forgo a country-wide day off.

Kat bumped into me and froze. "Oh, spank me," she whispered, her tone reverent.

Here they were, all of the slayers in all their glory. There was enough testosterone in the air to jump-start the deadest of hearts. Most of the boys were shirtless, displaying bronzed muscles honed from more than just weights—honed from hacking at the enemy. I saw wicked scars, sexy tattoos and piercings, and even a few house-arrest anklets.

The blond and scarily beautiful Frosty pounded his fists into a poor, defenseless punching bag. The rough-and-tumble Bronx held the thing in place, his feet planted firmly on the floor. There was no force on earth that could move him, even one as violent as Frosty. Collins ran on a treadmill, and Cruz lifted weights.

And Cole, well, he was in the boxing ring with a girl I didn't recognize.

There was an unfamiliar boy standing at the side, watching the pair. The only other females in the room were Mackenzie—Cole's very feral ex—and Trina, a girl Kat had yet to forgive for *not* having a summer fling with Frosty.

Don't ask.

Trina waved at me, and I waved back, but my attention quickly returned to Cole. He swung lightheartedly at the unknown girl, and she ducked before straightening and swinging at him. He ducked, too, and when she swung again, he caught her fist and jerked her against the hard line of his body, effectively disabling her.

She grinned up at him, all cocky assurance and feminine wiles—and she stayed right where she was, clearly happy to be there. A boy with a girlfriend should have released her and stepped back. Although Cole stiffened, the gleam in his eyes turning granite-hard, he remained just as he was, returning her grin with one of his own.

I wasn't sure what any of that meant. I only knew I didn't like it.

Time for Pep Talk Ali. *He's trained other girls. He's even smiled at other girls. This isn't romantic. This isn't sexual.*

Of course, Downer Ali wasn't fully convinced (yes, there are many sides to me). *He didn't pick you up because he didn't want to leave this girl's side.*

I shook my head. He was mine, my toy, and I wouldn't share.

But what if he wanted me to share him?

No! Stupid insecurity. Cole wasn't like that.

"Kitten," Frosty called, sounding more than a little surprised. "How'd you find me?"

Kat lifted her chin, the picture of female pique. "Don't flatter yourself. I'm not here for you. But just so you know, I used my phenomenal detective skills, coupled with Ali's mediocre directions. No offense," she said to me.

"None taken." Mediocre was actually better than I deserved.

"Don't be that way, baby," he replied, unwinding the tape from his fists. "You know I would have given you a ride on the Frosty Express. You just had to ask."

Bronx rolled his eyes. Several of the other guys groaned.

Cole's attention arrowed in my direction. Our gazes locked, and guilt filled those violet irises.

Guilt? Why guilt? Whatever the answer, it couldn't be good.

I will not stomp into that ring.

I will not pull the pair apart.

I will not beat them both into pulp.

He set the girl away from him. Once again I found myself waiting and hoping for a vision. I was back on my feet. Things should go back to normal. But a moment passed, then another.

Normal remained at bay.

A dash of dread joined a pinch of jealousy, a recipe for trouble.

The new guy whistled under his breath, and my attention shifted to him. Our gazes collided. A second later, the world washed away, just as I'd wanted it to do with Cole—

—we were in my bedroom, standing beside my bed. No, we were lying on my bed. I'd just pushed him down. I tilted his head with one hand and pulled at his clothes with the other. Then I licked my way down his throat. I was making strange little growling noises, as if I'd never enjoyed a taste so much and had to have more—

"—Ali!" Cole shouted.

I blinked, and the vision evaporated.

Cole appeared, his features tense. "What just happened?"

"Dude," Frosty said to the new guy. "Your brain just checked out for a bit. I haven't seen anything like that since Cole first met Al—and uh, yeah, never mind."

New Guy stared at me, looking suspicious and angry.

I stumbled back a few steps. I couldn't believe I'd just mind-cheated on Cole. Like, big-time.

"Cole asked a good question," New Guy croaked. "What just happened?"

So he'd had the vision, too. *No. No, no, no.* What did that mean? That strong of a connection had never happened with anyone but Cole. Why here? Why now? Why *this* guy?

"I have a better question," the new girl said with a sweet Southern drawl. "Will someone please introduce me to the newcomers?"

I had to make sure the vision never came true. It *couldn't* come true. It would mean Cole and I were over. It would mean the new life I'd carved for myself had crashed and burned.

A muscle ticked in Cole's jaw. "Veronica, meet Ali. Ali, Veronica. She's one of the slayers from Atlanta. Ali's friend is Kat."

"My girl," Frosty added, proudly thumping his chest.

"In your dreams," Kat replied.

They launched into a heated argument.

"Veronica is another of Cole's exes," Mackenzie piped up.

Oh, good glory, no!

"Not just any ex," Veronica added, offering me a grin as sweet as her voice. "I'm his favorite."

I stiffened, waiting for Cole to say the words *Actually, Ali is my favorite—and she's not an ex.* He didn't.

"Nice to meet you," I whispered, fighting panic.

Once I hadn't thought there was a girl more beautiful than Mackenzie. Now I knew how wrong I'd been. Veronica was. By far. She had perfectly tanned skin, dark glossy hair that was iron-board straight and fell to her shoulders and light green eyes.

Mackenzie had dark hair, though hers was curly, and dark green eyes. Put the three of us side by side, and you wouldn't have to ask who didn't belong. I had wavy hair so pale it could have been classified as old-granny white, and eyes so blue they bordered on freaky.

One of Veronica's perfect brows lifted. "So you're the infamous Ali Bell, huh? The girl with abilities no one can explain."

I could see the Blood Lines we poured around our homes, a mix of chemicals the zombies couldn't bypass. My body sometimes became a living flame, ashing every zombie I touched in seconds, while other slayers could only light their hands and needed several minutes to achieve the same re-sults. I could sometimes see into the future.

I wasn't sure why I could do these things, or what made me different. My slaying genes were no more special than anyone else's.

"Yes," I said. Cole wouldn't look at me. Why wouldn't he look at me? "That's me."

Veronica's head tilted to the side as she scrutinized me more intently. "Did you use one of those abilities on my friend?"

I stuttered for a response, but came up empty.

"So what if she did?" Kat called, always my backup. "She's got the boss man wrapped around her little finger. She can do what she wants, to whomever she wants."

How much did I love that girl?

Venom leaked into Veronica's sweetness. "No one wraps Cole Holland around their finger."

Cole left both comments alone as he hopped out of the ring. "Later, Ronny. Practice without me."

Ronny? He had an affectionate nickname for Mackenzie, too. Kenze, he sometimes called her. I hated both.

He stalked to an open treadmill, motioned me over and pushed a few buttons. "Before you hit the ring, you need to build your stamina back up. Do not—I repeat—do not overwork yourself."

I closed the distance between us. "You're right about the stamina, and I can tell you I have no plans to overwork my-self, but first we need to talk."

Still he refused to look at me. "Clearly, you had a vision with Gavin."

Gavin. The name of the boy I'd just mind-molested. "Y-yes. But that's not what I want to talk about. This Veronica girl—"

"What did you see?" he said.

"I, well, uh…" I couldn't tell him, and I wouldn't lie. So, where did that leave me? "Does it really matter? It won't come true." I wouldn't let it.

"It matters. It will come true. And we both know it." Cole walked away without another word—without ever looking back at me.

I watched him until he disappeared inside the locker room, my heart creating a staccato beat in my chest. Veronica—Ronny—followed him. She paused at the door, and *she* did look back at me.

To smirk.

CAN'T GO BACK TO YESTERDAY

While Kat and I had run the treadmills side by side, and I'd tried not to worry about the vision with Gavin and Cole's behavior before and after, Nana had been out buying me a big, puffy blue gown. *Not* from the thrift store. The shiny monstrosity had a lacy corset top, stripes on the skirt and a black hat to top things off.

I wasn't sure what I was supposed to be—other than a Southern belle magician on crack.

Normally, I wouldn't leave the house at night wearing anything with colors. And never anything this fantastical. I liked to blend with the shadows. Needed to. Tonight, however, I was making an exception.

I wanted Cole to see me in something other than the tee and shorts I'd sported the past few weeks, and the workout clothes from this morning. I wanted his eyes to light up, and for him to spend the night complimenting me, unable to keep his hands off me. We'd dance. We'd laugh. He'd kiss me. I'd kick myself for worrying about him and Veronica-slash-Ronny.

We weren't allowed to fight tonight, but I wrapped a utility belt around my thigh anyway, my daggers hanging from the attached sheaths. I never left home without them.

I wondered what costume Cole would be wearing. He hadn't said. Well, other than the naughty nurse, but I knew that had been a joke.

I stepped into the dress, hooked everything together and studied myself in the mirror. Not bad. Quite fancy. I wished my parents were here to see me. They'd—

I cut off that thought before it could fully form. I'd cry.

Something warm and wet trickled down my cheek. Great. I was already crying.

My cell phone chirped, signaling a text had just come in. I wiped the tears away with the back of my hand.

Cole McHottie: Sorry, Ali, but making plans w/U was a mistake. I need a break. Stay in & we'll talk 2morrow

I had to read the words three times before reality set in. He needed a freaking break? Seriously?

From what? I wanted to scream. And what, exactly did "need a break" mean?

My anger and disappointment were as sharp as a blade.

Me: WHY? What's going on w/you? Respect me enough 2 talk 2 me! Apparently that's how relationships WORK.

A minute passed. Two, three. He didn't respond.

I threw my phone across the room, and then had to rush over to make sure I hadn't cracked the screen.

What the heck was he planning to do on this "break"?

And whom was he going to do it with?

This can't be happening.

My cell phone chirped. Heart racing, I checked the screen.

Mad Dog: Where are U?

Me, pressing the keys a little too forcefully: Home.

Mad Dog: U ditched Cole??

Me: No. He ditched me.

Mad Dog: UH, HE'S HERE. Just walked in.

Wait, wait, wait. He'd meant he needed a break from *me?*

Yeah. He must have. He had to know Kat would contact me. He had to know I would find out he'd gone to Hearts without me.

He just didn't care.

I trembled as I typed What's he doing?

Mad Dog: He's talking w/Lucas, Veronica & that hobag Trina & get this: he's wearing a costume that says he's a bad mofo—meaning, he's not in costume.

Veronica again.

Me, grinding my teeth: He told me he needed a break from me.

Mad Dog: WHAT? Oh, I'll give him a break—in both of his legs!! 1st, of course, I'll spy.

For the next hour, I received nearly fifty texts from Kat.

He's talking w/Frosty now.

Just came out of shadows w/Justin S—what's up w/THAT?? Altho, he just had Frosty kick JS out of club & it wasn't pretty (4 JS).

Just rubbed his knuckles in2 Veronica's hair. She laughed, & I almost punched her teeth down her throat (don't 4get my fighting lesson 2morrow!).

Handed hobag Trina a drink.

Handed Lucas a drink.

Talking heatedly w/Gavin.

Walking away from Gavin (I hate the C-man right now, I really do, but he sure does have a nice butt).

Telling me 2 stop following him.

Telling me he knows what I'm doing & getting ticked when I ignore him.

Walking away as I flip him off.

Telling Frosty 2 control me (like that's really possible).

Becoming more agitated by the second, I stomped downstairs. I trusted Cole; sometimes I trusted him more than I trusted myself. But that didn't mean I was going to stay here and let him take a "break" without talking to me about it.

Nana was at the front door, handing out the last of the candy to a ghost, a cowboy and a Smurf.

"Nana," I said as soon as the door was shut. "This is probably the first time in history a teenage girl will pose this question to her grandmother, but, will you drive me to a nightclub? Cole's there," I rushed to assure her. "And Frosty and Kat."

She frowned at me. "I thought Cole was picking you up."

"I thought so, too," I said a little bitterly.

"What about the—" her voice lowered to a frightened whisper "—the creatures?"

"You don't have to worry. To my knowledge, they aren't out tonight. And even if they do make an appearance, your car is protected with a Blood Line. They can't get to you."

Her smile was sad and affectionate at the same time. "I wasn't worried about me, dear, but my inability to help you."

Oh. "Nana, it's my job to protect *you*."

The sadness drained from her, leaving only the affection. "No, that's not how things are supposed to be, but we won't get into that tonight. Will there be drinking at this club?"

I wouldn't lie to her. "Yes, but I won't be doing any and neither will Cole." Alcohol impaired judgment, and he took his responsibilities as leader seriously. Me? I'd watched alcoholism destroy my dad and was determined to avoid a similar fate.

"Well, I did buy you that…" She motioned to my dress.

What adjective was she looking for? Ginormous? Unforgettable? Behemoth?

"…unique costume," she finished, "and I want you to be able to show it off. You look so beautiful."

"Thank you. But, uh, what am I supposed to be, exactly?"

"Alice in Wonderland, silly. And you're supposed to give the hat to Cole so he can be your Mad Hatter."

"So you'll take me?"

She sighed, nodded. "I'll take you."

I threw my arms around her. "Thank you, thank you, and thousand times thank you!"

Fifteen minutes later, I was stepping out of her car, and she was driving away. I approached the club's entrance and gave the guards at the door Cole's name. They let me inside without a hitch—if you didn't count the people in line desperate to get in, complaining about my lack of wait.

Multicolored strobe lights flashed, and smoke wafted through the air. There were people everywhere, each in costume. For the girls, there was clearly a theme: slutty. A slutty devil. A slutty fairy. A slutty witch. I felt seriously overdressed. For the guys, there was no rhyme or reason. A shirt made out of cardboard. A toga with pictures of grinning waffles. Clown trousers paired with riding boats. Loud music blared, fueling the frantic motions of the dancers. I navigated up the stairs to the VIP lounge, the width of my skirt only tripping three people. I considered the low number of casualties a major win.

I scanned the top floor and saw all the faces I'd seen at the gym, plus a few extras.

Where was Cole?

Mackenzie Love caught my eye. Wearing a skimpy black dress with colorful peacock feathers stretching over her shoulders, she strutted over. "Well, well. Ali Bell. I'd like to tell you how awesome you look, and if I can figure out a way to sound sincere, I will. What *is* that thing?"

My cheeks flashed white-hot with embarrassment. "You can't guess?" I asked, using a scathing tone that suggested she was an idiot. "Wow. How sad for you."

She paled and stomped away.

"New drinking game, everyone," the new guy, Gavin, called. Blond and handsome—and dressed as a pimp—he was surrounded by a bevy of hot brunette vampires. "Anytime someone speaks, down a shot!"

Cheers abounded.

"And meanwhile, if anyone wants a free make-out session," one of the vampires shouted, "I'm giving them away."

More cheers as a laughing Gavin kissed her.

Then he kissed the girl next to her. He used tongue with both.

I watched, reeling. For once, a vision just had to be wrong. There was no way I'd be into a guy like him. He was beautiful, yes. I'd give him that. But no. Just no.

"Ali!" Kat rushed over and threw her arms around me. She had to be the cutest Little Red Riding Hood I'd ever seen. Her barely there dress was red, black and white, and hugged all of her curves. The tulle skirt flared at the waist and stopped a few inches below her panty line. Long white socks stretched to her knees. "You made it!"

Before I could respond, Cole stalked past us, grabbed my hand and tugged me away from her.

I tossed her a he's-going-to-get-it-now glance. She gave me a thumbs-up before Cole pulled me into a shadowed corner, and I lost sight of her. He crowded me against the wall, his arms at my temples, caging me in. His heat and scent surrounded me, drugged me.

Oh, no. I wasn't going to melt this time.

"What are you doing here?" he demanded.

How dare *he* use that tone with *me?* "I am so mad at you," I said, beating at his chest.

His aggressive stance softened in the slightest degree. "I know. And you have every right to be."

"You ditched me. You want a break from me."

"Yes. No." He scrubbed a hand down his face. "Not from you. You don't understand."

"Of course I don't! Moron! You haven't explained it to me. You ignored my text."

He glared at me, his anger heating back up. "I wanted to be with you, I did, but I couldn't not come here since I'm the D.D."

"And you couldn't bring me with you? Because, and I quote, making plans with me was a mistake?"

"It was. I don't want you here because I know…"

"What?" I demanded when he paused. I hit him again.

"Gavin is here, all right?" He flashed his teeth in a scowl. "I don't want you around him, okay? Get it now? I need a break from the jealousy. As long as you're near him, I can't get past it."

How could I want to slap him and kiss him at the same time?

But then, I already knew the answer. I'd been battling the green-eyed monster, too. "I promise you have no reason to be jealous."

His shoulders drooped. "I know that, in theory, and I'm sorry for the way I've acted. I've never felt this way, and I'm not handling it well. If you have another vision with him…"

I slid my hands to the nape of his neck and toyed with the ends of his hair. "It wouldn't make a difference. My feelings won't change. But I guess we need to talk about what I saw, even though I'd rather forget it."

"It's bad, isn't it?" he croaked.

I nodded, suddenly unable to speak.

"Then I'm not ready."

He faced monsters on a daily basis, but this was too much for him? *Oh, Cole. What am I going to do with you?* "Will you trust me, then? Trust my feelings for you?"

A moment passed before he nodded. It was a stiff acceptance, but an acceptance all the same.

I smiled at him.

He smiled back. His gaze raked over me, and his eyelids became heavy, staying at half-mast. "You look edible, by the way. You have no idea how badly I want under that skirt." His voice dipped huskily as he added, "I wish I had time to prove it."

Oh.

My.

"Nana said the hat is for you. I'm Alice in Wonderland, and you're the Mad Hatter."

With a laugh, he took the hat and settled it on his head.

"So, what are you doing that you don't have time to try and get under my skirt?" I moved my palms to measure the heavy beat of his heart.

His features closed up shop, displaying zero emotion. "*You* will just have to trust *me*."

A thousand questions sprang to instant life. I ignored them all. As his tone implied, I couldn't ask him to trust me about the vision if I couldn't extend him the same courtesy about this. Whatever "this" was. Besides, he could have lied and made up an excuse for his behavior. He hadn't. He wasn't that kind of guy. He gave truth, or he gave nothing. I'd always liked that about him.

"Do you have a few minutes to spare?" I asked softly.

He fisted two handfuls of my hair, his grip hard and unyielding, holding me still for his perusal. "For you?" The panic I'd noticed last night returned for one second, two, before he gave me the softest of kisses and whispered, "Anything."

"Yo, Cole," a voice said. A head peeked around the corner. "I'm taking off with Kira and Jane and—"

I turned to look, and my gaze locked with Gavin's.

The world disappeared. Cole disappeared—

—there was only here, now, and Gavin, and we were back inside my bedroom, on my bed, my body on top of his. One of his hands was in my hair. The other was sliding down my back to cup my bottom and urge me to grind against him, hard...harder—

—a low snarl snapped me back to the present. To Cole. The growl had come from him.

"Yeah, uh, I'll just be going," Gavin said, and beat feet.

Cole and I stayed where we were for a long moment, silent.

"What I saw with him..." I began, fighting for calm. I'd said it wouldn't make a difference, and now had to pray I was right. "It was the first vision all over again." Only a bit more vivid.

"Don't tell me," he lashed out. "Not tonight."

"Cole—"

"Not tonight, Ali. Please." With that, he walked away from me for the second time that day.

He watched me from afar the rest of the night, but at least he continued to wear the hat.

As the days wore on, I had to admit my relationship with Cole was unraveling.

Every day he grew a little more distant with me. Anytime I tried to talk to him about Gavin and the vision, he would shut me down, saying, "I can't do this right now."

I was trying to trust him like he'd asked. I really was. But the hot-and-cold treatment was wearing me down. Even though he'd always been lavish with his praise of me, I hadn't spent the past few weeks mutating into a secure person. Especially with matters of the heart.

Should I call him again?

What was considered good girlfriend behavior? What delved into Stalkerville?

I knew something other than the vision was bugging him. The few times I'd seen him, his features had been withdrawn and pinched. And what had the panic been about? But again, when I tried to talk to him about it, he shut me down and walked away.

I wasn't sure how much longer I could wait for an explanation about his odd behavior without banging on my chest like a gorilla and screaming.

Eventually, he stopped returning my calls. His replies to my texts were short and abrupt—if he bothered to reply at all. He stopped coming by Mr. Ankh's, and he stopped working out at his own gym.

Maybe Gavin had told him about the vision, and he'd decided to wash his hands of me?

Oh, good glory. No! I bet that was it, though. Dang it! The admission should have come from me. I should have grown a pair of lady balls and forced Cole to listen to me. Then I could have assured him I would rather die than allow my lips to touch any part of that he-slut's body.

I hadn't seen the Georgian slayer since Halloween, and I had no idea what would happen the next time we locked eyes. Part of me didn't want to know. Part of me *needed* to know. If nothing happened, I could assure Cole wires had somehow gotten crossed—twice, yes—and I was meant to lick and grind on *him.*

What should I do next?

I couldn't talk to Kat about this. She had her own problems, and I wouldn't add to them.

I couldn't talk to Reeve. I couldn't risk a slipup.

I couldn't talk to Nana. She'd just lost her husband.

I couldn't even talk to Emma. To her, kissing was gross.

I missed the days when I'd thought the same. I was alone in this.

A bell rang, loud and shrill, signaling the end of class. I stood on shaky legs and gathered my notebook and pencil. Earlier today I'd met the new principal of Asher High, an older black man with kind eyes—a nice change considering the last one had been the queen of ice-cold hearts. I'd turned in all the work the teachers had sent to my sickbed. I was finally caught up.

"Glad to have you back and dominating my assignments, Ali Bell," called Ms. Meyers as I strode from the room.

That was right. In my turmoil over Cole, I'd lost my excitement for my grade. I palmed my cell and texted Nana.

Got an A on my Creative Writing paper! I'd been working on my own at home, and it was nice to know the time and attention I'd put into everything had paid off.

A few seconds later, her reply came in. WTF an A!

I blinked, sure I was misreading. But no, the letters didn't change.

Me: Nana, do U know what WTF means??

Her: Of course, silly. It means "well, that's fantastic."

I swallowed a laugh. I luv U!

Her: Love you, too! Now get back to work.

I stuffed my things in my locker and made my way to the cafeteria. Along the way I ran into Mackenzie. I was as happy to see her now as I'd been at the club but still grabbed her by the arm to stop her.

She looked at my fingers, curled her red lips in distaste and jerked away. But she didn't walk off, as per usual, and I was grateful.

"What do you want?" she snapped.

Such a sweet, sweet girl. "Where's Cole?"

"What am I? His keeper?"

"Just tell me where he is," I gritted.

"He's gone."

"What do you mean gone?" He'd left without saying goodbye? Again?

"Is there more than one meaning for the word?"

Don't punch her. You can't afford a suspension. "What's the deal with Veronica? She and Cole are on such great terms, I'm curious about how long they've known each other." I should be discussing this with Cole, and only with Cole, but curiosity—and maybe a little anger—urged me onward.

"Cole dated her before me. I've heard rumors, but I'm not one hundred percent sure why they broke up. He never said."

Keep it together. Something about her tone… She knew something she wasn't telling me. "When he broke up with you, how did he do it?"

She stared at me as if I were a bug under a microscope—already dissected, ready to be sold for parts. Finally she averted her gaze, but not before I caught a glimmer of pity. "It was a few weeks after Bronx and I moved into his guesthouse, and a few months before you showed up. He got me alone, sat me down and told me we were over. I was absolutely blindsided. Even the day before, we were pretty into each other. Or so I thought."

Blindsided.

Into each other one day, but not the next.

Keep. It. Together.

Kat sidled up beside me, saying, "There you are."

She would help me, despite her problems.

"Well, well. Hello, Ally Kat." Mackenzie smiled with saccharine sweetness.

The two had never been friends, and probably never would be. Mackenzie, so protective of "her" boys, had tried to ruin Kat's relationship with Frosty a time or ten.

"Hello, Love Button," Kat replied, using the same tenor of falseness. Then she turned to me, putting her back to Mackenzie, as if the girl were of no consequence. Her cheeks were colorless, and her lips chapped from being chewed. "I'm blowing lunch and my last few hours and taking off. I'll pick you up for tonight's game. And I know you want to spend a few minutes explaining why you can't go, but I'll save you the time since there's no way you can win this argument. You're going and that's final."

I opened my mouth, but she kissed my cheek and bounded off before I could get out a single word. "What if I have to, I don't know, help Cole?" I called. A few slayers had to patrol the streets nearly every night, just in case.

She never turned back.

"You don't. You haven't been put on rotation," Mackenzie said, and bounded off in the other direction.

Cole still hadn't added me.

Trembling, I entered the lunchroom and headed toward the table I shared with Reeve and the slayers. Halfway there, I slammed into a brick wall. Or rather, a brick wall that went by the name of Justin Silverstone.

"Move," I commanded.

Big brown puppy-dog eyes peered down at me, beseeching. "Why would I? I'm right where I want to be."

"That's odd, considering your location might just get your testicles knocked into your throat." I wasn't falling for his innocent act. Not again. He'd once used me for information to feed to Anima. He might even have helped them bomb my house. No telling what he'd do next.

"Give me a chance to explain my side of things, Ali. Please. I had nothing to do with—"

"Save it." I took a step to the side, intending to brush past him, then stopped as a thought occurred to me. "First, answer a question for me. Did you talk to Cole on the phone last Saturday night?"

An emotionless mask descended—the same one Cole had been donning lately. "No. Why?"

If he was to be believed, I'd dreamed their conversation. My mind really was a mess.

"Watch me as I don't discuss that with you." I marched to the table and sat with more of a slam than I'd intended.

"What did Justin want?" Frosty asked, looking ready to commit murder on my behalf.

"To chat about old times."

Bronx ran his tongue over his teeth. It was his way of telling me he would be at Frosty's side, inflicting major damage on the boy. With his spiked hair now dyed an electric blue rather than green, and the piercings in his eyebrow and lip—and, okay, the tattoo peeking from under the collar of his shirt—he didn't have to say anything to scare the crap out of most people.

Frosty crossed his arms over his chest. "Want me to break his face?"

"That's sweet of you to offer," I replied, liking that I had such fierce protectors, "but if there's going to be any face-breaking, I'm going to be the one to do it."

"Well, if you change your mind…"

"I'll let you know." I picked at the lunch I'd packed—a bagel with cream cheese—and wondered where Cole had gone, what he was doing and if this day could get any worse.

What a stupid question, I told myself later that evening. Of course the day could get worse.

By five, a cold front had swept into Birmingham, and by eight I felt like a Popsicle despite my winter wear. I huddled on the stadium bleachers between Kat and Reeve. Neither girl seemed to notice the frigid temperatures. They were too busy bouncing up and down and celebrating. The Tigers had just scored their first touchdown of the game.

As the second quarter kicked off, Kat said, "So, get this. I'm, like, way more mad at Frosty than ever before. I may not ever forgive him."

"Why?" I asked. She was paler than she'd been at school, and despite her excitement over the game, her eyes were a little glassy. "What'd he do?"

"Last night he kissed some skank—right in my front yard."

"Oh, Kat. I'm so sorry."

"That snake!" Reeve exclaimed. "He deserves to die a thousand painful deaths."

Kat nodded, saying, "And that's not even the worst part. He put her on the back of his unicorn and rode off into the rainbow. He's *never* taken me to a rainbow."

Wait. "What are you talking about?"

"My dream last night," she said easily, then sipped her hot chocolate.

"Your dream." Reeve shook her head. "You're more mad at him than ever because of a dream?"

"Hey! I always behave myself in dreams," she said. "He should, too. And if he can't, he needs to apologize with more than my favorite flowers."

"He actually brought you flowers?" Stunned, I blinked at her. "For what he did in a dream?"

"Well, yeah. Wouldn't you?"

At the moment, I couldn't get Cole to say more than seven words to me. In real life.

Gavin suddenly plopped into the seat in front of me and though he grinned at me, he didn't look me in the eye.

Was this a nightmare?

A pretty brunette eased beside him, and she wasn't one of the girls from the club. She wrapped a possessive arm around his shoulders. A clear warning to me and my friends.

He had a girlfriend.

He frowned at the girl, removed her arm. *O-kay.* Maybe not a girlfriend.

"Ali Bell," he said with a nod of greeting. "It's good to see you again."

He hadn't shaved since the last time I'd seen him, and golden stubble now covered his jaw. Heart pounding unsteadily, I jerked my gaze to just over his shoulder, just in case he accidentally glanced up. "Uh, hi," I replied. "What are you doing here?"

"I came to see you."

"Hey, I remember you," Kat interjected. "From—" she caught herself before she admitted something she shouldn't and finished with a limp "—somewhere."

Reeve stiffened, as if she knew Kat was hiding something.

"You should," Gavin said. "I'm unforgettable."

"What a strange coincidence," Kat replied, fluffing her hair. "I am, too. So, are you a new member of the Asher High student body?"

The maybe/maybe-not-girlfriend snorted. "Does he look like he's in high school, kid?"

Her disdain irked.

Gavin, I'd discovered, had graduated last year. He was nineteen, not that much older than me, but he looked about thirty. The finest of lines branched from his eyes—either laugh lines, scowl lines or both. With slayers, you couldn't be sure. Most of the guys were as mean as rattlesnakes, but they were also quite warped in the humor department.

"Hillary," Gavin admonished.

"It's Belinda," the girl corrected tightly.

"Whatever. I wanted one night, you wanted two. I agreed to give you the second night if you promised to behave. You're not behaving."

She pressed her lips together and remained silent.

Are you kidding me?

He was casually discussing sex with a woman he'd called by the wrong name. I had no words.

"Since no one is willing to make introductions," Reeve said to break up the tenser-by-the-second silence, "I'll do it. I'm Reeve Ankh."

Gavin looked her over with unabashed interest. "You the one dating Bronx?"

"Not dating, no. We're not even on friendly terms anymore."

I caught the bitterness in her tone. She had no idea her father had threatened to pull his support from the slayers if one of the boys made a play for her. Every day Bronx had to choose between the girl he wanted and the friends he was determined to protect.

"I'm actually seeing someone else," Reeve admitted quietly.

"What!" Kat gasped. "And you didn't tell me? Who is it? How long has this been going on?"

"I'll share if you will."

Kat's excitement deflated. "I'm not sure I know what you're talking about."

From the corner of my eye, I spotted Wren Kyler and Poppy Verdeck making their way toward the concession stand. They made a striking pair, the beautiful black girl and the delicate redhead. A few weeks ago, Kat, Reeve and I would have been with them.

The moment I'd started dating Cole and she'd gotten back together with Frosty, they'd dropped us. We were now considered troublemakers, a bad bet, and they'd thought their futures would be brighter without us.

They were probably right.

Justin was dating Wren, and he walked behind the pair. He looked up, his gaze landing on me as if he'd known where I was all along. Just like before, his eyes pleaded at me.

I broke the connection.

"Hey, can I talk to you?" Gavin asked me. "Alone?"

Hillary/Belinda opened her mouth to protest, quickly closed it.

My palms began to sweat. Gavin wanted to find out if we'd have another vision, didn't he?

I nodded, trying to sound normal as I said, "Sure. Why not?"

We stood in unison. He led me up the bleachers, his hand on my lower back, making me uncomfortable.

"Here's good." He stopped at a secluded spot overlooking the parking lot, then motioned to the section we'd just abandoned. "I need to be able to see the girls."

Agreed. Emma hadn't formed a rabbit cloud, so I wasn't

worried about an attack, but I'd learned to err on the side of caution.

"Before you ask," I said, still not meeting his gaze. "I don't know what causes the visions—or, apparently, what stops them. I thought building emotional walls was the key, but I'd built what I considered an impenetrable fortress against you before Hearts and yet we had another one."

He pushed out a heavy breath. "Note to self. Take Prozac before talking to Ali."

That probably wasn't a bad idea. "I don't think we should look at each other. Not here. Just in case."

"All right. Where? When?"

How about…never? I ignored the questions, saying, "Have you experienced a vision with anyone else?"

"No. But you have."

"Yes." And I was clearly the only unchanging variable. Somehow, this was all my fault. "What did you see in the barn?" Maybe he'd seen something different. Maybe—

"I saw you tasting my neck."

I gulped. No maybe. We'd seen the same thing. "That's never going to happen."

"That's not what Cole said."

Fury rose inside me, even though I'd already suspected Gavin had spilled the worst of the details. "You told him?"

"Of course. I had to. He's my friend. You're his girl."

Was I? I licked my lips. "When did you do it? What'd he say?"

"The day after the incident at the club. And nothing. He stormed off."

Why hadn't he called me?

I had to talk to him. I had to explain...what? What could I say to make this better?

"I feel the need to reiterate—I'm never going to lick you or throw you on my bed," I said.

Gavin fingered a lock of my hair. "Honey, I have to agree with you on that one. You're not even close to being my type."

"What type is that? Easy?"

"Among other things," he said unabashedly.

I stepped away from him and gripped the railing in front of me. In the parking lot, darkness was chased away by the occasional streetlamp, revealing car after car.

"I just want to figure out what's going on," he said.

"Me, too. And by the way, you're not my type, either."

"You don't like sexy?"

I rolled my eyes. "I just like Cole."

"So you like moody and broody."

I kind of wanted to smile at that. "I—" The scent of rot hit me, and I wrinkled my nose. Stiffening, I searched for any other sign of the zombies. They couldn't be here. They—

Were here.

Red eyes cut through the night, and my heart skittered into a wild beat. Anyone who wandered through the parking lot would be unable to see the evil lurking nearby, and the odds were good they'd become dinner.

"They're here," I said, trying not to panic. "The zombies are here."

BLOOD AND TEARS

I beat feet to my friends. "Stay here. No matter what you see or hear, don't leave the bleachers until I come back to get you, okay?" The zombies might have braved the parking lot, but their sensitive flesh would sizzle up here in the lights.

Kat paled—she knew what was happening. "Okay."

"What's going on?" Reeve demanded. "I've seen Bronx, Frosty and Cole act this way. Heard them say these things."

Unfazed, Gavin pointed a finger in her face. "Do as you've been told or I'll make sure you regret it." He switched his attention to his two-night stand. "You, too."

We didn't say anything else to the girls. There just wasn't time. Together, we pounded down the rest of the bleacher steps.

"You up for this, cupcake?" Gavin asked.

"Always. Jack-hole."

He laughed.

As I ran, I withdrew my phone and dialed Frosty. There was no reason to try to reach Cole right now. He'd just send me to voice mail. But Frosty failed to answer, as well. I left a message. "We're at the game. The enemy has entered the parking lot. Send backup ASAP."

Justin appeared at my side, keeping pace as we closed in on the darkness. "How many?" he demanded.

"Go home," I snapped. "We don't need your kind of help. You'll feed us to the Hazmats the moment we're distracted." He had before.

"I won't. Trust me."

Trust him, when I was struggling to trust Cole?

"He works with the Hazmats?" Gavin slowed down, moving behind us. Without any more warning than that, he punched Justin in the back of the head, knocking the boy forward. "Then he doesn't work with us."

Justin tripped over his own feet and went down, his hands and knees absorbing most of the impact. He could have recovered, but Gavin kicked him in the center of his back, sending him flying onto his stomach. Then Gavin stomped over his body and continued onward.

Part of me wanted to protest his methods. I wasn't Justin's friend, but wow. The other part of me was kind of impressed. He-slut had skills.

The moment we hit the parking lot, I withdrew my favorite daggers from the purse hanging at my side, then dropped the purse on the ground, not wanting to give the zombies anything extra to grab onto. There were streetlamps to my far left and right, illuminating sections of the lot. Four kids I recognized from school were climbing into a red truck.

Another two were standing in front of a sedan, a girl leaning against the hood, a boy leaning against her.

"Get out of here," I shouted, cruel to be kind. Contrary to popular opinion, stupidity did not make a less-than-delicious brain.

A strip of darkness consumed the center, and that was where we headed. I looked for the glow of the Blood Lines, but...found none. Very well. None of the cars would be solid to us when we entered the spirit realm. We could ghost through—and so could the zombies.

The closer we drew, the stronger the scent of rot became, and I gagged.

"Let's do this," Gavin said, and stepped out of his body as if it were a suit of armor he'd gotten tired of wearing.

As Cole had once told me, people were spirits. We had a soul, and we lived in a body. The spirit was the power source. The soul was the mind, will and emotions, and linked to the power. The body was the house.

I, too, forced my spirit and soul to split from my body, and my body froze in place, unable to move until I reentered it. If anyone stumbled upon the motionless shell, well, they'd get no response and I was sure there would be trouble. *Can't be helped.*

Instantly the air became colder, and the light I'd admired only a few seconds ago was too bright, making my eyes water. A typical reaction to leaving the natural realm and entering the spiritual.

"Shout if you get into trouble," Gavin called.

I didn't reply. Sometimes it was just better to remain silent.

Whatever a slayer said while in spirit form came true.

Well, mostly. There were two caveats. We had to believe it, and we couldn't violate someone else's free will.

Some things happened instantly. Some took a while. As long as the words met the requirements, they happened. No exceptions.

Gavin picked up speed and moved in front of me. He extended both his arms, fired two SIG Sauers—and bonus points to me for knowing the type...or brand...whatever! Sparks exploded from the barrels, and the ensuing *boom, boom* made me cringe. Not that anyone around us would hear it.

The fight was on.

The two zombies closest to us went down. But a heart-beat later, they were climbing back to their feet, ready for more. I frowned. The bullets should have slowed them, at least a little. Zombies felt no pain, but their spiritual bodies *were* subject to injury, just like ours.

"I didn't miss," Gavin gritted. He fired the guns until they ran out of bullets.

He reached the creatures first, using the two he'd deco-rated with holes as punching bags.

I reached my own target and gave a wide slash of my dag-ger, clipping his spine, nearly removing his head. An action that would merely disable. There was only one thing that could forever end these creatures, and it was the fire from a slayer's hands. But I could have a lot of fun beforehand.

I kicked the next one in the stomach, knocking him back-ward and revealing the zombie coming in behind him. Too late. He moved too quickly. The new addition pushed me, and I pinwheeled over a body, landing with a hard thud, my side throbbing. I was jumped and pinned a second later, teeth going for my neck. I broke his nose and his jaw and wiggled out from under him; he ended up gnawing on pavement.

As I stood, I swiped out my blades, the tips slashing into his neck once, twice, going deeper and deeper, into spinal cord, buying me a temporary reprieve. From him, at least.

I tried to summon my fire the same way I'd left my body, believing I could and thereby gaining the inner strength to actually do it, but I was so new to this, didn't have as much faith as the others and could only stretch myself so far. And multitask? Forget about it.

As expected, no flames.

Another zombie lunged at me, black-stained teeth bared. I spun and kicked, my booted heel slamming into his side. He stumbled away from me as yet another zombie lunged at me. I popped her in the nose and spun again, elbowing her in the temple when I lined up to her left. She went down, but quickly twisted and reached for my ankle.

I don't think so. I hopped up and stomped on her hand. Saw two more coming at me from the right. With a twirl of my dagger, I pressed the blade against my wrist, then punched one creature and kicked the other. At my side, a gnarled arm stretched out. I grabbed and bent it, forcing the zombie to hunch over as I jerked up my knee, barreling into his face. When I released him, he fell to the ground.

But like his brethren, he recovered in a rush. I performed another spin—*am getting so good at those!*—whipping out my leg to shove him back several feet. Before he could rise a second time, I swung my arm around and launched one of the daggers. The tip soared past his open mouth and embedded in the back of his throat.

Bull's-eye.

On instinct, I turned, realized a pack of zombies had launched a sneak attack. I arched left, right, narrowly avoiding nails and teeth, my blade constantly swinging, slicing through rotting flesh. Cold black goo dripped down my hands.

I grinned. Some people got off on drugs. I got off on this.

Something solid pressed against my back, and I threw an elbow, raised the blade. As I sliced in a downward arc, Justin ducked, barely avoiding impact.

"Idiot," I screamed. He knew better than to creep up on a slayer.

"Incoming." He motioned to just over my shoulder.

I drank in the scene as quickly as possible and decided what to do. A zombie had used my distraction to his advantage, stealing in close and preparing to sink his teeth in my upper arm. I could dive away, but Justin's nearness would put him in striking range. I could arch, but the creature's momentum would draw him back with me. We'd fall. His weight would cage me. I'd be more of a target, and he could go for my neck.

I had to take the bite in my arm and pray Justin or Gavin injected me with antidote right away, so I could jump back into battle.

Gonna sting.

"No!" Justin reached out, flames springing from the pores in his hand, the light shining as brightly as the streetlamps. The zombie bit into that light, and both Justin and the creature dropped.

The zombie frantically patted at his mouth, his throat, his

stomach, as if experiencing pain for the first time. But that wasn't possible. Was it? Even still, he hadn't been exposed to Justin's fire long enough to die.

On the opposite end of the spectrum, Justin *had* been exposed to enough toxin to die. A single drop was all it took. He writhed, the poison already pouring through him, a river, pulling him down, down, down, washing over him, drowning him.

I wanted to help him, meant to inject him, but there just wasn't time or opportunity. All I could do was stand over him and fight, protecting him from further harm, reeling that the boy I knew as a traitor had taken a blow meant for me. Maybe I should have been nicer to him.

Zombies, zombies, zombies, everywhere I looked; so many grotesque bodies I lost count. They were like a swarm of flies, moaning instead of buzzing. I hobbled one, and two more replaced him—and then the one I'd hobbled rejoined the party.

My inhalations were too shallow, my exhalations too quick. I trembled, the blades seeming to gain ten pounds with every move I made. I'd been without physical activity for too long. This was too much, too soon. I wasn't sure how much more I could take and still remain on my feet.

Can't let Justin's sacrifice be in vain.

Must avenge my family.

As I fought, I caught a glimpse of Gavin battling his own horde. He moved with the grace of a panther, his every action fluid, nothing without a purpose.

Should I call for help?

A clawed hand swiped at me. I barely managed to duck.

Teeth snapped at me. Hissing and snarls filled my ears. I swung, but an elbow jabbed into my middle, and I lost what little air I'd managed to take in. I doubled over. Fingers tangled in my hair, and hello, joyride to the ground.

"Gavin."

"Ali!" he shouted.

I kicked out, but two of the creatures managed to grab my ankles. I lashed out with my fists, but two others managed to grab my wrists. I bucked, but couldn't free myself.

Don't panic. Panic would prevent me from acting rationally. I could get out of this. I just had to... What?

"Ali!" another voice shouted.

Cole! Cole was here!

Cole, the light of my life.

Light. Yes.

"Light up, dang it," I commanded my hands. I could do this. I *would* do this. I believed. "Now!"

As Gavin ripped a zombie off me, flames at last burst from the ends of my fingertips.

The zombies still holding me instantly turned to ash.

"Help the kid," Gavin commanded, returning to finish off his own horde.

I looked over my shoulder—saw the creatures eating at Justin. Horrified, I scrambled over and performed an inelegant dance of touch and destroy, freeing him from grasping hands and too-sharp teeth.

Back on my feet, my arms glowing brightly, I ripped through the remaining zombies, touching this one, touching that one, destroying all. When the last one exploded into tiny pieces of ash, my knees collapsed, and I fell. On impact, the flames vanished, and my skin returned to normal.

Victory.

Face splattered with black goo, Gavin closed the distance and grinned at me. "Now that's the kind of ability I can encourage."

Cole misted through the car beside me and stopped short. Fear radiated from him. Violet eyes I'd missed with every fiber of my being scanned me, searching for injury. "Were you bitten?"

"No, I'm good. But Justin isn't."

He frowned. "Justin?"

"He took a bite meant for me." I crawled to Justin's side and felt for a pulse. The beat thumped so swiftly I couldn't keep count. "He needs the antidote."

"I'll give him mine," Cole said, bending down as he withdrew a syringe from his back pocket.

"Justin," I said, patting his cheek. "We're here. We'll take care of you."

His eyelids split apart. Rivers of red ran through his irises. I gasped. Surely he wasn't... Couldn't... Not that quickly.

His head whipped toward me—and he sank his teeth into my wrist.

He quickly released me to curl into a ball and vomit, but the damage was done. I screamed. It was like electric paddles had been strapped to my chest, jump-starting a second heart, making it beat for the first time, but never in rhythm with the other one.

Suddenly there were two Alis, and both were in pain.

One hated it. One liked it.

That one was hungry. *So hungry.*

Cole loomed over me, his features tortured with concern. His mouth was moving, but I couldn't hear him. My attention caught on the pulse at the base of his neck. *Thump, thump. Thump, thump.*

Hypnotic.

Delicious.

Radiant light seeped through his pores. A light that didn't hurt my gaze. A light that drew me, every part of me. I licked my lips. If I could just get past his skin, I could reach that light. I could touch it. Taste it.

Consume it.

Desperate, I grabbed him by the shoulders and tugged him down, baring my teeth. Just before I could bite into him, a fist slammed into my temple. From the corner of my eye, I saw Gavin, raising his arm to deliver another blow. Cole stopped him.

It was the last thing I saw before darkness swept over me.

THE KING TAKES THE PAWN

I had spent the first sixteen years of my life under the watchful eye of a man who'd seen monsters no one else could see. I'd thought him insane, and part of me had resented him for the rules he'd enforced, the trouble he'd caused.

He'd built a house to protect us, a fortress of solitude, really, with iron behind the walls and bars over the windows. My sister and I had left our prison to attend school and church, and the occasional lunch date with our grandparents, but that was it. Every other second had been spent in confinement.

Now I knew more about the invisible world around me, more than Dad had ever known, and I knew the iron and the bars wouldn't have kept the monsters at bay. Only Blood Lines could. I knew zombies were drawn to life—the very thing they'd lost. I knew they hungered for slayers first, and average Joes second. We were tastier dishes, I guess. I knew they found fear to be an aphrodisiac and fury to be a dessert.

Emotion added spice.

As miserable as I'd been back then, I missed the life I used to lead. I missed the hours I'd spent holding my sister while she drifted to sleep. I missed the hugs my mother had so freely given. Missed the smiles she and my dad used to share. The food she used to cook. The notes she used to leave under my pillow.

I love you, Alice Rose.
Thinking about you today, darling girl.
You're so strong and beautiful. How'd I get so lucky?

Remembering caused pain to scrape at my chest, over and over, again and again, razor-sharp claws tearing into flesh and muscle, even bone, leaving me raw and bleeding. I hurt. Oh, glory, I hurt with a hunger no one should ever have to endure. It was as if I'd never eaten. As if my body was destroying itself, cell by cell. And all the while, those two hearts pounded in my chest.

I unleashed a terrible scream.

The pain only expanded, razing my mind, pooling even in my toes. I tried to burrow my fingers past my skull, my chest, somewhere, anywhere, desperate to reach the pain and snatch it away, but I failed miserably.

My blood turned molten in my veins, burning me from the inside out. But a second later, a chill danced over my skin, causing me to shiver. *Cold.* My teeth chattered as I burrowed deeper under the blanket. *Hot.* I kicked the stupid blanket away. *Cold.* I pulled my arms into my chest, trying to curl into myself for warmth. *Hot.* I tore at my clothing.

"Ali," called a voice I knew I should recognize. Male. Raspy with concern.

Cole, maybe. I inhaled deeply, and oh, he smelled so good. Pure and crisp and crackling with energy. The hunger overwhelmed me all over again. My mouth watered. "Feed me," I croaked.

Gentle hands smoothed over my cheeks, offering a comforting stroke.

My nerve endings went haywire, agonizing me further. I jerked away. "No. Don't."

"Ali."

Grab him. Devour him. You'll feel so much better.

"I administered a double dose of the antidote hours ago. Why isn't she better?"

Definitely Cole. He was here. He was with me.

"Give her another."

"Can she take it?"

"Do we have a choice?"

A sharp sting in my neck, a cool rush through my veins, and the pain and hunger at last died. The second heartbeat slowed, softened, but didn't disappear completely. Still, it was enough. I sagged into a boneless heap.

"Ali, I need you to wake up, okay?"

Anything for Cole. I ripped my way through the veil of darkness shrouding my conscious and pried open my eyelids. At first, I saw only a haze of white clouds.

Clouds.

Emma.

But…she wasn't here. Where was *here?* I frowned.

"Good girl, that's the way," Cole said. "Come back to me, sweetheart."

Sweetheart. An endearment.

He wasn't upset with me anymore.

Blinking rapidly shooed away the haze. Cole leaned over the side of the bed, peering down at me. Black hair shagged over a forehead furrowed with a mix of worry and relief. His eyes were glassy and bloodshot, making me think he'd been denied sleep. The shadow-beard he always sported was now thicker.

"Hey there," he said softly.

"Hey." My voice was damaged, as if my vocal cords had been cut and only recently sewn back together. "I'm glad you're speaking to me again."

He frowned, and suddenly I could see the storm brewing beneath his exhaustion. "I wasn't ever *not* speaking to you."

"You were avoiding me, then."

A stilted pause before he admitted, "Yes."

A second later, the world around me tunneled so that only Cole existed. Elation speared me—finally we were having a vision—

—in the Ankhs' game room, Cole stood across from me. He was smiling at something Veronica was saying. I stood in front of Gavin, my hands cupping his cheeks.

"You are a better man than I ever gave you credit for," I told him.

"I know," Gavin replied.

"And you're *so* modest."

He chuckled. "Are you happy with the way things turned out?"

My gaze strayed to Cole. The tension he'd worn like a second skin all these weeks had utterly vanished. "Yeah. Yeah, I am—"

—the vision vanished in a blink, right along with my elation, and Cole let his head drop into his upraised hands. He scrubbed his fingers through his already disheveled hair.

"Gavin's a man-whore, you know. Never been with the same girl twice. And he's never liked blondes. He won't stay with you for long."

There was ice in his tone, and it scared me. "I'm not interested in Gavin." I struggled to sit up. "Cole, you have to—"

"Don't say anything. Just…don't." Motions jerky, he shoved two pillows behind my back and reached over to lift a glass of water from the nightstand.

I was in my bedroom, I realized. Determined sunlight shoved its way through the curtains. The iPod Cole had given me was stationed in its dock on the desk and turned on. Soft music filled the room.

He placed the straw at my lips. "Drink."

I obeyed, the cool liquid sliding down my throat, soothing for a moment only to churn in my belly, frothing up acid. "Thank you."

He nodded stiffly and set the cup aside. "Let's talk about what happened with Justin."

Yes. Okay. A safe topic. "Has he recovered?"

"Yeah, and a lot quicker than you."

The accusation in his voice threw me, and I glowered at him. "Hey, don't blame me. I'm the victim here."

He massaged the back of his neck, somewhat contrite. "Yeah. I know. Sorry. It's been stressful, watching you suffer and not being able to help."

Slowly I relaxed. "Has a slayer ever bitten another slayer like that?"

"Not to my knowledge. Not while both are still human."

Why Justin? Why me? What had been different? "Did I try to bite anyone while I was...out of it?" The moment I asked, memories came flooding back to me. Cole. I'd tried to bite Cole.

"Just me," he said without any hint of emotion.

I soaked in horror like a sponge. "I'm sorry," I rushed out. "I know I failed. Wait. I failed, right?"

He gave one, sharp nod. "You did."

I relaxed again, but only slightly. "I'm so sorry, Cole. I don't know what came over me, but I do know I'm not going to do it again. I promise you."

He shrugged—and I wasn't sure whether he was trying to tell me he believed me...or that he didn't.

"I mean it," I insisted.

"You tried to bite me more than once," he said flatly.

Oh. I didn't remember the other times. "I'm so sorry," I repeated. "I didn't realize..."

"I know."

I gulped. Was he disgusted with me now? "Do you think Anima put Justin up to hurting me? Causing this kind of reaction, thinking we'd destroy each other?"

"Maybe, but like you, I don't think Justin knew what he was doing."

Agreed. The red I'd seen in his eyes... "Where is he now?"

"Ankh kept him below, in the dungeon, as you like to call it, for a few days to make sure the antidote was working and he wouldn't try to attack anyone else. Tests were run, and a strange toxin was found in his blood. Not zombie, but actually antizombie. Different than what's in the antidote. We think it's what made him vomit."

Wait. Hold everything. "A few days? How long have I been out? Did you check my blood, too?"

Used to my rapid-fire questions, he easily followed. "About a week. And yes. You had—have—the same anti-zombie toxin, only you have a lot more of it, which makes us think you shared it with him when he bit you."

Crap. I'd lost another week of my life. My poor Nana. Ugh, my poor grades. "How and where would I have gotten an antizombie toxin? And why is it in my blood, rather than my spirit?"

He shrugged. "Could be an ability, like the visions. And if it's in your spirit, it's in your blood. We have to test what we can."

Yes. Okay. All of that made sense.

When I'd first moved in with Nana, I'd found a journal written in a strange numbered code that always seemed to unravel by itself. Through it, I'd learned some slayers were born with strange abilities no one could explain. A poison-ous spirit, and thereby blood, had been on the list—which was actually a good thing. Like Justin, the zombies sickened soon after biting me.

"Just so you know, we told everyone you'd overdone it and reopened your wound," Cole said. "Both of which are true."

"Thank you."

He nodded, moved to the door.

He was…leaving me? Just like that?

"Cole," I called. "We need to talk."

"You need to rest."

"Cole." My voice lashed like a whip. I wasn't letting him get away. Not this time.

He paused, faced me. His features were blank.

"This has to stop."

He gave a single nod, and the formality of the action worried me.

"I tried not to push you, but you have to give me something. Your silence is driving me crazy."

He crossed his arms as if preparing for battle. "Some things aren't meant to be discussed, Ali."

Today, I just couldn't accept that. I'd come this far… "At Hearts, you couldn't spend time with me. Why?"

He ran his tongue over his teeth. "I've already told you all I'm willing to say on that subject."

"You asked me to trust you, and now I'm asking you to trust me with the truth. Why?"

Silence.

Argh! I tried a different approach, saying, "You told me you wanted me to stay away from Gavin, and yet you have been the one to stay away from me. Why?"

Again silence.

Dang him! I was giving, but he wasn't giving anything back. "What we just saw in the vision—"

"Will happen." Fury blazed in his eyes, making me miss the expressionless mask. "You know it will. It always does."

I'd denied it to myself, but I couldn't deny it to him. He'd call my bluff. "Maybe it doesn't mean what we think it means."

His head tilted to the side, and he studied me intently. Hopefully? "What do you think it means?"

"I…don't know." I wasn't at my best just then. But I knew that just because I'd stood with Gavin, and Cole had stood with Veronica, and just because I'd had my hands on Gavin and Cole had been smiling so peacefully at Veronica, didn't mean we belonged with Gavin and Veronica. "What do *you* think it means?"

Please tell me what I want to hear.

He would. He had to. Not many people were as layered as Cole. A hard outer shell covered razor blades, and razor blades covered steel. But for those willing to dig—and endure the injuries and bleeding—a soft, gooey center could be found. I'd dug. I'd found it. He wouldn't let me go, wouldn't turn to Veronica.

"I think it means…we're over," he said, and closed his eyes.

He would. He really would.

He might as well have slapped me. "No," I said, shaking my head. "No."

"Okay, let me rephrase. I *know* it means we're over. We have to be. I've almost lost you twice, and I'm going to lose you for good when the visions start coming true. I'm not going to hang on to a lost cause, Ali."

Panic set in. I had to make him understand. "I'm not a lost cause. *We're* not a lost cause. I don't like Gavin."

"But you will."

No! "Don't do this," I said. "Please. You have to trust me. Please," I said again, and I didn't care how desperate I sounded. "There are some things you can never take back, and this is one of them."

A terrible stillness came over him. I wasn't sure he was even breathing. Then he was stomping to the wall, throwing a fist.

Boom! I flinched. Plaster gave, leaving a hole. Dust mushroomed through the air.

Here was the dangerous boy I'd been warned about in the beginning. The one mothers wanted to hide from their daughters. The panty melter, I'd heard a few girls at school call him. The boy others feared. The violent criminal. The hard-hearted machine.

"I'm not going to look at Gavin and suddenly start wanting him," I whispered. I couldn't even imagine it. "You're the one for me. And this isn't like you," I added. "You never back down. You never walk away from a fight." *Fight for me.*

He pressed his forehead into the damaged wall.

"Cole," I said quietly. *Must get through to him.* "Do you want Veronica?"

"No," he said, and I could have sobbed with relief. "Not even a little."

"See!"

"Ali, I..." He straightened, turned toward me. I saw the panic a split second before a sheet of ice fell over his features, and that ice was far worse than the fury he'd displayed earlier. "Our feelings right now aren't the problem. One day I hope you'll forgive me. I doubt I'll ever be able to forgive myself. But...we're done."

Done.

Just like that.

Over. Finished.

"Cole."

"We're done," he repeated more firmly. "We're done."

How finite he sounded. How sure.

For the second time in my life, my heart broke into thousands of pieces. I thought I would die. But this time, I had the second heart, the new one, whatever it was, to pick up the slack, to keep me alive.

Silent now, he backed up, away from me.

"I won't come crawling after you," I croaked.

"I don't want you to."

With those five words, he shredded the rest of me. Spirit, soul and body. I wouldn't give him the chance to do it again. I couldn't. "I won't take you back even if you come crawling back to *me*."

"I know," he said, despair creeping into his tone. "And I won't.... I can't...." He shook his head. "There's nothing I can say to make either of us feel better about this, and I'm sorry about that. You'll probably never know how much. But that's not going to change my mind. It has to be this way."

He turned and left.

6

WELCOME TO
YOUR NIGHTMARE

I…

Broke…

Down.

Somehow I found the strength to stand. My legs shook. With fury. Sorrow. Helplessness. Regret.

Pain.

I wanted to chase after Cole and tear into him the way he'd just done to me. I wanted to hit him. I wanted to scream at him.

I wanted him to hurt the way I was hurting.

I wanted to cry and beg him to come back to me.

I wanted his arms around me.

I wanted to hate him.

Maybe I did hate him. Today he'd proved he wasn't the admirable boy I'd thought he was. How could he be? He'd cut me loose the same way he'd cut Mackenzie loose. As if

I meant nothing. Only difference was, I'd had a little warning. I just hadn't wanted to face the truth of it.

I wanted to avoid him forever.

I'd see him again. Of course I would. We would even talk to each other. We'd have to. In a way, he was my boss. He set the nightly rotation schedule. He headed up all training. But the easy camaraderie we'd shared was over. The bantering. The kissing. The touching.

Over.

He'd wanted to protect himself, and me, from further hurt, from fighting a losing battle, from whatever mystery he refused to discuss, from the devastation and shame of falling for other people while we were still together.

I'd been willing to risk it.

He'd decided I wasn't worth the effort.

I looked around the room that wasn't mine. It was only a loaner. The only things I owned were the clothes in the dresser and closet. I stumbled to the dresser without knowing why—until I felt my fingers curl around the edge and my arms push forward, sending the piece of furniture crashing into the floor.

I grabbed a drawer and tossed it, then another, and another. Socks and underwear went flying in every direction. Seeing them lying on the floor only made me madder. I was just like them. Tossed aside. In a place I didn't belong.

Cole had just changed the entire course of my life, and I'd been helpless to stop him. Just like I'd been helpless to stop the car crash.

How many other changes would I be forced to endure?

Everything changed. The world. The seasons. Time. Peo-

ple. Nothing and no one ever stayed the same. Accepting another change should be easy. After all, even I would change.
One day, I would forget about Cole and the feelings I had
for him. I would move on.

And so would he.

He would date another girl.

My gaze drifted to the picture I kept on my nightstand.
Kat had snapped it when I'd been too distracted to know
anyone else was around. In it, Cole stood behind me, his
arms wrapped around me. His chin rested on top of my
head, and he appeared utterly content. I was smiling with
the dreamy confidence of a girl rushing headlong into love.

Love.

I refused to love him.

I picked up the photo and launched it across the room, my
new heart racing with dangerous speed, my lungs burning,
no longer able to pull in enough oxygen—as if something
inside me was stealing it. My stomach curled into a ball and
hardened into iron—but the iron was hollowed out and
desperate to be filled. I was hungry again, so danged hungry...but not for food. For... I wasn't sure. But whatever it
was, I needed it.

Now.

A high-pitched ringing scraped at my ears. Sweat broke
out over my brow and my palms and trickled down my
back. The room spun around and around, my equilibrium
shot, and I flailed for balance...tilting anyway...and felt a
sharp sting against my entire right side. I must have fallen
to the floor.

Help me, I tried to call, but no words emerged. My heart

sped up, faster and faster. My lungs constricted far more tightly, the burn intensifying. My hands and feet mutated into blocks of ice.

I…was dying? I had to be dying.

I crawled to the desk, reached blindly for my phone and knocked down the lamp. Glass shattered on the floor.

Had to text Co—no, Nana. Yes, Nana. She would come. She would take care of me—*she* loved me. But I couldn't see the keypad. The room was still spinning.

Hinges squeaked. "Ali? Are you okay? What happened to your room?"

Male voice. I recognized it. Mr. Ankh?

Help, I tried to say, but again, no sound emerged.

Footsteps. Strong arms slid underneath me, lifted me. I floated for a few seconds before the mattress pressed into my back.

"Is it the toxin?" he asked, even as he stuck me in the neck with a needle. Yes, it had to be Mr. Ankh. Like the rest of us, he carried the antidote in his pocket, just in case.

A cool stream raced through my veins, and the hunger simmered.

"Breathe," he said gently. "In. Out. Yes, just like that. Again. Again." Hands smoothed over my brow, offering comfort I so desperately needed. "Again."

At last, my heart…hearts…began to slow. My lungs began to fill. The sweat stopped pouring, and the chill kissed me goodbye.

I blinked open my eyes, and saw Mr. Ankh sitting at the side of my bed. Concern bathed his still-handsome features.

"That wasn't just about the toxin, was it?" he asked, the concern giving way to sympathy.

I remained silent.

"Has that ever happened before?"

"Wh-what?" Almost dying?

"A panic attack?"

Panic attack? No. "That's not what just happened." I'd weathered the death of my family. A breakup wouldn't ruin my mental stability. I wouldn't let it.

"Ali, sweetheart, I'm a doctor. More than that, for several years I was married to a woman with an anxiety disorder. I know a panic attack when I see one."

Anxiety disorder. No. Not that, either. "I'm fine," I said, my voice ragged. "Just tired."

His smile was sad. "Did something happen to trigger it?"

Something like losing the other part of me? "I told you I'm fine," I replied stiffly, then regretted my tone. He was being nice, trying to help me. He didn't deserve my rancor.

He sighed, pushed to his feet. "The more you know about the triggers, the better you'll handle the episodes. If you ever want to talk about it…"

"I don't. I won't. I'm fine, really."

"All right. Well, don't worry about the room. I'll send someone up to clean."

"No! No," I said more gently. "I'll take care of it."

A pause, then, "If that's what you prefer." Like Cole, he left the room.

Left me alone.

My new heart sped up all over again.

★ ★ ★

I righted the furniture and cleaned the room, even patched the hole in my wall. The one Cole had caused. It had reminded me of him, and I wasn't fond of reminders right now. I threw our picture in the trash.

The next week passed in a daze. Every day I had to bury my emotions as deep as they would go and pretend everything was peachy, just to make it through school. Kat and Reeve treated me the same; they had no idea Cole and I had broken up. I hadn't told anyone, and for some reason, neither had he. I think the girls were onto me, though, and I expected questions very, very soon.

I stayed away from Cole's gym and worked out with Kat in Mr. Ankh's. I still hadn't been put on rotation, but I hadn't pushed because the zombies hadn't made another appearance.

I wasn't eating, wasn't sleeping.

I couldn't go on like this.

"Emma," I said as I burrowed under my covers. "Emma." I needed my baby sister.

I wasn't sure how much time passed before she materialized in the center of my room.

"Oh, Ali." She stretched beside me on the bed, ghosting her hand through my hair. Somehow she calmed me, the weird heartbeat evening out, the hunger pains that always seemed to hover at the edge of my conscious ebbing. "I hate seeing you like this."

"I'm better now that you're here."

"I'm glad. And I'm glad you called me." Her dark eyes were luminous as she said, "Would it help to know I've been watching Cole? He's miserable, too."

"Maybe," I said with a sniffle. "Why have you been watching him?"

"I think he's spying on the other slayers."

Why would he do that? He trusted the people around him, everyone but me, that is, and—

Wait. "I don't care anymore." I changed the subject. "The night I was bitten, you didn't put a rabbit cloud in the sky. Why?"

"I had been watching the zombie nests, and none of them had stirred. The ones that attacked you came out of nowhere."

No, they'd had to come from somewhere. But where? And what did this mean…for the…future? *Can't concentrate. So tired.*

"I'm losing you," she said with a chuckle. "Rest now."

I must have fallen asleep at long last; the next time I opened my eyes, she was gone.

Thursday, Nana tried to talk to me about my sudden withdrawal. She was worried I was sick. I assured her I was the picture of health.

Friday, Mackenzie and Trina insisted on driving me home from school, and I buckled in back of a beat-up Jeep. They knew my situation without being told.

"I recognize the glaze in your eyes," Mackenzie said, twisting in the passenger seat. For once, there was no heat in her tone. No condescension or anger on her face. "I know we've never liked each other, but I do mean it when I say I'm sorry for what you're going through. And maybe I should have warned you. This is what he does. This is what he's always done."

I peered out the window. The sun was bright today, making my eyes water. "What do you mean? What does he always do?"

"He cuts and runs when things get serious, and I don't think he even realizes he's doing it. He just looks for an excuse, and then boom, it's over."

I remembered the panic I thought I'd seen in his eyes. I'd convinced myself I'd imagined each instance, but what if they had been the start of the demise of our relationship? *Not* the visions.

"Yesterday I asked Veronica straight-up," Trina said. "When he broke up with her, he told her he couldn't do the long-distance thing anymore."

I wondered what he would say about me, when he finally started talking.

"He's a great guy," Mackenzie said, "but he's never been in a relationship for the long haul."

"I think his friendships are the same way. Don't get me wrong, I know he loves us slayers." Trina maneuvered the car onto Reeve's street. "I'm never in doubt of that. But I'm always aware of the fact that he keeps me at a bit of an emotional distance. He does it with everyone but Frosty and Bronx—they're like brothers with other mothers or something. Frankly, I was shocked he let you get as close as you did, as fast as you did."

I thought I understood. Cole had lost his mom to the zombies. He knew he would lose his dad the next time his dad was bitten, since the man had developed an immunity to the antidote. If he let someone else all the way in, like, say, a girlfriend, and then he lost her, too, he probably didn't think he would survive.

The fury returned—the roots had never withered. How dare he? How dare he lead me on, making me want more, when he'd never planned to see this thing through? And then to throw me away because of what might happen at some later date… Because of fear…

"There's the spirit we're used to seeing," Mackenzie said with a nod of approval.

No, this was something else. Something sharper. But I didn't correct her. "Has he ever gone back for seconds?"

"Never. Not even when we get desperate and try to steal his attention by messing around with someone else," she added bitterly.

There was a story there, but I wouldn't pry.

"So…what excuse did he give you?" Mackenzie asked.

"Have you heard about my vision with Gavin?"

She nodded. "Gavin has been soliciting advice."

"That's why."

Anger glazed her eyes. Anger on my behalf? "Someday some girl is going to come along, and he's not going to be able to let her go. Maybe she'll dump him, and he'll learn what rejection feels like."

Maybe. But that would mean he loved her. My nails dug into my thigh.

"I'm guessing your vision with Gavin is the reason Cole has stayed silent about the breakup," Trina said. She parked in Reeve's driveway. "He doesn't want Gavin coming to you for information about your ability, something he would do if he knew you and Cole were over."

"Which isn't like him," Mackenzie said, a little confused now. A lot intrigued. "Cole doesn't usually care what a girl does or who she does it with once he's done with her."

Part of me wanted to thrill over this knowledge. Maybe he still cared about me. The other part of me scoffed. I wasn't so pathetic…was I? "He and I are over, and that's that. I'll be fine," I said tightly. "Thanks for the ride, girls. And the conversation. I appreciate it."

Mackenzie grabbed my hand to stop me before I could emerge. "We're here if you need us."

I had the dream again.

My mother reached for me. Warmth spread through me. She shook me, shouting, "Alice. Wake up!"

I didn't. Not this time.

The zombies came for her, dragged her off and threw her on the cold, hard ground next to my dad. Then they fell on her, disappearing inside her, eating her spirit right out of her body. At first, she screamed and fought. Then she quieted and writhed. Then she stilled. Black boils appeared all over her skin, the zombie toxin poisoning her from the inside out.

I watched, helpless, sobbing.

And when I woke up, my cheeks were actually wet.

Had she died that way? Even the thought filled me with a terrible, dark rage. She had been such a gentle, loving woman. She'd never knowingly hurt anyone. For those creatures to torture her that way…

Can't deal with the past. I crawled out of bed and into the shower, not leaving until my fingers and toes were like prunes. I towel-dried, swiped a shaky hand across the steam-covered mirror. My gaze caught on my reflection, and I stumbled backward, shocked. I was… There was… *Impossible.*

Tick, tock. Tick, tock.

The sound whispered through my mind, keeping time to the beat of my new heart. I stepped as close to the mirror as I could get, until the round edge of the sink prevented me from going any farther. There were dark smudges under my eyes and around my lips, and a black dot the size of my thumb streaked over my heart. Though I scrubbed with all my strength, leaving welts and nearly peeling off my skin, the splotches remained.

Could stress do this?

Maybe. Probably.

I turned away from the glass, and the sound of the *tick-tocks* died. My hands shook as I dressed in a T-shirt, jeans and butt-kicking boots and sheathed a dagger at each ankle.

I picked up my cell and texted Kat.

Me: How soon can U get here? Time 2 work out.

It was just after noon on Saturday. I was done avoiding Cole. I was going to his gym, and I was moving on with my life. Self-inflicted incarceration had done me no good. Obviously.

Mad Dog: Like, NOW. I'm here! Come 2 Reeve's room.

Me: On my way.

Mad Dog: Walk faster. Reeve's annoying me.

Reeve: SHE LIES! I annoy no 1.

I stalked down the hall and up the stairs. Reeve occupied the entire top floor. I cleared the landing and sailed inside the first sitting room, an area decorated with pink, pink and more pink, coupled with mounds of lace and rows of ruffles.

Every time I came up here, I thought that maybe Valentine's Day had thrown up and this had been the result.

The bedroom door was open. The girls sat at the edge of the four-poster king (draped in pink satin). Reeve had her hand on Kat's forehead. Kat was shaking her head in denial of something, her cheeks pale, dark circles under her eyes.

"Are you okay?" I asked her.

Hazel eyes found me, only to skitter away. "Not you, too. I missed out on my beauty z's, that's all."

No. It was more than that. Lately, she'd had more bad days than good.

She returned her attention to me, looked me over and frowned. "But, uh, what's wrong with *you?* I mean, I know you've been going through something you haven't had the decency to share with us, but wow. You're like death walking."

"Kat!" Reeve said.

"What? It's true."

I attempted to scrub the discolorations from my skin. "I don't know what happened, but I can't get the smudges off."

"Smudges? What smudges? You're the same shade of snow-white as always—and that's a compliment, by the way. You're like a winter wonderland fairy, and I'd be eaten up with jealousy if—"

"You weren't so in love with yourself," Reeve interjected with a laugh.

"Exactly! You've seen me, right? God was on His A game when He made me, all, like, a dash of sexy here, a sprinkle of awesome there. It's just...your eyes," Kat said to me. "They're more haunted than usual."

The smudges had faded? That quickly? I stalked to the vanity mirror and leaned over, planting my palms on the surface scattered with makeup. My reflection stared back at me, the smudges just as dark as before. Disappointment hit me a split second before I realized something else was wrong. Something far worse.

I wasn't smiling—but my reflection was.

Tick, tock.

I shook my head, blinked, but the image remained the same. *Tick.* Reeling, I reached up and patted my lips. *Tock.* The corners hadn't somehow lifted without my knowledge. *Tick.*

No longer able to catch my breath, I straightened and turned away. What I'd just seen... The fault of my imagination, surely.

"I look normal to you?" I demanded.

"Sure. But you've lost a little weight your Nana's chocolate chip cupcakes would fix—hint, hint, I want chocolate chip cupcakes," Kat said at the same time Reeve said, "Totally."

Confirmation. My imagination *was* at fault.

No big deal, I decided. Everything would calm down once I'd dealt with my stress load.

I licked my lips. First step: I had to stop pretending. "So... Cole and I broke up. We're one hundred percent over. There's no hope of us ever getting back together."

"What?" Kat gasped, jolting to her feet. "What'd he do? And I know it's all his fault, the jerk! I'll kill him. I swear I will! Reeve, where are your Skittles?"

Reeve ignored her, her hand fluttering over her heart. "Oh, Ali. I'm so sorry."

I jutted my chin, somehow able to maintain my calm. "Don't be. That's life."

"But you guys were so happy. And he was spending the night with you," Kat said, clearly reeling. "Bronx told Frosty he caught Cole sneaking out to come see you multiple times."

I shook my head. "He might have snuck out and spent the night, but we never actually had sex." Not even before my injury.

Mom had told me to wait for someone special. Someone who loved and appreciated me for more than my body, and wouldn't run tattling to all his friends. Or hurt me. Or push for more than I was ready to give. Or abandon me if things got rough afterward. I'd thought Cole was that boy, but I must have sensed, deep down, he'd been holding a part of himself back.

Go me.

"He didn't think we'd last," I said, "and he didn't like me enough to fight for me. It hurts, I'm so mad I could do serious damage to him, but I'm not going to break down." Not again.

"Well, boys suck!" Kat flicked the length of her dark hair over one shoulder, truly angry on my behalf. "Ali, forget working out. Reeve, grab your keys and your dad's credit card. We're taking a girls' day, and since he's one of the enemy, he's paying."

"That seems fair. We just have to be back by six," Reeve replied, standing. "I have a date—I mean, uh, I'm sorry, Ali." Her dusky skin flushed, and her shoulders drooped with shame. "I shouldn't have mentioned my date while you're suffering and...I'm just so sorry."

Oh, no, no, no. We weren't going down the pity road. "Don't you dare stop talking about your love life just because mine went up in flames."

"Yeah. What she said. Even though I have a feeling mine will be going up in flames, too." Kat toyed with the ends of her hair. "I don't think Frosty will be willing to become a girl for me, and right now I'm totally giving up on dudes."

Reeve shook her head in exasperation.

Me? I suddenly saw Kat through new eyes. She only ever talked about axing Frosty when she looked pale and withdrawn. In other words, when her kidneys were acting up. Fear was driving her, I realized, just like it had driven Cole. She probably felt vulnerable, desperate to protect herself.

Poor Kat. One day, Frosty might get tired of the hot-and-cold treatment and leave her.

Kat pointed a finger at Reeve. "Don't think I've forgotten you've been sidestepping my questions about your mystery guy."

"Maybe I'll tell you about him. Maybe I won't." Dark amber eyes gleamed with challenge. "You guys aren't the only ones who can keep secrets."

Kat backed down; what else could she do? "I don't know what you're talking about. I'm probably the most open and honest girl in the world," she muttered. "Just ask Ali."

Both girls peered over at me, expectant.

Kat wanted confirmation. Reeve wanted me to spill our secrets.

"Didn't someone mention a girls' day?" I asked.

★ ★ ★

We had our hair cut and styled, had facials and bought makeup, perfume, clothes and shoes. Or rather, they bought those things. I was still saving my money and refused to spend Mr. Ankh's. That didn't deter the girls. Every time my back was turned, they purchased something else for me and stuffed it in my bag.

Through it all, I avoided mirrors. I couldn't bring myself to look at my reflection, even though the girls raved about my appearance.

Sadly, I almost hyperventilated when Kat said, "A new you, for a new direction in life."

Fine. I did hyperventilate, and it freaked out both girls. It was just, terror had wrapped cold, clammy hands around my neck and squeezed, shutting off my airways. The second heartbeat had become more noticeable, and the intense hunger had returned.

Reeve splashed water in my face, but that wasn't what jolted me out of terror's grip. As close as she was, I could smell her—such a sweet, mouthwatering perfume—and I wanted to bite her. *So bad.* The desire threw me into another tailspin. I plopped into a chair, holding on to the arms for dear life...her life...again struggling to breathe.

Kat called Frosty, thinking I needed medical help only the slayers could provide.

Frosty, Bronx, Lucas and Cole—*please, anyone but Cole*—arrived at the store fifteen minutes later, and all heads turned in their direction. Eyes widened. Women muttered excitedly. Grown men backed away.

"What's he doing here?" Kat hissed.

The ringing in my ears was finally fading, allowing me to make out her words.

"Sheathe the claws, Kitten," Frosty said. "We weren't sure what we were dealing with. And what did you do to your hair?"

"Duh. I fixed it."

"But I liked it the way it was."

"Say one more word, I dare you, and I'll shave it all off. Your ex-girlfriend will be bald."

"You aren't my ex," he said flatly.

I'd never heard him use that tone with her. And yet, their familiar chatter helped soothe me, and the urge to bite Reeve at last diminished. What the heck was wrong with me?

Then Cole was crouching in front of my chair, and the rest of the world was forgotten. Embarrassment burned my cheeks. Wet strands of hair stuck to my forehead and cheeks. My T-shirt had a water ring around the collar.

I met his gaze, not expecting a vision this time and not getting one. I was careful to keep my features blank. Seconds…minutes…maybe hours passed…but he didn't do what I needed him to do and leave.

Please leave.

Then something happened. The same something that happened every time we were together.

The air around us came to life, thickening with awareness. My skin prickled in the most delicious way.

I didn't like it—because I liked it so much.

He must have felt it, too, because he looked away.

Thankful for the reprieve, I scrutinized his body language. His fingers were next to mine, twitching on the arms of the chair, as if he wanted to reach for me but was fighting the impulse.

Did he want to reach for me?

My gaze lifted of its own accord.

He was staring at me again. Only he was staring far more intently, that violet gaze drilling into me, trying to burrow past skin and into soul to search for answers I didn't have.

"I didn't need the dark knight to race to my rescue," I sniped. "I'm fine."

"Ali," he said on a sigh. "You're not fine. Kat said you couldn't breathe."

"As you can see, I'm over it." I was proud of my seeming calm. "You can leave now."

Concern darkened his features, poking at my anger.

He had no right to feel concern for me.

"Why couldn't you breathe, Ali?"

"Does it really matter?"

At last he reached up, intending to cup my cheeks the way he used to. Just before contact he caught himself. His hands returned to the arms of the chair, caging me in, making me shiver—and hate myself. "Let Ankh run a few tests."

"No." I had been wrong to think I could face Cole today. It was too soon. Especially if he was going to be nice.

Why was he being nice?

"We're done here." I pushed him out of the way and stood on shaky legs. Frosty was scrubbing his knuckles into Kat's scalp while she laughed and batted at his arm. Bronx and Reeve were in the midst of a glaring contest.

"We have more to do," I said to the girls. Then I marched

away without another word, my coat and bags hanging at my sides.

Both Kat and Reeve followed me, ditching the boys without hesitation.

"So…did you know that sleeping with twelve different guys is the same thing as sleeping with, like, four thousand?" Kat asked, breaking the silence, the tension.

I could have hugged her. She hadn't mentioned *our* guys, and wasn't going to. She was trying to distract me.

"No way," Reeve said.

We cleared the doors of the mall, entered the coolness of the day. I pulled on the coat.

Kat nodded. "I crunched the numbers myself. I'm eighty-three percent sure that I'm one hundred percent sure that my math is perfect. See, if you sleep with a guy, you've then been with everyone he's been with and everyone his other partners have been with and everyone their partners have been with. It goes on and on." She held up one finger. "Frosty is my only, but he's been with others and I'm sure they've been with others, so, I'm guessing I've been with at least fifty people—is there a scarlet letter on my forehead?"

"I wonder how many girls Bronx has gotten into bed," Reeve muttered.

"Bronx? Did you say Bronx? Because I could have sworn you told me you're over him and seeing someone else," Kat quipped.

Reeve pursed her lips.

I took a breath—held it. Exhaled, slowly. Mist formed in front of my face. My first real post-breakup encounter with Cole was now history. I'd survived with the tiniest shred of dignity, and that was more than I'd expected. I was going to be okay.

A twentysomething guy stepped into our path, blocking us. We drew to a halt as he said, "Hey, pretty girl," with a wide, toothy grin aimed at Kat. "How about some company, hmm?"

Another guy pressed into his side. He eyed Reeve up and down as if she were a stick of cotton candy and he was dying from a sweet tooth.

"No, thanks," she said, and tried to inch around him.

He moved with her, continuing to block her. "Wait. You don't want to go until we've exchanged numbers, do you?"

The other guy leaned down to sniff Kat's neck. "My own personal brand of crack, right there."

"Quoting romance novels?" Scowling, she leaned back, out of reach. "Lesson of the day—you don't smell a girl until she gives you permission. Ever. It makes you a creeper."

He pouted.

I doubted the two were dangerous. I actually thought they were going for sexy and charming rather than disturbing. And maybe I could have tried to reach a verbal resolution with them. Maybe not.

Despite being "okay," anger still pulled at an already thin tether.

Nope. Wrong. The tether snapped.

I jabbed my palm into his nose, and cartilage shattered. Blood spurted. Cursing, his friend grabbed hold of my arm. To stop me from running—unnecessary—or to stop me from another attack, I wasn't sure. I only knew he'd made a mistake. I clamped onto his wrist and twisted with all of my strength, forcing his body to turn with the motion to save the bone from breaking.

Before he could lurch free, I kicked the back of his knee, sending him to the ground. An elbow to the temple finished him off, and he collapsed the rest of the way. He sprawled on the concrete, motionless.

Satisfaction filled me, followed swiftly by guilt.

"Come on," I said. I tugged the lapels of my coat closer as I walked away.

"That was both cool and frightening," Kat said with a shudder, keeping pace with me. "I don't know whether to pat you on the back or run and hide."

"Where did you learn how to do that?" Reeve asked, her gaze darting back to the boys.

"Col— Around." My gaze landed on the tattoo shop across the street. Bright red letters—TATTIE'S INK—flashed on and off.

I stopped.

The girls backtracked.

"I want one," I found myself saying.

"One what?" Kat asked.

"A tattoo." The slayers marked themselves with the names of the loved ones they'd lost in the war against the zombies, or symbols to represent them. I had none, yet I'd lost my parents, my sister and my grandfather.

Bad Ali.

"I want one," I said again, more confident this time. I headed across the street.

The girls followed after me.

"What are you going to get?" Kat asked, clapping happily. "A skull and crossbones? Snake fangs dripping with blood? A unicorn?"

"This is a mistake," Reeve said.

A bell jingled over the door as I entered. The walls were covered with art, pictures of lions and tigers, dragons and aliens. Hearts. Stars. The sun, the moon, fish and lightning. Naked women. It was overwhelming.

A heavily tattooed man with piercings all over his face stood behind the counter, cleaning equipment. He glanced up, grunted with disdain. "You guys even close to eighteen?"

"No," Reeve and I said in unison.

"Yes," Kat said, and elbowed me.

He dried his hands on a rag. "You'll need a permission slip from your parents, and you'll need at least one parent present."

Kat offered her sweetest grin and wound her arm around my waist. "We knew that. That's why I'm here. I'm her mother, and I'll sign whatever form you've got."

A gleam of amusement in his eyes. "She must take after her father."

"All of my children do," Kat quipped.

His gaze landed on me. "Let me guess. You want a flower. Or a butterfly."

Not quite. "I want a white rabbit," I said.

He thought it over, shrugged and slid a pad and pen in Kat's direction. "Fill this out all properlike for your *daughter,* since I'm guessing your IDs will tell me you have different last names, and you," he said to me, "come on back. I think I have something you'll dig."

"Ali," Reeve said, latching onto my wrist. "A tattoo is permanent."

Yeah, and mine would be the only permanent thing in my life. Nana wouldn't live forever. And, as I'd been told time and time again by Mr. Ankh, the moment Reeve learned about the zombies she would be ripped out of my life. Not even the vivacious Kat was guaranteed a tomorrow.

"I have to do this." I pulled from her grip to trail Artist Guy behind a crimson curtain. There were several rooms, each blocked by one of those curtains. He led me to the one in back, swept the fabric aside and motioned to a lounge chair. I sat.

He flipped through an art book. When he found what he was searching for, he showed me the page. "What do you think?"

"I like the ears of this one," I said, pointing. "But the body of this one, and the tail of that one." Perfect for Emma. "Also, I'll want a second tattoo. Two daggers in the shape of a cross." I could think of no better representation of my parents. I wasn't sure what I'd get to represent Pops, though. His would have to wait.

Artist Guy frowned and set the book aside. "I'll have to draw both from scratch, and that's gonna cost extra."

"I'm fine with that." For the first time today, I wasn't going to worry about spending the allowance Nana had given me. I removed my coat, pushed up the sleeves of my shirt.

He peered at my pale, unmarked flesh and shook his head. "All right, then, where do you want them? Exactly?"

"One on each wrist. And I want them to face me, not the

people looking at me." I wanted to be able to see the designs without having to contort.

What would Nana say when she saw them?

"I've got to sketch what you want, so give me about…oh, half an hour." He left without another word.

An opportunity to leave. *Not going to happen.*

I closed my eyes and counted.

By the time he returned, I'd reached 1,532. I wondered what Kat and Reeve were doing in the lobby.

He gathered the necessary supplies and sat beside me.

"Still want to do this?" he asked. "Because once I start, there will be no backing out."

"Absolutely."

He used a piece of paper to transfer the first image onto my wrist. I saw big ears standing tall, a fat body and a bushy tail, just like the rabbits Emma had created in the sky time and time again to warn me of coming zombie attacks.

"Perfect," I said, a bit surprised.

"I only do perfect work." He sounded offended.

"Prove it."

My snark clearly surprised him, and he shook his head. "You know this will hurt, right?"

"I've known hurt. This will be nothing."

He snorted. "Sure, princess. Whatever you say."

Leaning over me, gun in hand, he got to work. And okay, it hurt more than I'd anticipated, stinging and throbbing, but a part of me welcomed the pain. I liked that I was feeling something other than anger and panic.

Panic. The word got stuck in my mind, echoing.

I'd panicked earlier.

I'd panicked big-time.

Mr. Ankh had been right, hadn't he? The episodes were panic attacks, triggered by…what? Emotion? Maybe. I was living with the guilt of knowing Emma's life would be forever unfulfilled. The ache of forging a new one for myself as the old one burned behind me. The uncertainty of navigating a spiritual world I'd been unprepared for. The fear of the unknown.

But emotions couldn't be the full story. Otherwise I'd never have moments of calm. I thought back. Lying in my bed, after Cole had walked out on me, I'd lamented about the new direction of my life. Then, boom, the panic had come. Then, later on, Kat had mentioned the newness of my appearance and boom, panic again.

New things.

Change, I realized. The thought of change had to be the trigger.

And okay. All right. Now that I knew, I could deal. But…

That wasn't the full story, either. It couldn't be. Panic failed to explain the double heartbeats…the hunger…and the fact that I'd wanted to bite Reeve. And what if I'd been wrong about the smudges? What if they weren't part of my imagination, but this…whatever *this* was?

That would mean…what?

I didn't know, but one thing was certain. More changes loomed on the horizon.

Just like that, perspiration beaded on my brow and upper lip, and an invisible elephant sat down on my chest. The pressure… I struggled to breath, barely even able to wheeze.

"Hey, are you okay?" the guy asked me.

"Fine," I managed to huff. "Just hurry."

"You don't rush quality. And I told you it would hurt."

My sister was my calming force, so I drew her image to the front of my mind, concentrating on her. I saw a mass of straight, dark hair. Sun-kissed skin. A mischievous gleam in her dark eyes.

"You're the prettiest girl in the whole world, Alice," she said, *beaming up at me.*

"No, brat, that would be you," I replied, *gently tapping the tip of her nose.*

"No way. A boy at my school told me he heard his dad say only blondes are worth doing."

"First, I never want to hear you say the words worth doing *again. Do you even know what that means? Second, that boy's dad is an idiot. And a pig!"*

So hungry… Must eat…

The whispery voice intruded on the memory, and I frowned at Artist Guy. "Did you say something?"

He didn't glance up, even as he moved to my other wrist. "Nope."

Hungry. Hungry! HUNGRY!

I shook my head, as if my mind had somehow locked on a different radio frequency and a little motion would change the channel back. But it didn't, and I found I couldn't tear my gaze away from the vulnerability of Artist Guy's now-glowing neck.

"Be still," he commanded.

"I'm sorry. I just… Did you hear that?"

"Hear what?"

"That voice. That whisper."

He paused long enough to dab at a bead of blood with a cotton ball. "Great. The pretty princess is one of the crazies. I should have known."

Bite him. Feed on him.

"Emma," I said.

"You want me to add a name?" he asked.

"No."

My sister appeared a few seconds later. "You're getting tattoos?" she squealed. Then she saw my face, and the excitement was replaced by concern. "Alice?"

"Something's wrong with me," I told her.

"I know." Artist Guy sighed. "That's what I just said."

"Cole?" she asked.

I snapped my teeth, then glanced at Artist Guy, trying to show her what the problem was.

"You want to bite him?"

I nodded.

Frowning, she traced her fingers through my hair, and the urge to bite instantly vanished, thrilling me...baffling me. "I'll ask around and return when I've learned something."

She disappeared. And maybe I passed out from relief. I don't know. One moment I was relaxed in my seat; the next Artist Guy was saying, "All right. All done. What do you think?"

I opened my eyes to see he was setting the equipment aside. I waited for the voice or urge to return, but...there was only silence. No hunger. I uttered a quiet prayer of thanks.

He crossed his arms and watched my expression. "Well?"

The ink was perfect, as promised, and exactly what I'd wanted. The white rabbit was on one side, and the daggers on the other. The skin around the ink was red and swollen, though, and throbbed insistently.

"They're wonderful."

Grunting with satisfaction, he smothered each with ointment, then covered them with bandages. "Remove the dressing in about an hour and add more ointment. Keep the ink clean, but don't take long showers or baths for at least two weeks."

"Okay."

He ushered me to the front of the building, where Kat and Reeve waited.

Grinning when she spotted me, Kat jumped up and clapped. "Let me see, let me see!"

Reeve stood more slowly, as if she wanted to avoid looking at the tattoos as long as possible.

"Give me a minute to pay," I said.

The moment we were outside, I peeled back the bandages.

"Very cool! Cole will regret the day he let you get away," Kat said. As we climbed into Reeve's Porsche, she added, "I'm making it my life's mission. Well, that, and torturing Frosty."

I claimed the center of the backseat and buckled up. "Where are we going now?"

"To Reeve's. Then you and I are going to Cole's—uh, house, yes, to his house to work out," Kat said. "You're going to train me, as promised. No more treadmilling. And yes, I just turned a noun into a verb."

"Train you?" Reeve eased the car into traffic. "For what? I mean, I know you guys have been working out a lot, but I'd had no idea there was a purpose to it."

"Self-defense," I replied. "Like what I did today."

Kat nodded. "Only maybe not so hard-core."

"I promised I'd teach you," I said, flickers of dread lighting me up, "and I will. Just…not today." I wanted to go home and wait for Emma.

"Well, I'd like to learn, too," Reeve said.

"Uh…hmm." I peered out the window, watching as cars whizzed past. Trees. Power lines. "I'd love to include you, but you'll have to get permission from your dad first."

Her brow furrowed. "He'll say yes."

Not even if she begged him.

"I mean, why would he say no? Especially after what happened today," she added.

My gaze snagged on a cloud in the sky—a cloud cut in the shape of a rabbit. The zombies would invade tonight. I frowned. Was I ready?

Better question: Would I be invited to help?

"Uh, guys. I think someone's following us," Reeve said, her voice trembling with apprehension. "What if it's the guys from the mall? What should I do?"

I turned in my seat, peering out the back window. "Call—" I stopped myself before I said his name. "Which car?"

"A black SUV, dark-tinted windows."

It was two slots back, on the left. As big as it was, six people could be inside. The odds weren't great, but they weren't terrible, either. "Take the next exit ramp and pull over."

"What!" she and Kat demanded in unison.

"Just do it. Please." I was armed. I was also in a terrible mood. If Anima hoped to scare me, they'd soon learn the error of such a fruitless endeavor. If the guys from the shopping center craved revenge, I'd give them something else to cry about. If this was just one big misunderstanding, I'd make sure it never happened again.

Reeve obeyed, reluctantly, and the moment the car came to a stop, I palmed my daggers and jumped out of the car. The SUV had tracked us off the highway and slowed down as it approached us. A window rolled down.

"Miss Bell," said a man I'd never before met. He was old enough to be my grandfather, with a full head of salt-and-pepper hair, thick glasses, an aquiline nose and dark brown skin. "I'd like a word with you."

He knew my name, and he'd come at me in the most secretive of ways. He had to be a Hazmat.

I didn't need to know any more than that. I threw one of my daggers, just as Cole had taught me, and the tip embedded in one of the SUV's tires. Air hissed out.

The man scowled at me. "Was that really necessary?"

"Probably not." I held up my other dagger. "I doubt what I do next will be, either, but I'm sure it'll be fun."

He flashed me a look full of disappointment. "Very well. When you're curious about your condition, you'll have to come to me." He tossed a card out the window, and as the paper floated to the ground, the SUV sped away.

OF ROTTING MONSTERS AND TASTY MEN

Normally, I would have hunted Cole down and told him what had happened. Today, I decided to tell Mr. Ankh.

On my way to his office, I ran into Nana. "Ali, honey, I have a surprise—"

"I'm sorry, Nana," I rushed out. "But I have to talk with Mr. Ankh about something. Rain check?"

Disappointment clouded her features. "All right. No problem."

Instant guilt. I'd hurry here and spend the rest of the day with her. I marched into the office without an invitation, a first for me, and shut and locked the door. He glanced up from the stack of papers on his desk.

He had dark hair and eyes, like Reeve, but he was almost always tense and formal, and I rarely left his presence feeling better about my circumstances. Right now, though, he was my only choice.

"Good," he said, "I've been wanting to talk to you. Sit down."

I obeyed, saying, "There's been an incident."

"All right," he acknowledged, folding his fingers together. "How bad is it? Does it need to be covered up?"

"No, nothing like that. It's just—"

"So there are no dead bodies?"

"No."

"No zombies?"

"No. Just—"

"Then listen," he said, once again cutting me off. "I've been told you've been cleaning up the house and only eating bagels and cream cheese. That isn't acceptable, Miss Bell. I pay someone to take care of the house, and I have enough food for an army."

"That's wonderful, but I'm not going to take advantage of you. Now. We went to a strip mall today and—"

"Does your grandmother know what you're doing? How you're starving yourself?"

"I'm *not* starving myself," I said. Then I told him what had gone down, described the SUV, the man who'd hoped to talk to me and what I'd done to his tire. The only detail I kept to myself was the business card currently burning a hole in pocket.

I'd grabbed it with every intention of handing it over to Mr. Ankh, but now, peering into his stern features, I just… couldn't.

When you're curious about your condition…

Did the man know what I didn't? Did he know what was wrong with me?

How could he know?

And what would Mr. Ankh say if I told him about the smudges and the heartbeat and the hunger? How many tests would he want to run? Would he lock me away?

He popped his jaw. "That is Anima's M.O. I'll put a security detail on—"

"Oh, no," I said, tugging at the sleeves of my shirt, making sure my bandages were covered. "No one's following me around." No telling what they'd see me do.

He frowned at me. "Privacy means nothing in the face of safety, Miss Bell. I'm sure your grandmother would agree with me."

Low blow. One I ignored. "No guards," I insisted. "Reeve might notice them and start asking more questions."

He relented. As I'd known he would.

He really did love his daughter.

For the first time, I began to wonder about this man's life…his past. "The woman you mentioned… The one who had the anxiety disorder… Was she Reeve's mom?"

"Yes." His tone was short, clipped, letting me know he'd said all he wanted to say on that subject.

We don't always get what we want. "Did she know about the zombies? Is that why she was afraid?"

He hammered his elbows into the desk, rattling the entire piece. "Yes, Miss Bell. Yes. She knew about them, but she couldn't see them, and so she began to imagine them around her every second of every day, and it was more than she could deal with. Finally she killed herself."

How awful. Poor Mrs. Ankh, to feel death was the only way. Poor Mr. Ankh, left to pick up the pieces. Poor Reeve, a little girl drowning in sorrow and confusion. No wonder he insisted she be kept in the dark. He didn't want the same fate to befall her. "I'm sorry."

He waved my sympathy away. "The past is the past, Miss Bell."

Such easy words to offer—but was he actually living them? "Just so you know, I saw a rabbit cloud in the sky. Zombies could be coming out tonight."

He arched a brow, saying, "And you want in the rotation."

I'd told myself I wasn't ready to see Cole again. I'd even questioned my ability to fight. And still I found myself saying, "I do." I couldn't waste an opportunity to slay my enemy.

Mr. Ankh grilled me about my health. Was I feeling okay? Had I had any moments of weakness? Had I had another panic attack?

I answered the first two bluntly but sidestepped the last one. "Look, I was born to kill zombies. So, tonight, that's exactly what I'm going to do. Whether you're on board or not. And yes, that's a threat."

He grinned at me, but it wasn't a nice grin. "You can't do anything if you're unconscious."

He would drug me? "Try," was all I said.

He studied me for a long while before sighing, nodding stiffly. "Fine. You're determined. I get it. And this time, I'll let you have your way. You'll have to hurry, though. The slayers are at Cole's gym, and rotations are about to be decided for the week."

Crap. My day with Nana would have to wait. "Slight problem," I said. "I don't have a license or a car."

He released another sigh. "Be ready in five. My driver will be waiting out front."

"Thanks, Mr. Ankh." I stood and walked to the door.

"By the way, I wasn't teasing about the cleaning and the food."

"I didn't think you were." And he would learn I hadn't been teasing, either. I paused and glanced back at him. "I admire the way you're protecting Reeve, I do, but all our secrets are hurting her. She's already suspicious, and those suspicions are making her unhappy. There's got to be another way."

"Miss Bell," he said, slamming his pen on the desk.

I knew a very stern lecture was coming, so I hurried into the hall.

In my room, I changed into battle-ready clothing and gathered everything I'd need. More daggers, a syringe filled with the antidote, a pocketful of throwing stars and my phone.

I tucked the business card the man had given me in the bottom drawer of my desk and saw there was a note resting next to my computer.

I was going through the things that survived the fire, and I found my great-grandfather's journal. I had given it to your mother years ago. A few of the pages are now singed, but that's the only damage. I know it's weird, but I thought you might like to have a family heirloom.
Love, Nana

The journal!

I'd thought it had come from my dad, that *he'd* given it to my mom. How had my great-great-great-grandfather known to write it? I mean, the ability to see the zombies was passed through genes just as easily as blue eyes, but my mother had never seen them. Neither had Nana.

What could this mean?

No time for puzzles. Right.

But this had to be the surprise Nana had mentioned. And what an amazing surprise it was.

I owed that woman a million hugs.

I didn't mean to, but I glanced at the vanity mirror as I opened the door. A habit I'd developed after first meeting Cole. I'd always wanted to look my best for him. This time, my reflection caught me completely off guard.

Tick. The girl in the mirror—me!—had her hand lifted and pressed against the glass, as if reaching for me.

Tock. How could… How was… *Impossible.*

Tick. In a daze, I walked toward her—toward me.

Tock. She never moved. I mean, *my reflection* never moved.

Tick. I pressed a trembling hand against the coolness of the glass.

Tock. Her hand fell away.

A thousand different thoughts raced through my head.

I'd decided she was real rather than a figment. So…what was she? A part of me?

Another me?

The smudges under her eyes curved and seemed to drip onto her cheeks. A *dying* me?

Trembling, I swiped a tube of red lipstick from the bathroom and wrote over the glass. **Who Are You?**

I slammed the lipstick on the vanity surface and marched to the door. As I stepped into the hall, I glanced back. Breath caught in my throat. I read **Your Doom**.

Running back inside and smearing the words gave me no satisfaction, only increased my shock. Whatever she was, she didn't like me.

Can't worry about this right now.

I raced from the room, and this time, I didn't look back. I wouldn't think about anything I'd seen, about the change… the change… *No!* I wouldn't allow another panic attack to swoop in and carry me away. Mr. Ankh would find out, and I would be banned from the meeting at Cole's.

I checked the halls. Empty. Good. Reeve must be in her room, and I wasn't sure where Nana had gone. Even the housekeeper was nowhere to be seen. As promised, the driver was waiting for me at the front door. I sailed past him without a word and buckled into the backseat of the dark sedan. I held my breath as he slid into the driver's seat. He started the engine. Eased forward.

I exhaled.

Along the way, I checked the sky. The rabbit cloud was still there.

My phone rang, startling me. I recognized the number and experienced a conflicting tide of emotions, from uncertainty to gratitude. "Justin," I said. "I should have called you. Thank you for helping with the fight and taking what was meant for me."

"Hey, I owed you." Then, "How are you, Ali?" His voice

was low, as if he wasn't sure of his welcome and was determined not to spook me.

"I've been better."

He groaned. "Yeah, I'm sorry about that. I'm sorry I bit you. I don't know what came over me. You were there, and you smelled so good, so clean and pure, and my mouth was watering, and the urge hit me, and it was so strong, so intense, I couldn't fight it." The words spilled from him with barely a breath. "I didn't *want* to fight it."

Some of what he'd said really jelled with me. A clean, pure scent. An unwillingness to fight. An unquenchable hunger. "Has anything else happened to you since that night?"

A crackling pause that set my nerves on edge. "Like what?"

Yeah, like I was really going to confide in him. "You tell me," I said, using a tactic Cole had once used on me.

Cole. I ran my tongue over my teeth.

I had to stop thinking about him.

"To be honest, I've been normal," Justin said. "Nothing's happened. To me, at least," he added. "I'm guessing something's happening with you, though."

The brakes on the car squeaked, and I peeked out the window to see we'd reached our destination. So soon?

"I have to go," I said.

"Don't want to talk about it?"

"I'm kind of busy." *And yes.*

Another pause. "We'll talk again, though?" he asked, hesitant.

"Yeah. I think so."

I hung up and stepped into the cold of the evening. The

sun would soon disappear, and the moon would take its place, full and golden in the sky. Even though darkness had yet to fall, the path to the barn was lit by small halogens meant to discourage any zombies from drawing near.

I used the code on the ID pad to open the door. Before our breakup, when I'd come here and he hadn't, Cole had finally broken down and given me the "key." I pushed my way inside, only to discover the meeting was already in full swing. A chair had been carried to the center of the boxing ring, where Cole was perched.

Veronica sat in his lap.

His arm was wrapped around her waist.

The girl was relaxed against him, completely at ease, as if she had no doubts about her reception.

Cole was disheveled, but also perfectly at ease. As if they'd messed around before settling down, and he'd never been happier.

The details hit me like bullets, one at a time, fast and sure. He'd always liked touching me. Sifting the ends of my hair through his fingers. Ghosting his knuckles across my jaw. Pulling me into the hard line of his body for a kiss. Seeing him act that way with someone else…

Pain? Yes, I felt pain. Betrayal? Jealousy? Yes, I felt those, too. Felt them so deeply I wasn't sure how I remained on my feet—or out of that ring. I think a part of me had hoped he would eventually come crawling back to me, no matter what I'd told him. No matter what I'd told my friends. But he wasn't going to, was he? We were done, just as he'd said. Just as I'd agreed. Only he'd already moved on.

Breathe. Just breathe.

I wouldn't freak out over this.

I'd come here to do a job. So I would do it.

I switched my focus. The rest of the crew leaned against the ropes. Frosty, Bronx, Mackenzie, Derek, Trina, Lucas, Collins, Cruz and Gavin, each hard bodied and dressed in black, ready for action. No one seemed to care that Cole— a guy who had only split from me a short while ago—had already forgotten about me.

Okay, so I hadn't exactly switched my focus.

Threads of fury joined an already toxic mix of emotions, whooshing through me. This wasn't right. This wasn't fair. How could he do this to me? Was he trying to punish me for the vision I'd had? A vision I couldn't control? A vision I wouldn't allow to come true?

No. This wasn't for my benefit and wasn't a punishment. He hadn't known I would show up. This was for him. He wanted that girl in his lap.

My hands fisted. I'd been wrong about his sense of honesty. He'd lied to me.

I remembered what he'd said to me.

Me: *Do you want Veronica?*

Him: *No. Not even a little.*

Liar! I longed to shout.

How easy it would be to stalk into the ring, sink my teeth into his spirit and—

His spirit?

Oh, good glory. Was I thinking like the zombies now?

I raised my chin, squared my shoulders. I'd rather die.

I forced myself to concentrate for real.

"—report every detail," Cole was saying. "I don't just

want to hear that you survived the night, or that you did or didn't see any zombies. I'm not kidding, I want every detail. In writing. From all of you. Two partners can't turn in one report. I want two from two, and I want you to write them separately. After what happened to Justin and Ali, I'm in an information-gathering mood." Shadows and light battled for dominance on his face, giving him a sinister bent. "Got me?"

He scanned the murmuring crowd, bypassed me and quickly returned. Guilt flashed in his eyes, only to be extinguished, leaving the cold, blank mask. He stood, forcing Veronica to stand as well, and dropped his arms to his sides. She remained only a whisper away and frowned when she noticed me.

I held Cole's gaze, again not expecting a vision, but wanting one—no, I didn't want one, shouldn't want one, but...

It never came.

Disappointment grew wings of sharply honed iron and flew through every inch of me, cutting at me.

Cole cleared his throat, clearly uncomfortable.

Don't give him a reaction.

He looked away. "From now on," he said, voice harder now, harsher, "if your partner gets bitten, administer the antidote the moment you're able. Don't wait until the fight is over. And if your partner bites you, don't try to hide it from us. We're not going to blame him."

"Or her," Mackenzie called, and snapped her teeth.

"Now you're just giving the girls permission to take a nibble anytime, anyplace," Frosty retorted. "I've got enough trouble keeping them off me as it is."

Chuckles resounded.

I couldn't force myself to laugh.

"You know who your partners are," Cole said, "and where you've been placed in the schedule. Do what you have to do to get ready."

The group broke apart; some kids were to walk the streets, hunting zombies; some were to go home and rest, catch up on schoolwork; some were to stay here and guard the bodies of the slayers, also waiting in case backup was needed.

Veronica rose on her tiptoes and whispered in Cole's ear.

The fury returned, expanded, but I managed to calmly say, "What about me?" and step up to the ring.

All eyes darted in my direction.

"Ali Bo Bali," Frosty said, throwing his arm over my shoulder. "I didn't think we'd see you tonight."

I appreciated the show of support.

"What about you?" Cole replied, hesitant.

Steady. "I want in."

A muscle ticked below his eye as he approached me. "After what happened today? No."

"What happened today?" Veronica asked, coming over to rest her head on his shoulder. Staking a claim? Digging the knife deeper?

If anyone told her what I'd gone through…

Cole eased away from her and massaged the back of his neck, a habit of his. Right now he was more than uncomfortable. He was discombobulated.

Good.

"You're injured," he said.

"I'm healed. Besides that, others have fought injured and you never complained."

"Others have had more training. And why do you have bandages on your wrists?"

He'd noticed them, even though I wore long sleeves?

Trying to control my sudden trembling, I pulled the bandages off for good. My skin was more reddened than before, and far more swollen, but the ink was still pretty.

Veronica leaned toward me, shrugged. "Don't take this the wrong way, but those are too big for your bone structure."

There was a right way to take that? I knew the tattoos were beautiful and just the right size for me.

I wouldn't give her the satisfaction of a response.

No, that wasn't true. I would. "I'm seconds away from giving *you* a brand-new bone structure."

She blinked at me as if I was missing a few screws. "I've been nothing but nice to you, and you want a go at me?"

That was *nice?*

"I think the tattoos are perfect." Cole stepped between us. His narrowed gaze roved over me, lingered in a few select places. I had to fight a shiver. "Tattoos. New hair. New makeup. I didn't notice it before. You were too wet. I'm noticing now."

"Wet?" Veronica said, the word almost strangled out of her. "Wet how?"

Scowling, Cole pushed her toward the rings. "Go. Now."

I kind of wished the floor would open up and swallow me.

She flicked me a confused glance over her shoulder but did as he'd commanded and left us alone.

Getting back on track. He had a problem with my makeover? "Are you saying I'm eye broccoli?"

Frosty barked out a laugh. "Where do girls get this stuff, man?"

"I'm not even sure what eye broccoli means," Cole said. "That you look bad, and I shouldn't want to eat you, or that you're loaded with vitamins and I should."

Kill me.

Please.

"That I look bad," I gritted.

"You don't. You never have." Cole lifted my wrists and traced his thumb around the designs. When he realized what he was doing, he scowled and dropped his arms. "So. Tell me. Why'd you make all these changes?"

Changes.

The C word overshadowed any pleasure I might have taken from his compliment…his touch. What would change tonight? Tomorrow?

Both hearts sped up, and my nasal passages seemed to clog with cotton.

"Easy, now," Frosty said.

Cole released my arms to cup my cheeks. "Breathe, Ali. Just like that. In and out. Good girl."

The moment I calmed, I pulled out of Cole's hold and shrugged away from Frosty's. Another rush of embarrassment washed through me. I couldn't allow myself to rely on these guys in any way.

"What was that about?" Cole asked.

"To answer your other question, the only one I'll acknowledge," I said tightly, "I made a few improvements. I wanted to look hot for the night my vision with Gavin comes true."

Direct hit—a shocker. Cole flinched, even paled. "You were hot the way you were," he said, staring deep into my eyes. "Whatever you think of me, whatever's happened be-tween us, that was never up for debate."

Pretty words, nothing more, and yet the air between us charged, just like before, becoming electric with awareness. Every nerve ending in my body perked up, waiting for… something. Another visual caress. A hand on my shoulder. The nudge of his knee. *Anything.*

He backed up a few steps, and the charge fizzled. I could still smell his scent, though, soap and something woodsy, a hint of the animal he could sometimes be. Rough, wild, untamed. But underneath it all was the scent of roses… Veronica's scent.

Maybe I'd consume *both* their spirits.

"Did you really do all this for Gavin?"

His tone was dead. As if he didn't care.

As if he'd never cared.

"I did it for me," I said, and left it at that. I would never let him know how much he was hurting me.

He nodded, some of the tension leaving him.

Tension? I hadn't noticed it. I wonder what had calmed him. Because it certainly couldn't have been my admission. He didn't care, remember? "Where am I in the lineup?"

"You'll be on patrol tonight. Sunday you'll rest. Monday you'll stay here in the gym, in case you're needed. Tuesday, patrol again. Be ready to go in ten." He stalked into the locker room.

I remained in place, trying to control my inner turmoil.

Veronica stood in back, watching me.

I scowled at her, daring her to approach. No question she'd come to *my* Bama expecting to win Cole back by fair means or foul. Well, she'd done it. And she hadn't even had to work that hard.

"Enjoy him while it lasts," I called. "Apparently he has Girlfriend ADD."

She looked away, but not before I caught the blush staining her cheeks.

A blush from her. Why?

Frosty cleared his throat, a demand for my full attention. "Hate to stop you when you're going balls to the wall, but you need to talk to Reeve," he said. "Tell her to drop whoever she's seeing. This keeps up, and Bronx might just snap and play Prison Rules with the guy."

"How do you know about Reeve's new boyfriend, Ethan?" I demanded, searching for Bronx.

He hammered at the punching bag with so much force I was afraid his knuckles would crack. Dark hair streaked with blue was wet and plastered to his scalp. Sweat dripped from his temples to his bare shoulders, then down the ripped cords of his abs, and if I'd been with Cole, I wouldn't have watched those droplets, mesmerized.

Lucky Reeve.

Poor Ethan.

Frosty patted me on top of the head. "Aren't you cute? As if you don't know the answer to your own question."

Right. Kat. "Forget Reeve. Her life, her decisions. Your problem is the fact that Kat wants self-defense lessons, and I promised to give them to her. I know she would love it if you helped." And with my new…urges, it would be better all the way around.

Uncomfortable with the new direction of the conversation, he shifted from one booted foot to the other. "No. And you're going to tell her you changed your mind."

"Are you kidding me? No, I'm not."

"It's not that I don't want her trained. It's that I want her stronger first. You could break her. I'd definitely break her."

"Cole didn't break me, and I'll be a much gentler teacher. So will you. I've seen you with her."

That earned me another head pat. "Cole went easy on you, sweet cakes. And I'm the worst coach the slayers have ever seen. Just ask them. I'm too impatient with failure, and I'd hurt Kat's feelings."

I got snagged on his first words. "Cole did not go easy on me."

He tsked. "Pretty, but delusional. A smoking-hot combination. No wonder all the boys want a go at you."

Hardly. "You're seconds away from a busted nose, Frosty."

He laughed. "Unlike Cole, I give back whatever's dished. Just remember what I said about Reeve." And he ambled away.

As if! "Who's on patrol tonight?" I called.

Frosty grinned over his shoulder. "There are two patrols going out. Gavin and Mackenzie, and Cole and Lucas. Want to guess who you'll end up with?"

A BEAUTIFUL
DISASTER

For several minutes I stood where Frosty had left me, all by myself, feeling forgotten, abandoned. Finally the most unlikely source took pity on me and strode over.

"It won't always be this hard," Mackenzie said with a sad smile.

A show of compassion. One I didn't deserve. Not from her. I guess she'd meant what she'd told me before, about being there for me if I needed her.

I'd find a way to make up for every bad thing I'd ever said to her.

"Here's hoping," I replied.

She patted my shoulder before walking away.

A few seconds later, Trina took her place. "When you're ready, let me know and I'll take you out to meet someone outside our little circle. You'll have fun, I promise. It did wonders for Mac when she was in this same situation."

I nodded, and she was off. I wasn't sure I'd ever be ready.

Cole exited the locker room. He'd painted black half circles under his eyes and strapped weapons all over his body. I'd always loved seeing him like this. Strong. Ready for action. Just a little naughty, capable of any deed. Had we still been together, I would have thrown myself into his arms and kissed the breath out of him.

You know what wistful thinking gets you? A whole lot of nothing.

"What are my instructions?" I demanded.

He stopped in front of me. Avoiding my gaze, he withdrew a black bandanna from one of the pockets in his combat pants and covered my hair. "You'll stay with Gavin and Mackenzie, and you'll be careful."

"Wait. What?" Frosty called from the sidelines.

Yeah. What? Frosty had led me to believe Cole would want me to be with him.

Cole frowned at him, and I think the two somehow engaged in a silent argument with their eyes.

"Can't wait," I said, drawing Cole's attention back to me.

"I wish… Well, it doesn't matter." He rolled his shoulders, the tension back and clearly too much. "I have to be with Lucas tonight, and I have to be alone."

Something about his tone… It was the gruff one he used whenever he spoke about his secret. He had to be with Lucas because…he was spying on him? Emma had mentioned spying.

Or was I just giving him an excuse for not wanting to patrol with me?

Ugh. I hated this. Hated that I was taking everything he said, everything he did, and dissecting it, looking for hidden meaning, trying to give myself a reason to hope for reconciliation I knew wasn't going to happen.

Stupid. Put your hope in the right thing, and it would be a lifeline. Put your hope in the wrong thing, and it would be a noose.

"I was serious. Be careful out there." He ghosted his knuckle across the curve of my jaw. "Stay alert."

I stepped back, out of reach. I wasn't sure what he'd meant by the touch—and I wasn't going to try to figure it out. I also wasn't allowing him to touch me like that anymore.

He frowned.

"By the way," I said, "I saw the rabbit cloud. I'm pretty sure the zombies will be out tonight."

His features hardened, chilled. "You tell me *now,* after I decide to send you on patrol?"

What, he'd thought the zombies would stay in tonight, and that was the only reason he'd opted to send me out? Anger sparked. "If you hadn't already broken up with me, I would absolutely be breaking up with you right this second. You're a grade-A douche bag, Cole Holland."

"According to your grandmother, it's douche purse. And if I'm going to do something, it's good to know I'm giving my best," he replied, unfazed by my insult. "You're a great fighter, and I have no problem throwing you into the heart of battle—when you're well—but you're still recovering from Justin's bite, on top of everything else. Tonight, you'll stay in."

I felt my hand curl into a fist. Felt my elbow draw back. Felt my arm dart forward, my knuckles crack into Cole's jaw. I couldn't stop myself.

His head whipped to the side, and blood leaked from a cut in his lip.

Behind me, gasps of shock abounded.

"I'm recovered," I said. "Believe me now?"

Those violet eyes slitted when they found me. "Assault and battery is illegal."

"So have me arrested."

He closed what little distance there was between us. Suddenly I could feel the warmth of his breath caressing my skin, could smell the decadence of his scent, the heat of his skin. "How about I put you over my lap and spank you instead?"

"How about I knee your balls into your throat?"

"If you're going to play with that particular area, I'd rather you use your hands."

"My hands aren't going near that area ever again."

A pause. Then, "I bet I could change your mind," he whispered huskily.

"I bet I could bash yours." I drew back another fist, but he was ready and caught me midswing. His pupils dilated, a sign of arousal. Another sign: he began to pant. He was acting like I'd just tried to unbuckle his jeans rather than smack the fire out of him.

"Hit me again," he said, still using that same whispered tone, "and I'll take it as an invitation."

I was just as bad. I trembled with longing I couldn't control and struggled to catch my breath. "An invitation to do what?"

His grip loosened, his fingers rubbing my skin. A caress, not a warning. "I guess we'll find out together."

What the heck are you doing?

The words screamed inside my head. This…whatever this was—flirting?—had to stop.

I dropped my arm and stepped back, only then noticing the silence inside the barn. Were the others watching, listening? My cheeks heated. "Look, I know you stayed friends with your other exes," I said, "and if you want to be friends with me, fine. I'll try. I just don't want to play this game. Understood?"

He opened his mouth, closed it with a snap. Then he nodded resolutely.

I spun away from him before I did or said something worse, and stalked to the wall of weapons. Gavin was there, weighing a semiautomatic in his hand.

"Nice right cross, Als," he said.

Finally. A cute nickname. Why did it have to come from *him?* "Thanks." I lifted an ax.

He took it from me. "Sorry, honey, but if you want a big boy's weapon, you'll have to fight me for it. Spoiler alert—I'll let you restrain me on the floor as long as you're straddling my waist."

I think my lips were curling at the corners. "I'm not straddling you," I muttered, selecting another, lighter ax.

"Too bad." He reached over and pressed a button on the bottom of my weapon. It was a lever of some sort and triggered metal spikes that popped out at the sides of the blade. "Do you know how to use this thing?"

"I have an arm, and I can swing. I figure that will do the trick."

"If you don't get yourself killed tonight, it'll be because

of a miracle," he said. "Good thing my middle name is Miracle."

"You've seen me fight. You know I'm good."

"True." He bumped my shoulder with his own. "So... have you ever thought about dyeing your hair punk-rocker-chick black? As I'm sure you've heard, I have a thing for brunettes and always avoid blondes."

"I've heard. And no."

"Too bad. Because you're making me rethink my stance about not doing my friends' exes."

I snorted, not even trying to hide my...incredulity? Surely I wasn't amused. "You're making me rethink my stance against cold-blooded homicide." I didn't wait for his reply but marched away.

Laughing, he followed me. "Are you always this on edge?"

"I didn't used to be, no." I sighed. "Look, I'm sorry if I hurt your feelings." I tried to sit down in one of the cushioned chairs in the back of the room, but he caught my arm in a gentle vise and forced me to face him.

"First, you didn't hurt my feelings. I doubt anyone could, considering the fact that I don't actually have any. Second, I believe we have some unfinished business."

I stared at his feet to avoid his gaze. Like Cole, he towered over me—which was not an easy feat. I had the legs of a giraffe.

"Cole assigned you to my team, and there's no way we'll be able to avoid each other. We can't risk having a vision during a fight with the zombies."

I nodded, but I still didn't look at him.

He placed two fingers under my chin and forced my head to lift. "Let's get this over with."

No, no, no.... But I couldn't avoid it, and our gazes locked. Annnd...nothing happened.

We both exhaled with relief.

"Well, that was certainly anticlimactic," he muttered.

"The on-and-off thing is kind of annoying, isn't it?" First with Cole, now Gavin.

"Maybe you need a tune-up."

I rolled my eyes. "I'll just pop into the supernatural ability repair shop sometime tomorrow."

He grinned, his fingertips tracing the line of my jaw. A patented Cole Holland move. The contact unnerved me, and I turned away.

"Sit down," Cole shouted. The harshness of his voice echoed off the walls.

I ignored him. It was either that, or tell him to suck it in a thousand different ways.

"Yeah, stop flirting. It sickens me," Mackenzie said loudly enough for everyone in the room to hear. She came up beside me and winked, and I realized she'd wanted Cole to hear, probably thinking he would erupt with jealousy.

Sweet of her, but she couldn't have been more wrong. I knew his attitude stemmed from my refusal to leave the fighting to the others.

Cole stomped past our group, viciously shouldering Gavin out of the way, and took his seat. Lucas blew me a kiss before taking his.

Frowning, Gavin sat. Mackenzie plopped into the chair next to his and motioned for me to take the one next to her.

"If there's any hint of trouble," Cole said to no one in particular, "I want to know about it immediately."

"Wow. Micromanage much?" Gavin muttered.

I tuned them out and closed my eyes. I could do this. A deep breath in, hold, hold, then release, and as the air left me, my spirit rose from my body. Chilly air wrapped cruel arms around me, squeezing me.

I turned and looked down. My body still reclined against the cushions, my eyes closed, my features relaxed.

Gavin tapped me on the shoulder.

My gaze lifted to his, and I arched a brow in question.

He motioned to the door with a tilt of his chin. I nodded. Right now, as emotional as I was, I would have to be more careful than usual about what I said.

Cole moved in front of Gavin and whispered a command, his expression fierce. I was able to make out the words *take care* but no others.

Take care of...me?

Gavin whispered something back, and I thought I heard the word *crazy*.

Me again?

Or was I being just a tad narcissistic? Not everything was going to be about me.

We left the barn using the door Frosty held open for us. Blood Lines surrounded the property, the house, the barn and everything inside it. Meaning all of it was solid to our touch.

Once we entered the forest, my group branched away from Cole's. Unable to help myself, I looked back. Cole's gaze was already on me, watching me with confusion…longing…until he snaked the corner and the moment was lost.

I wasn't sure what the attention meant, or if I'd misread him, or how—

I slammed into a tree, ricocheting backward and landing on my butt.

Mackenzie laughed. "That, when she can see the Blood Lines."

"That true?" Gavin asked, helping me stand. "You can see the Blood Lines?"

"They glow," I replied through gritted teeth. I'd deserved to be pimp-slapped by a tree, I really had. No more Cole. Just. No. More.

Intrigued, Gavin said, "So…you, a girl who has never been on patrol before, a girl who has never been shown the proper path to take, could get us out of the forest using our preferred path?"

"Watch me." I took the lead, getting us out of the wheat fields and into the forest, maneuvering around every tree wiped with a Blood Line and ghosting through those that weren't. Within half an hour, we cleared the foliage to stand at the edge of a dirt road. I spread my arms in a look-at-me gesture.

"Impressive," Gavin said.

Even Mackenzie muttered her approval.

"Now what?" I asked. How much ground could we cover on foot like this?

"Now, we hunt." He took only two steps, but suddenly he was at the end of the road.

I whipped to Mackenzie, questions poised at the edge of

my tongue, but she followed Gavin, beside me one second, beside him the next. Shock beat through me. I took a step, then another, and…

I was only two steps away from where I'd started. What the heck?

I took another step, another and another, but I never gained extra ground. Frustration surpassed my shock.

"You will stop messing around," Gavin called. "Come on."

It was a command that did not violate my free will—I wanted to stop messing around. I stepped toward him and a second later, my surroundings blurred. A second after that, I was standing beside him.

"How did I do that?" I gasped out.

"Spirits are bound by spiritual laws, not physical," Mackenzie explained. "Just tell your feet to dash, and hello, they will."

"We're hitting neighborhoods tonight," Gavin said, pointing in the direction he wanted us to go.

He moved forward at that impossible speed, Mackenzie right behind him. I looked down at my booted feet and snapped, "You will move just as quickly!"

They obeyed, shocking me all over again. I quickly caught up with the twosome, and we soared through neighborhood after neighborhood, searching for any sign of zombie activity. I lasted one hour…two…three…before the swiftness of my movements began to take a dangerous toll.

My limbs trembled lightly at first, then more noticeably, then more violently. After a while, I was barely able to remain upright.

"Guys," I huffed, and stopped.

A mistake.

Suddenly I could feel the heaviness of my feet and could barely maintain my grip on the ax.

I hated to admit it, but Cole and Frosty were right. Stamina was important. I needed to up my training.

Gavin slowed and turned to face me.

"Rest," I said.

So hungry, a ragged voice whispered, claiming my attention.

I spun, but no one stood around me.

Will eat. Food will scream. Yes. Yes!

Hmm, what's that smell? Must have.

Hard bands wrapped around my upper arms. Instinct took over, and I raised my fist to attack the culprit. I turned.

Gavin ducked, avoiding impact. Straightening, he frowned. "What's wrong with you?"

"I—I don't know."

Your condition, the man in the car had said.

"The smell of rot is in the air." Excitement bubbled in Mackenzie's tone.

Smiling, Gavin released me. He shot a flare in the sky to alert Cole and Lucas, then palmed two daggers. "Yeah, baby. The zombies are nearby."

I inhaled deeply, but I smelled only the pine of the trees. And…Gavin. I smelled Gavin, and it was better than the pine. It was delicious. Mouthwatering.

"You able to fight?" he asked me.

I wasn't actually sure, wasn't even sure I cared. I leaned into him and sniffed. *Hmm. Snack time.*

He looked as if he wanted to question me, but a male with a hunched back and a twisted ankle ambled from the side of a house, drawing his attention.

The zombies weren't just nearby; they were here.

This one wore a dirty, ripped suit, and his tie was askew.

Three other zombies moseyed out behind him, and five more behind them.

Must have, must have, must have.

Mine, all mine.

Gonna be so good!

The voices stacked one on top of the other, insistent and loud. I shook my head and tugged at my ears, even as I licked my lips and stared at Gavin's neck.

He tossed something small and black at the zombies and shouted, "Down!"

He hit the ground. Confused, I remained standing.

Boom!

A minigrenade exploded, ripping through the first line of zombies. Arms flew one way and legs another, minus the bodies. A white-hot blast of air shoved me backward. When I landed, twigs and grass and body parts rained over me.

Gavin and Mackenzie hopped up and rushed headlong into battle, hacking and slashing at the creatures still standing.

I gritted my teeth and forced myself into motion. "I can do this. I can do this."

But...as I carved through the spine of a female zombie, she reached for Gavin, ignoring me. As I cut off the arm of another, he bit at Mackenzie, as if I wasn't even there.

WILL TASTE.

MINE, MINE, MINE.
HURT. MAIM. KILL.
GOOD, SO GOOD.

Argh! The voices. Louder now, screaming at me. I dropped the ax to clutch at my ears. *Stop. Please, stop.* But they didn't. They only grew louder. My knees gave out, and I collapsed to the ground. The zombies stepped over me, desperate to reach Gavin and Mackenzie.

What are you doing? Get up. Fight. Help your friends. You're better than this.

Finally Pep Talk Ali, a voice of reason. Barely discernible over the noise. I palmed a dagger with a trembling hand and stood. My legs quaked, and I swayed, but I somehow found the strength to lumber forward.

Splattered in black blood, Mackenzie presented a macabre picture as she spun and sliced the throats of the three zombies attempting to latch onto her arms. Gavin jumped over a pile of headless, writhing zombies, avoiding grasping hands, to press against Mackenzie's back.

I lifted my blade. I would help them…touch them. They glowed. Soft light pulsed from their pores. Such pretty light. Drawing me.

Mine.

I had to taste it. Them.

Taste. Yes. Mackenzie was closest, and she would be the first to feed me. I would gorge on her. She would scream, and I would laugh, because I would be full for the first time in my life.

"Ali," she growled. "There's one behind you!"

One…a zombie. Behind me. He didn't care about me. Bypassed me.

But she'd warned me. To help me…the way I was supposed to help her.

So many times I'd wanted to help the people I loved, and I'd failed. My dad, my mom, my sister, my grandfather. I couldn't fail again. I blinked, my wits returning. Realization—and horror—slammed into me. I'd come close to harming my friend.

I bit my tongue until I tasted blood, dropped the blade and backed away from her. How could I have entertained such dark thoughts?

"Ali, light up!" Cole called.

He was here. I turned, our gazes meeting. He was sprinting toward me, moving as quickly as I had done. And yet I easily tracked his movements. Could even see the concern on his face.

What if I decided to hurt him? What if I attacked him?

As much as I currently disliked him, I couldn't take the chance.

Panicked, I ran in the opposite direction, away from Cole, from the fight, from everyone and everything. I ran and never looked back.

DRINK ME

Gasping, I jolted upright. Panic cloaked me as I scanned surroundings I didn't remember stumbling upon. I was…

On the cold, hard ground in front of my old house. The house I'd lived in most of my life. The house my father had built. The house I hadn't visited since the death of my family.

Tremors rocked me. How had I gotten here? I'd run from Cole, from the zombies and the voices, yes, yes, that was right, and then I'd…blacked out, maybe. I remembered nothing else.

Now the sun was in the process of rising, though it was hidden behind a thick wall of clouds—one of which was shaped like a rabbit. I gulped. Looked away. The tree swing my dad had built for Emma had been removed. The rose garden my mom had poured her blood, sweat and tears into maintaining was now a pile of rocks.

Corrosive acid filled my veins, threatening to spill over.

Change, change, all around, here and there and everywhere, reminders that nothing and no one was safe from its clutches.

Familiar sensations pricked at me. The speeding up of my heartbeat—both of them—the beading of sweat on my brow, the constricting of my lungs. Knowing I was losing control of my body and my reactions only made everything worse.

Stop! Just stop. I wasn't this girl, wasn't some scared little mouse. I was stronger than this, forged from fire and sharpened by steel. *In*—I inhaled. *Out*—I exhaled. *In. Out. Good.*

Something soft shifted through my hair, tickling my scalp. "Oh, Alice. I hate to see you like this."

My gaze traveled up a pair of ballet slippers, stockings, a fluffy tutu and a glittery pink leotard. The remaining panic went head-to-head with a sudden burst of happiness, and, miracle of miracles, the happiness won.

"Emma." I leaped to my feet and gathered my baby sister in my arms. Wait. Something wasn't right. "I can touch you," I said. "I can actually touch you." Shock sent me careening backward. "How can I touch you? Am I dead?"

Golden eyes twinkled merrily, and perfect heart-shaped lips edged into a smile. "You're in spirit form, silly." She flicked the end of her pigtails over her shoulders, a familiar gesture. "Your body is waiting at Cole's barn, and your friends are, like, superworried."

The barn. That's right.

I didn't care. "I want to stay this way forever." I couldn't lose the feel of her again.

"You can't. Your body will die."

Just then, I didn't care about that, either. "Your point? We'll still be together."

Her smile slowly fell. "I don't think we would." Looking down at her ballet slippers, she said, "Once we promised never to lie to each other, and right now I'm going to keep that promise." A pause. A sigh. "You're in trouble, Alice, and it's getting worse every day."

"No." I shook my head. "I'm handling things."

Her gaze met mine. "I can see the smudges."

I gulped. "What are they?"

Expression filled with tenderness, she reached up and brushed one side of my face. "I told you I would talk to people, and I did. But, Alice…I don't think you're going to like what I learned."

"Tell me anyway." I had to know.

"Very well. Have you ever heard the story of the two hungry wolves living inside every man? One is good, one is evil and both are fighting for control. In the end, the one that's fed will end up the winner."

I shook my head.

"Well, that is what's happening. That night inside Anima Industries, when you were stabbed, you had so much zombie toxin inside you the antidote couldn't eradicate all of it. Your spirit was strong enough to fight it, though, keeping that part of you safe, but not your already weakened body. And the toxin, well, it was a mutated version and created something new, something born of you. Another spirit. That means there are now two spirits battling to the death for rights to live inside you. Yours, the human Alice. And the other…zombie Alice."

Pausing, she waited for those words to sink in.

I wrapped my arms around myself, as if I could protect

myself from such a terrible invasion. Zombie Alice. Fighting for control. My smudged reflection… The desperate whispering voices… The sickening urges… I nearly dropped to my knees.

"You're saying I've become a host to a…to a…zombie. But that can't be. I've had long moments without the darker urges. Like now. I don't want to bite you."

"That's true, but you have to think of this as a disease. Your human spirit is fighting the zombie spirit, even though you may not be aware of it, and the human one is mostly winning right now. But because your human spirit, and therefore your body, produces a poison for the zombies, and you now have a zombie inside you, you are basically poisoning yourself. You're allergic to yourself and weakening because of it."

"No," I said, shaking my head.

"You know I'm right," she said, and I could tell she was battling tears. "The darker side of you is sometimes strong enough to manifest *outside* you."

No. "I'll use more antidote."

"And that will help in the short term, but it's not a solution."

"What is?" I croaked.

"I…don't actually know. When Justin bit you, he woke this new side of you. Breathed life into it."

Finally I did fall to my knees. I couldn't deny her words anymore, could I? Seconds after Justin had bitten me, the new heart had started beating.

The new heart.

For the new me.

"What happens if she wins?" I asked.

"You know the answer to that."

I did. I just hadn't wanted to admit it.

I would become what I hated most.

"How long do I have?" I asked, trying not to sob.

"Longer than most. Do you remember when Mom put her hand on your leg after the crash?"

My eyes widened. I couldn't form words, could only nod. The dreams hadn't been dreams, then, but memories. Having it confirmed ripped me apart. She'd suffered. My mother had suffered.

"She didn't realize she was doing it, but she passed on her zombie-slaying abilities. Her…power, I guess is as good a word as any."

Hers. Not my father's. "But she never exhibited any abilities."

"You know better than anyone you don't have to see something for it to be there." She settled in front of me, squeezed my hand. "You inherited Dad's abilities, too. That's why you're so strong, and one of the reasons you can do things others can't. One of the reasons your body hasn't already died. If anyone can beat this, you can."

"How?"

"I don't know that, either," she said. Her shoulders drooped. "I'm sorry."

I tried to smile. I wasn't sure I succeeded. "Hey, don't worry about me. I'll find a way."

She nodded, and I could see that she wanted to believe me. And then she kissed my cheek, said, "I'm still searching for answers. I'll be back," and vanished.

I crouched there, breathing in and out, my hands fisted. No matter what, I wouldn't allow myself to become a zombie. I would fight this, and I would try to find a cure, but if I failed…

No. Not an option. I formulated a to-do list and calmed. *Find a way to decode the entire journal. Learn how to kill the zombie inside me. Actually kill her.*

Simple, yet amazingly complex. Whatever. I'd done worse.

"*Ali!*"

My brow furrowed. That was Cole's voice.

I stood and turned left, saw a car speeding through the neighborhood. I turned right, saw a woman walking to her car, a cup of coffee in hand.

"*Ali!*"

Suddenly a sharp sting pierced my cheek.

Had Cole just *slapped* me? I marched forward, setting a collision course for the barn and all my problems, annnd… the world around me blurred, only coming back into focus when I spotted the big red building where I'd left my body. Someone had left the door open for me. Inside, I caught a glimpse of Cole, Mr. Holland and all of the slayers crowding in front of my chair.

Cole lifted his arm, palm flat, ready.

He had. He really had.

I slipped into my body with a gasp. "I'm here."

He straightened. His gaze found mine and narrowed. It was a new day, but I was no longer surprised when a moment passed without a vision.

His father pushed a needle into my neck. "Antidote," he explained.

"Are you okay?" Cole demanded.

Okay? No. Even with my to-do list hovering in the back of my mind, I wanted to curl into a ball and cry. I wanted to tell him what I'd learned. I wanted…everything I couldn't have. His arms around me. His voice in my ear, telling me everything would be all right.

He was the only person I would believe.

It was odd, and probably just the moment, or my shock, but now that limits had been placed on my future, none of the fury I'd harbored for Cole remained. I was still hurt by what he'd done, and the way he'd been treating me, but none of that mattered just then.

A single night had changed me irrevocably.

Change.

I laughed without humor. Another change had come for me.

"Give the girl some breathing room." Mr. Holland shoved the slayers out of the way.

"I'm sorry," I said, my voice nothing more than a whisper.

Cole shrugged off his dad's attempts and planted his hands on the arms of my chair, leaning into me, putting us nose to nose. "Where were you? What the hell do you think you were doing out there? Do you have any idea how much worry you caused m—us?"

I blinked at him. Gone was the gentle Cole, the one who had tended me after my panic attack. The one who had sweetly covered my hair with the bandanna.

"I can guess about the worry," I said, and looked away from him. I was too raw, too susceptible to his concern and his mood, torn to shreds all over again. "And I'm sorry," I repeated.

"Where were you?" he demanded a second time.

"At my old house."

"Why did you go there?"

"I don't know. I woke up, and there I was."

Mr. Holland opened his mouth, but Cole cut him off.

"You don't know?" Cole snorted, his anger far from assuaged. "How can you not know?"

What had brought about this transformation in him?

Gavin slapped him on the shoulder. "Dude. Let's give her a minute to explain."

Cole whipped to him, snarling, "You'd like that, wouldn't you?"

"Uh...yeah. We'd all like that." Confused, Gavin looked to me, probably expecting me to explain Cole's odd behavior. I couldn't.

And then I didn't want to. The world faded—

—Gavin was in my room, standing in front of me. I spun him and pushed him down on the bed, then climbed on top of him. I forced his head to the side, baring his neck. My tongue swiped over his skin as I tugged at his shirt, trying to pull it off his body and—

—*smack!*

I blinked into focus, the here and now returning just as quickly as it had vanished, only to realize Cole had just punched the partition over my head, leaving a gaping hole. Dust filled the air, making me cough. Then he pushed Gavin.

Gavin stumbled backward and scrubbed a hand down his face.

"What did you see?" Cole demanded. "Tell me, before I—"

"Get control of yourself, son." Mr. Holland grabbed him by the arm and thrust him toward the door. "If you can't, leave."

Cole took only a moment to decide. He stormed out of the barn, the door slamming shut behind him. Frosty and Bronx tossed me a sympathetic glance before following him. A few seconds later, I heard the squeal of tires and the spray of gravel.

"The rest of you need to leave, as well," Mr. Holland said. "Except you, Gavin. You stay."

All of the slayers filed out, except for Gavin. Mackenzie threw me a puzzled glance.

I'd left her in danger last night.

"I'm sorry," I said again, wrapping my arms around myself. Tears beaded in my eyes. "Did anyone get hurt?"

"No." Mr. Holland stared at me, his crystalline gaze boring into me like a laser. "I'm not going to ask what you and Gavin saw in your vision. Judging from your expression, I can guess. What I want to know is what happened to you last night."

Not too long ago, this man had found me utterly unreliable. He hadn't wanted me here. What would he do if he learned the truth, that I was rotting from the inside out?

Soon I could very well be a hazard to everyone we loved.

"I blacked out," I said.

"I was told the zombies wanted nothing to do with you."

"That's right." I shuddered with revulsion. They must already consider me one of their own.

"I want Ankh to check you out," Mr. Holland said.

I wouldn't protest. "Okay." Just what would he find? Would he discover the source of the problem? He hadn't yet.

"And I want you off rotation until this is figured out."

A denial rose immediately. One I quickly swallowed. I'd almost hurt Mackenzie and Gavin. I'd left my team to engage in battle without me. I deserved this, and worse.

I looked down, ashamed, and nodded.

Mr. Holland faced Gavin. "Drive her home." Then, having said his piece and issued his orders, he stomped out the door.

As soon we were trapped in his car, alone, Gavin said, "Why do we keep having the same vision?"

"I don't know. With Cole, we usually only had the same vision a few times before a new one took its place."

"Maybe this one is important."

I knew he didn't mean that in a conceited way. His tone was too confused. "Maybe we're not getting whatever it wants us to get."

"So the visions are alive? Sentient?"

"No," I said with a shake of my head. "But our minds are at work here, and they know what we get and what we don't."

He tapped his fingers against the steering wheel. "Let's forget the vision for a minute. You remember grabbing your ears during the fight, as if you were hearing something you shouldn't?"

I squirmed in my seat. I'd either heard Zombie Ali—

Z.A., I thought, because I hated pairing my name with that description—or the other zombies. Both options sickened me.

"Yeah." He turned the key, gunned the engine. "You remember. What'd you hear?"

"I'm not going to talk about it."

"Fine. Whatever. Just know I won't rat you out. You're a good girl, I can tell, and I'm sure you've got your reasons for keeping quiet about such an interesting development."

An unlikely ally. I desperately needed one. "Thank you."

He shrugged, and merged into traffic. "I guess I owe you."

"What do you mean?"

"After the way you were going at me, acting like you were on life support and my body had the oxygen you so desperately needed, I—"

Suddenly feeling a little more like my old self, I reached over and smacked him in the chest. "Shut up."

He grinned, his entire face lighting with amusement. "We have another vision like that, and Cole might just kill me in my sleep."

"Highly doubtful. I think he was just upset that I stayed out all night, making everyone worry."

His snort echoed through the cab. "Yeah, that's why he spent hours looking for you."

He had? Not for my benefit, surely, but for the team's. "Plus—and please hear me when I say this—I've been serious every time I've told you I have no interest in you."

His grin only widened. "You realize you're just making yourself more attractive to me, right? First, do you really not understand how beautiful you are? Even to a guy like me. And second, there's never been a female I couldn't win over."

Me? Beautiful? "Maybe you've gotten the women you've wanted in the past, but there's always a first time for failure."

He clutched at his heart, as if in pain.

I rolled my eyes. "Don't pretend you like a challenge. I had you pegged at moment one, remember?"

His laughter proved to be infectious, and I reveled in the burst of hilarity with every fiber of my being. I wasn't sure I'd have many more opportunities.

"A guy can change, you know."

Change.

"Yeah. A guy can. So can a girl." I cast my attention to the hills outside and ignored him for the rest of the drive.

Gavin followed me inside the mansion, citing, "I was told to see you home safely, and I'd be remiss in my duties if I failed to walk you to your bedroom door. Who knows? Maybe you'll even try to kiss me goodbye."

"Stay away from my bedroom, you dirty he-slut."

He grabbed my hand and twirled me, as if we were dance partners. "I'm liking you more with every second that passes, Als. Maybe there's some truth to the visions, after all. Seriously. Think about it."

"Will you shut up about the you-knows? This isn't a conversation safe zone." I stalked to the staircase and found a note taped to the banister.

My office, Miss Bell. Now.

Guess I wouldn't be reading the journal right away. I balled up the paper and threw it at Gavin. "You're dismissed.

Apparently I already have a date." Mr. Holland must have called Mr. Ankh, and his other personality, Dr. Blood and Guts, must have jumped into action.

"Dismissed," he said. "That's another first."

"You're welcome." I switched directions and trudged inside Mr. Ankh's office.

"Shut the door," he commanded from the desk.

I obeyed without protest or comment.

"Take a seat."

Again, I obeyed, my nerves razed more with every second that passed.

He walked around the desk to claim the seat across from mine, then opened a black bag filled with needles, tubes, cotton balls and a ton of other paraphernalia I was sure I didn't want to know about. There was another black bag in the far corner of the room, filled with vials of the antidote. He kept it there for emergencies.

"Try not to scream," he muttered, reaching for the tourniquet.

"Sure. You try not to poke something you shouldn't."

"I'm a doctor. I know what I'm doing."

"You're a surgeon. You know how to cut and sew."

He pursed his lips the same way Reeve did. "After a thousand years of medical school, as my daughter says, I think I can do a little more than cut and sew."

He set the needle in place and pushed, and my vein rolled. My entire arm felt the sting, and I hissed in a breath.

"Sorry," he muttered, trying again. And wouldn't you know it, he missed a second time.

I could only bite my tongue and content myself with glaring at the top of his head.

"Sorry," he muttered. Finally he succeeded.

A few minutes later, he was labeling the packed tubes. "I'll have the results tomorrow."

What would he find? I rubbed my hand over the second heartbeat and forced myself to breathe. "Thanks."

My stomach growled, embarrassing me. I snuck into the kitchen and searched for my bagels. They weren't where I'd left them, and they weren't in the pantry. Someone must have eaten them. I gazed longingly at the boxed desserts and even the jars of vegetables, but still backed out without touching anything I shouldn't and made my way to Nana's room. I'd never thanked her for the journal. I knocked, waited.

"Your grandmother went to church," a soft voice said from behind me.

I turned and saw one of the maids dusting a side table. "Thanks."

Nana and I always went to church together. I hated that I'd missed. Especially since it probably seemed like I'd blown her off. Again. I hoped she wasn't upset.

I trudged to my room. Avoiding the mirrors, I sat at my desk and thumbed through the journal. I expected to start by rereading what had already been decoded. Instead, I found that every word was once again hidden from my understanding. But...how could that be?

Frowning, I went through every page slowly, line by line, studying every symbol, every number. Nope. No miraculous unveiling.

Must simplify the to-do list: *Learn how to kill the zombie inside me without the journal. Actually kill her.*

Where to start? My sister? Maybe she'd learned something else about my situation. "Emma. If you can swing another visit, I'd love to see you."

I had to wait longer than usual, but she did, eventually, arrive. "Hey there," she said.

I smiled at her. "You came."

"I told you. I'll always come." She stood beside the desk, fingering the ends of her skirt. "You look better."

"Thank you."

"So…whatcha doing?"

I lifted the book. "Apparently our great-great-great-grandfather wrote a journal about zombie slaying. Only he wrote it in some kind of code, and I can't decipher it. So I started to wonder whether you'd learned anything new."

"Not yet." She rubbed her hands together. "But let me take a crack at the journal."

Leaning over my shoulder, she scanned the pages and pouted with disappointment. "I was hoping to crack the code with my genius mind and rub it in your face forever, but I can read the words no problem."

I stared down at the still-coded pages. "How?"

"I don't know. I just can. Everything just looks normal to me."

"Read something to me, then."

"Okay…how about there?" She pointed. "The words are flashing at me."

Flashing? I nodded.

"'I've heard we need darkness to balance light,'" she read,

"'and light to balance darkness. I say we have no need of darkness, period. It confuses. It hurts. It tortures. It ruins. And really, darkness cannot remain with light. Light will always chase it away. Think about it. We kill the zombies with the fire from our hands—fire produces light. And they, the zombies, are the ultimate darkness. With a touch, they can be extinguished for eternity.'"

I let the words settle in my mind before turning them over again and again. Could Z.A. be killed by the fire the slayers produced? *My* fire? If so, if a slayer pressed his—or her—palm against my chest, would I die, too?

There was only one way to find out.

Was it worth the risk, though?

"Want me to read more?" Emma asked.

"Not right now." There was a tremor in my voice. *Crap.* I didn't want her to know what I was contemplating.

"Well, then, I better get back to my research."

I nodded, offering her as bright as smile as I could. Then she was gone.

Put-up or wuss-up time. I eased to the foot of the bed and rested the backs of my hands on my knees. My breathing was fast, too fast, as a bead of nervousness rolled through me, picking up steam.

I was a slayer. I could produce the fire.

I could kill Z.A.

And maybe myself…

Yeah, but maybe not.

I closed my eyes to concentrate. Before I could step out of my body, a thought bloomed, and I couldn't shake it.

Would Nana come in here and find a pile of ash, then blame someone else? One of the other slayers?

Should I leave a note?

Shaking, I scribbled a quick goodbye at my desk. *Did this to myself. Love you so much.* Just in case. And maybe I should have spent more time on it, explaining everything, but I didn't want to take a chance I'd talk myself out of such a necessary action.

So…without further ado, I forced my spirit to rise. I looked at my hands, and willed the fire to come. Little white flames sparked at the ends of my trembling fingertips. Not giving myself time to think, I turned and pressed those flames into my body's chest. Then I waited. I watched my own face as a muscle ticked under my eye…but nothing else happened.

Disappointed, a lot angry and just a little relieved, I dropped my arms to my sides.

Why hadn't that worked?

I rejoined spirit and body. Maybe…Z.A. had left my body with me?

Would she always?

I had to find out. But how?

Temples throbbing, I stalked out of my room and hunted for Reeve. I needed a distraction. Only, she wasn't in her room. Or the kitchen. I headed to the second floor, bypassing antique chairs and tables, each surrounded by colorful vases and paintings of flowers. The closer I got to my gym, the more grunts, groans and girlish laughter I heard. She was there.

I reached the open doorway and ground to a halt.

Veronica was in the process of teaching my friends how to defend themselves from an attack.

"—proper fist," she was saying. "Like this. That way, when you throw a punch, you won't break your thumb."

Reeve and Kat nodded eagerly.

"Show me," Veronica commanded.

The pair spent the next few minutes punching air.

"Excellent."

"I feel sorry for whoever makes a play for me," Kat said, flexing her arms. "Do you see the amazingly sick biceps I'm developing?"

Grinning, Reeve said, "So, how did you learn to fight like this, Ronny?"

Ronny. Just like that, I felt utterly betrayed. This was *my* home. They were *my* friends. And I'd had enough. Before the girl could reply, I stepped deeper into the room. "What are you doing here, Veronica?"

Three sets of eyes looked over at me.

"Frosty sent me," Veronica explained, tone now cold.

"He said you were fine with it, that you'd suggested he take care of it," Kat said with a frown. "But, uh, judging by your expression, I'm thinking he must have misunderstood."

Veronica glared at me. "Would you care to join us and learn something, Ali? A few skills could give you the confidence you need to actually engage in battle rather than run away."

I sucked in a breath. *Such* a low blow.

"What are you talking about?" Reeve demanded.

Kat threw the girl a dagger-sharp glare. "Oh, no, you didn't."

"You have no idea what went down, Veronica," I gritted. "Therefore, you have no right to comment."

"What went down?" Reeve asked. "And how do you know our self-defense instructor?"

My attention remained on Veronica. "You can leave now. I'm taking over."

"Uh, that would be a big fat no. Frosty wants these girls trained right."

Are you going to let her speak to you that way?

I didn't have to think about my answer. No. No, I wasn't.

Threatening her won't do you any good. You'll have to force her to zip her lips.

Yes. I could. I would.

Then do it. Here. Now.

A strange, almost stinging anticipation wound through me as I stalked forward. "I don't know about you, but I teach through demonstration."

MIRROR, MIRROR
ON THE BLOODY WALL

I'd been taunted by one of Cole's exes before, and there was no question I would be taunted again. I'd always—okay, mostly—chosen to walk away. I'd had what the other girls wanted: Cole. They'd just been lashing out, and I'd understood.

In that moment, I didn't understand anything but rage.

This girl thinks you're weak, someone to scare away.

She would learn better.

She probably spent the night with Cole.

She would suffer.

She probably laughs at you behind your back.

She would never laugh again.

I increased my speed. Kat and Reeve backpedaled, moving out of the way. Not Veronica. She met me in the middle. I threw a punch, but she leaned to the side, avoiding impact;

I swiped air. She returned the gesture, and I lifted my arm, blocking her, and went at her with my other fist.

Finally. Contact.

Impact sent her stumbling to the side. Unfortunately she recovered quickly and as I approached, threw a right. I ducked, and she nailed me with a left in the center of my scar, using my own trick against me.

As I struggled for purchase, she clipped my jaw with every bit of her strength—*as serious as I am*—and I whipped to the side. I stumbled back, but caught myself before I went down. Didn't matter. She threw herself at me, and we flew to the floor. I took most of the impact, and whatever oxygen I'd managed to suck in was once again stolen. *Don't care.* I rolled on top of her and landed a blow to her chin before she was able to kick me off. We stood.

Panting, she circled me.

"You've proven yourself to be toxic," she spat. "I'm not going to let you hurt my friends."

That stinging anticipation pulsed in my chest, almost as if it were a living thing. *Hurt...*

The rage magnified.

Hurt HER.

When she made her next move, I was ready. She launched at me, throwing another punch. I twisted to avoid her fist, moving behind her, and, with my back to her, kicked out my leg, buckling her knees. As she dropped, I elbowed her in the back of the head. Yeah. Forget honor. I'd go with dirty.

She attempted to rise. Grabbing a hank of her hair, I rolled her over, then wasted no time straddling her waist, pinning her shoulders to the floor and whaling on her. Again and again…and again.

"Stop," Kat called. "Ali, you have to stop. She's bleeding. There's blood. Ali, stop. Please!"

"Ali," Reeve screamed. "Enough!"

I stilled only when Veronica's eyes closed, signaling she was out cold. Blood leaked from her nose. I might have broken it. Her teeth had cut into her lips, and had already swelled to three times the normal size.

Such a delicious buffet, unable to defend itself…

A wave of hunger hit me.

Kat ran over to push me away from the girl, but I batted at her hands and leaned down to sniff Veronica's neck. How sweet she smelled. Not as good as Cole or even Mackenzie, but she would do. I licked my lips.

One taste wouldn't hurt.

Muscled arms banded around me, jerking me backward. I struggled for freedom, desperate to return to the girl.

"Hey, now," Gavin said. "I've always thought there's nothing wrong with a little bloodshed between friends, but I draw the line at murder."

"Just want to—" *Bite her,* I realized. I wanted to bite her. Horror bathed me in ice, the hunger instantly forgotten.

"I'm so sorry," I said, my entire body beginning to tremble. "I wasn't thinking… Wasn't myself—" Oh, heaven help me, I'd been zombie. Almost fully zombie.

Want to die.

"Calm now?" Gavin set me aside and crouched beside his friend. Gently he smoothed the blood-soaked hair from her brow. "Veronica, honey. You okay?"

I backed out of the room, too ashamed to look anyone in the eye. In fact, I kept my gaze downcast until I reached my room. I shut and locked my door and tripped my way to the vanity. I closed my eyes. My chin wobbled, tears cascading down my cheeks.

I remembered what a sad little girl I'd once been, trapped inside my home, peering out my bedroom window while other kids played in their yards. Social Services had come once. They'd questioned my parents, questioned me, maybe even considered taking Emma and me away from the only home we'd ever known. Maybe we would have been separated from each other. Maybe not. I hadn't wanted to risk it, so I'd done something totally against my nature. I'd lied. I'd told them we were private people, that was all, and we enjoyed our family time and wouldn't sacrifice it. I'd laughed at their concerns of abuse.

In junior high, my friends had called me Nolice. *No, I can't go out with you. No, I can't stay the night. No, you can't stay the night with me.* One day, invitations had just stopped coming.

I'd wanted normal, give-and-take relationships more than anything. Now I had them, but I might have to walk away from them.

I was a menace. Dangerous.

Look. See who you're becoming.

Slowly I pried my eyelids apart. The mirror—and my reflection—came into view. Revulsion made me shudder. My eyes were red. The girl peering back at me wasn't me. Not anymore. Not in any way. She couldn't possibly be me. The smudges had spread, grown darker, and a black spiderweb of veins stretched over her forehead.

That. Quickly.

Her cheekbones were gaunt, her hair tangled.

Tick. She reached toward me with a smudge-stained hand, and I reared backward. Trembling, I waited for her next move, part of me expecting her to mist through the glass. But she merely pressed her palm against the surface, and I calmed enough to ease back into my seat.

Tock. "It is nice to finally have the strength to speak," she said.

Tick.

Oh. Good. Glory. I could hear her voice. *My* voice. But *I* wasn't speaking. "I know you're a zombie."

Tock. She lifted one shoulder in a shrug. "You say zombie, I say better half."

Tick. What *was* that? A clock? Yes, I realized. That was exactly what the strange *tick-tock* represented. A clock, and time was running out.

I steeled myself to ignore it.

"What do you want from me?" I demanded.

"What do you think?" she said with a grin. "I want *everything.*"

Everything. My body? My life? "I won't let you win." *I have a to-do list, and failure isn't on it.* Shaking, I reached out and pressed my fingers against the coolness of the glass.

She laughed. "You won't be able to stop me. I grow stronger every day."

"That means strength is measurable. So, if you can grow stronger, you can be made to grow weaker."

That wiped away her amusement. "Look how easily you gave in to my desires. Soon biting will be second nature."

"No." Never.

"Once your human spirit has been destroyed, I'll have control of your body. I'll be the first of my kind."

Breath crystallized in my lungs. "You can't—"

A knock sounded at the door, and a sweet, trembling voice said, "Ali. Is someone in there with you?"

Kat.

"No," I shouted a little too loudly.

A pause. "Will you let me in, then? Please. I need to know you're okay, and we need to talk about what just happened. I've never seen you act like that, not even when you were beating up those boys, and it scared me."

"I'm okay, and I'm sorry I scared you. But we'll talk about it later. I just… I need to be alone right now."

I heard her sigh even through the obstruction. "You're upset, and I want to comfort you—it's my specialty. Just don't hurt me, okay?"

I think she meant the words as a joke. I hoped she did. "I would never hurt you," I said, tears beading in my eyes.

"Ali, I know that, but you have to—"

"Please, Kat. Not now."

I waited several seconds, heard only silence. I turned back to the mirror.

My reflection was just as grotesque but no longer moved contrary to me. "Are you still there?" I whispered, watching my lips move.

My reflection offered no reply.

I bit my tongue as I injected myself with the antidote, just to be safe. Then I withdrew the business card from my desk drawer and peered down at the number. This man knew something about what I was going through. Maybe he could save me.

How sad. Right now a stranger was my best shot.

Alter list: *however proves necessary, kill Z.A. ASAP.*

Though I didn't like the idea of using my cell and letting caller ID reveal my number, there was no other phone I could use. Not without alerting Mr. Ankh, and therefore Mr. Holland, and therefore Cole. I dialed before I could change my mind.

A man answered after the third ring. "Hello, Miss Bell."

He freaked me out, his welcome too much, too soon, and with a gasp, I hung up.

Stupid, stupid, stupid. I redialed.

He answered on the second ring. "I hope you'll actually say something this time."

"Who are you?" I demanded.

"Your new best friend," was the casual reply. "I am Dr. Bendari."

I wrapped my fingers around the edge of the vanity and squeezed, trying to relieve a little of the pressure building inside me. "Enough games. You should know straight-out that I don't trust you."

"Believe me, I received that message loud and clear when you slashed my tire," he replied drily.

"You're probably wondering why I called."

"No. I know. You're desperate."

Well, okay, then. We were on the same page. "How do I know you have the answers I seek?"

"Were you bitten by a slayer who'd been bitten by a zombie? Are you now seeing things? Hearing things? Experiencing unusual emotions and reactions?"

He knew. He really knew. "Yes," I whispered. "How did you know that?"

"I have a source on the inside. I also have the answers you seek."

"Tell me." A command. "And who is your source? Is he one of my friends?" Who would betray me?

"The source matters little. I will tell you everything else you wish to know, but I won't do it over the phone. You won't believe what I tell you. Not without pictures."

Anger infused every cell in my body. He could be lying, trying to draw me out, make me an easier target. "You want to meet," I said flatly.

"I do. Tonight. Midnight."

He could be playing me, could be planning to murder me. But honestly? I didn't care. Right now death was preferable to uncertainty. If I walked into my own personal horror movie, oh, well. "All right. Where?"

"There's an all-night Chinese buffet in Birmingham called the Wok and Roll. Come alone, and I'll be there. Come with someone else, and I'll leave before you can spot me. That happens, and you will never hear from me again."

He hung up before I could agree. Or yell at him.

I paced my room for the rest of the day. Nana came to my door with lunch, then dinner, and both times I asked her to set the tray on the floor. Earlier I'd wanted to talk to her—I still did. Now just wasn't the right time. At the moment, I couldn't trust myself to behave.

"You're going to tell me what's going on, Ali," she said

through the door. Never before had she spoken so sternly with me. "The boy, Gavin, he told me you beat another girl unconscious. How could you do something like that?"

"I'm asking myself that same question," I replied, my chin trembling.

A heavy pause. "Let me in the room. I want to look into your eyes while we talk about this."

She would see was my horror, my remorse. My tears.

My new nature?

"I...can't. I'm sorry."

"Is it the upcoming holiday?" she asked, hesitant. "Are you missing your parents?"

"No." To be honest, I hadn't given Thanksgiving a single thought.

Another pause, this one writhing with tension.

"Ali, you're shutting me out and it's hurting me."

Yes, I could hear the pain in her voice.

I stepped up to the door, reached for the knob, stopped myself. Hot tears cascaded down my cheeks. "I'm sorry," I repeated. "I would rather die than hurt you, but if I open that door I could hurt you worse. I just... I need a day to work through this, okay?"

Several minutes passed in silence before she said, "You've got one day." Footsteps resounded.

I picked up the tray, placed it inside my room, my stomach a twisted mess. I couldn't bring myself to eat.

Finally eternity came to an end and eleven-thirty arrived. I loaded myself with weapons and sneaked through the secret passages Mr. Ankh had built throughout the house. He'd wanted his daughter to have an escape route if ever it proved necessary—not that she would know what chased her.

Reeve. I frowned. My nose wrinkled after I inhaled. I smelled her perfume. She must have used the passage, and quite recently.

Huh. The passage led to a hatch just beyond the front yard, seconds from the road. Still. I'd have to be careful. Mr. Ankh had cameras everywhere and—as I eased my out, I caught movement several yards away.

Gaze zooming in, I palmed a blade. Was that...Reeve? Had to be. Dark hair swished as a slender girl matching Reeve's height and build walked north. She'd sneaked out.

Dang you, Reeve! No matter how badly I wanted answers, no matter how dangerous I currently was, I couldn't let her wander the streets without backup.

As I followed her through the shadows, I dialed Bronx.

"What?" he snarled.

"Reeve snuck out. I'm a few yards behind her. I just thought you'd like to know."

He spewed a mouthful of curses. In the background, I heard a girl giggling.

"You're with someone?" I asked, shocked.

At the same time he said, "Where are you?"

I gave him our current location, and he hung up.

Thank you, Ali, I inwardly mocked. *I appreciate your help.*

A car drove past, and Reeve darted behind a tree trunk. I did the same, only to stiffen when the car slowed, stopped.

Reeve stepped from the shadows. "Ethan?"

"It's me, sweetheart."

Sweetheart. Hello, new boyfriend.

"Thank goodness! I realized the car was slowing down, and I almost peed my pants." She walked around the car and opened the passenger side door. "I thought you were meeting me at 7-Eleven."

"You were late, and I worried."

Bronx, who was in spirit form, moved through the trees and swept up beside me. The hair he'd dyed blue was now green, but it wasn't spiked. Tonight, it shagged over his forehead. There were several lipstick stains on the collar of his shirt—and not all of them were the same color.

"She just got into the car," I said, beyond grateful a slayer's ability to see spirits extended to human ones. Although…

Would this make my dark urges worse?

I tensed. Backed away.

No hunger pangs.

I stopped, unsure. I was…better? Once more safe to be around?

Look how easily you gave in to my desires.

That was what Z.A. had said. And she had been right. I did. Because I'd been mad at Veronica, my defenses weak. And every time before, I'd been a mess about Cole.

If I remained calm from now on, focused, I wouldn't have to ditch my friends or my grandmother. I could be around them without worry.

I wanted to shout with the force of my relief.

Scowling, Bronx waved me away. "Go home. I've got this."

His tone grated—my first test. *Calm.* "Are you sure you don't want to go back to bed and cuddle?" I asked sweetly.

He leveled me a look that would have frightened the most violent criminals. "The girls caught me at a bad time."

Girls. Plural, as I'd suspected. "Pig," I muttered. Could no guy stay faithful anymore? Sure, Bronx and Reeve weren't actually dating, and she was currently seeing another guy, but come the freak on.

"Whatever."

I heard the self-castigation in his voice and flinched.

"Sorry," I said on a sigh. "I didn't mean that."

He shrugged. "Do you really believe I'd be with anyone else if I could be with Reeve?"

No. I didn't. And when I thought about it, I understood. Sometimes the loneliness probably got to be too much and anyone seemed better than no one. He had no parents. They'd dropped him off in a forest, at night, when he was just a kid, hoping the wild animals would kill and dispose of him. He just wanted to be wanted, to have someone to call his own.

Earlier, as unstable as I'd been, I might even have settled on comfort from Gavin.

The driver—Ethan—turned the car around. Bronx stiffened, gearing to pursue.

He shouldn't do this on his own. I knew that. He could call for backup, but I also knew he wouldn't.

I looked behind me, in the direction I needed to go. I looked back at Bronx, at the anger and frustration shining from his features. He was distracted. He would probably get into trouble.

As the car sped away, Bronx arrowed forward.

I couldn't leave him.

With a mental push, my spirit left my body, which would remain hidden in the trees. I trailed after him, maintaining proper speed, just as Gavin and Mackenzie had taught me, keeping up without a problem.

We ghosted through other cars, and yeah, it freaked me out every time.

"Where's Cole?" I asked, barely panting.

"Taking care of Veronica."

I flinched as if I'd been punched.

"You really messed up, Ali," he continued, unaware of the pain his words had caused. "Beating on one of your own is never okay." His gaze raked over me, and he finally became aware. "He's not with her for that. He doesn't like her the way you think."

"It doesn't matter."

"To you, I think it does." But he offered no other words of encouragement.

About ten minutes later, the car parked in the driveway of a secluded house. Ethan emerged—leanly muscled, with blond hair and a handsome face—then rushed around to open Reeve's door.

"Thank you," she said with a grin.

He leaned down and kissed her cheek. "My pleasure, sweetheart."

Bronx growled low in his throat, a feral sound. He stalked forward, as if he planned to attack the guy, but crashed into a tree and ricocheted backward. He came up sputtering.

"Blood Lines." He looked left, right. "The guy has Blood Lines."

So…the guy knew about the zombies. And yet he couldn't

see them. Otherwise he would have seen us. And if he'd seen us, he would have reacted.

Ethan ushered Reeve into the house. Bronx trailed close to their heels, but the door closed before he could sweep inside, and he once again ricocheted backward. He cursed.

Bronx tried to bypass the walls and windows to no avail. We paced the front yard in unison, waiting for Reeve to come out, ticking off the nearly unbearable seconds.

"I have his address," Bronx snarled. "I'll find out who he is. Every detail. Every girl he's ever banged."

Only he didn't use the word *banged*.

"I'll know every secret."

Man. Bronx really liked Reeve, really wanted her. Her protection mattered to him. He was simply trying to respect her father's wishes, as well as the needs of the slayers.

Watching him, I knew this was how a boy should react to the idea of being separated from his girl. The way I'd wanted Cole to react.

The way Cole *hadn't* reacted.

Had he ever felt so strongly for a girl? Had it ever bothered him to walk away from one? Or was self-preservation wrapped so tightly around him it strangled any of the deeper feelings he had?

I wondered what he thought of me—if he thought of me at all.

"Ali," Bronx snapped, and I jolted back to awareness.

"Yes?"

"Go home. I've got this."

"No."

"You're making little growling noises in the back of your throat, and it's distracting me. Not in a good way."

Fear began to claw at me, because I knew what those growls meant. I had to do a better job of focusing—or else. I squared my shoulders. "I've already let one slayer down today. I'm not letting another. I'm staying."

He glanced at me, and I could see a new gleam of respect in his eyes. But all he said was "Whatever. Do what you want."

That respect…

It meant more to me than money.

And I knew how to get more. The list. *However proves necessary, kill Z.A. ASAP.*

You're going down, fiend.

When dark went against light, light always won. I was light—as long as I didn't let my fire get snuffed out.

I would win. Right?

Bronx bumped my shoulder. "You panicking over something, Bell?"

"No, I'm calm," I said. "From now on, I'm going to be a walking sedative."

11

ROT in PEACE

The next morning, I climbed into Reeve's Porsche and bucked my seat belt. Our ten-minute drive to school couldn't end fast enough. I was ready to hide in the back of my first class and fall asleep.

She clearly concurred, gunning the engine as she shot from the garage. I wanted to rapid-fire questions at her, now that we were alone, but I was too tired. I leaned against the door instead, the sunlight streaming through the window warming me, lulling me.

Singing along to the radio, she merged into traffic. There were shadows under her eyes, and for once, she wore wrinkled clothing, as if she'd just rolled from bed and called it good.

I happened to know that she had.

As promised, I hadn't left Bronx alone. I'd waited for Reeve to exit Ethan's house. And she had, at 3:00 a.m. Ethan had driven her home, dropped her off in the same spot he'd picked her up and kissed her on the mouth before driving away. Bronx hadn't said another word. His body language had said plenty, though.

Ethan was lucky to be alive.

The first moment I'd been alone, I'd called Dr. Bendari to reschedule, but the number had been unavailable. I had screeched with frustration, knowing I'd blown my best chance to talk with the only person with concrete answers.

Then I'd chastised myself for letting an emotion get the better of me.

Walking. Sedative.

"Wishing you hadn't gotten the tattoos?" Reeve asked.

"Of course not," I said. "Why?"

"Well, look at yourself."

I gazed down. I was absentmindedly rubbing my thumb over the daggers. *Oh. Well.* "They comfort me."

Reeve gasped and stomped on the brake. The car jerked to a stop, throwing me forward as much as the belt would allow.

"What the—"

"Bronx," she screeched, tearing off her belt and stepping into the daylight.

Just in front of her car, right in the middle of the road, was Bronx's old, rusted truck. He leaned against the hood, arms crossed.

I should have expected this.

"What do you think you're doing?" she demanded.

"What do you think *you're* doing?" he spat. "Sneaking out in the middle of the night, meeting some strange guy and going to his place. Do you know how dangerous that is?"

"How did you—argh! It doesn't matter." She grabbed a rock and threw it at him.

Reflexes honed, he ducked.

She shook her head, as if she couldn't believe what she'd just done. More calmly, she said, "He's not some strange guy, he's my boyfriend, and what I do with him isn't your business."

"Everything about you is my business."

Her back went ramrod straight. "Screw you. I'm not doing this with you, Bronx. Not anymore." She turned.

He grabbed her arm, spun her around. "Did you sleep with him?"

Very calmly, she said, "I told you. What I do with him is none of your business."

"And I told you everything about you is my business, but neither of us seems to be listening."

The forced calm vanished as she jerked away. "You can't do this to me. Can't pretend you care. Tomorrow, after I've dumped him, you'll change your mind." She shoved him, a puny action, really, when comparing a six-foot-five gigantor to a five-foot-five fairy princess, but he released her anyway.

"Does Daddy Dearest know about him?" he asked quietly.

She pointed her finger in his face. "No, and you won't say a word. You don't get to play any part in my love life. We've been sniffing around each other since junior high. You were so sweet to me at first. You made me things. You were my first kiss. Then suddenly you wouldn't look at me, wouldn't even talk to me—until I turned my sights to someone else and tried to move on. You'd come on strong, and I'd always fall back into your arms, but it wouldn't take long for you to start ignoring me all over again, and I'm tired of it."

I shouldn't be listening to this. I would have hated it if anyone had heard my arguments with Cole, especially the final one.

Trying to distract myself, I turned up the radio. Taylor Swift, "I Knew You Were Trouble." Fitting. I texted Nana. Can we talk later? Just U & me?

If my emotions started to go haywire, I'd adios.

Her: I would love that.

Me: I'm sorry I've been so weird lately, & I'm sorry about the fight w/the girl.

Her: We can talk about the reason at dinner. And just to make you happy, I promise I won't spend too much on groceries.

I laughed.

Her: BTW, do you want to tell me why I found a note in your room saying "Did this to myself"? WHAT DID YOU DO?

Uh-oh.

Me: Almost @ school. Gotta go. Love you!

Hey. Not a word of that was a lie.

"—can't be with you the way I want," Bronx was saying, drawing my attention back to the conversation.

"Why?" Reeve demanded. "For once, give me a straight answer. You do, and I'll never see Ethan again."

Bronx pressed his lips together.

"Yeah, that's what I thought." Bitterness tinged her tone.

Reeve stomped to the car. Bronx stomped to his. His tires squealed as he turned the vehicle around. Dirt sprayed as he shot forward.

"That boy," Reeve said, her body trembling.

"He cares about you."

"Yeah, just not enough."

I reached over, patted her hand. "Believe me, I get it."

She tossed me a sad smile before resuming the drive.

A few minutes later, she was parking in her usual spot. The lot could be overflowing, but no one, not even teachers, would dare encroach on her territory. Not because of her or her father's money, but because of Bronx. I heard someone made the mistake of parking here only once; Bronx had hot-wired the car and crashed it into the trees the students had spray-painted gold and black to proudly display our school colors.

Silent, we strode over the tiger paws mowed into the grass and headed inside the building.

Trina and Mackenzie were leaning against a locker, snarling at anyone stupid enough to approach them. When I walked past—*never said I was smart*—they pushed away from the wall and flanked my sides, shouldering Reeve out of the way.

"You have to talk to Cole," Trina began.

"I never thought I'd say this," Mackenzie said, "but I want you to do more than talk to him. I want you to seduce the hell out of him. I don't know how much more post-Ali drama I can take."

"O-kay. Cue my exit," Reeve said, branching away from us. "See you at lunch, Ali."

"Yeah. See ya." I sighed. "What's the problem?"

Trina twisted the ring in her eyebrow. "For starters, he's meaner than my stepdad's Yorkie."

"Your stepdad has a Yorkie?"

Mackenzie slashed a hand through the air. "Forget the tiny terror dog. Cole lashes out at everything we say, and has for weeks."

For weeks?

Until two nights ago, he'd shown me only his gentler side.

"He busted Lucas's nose during training," she continued. "Last night, he punched a window and needed eight stitches."

Last night? While he'd been with Veronica. "It has nothing to do with me," I assured them. If I'd had claws, I would have scraped them over the lockers.

Calm.

"I happen to think it has everything to do with you," Trina said. "I've seen the way he watches you when you're not looking."

"And I swear vessels burst in his forehead every time Gavin mentions your name," Mackenzie said, nodding.

"Guys. Cole broke up with me. I told him I'd work on being his friend, and I will, but that doesn't mean I'm going to stroke his…uh, ego and make him smile."

"Fine," Trina replied. "We'll stop trying to convince you to sex him up, but you still gotta talk to him. You're the only one he'll listen to."

"I don't think that's true."

She ignored me, saying, "He disappears for hours at a time. No one knows where he goes. He's paranoid we won't keep detailed records about what we find on patrol. He gets phone calls from blocked numbers and steps out of the room so no one will overhear his conversations. Before, he kept us in the loop about everything."

So he was still spying on the slayers. But what was it, exactly, that he was trying to uncover?

I reached my destination, freed the lock on my locker and stuffed my bag inside. "I'll talk to him about his weirdness, but that's all I can promise."

Mackenzie shocked me to my bones when she hugged me. "Thank you. We, like, seriously owe you one."

As if our conversation had summoned him, Cole turned the corner and strolled down the hall toward us. He was wearing a red baseball cap and had his hands in his pockets. I couldn't see his newest wound. He walked past us, nodding at Trina, then Mackenzie—avoiding me. My chest constricted.

"Or maybe I won't be talking to him," I muttered, and took off for my first class.

Just before Cole turned the corner, he looked back at me; our gazes locked. I tripped over my own feet. No vision. But I saw hunger. Fury. Regret. Remorse. Fear. Then he was gone.

Someone laughed, breaking me from the spell he'd woven. Dazed, a little angry with myself—*calm, dang it*—I looked to see what was so funny. Wren and Poppy stood with a group of girls making fun of a tall, skinny redhead with freckles and braces. Wren and Poppy weren't laughing, but they weren't stopping the taunts, either. The redhead was doing her best not to cry.

I stomped over and, to a chorus of "Hey" and "Watch it," shoved the girls out of the way. Glaring, I said, "You have five seconds to leave, and then I get mad."

I wasn't ever going to be a sedative, was I?

They might not know how good I was with my fists, but they certainly knew the people I ran with, and, paling, they left without another word. Poppy cast a remorseful look over her shoulder. Wren, too. Only she mouthed, *Thank you,* baffling me.

"Thank you," the redhead said, then swallowed a sob. "My shirt… I didn't bring a jacket today, so I can't cover up."

It was white and soaked with water, revealing every stitch on her bra. "Why don't we trade?" I didn't want her sitting in the cold and the wet and thinking about what had happened. "Your shirt goes better with my jeans."

"Really?"

"Really."

She brightened, and we raced to the bathroom.

"Thank you so much," she said after we'd made the switch.

"Don't worry about it." Shivering, I darted to class to avoid a tardy I couldn't afford.

To my surprise, Justin was waiting at the door. "Hey, Ali."

"Hey."

He opened his mouth to say more, closed it. Opened it. Snapped it closed. Finally he settled on "How are you?"

"I've been better." I headed toward my seat, and he followed me. "You?"

"Fine. I'm fine."

I studied him, saw dark circles under his eyes, gaunt cheekbones and lips that had clearly been chewed. He wasn't fine. "I know you told me nothing abnormal had been happening to you. Is that still the case?"

His brow furrowed, becoming a slash of anger. "Want to

tell me what's been happening to *you?* Because something has, right?"

I still wasn't sure what his motives were, but at the moment I had nowhere else to turn. "Possibly."

"Possibly?"

I sat down. "That's all I'm willing to say." *For now.*

He sat down beside me. "Okay, but I can't help you if I don't know what you're dealing with."

"*Will* you actually help me, though?"

His shoulders wilted, and he said, "I guess I deserved that."

Yeah, but I didn't have to be so crabby about it, did I? "Do you know someone by the name of Dr. Bendari?"

"No. Why?"

Crap. So...maybe Dr. Bendari wasn't with Anima, after all. Maybe Justin was lying. Or maybe Justin just hadn't met him. "Forget it."

"Ali. Please. Talk to me."

How many times was I going to hear those words?

The bell rang, saving me from having to reply. "Later," I said. *Maybe.*

Lunchtime arrived. I'd successfully managed to avoid Justin after first and second period. Trina and Mackenzie, too. But not Cole.

He cornered me in the girls' bathroom.

I was washing my hands as he stepped inside. A classmate of mine was in the process of closing a stall door when she spied him and squealed.

"Out," he said, and she took off, leaving me alone with him.

My heart thundered as I dried my hands with a paper towel. "If you plan to yell at me for hurting your girlfriend, let me save you the trouble. My anger got the best of me, but it's not going to happen again."

"She's not my girlfriend."

"It's okay if she is. You don't have to try and spare my feelings. I've moved on."

He did *not* appear grateful.

I tried to bypass him, deciding to talk to him about Trina and Mackenzie's allegations later, in a place without mirrors. He stepped into my path. "Stay," he said.

"Orders?" I glared up at him. "You know I'm not afraid to punch you, right?"

"Do what you want to me. I'm not leaving until you've listened to me."

Sometimes I really hated my curious nature. "What?"

When I backed off, he leaned against the sink, raked his gaze over me and frowned. "You're wearing a different shirt."

"Yes," was all I said, struggling with the sudden need to cover my chest.

"Why?"

Struggling—and failing. I covered my chest with my hands. "Is that why you're here? Because my reasons don't concern you."

His frown deepened. He shook his head, as if to get back on track. "I'm worried about you and want to discuss it like rational people."

"I don't have anything to say to you."

"Why? You said we could try and be friends."

Lesson learned: it was better to think before I spoke. "Fine. Discuss away."

He muttered something under his breath before saying to me, "Ankh told me you've been eating bagels at his house."

Wait. "This isn't about what happened on patrol? Or Veronica?"

"The bagels," he insisted.

What was with the freaking bagels? "Yes. I have been eating bagels. Last I heard, that wasn't a crime."

"It is when it's all you're eating."

I anchored my hands on my hips. "Why do you even care about this?"

He ignored the question, saying, "You didn't bring your lunch and you weren't planning on getting anything in the cafeteria today, were you? I know, because you didn't get anything last week, either. You're going to starve."

He made it sound worse than it was. "I'm saving to buy Nana a house of her own."

"Then bring food from Ankh's. He has more than enough."

"I'm living in his home free of charge. I'm not going to be any more of a burden and take more from him."

"You're not a burden."

"So you say."

"Ali."

"No," I said.

"Take from me, then." He withdrew a brown leather wallet with a chain at the end. "Please."

I violently shook my head. What the heck was happening here? "I don't want your money."

"Ali," he repeated, his tone ragged. "Friends share."

"We're not that close anymore."

He flinched. "You have to eat."

"I will. I promise."

"More than bagels," he insisted.

I nodded, anything to move this conversation along. After school, I'd walk to the convenience store close to the Ankhs' and buy bread and deli meat.

"Not just later, but now, at lunch," he said, as if he'd heard my thoughts. "Please."

Please.

His concern was doing something to me, weaving one of his spells around me, making me forget the world around me, the problems, taking me deeper and deeper into an obsession that had only gotten me hurt. I wanted out. I needed out.

"It's better that we broke up, you know." I said the words for my own benefit. "Our connection was so fast, we never took the time to get to know each other. Not really. And how would we ever have known if we truly cared about each other or if the visions had simply convinced us that we did?"

He smacked a hand against the mirror and leaned toward me. Glaring, he snapped, "I knew how I felt."

Past tense. Why did that hurt? "I know how you felt, too. Not strongly enough to fight for me."

A muscle ticked below his eye as he straightened, backed me into the black-and-gold-tiled wall. The warmth of his breath fanned over my face, as sure and sweet as a caress. His gaze took in every detail of my expression, lingering on my lips. Lips suddenly aching for the kisses he'd denied me during my recovery.

"We both know why I walked away," he said. "We both know what's going to happen."

"Yes, so what the heck do you think you're doing, closing in on me like this?" Good. I'd shaken off the melancholy and welcomed a bit of mettle.

"I don't know," he snarled, and I was suddenly face-to-face with Cole the Yorkie. "I never know anymore."

For my own good, I forced myself to say, "That's your problem, not mine." Then I angled around him and walked away.

This time, he let me go.

I was getting good at not looking back.

In the cafeteria, I spent three precious dollars on a me-diocre hamburger. Cole was at the table by the time I eased beside Kat and Reeve, and he watched me eat half…and try to save the other half for later.

Scowling, he planted himself at my side, scooting Kat out of the way, then unwrapped the burger and put it back in my hand. I suspected he would try to force-feed me if I resisted, so I ate the rest. My stomach nearly wept with gratitude.

He pushed a Gatorade in my direction. His? Half the contents were already gone. I'd forgotten to buy a drink, I realized, and gratefully swallowed one mouthful, then another.

"Thank you," I said, trying not to care that he cared.

"That's what friends are for, right? Even if they're not close." He put his mouth where mine had been and drained the rest.

After school, Kat and I piled into Reeve's car. The three of us had one class together, and Mr. Toms, the teacher, had allowed us to group up for a special humanitarian project. For it, we drove to Party Palace and bought a handful of Get Well Soon balloons.

"On a totally unrelated subject," Kat said, "do you guys want to go threezies on a gift for Aubrey Wilson's baby shower? And by threezies I mean your dad will pay the bulk of it, Reeve. We want to get her something totes amaze-balls."

"She mentioned needing a crib," I said. Poor girl. She had just started showing, and her boyfriend had dumped her.

Reeve nodded. "Count me in."

As we meandered along back roads, searching for the next object we needed to complete Kat's "most brilliant idea ever," I checked the clouds. The sun glared at me, making my eyes water, but I still caught sight of a rabbit and moaned. *No, please no. Not tonight.* I wasn't ready to face the zombies—and my reaction to them—again.

Tonight I was supposed to stay at Cole's gym and guard the bodies the slayers left behind. But. Yeah, there was always a *but* with me, wasn't there? I'd be called out just as soon as the zombies were found—and they would most certainly be found.

Would I hear the voices again? Should I just call in sick?

"I'm sure we're going to get a terrible grade for this," Reeve said with a groan.

"If anything, we'll receive a certificate for awesomeness," Kat replied.

My phone beeped. I checked the screen and stiffened.

"What's wrong?" Kat asked.

"Cole wants to meet with me," I said without any inflection of emotion.

Inside, I churned.

I read the text again. My house. Five. Be there.

Dang it. I'd planned to have dinner with Nana before heading over.

"When? Where?" Reeve asked, and I gave her the details.

"Are you going to go?" Kat wondered.

Hands shaking, I texted Nana. Can we reschedule? I'm so sorry, but something's come up w/Cole.

I waited, but a response from her didn't come.

To Cole, I texted Why?

Cole (I'd deleted the part about McHottie): Do I really need a reason?

Me: 2 talk? Yes. We've said all we need 2 say.

Okay, so that wasn't exactly true. I still had to drum up the courage to mention his odd behavior, as promised.

Cole: Who runs this show? Just be there.

Me: Fine.

Cole: Your enthusiasm is humbling.

Me: Go screw yourself.

Cole: I have. I prefer 2 have a partner.

I think I gasped.

"Yeah. I'm going to go," I said. I wasn't going to call in sick. I had responsibilities. I'd keep them.

"Hold everything." Kat bounced up and down in her seat and clapped. "I think I see one."

"Where?" Reeve demanded.

Kat pointed. "Pull over."

Groaning, Reeve slowed the car, eased to the side of the

road and parked. I freed one of the balloons and exited. The girls joined me, and together we approached the centerpiece of our project—a dead raccoon, its arms and legs stiff and pointing in the air.

"Gloves," Kat said, holding out her hand.

Reeve dangled a pair just beyond her reach. "These are cashmere, you know."

"I'm sure the raccoon will be thrilled," she replied drily. "Even though I told you to buy latex."

"I thought you'd appreciate something softer." Sighing, Reeve relinquished the gloves, and Kat tugged them on. "I bought hand sanitizer instead."

"Balloon," she said next.

I handed it over.

Then Kat crouched over the poor dead animal and tied the ribbon to one of its wrists. There was no wind, so the Get Well Soon balloon stayed perfectly straight, flying proudly over the motionless animal.

"Your family will thank me for this one day," she said with a nod.

"As if we're really doing any good," Reeve said.

"Hello, we *so* are. People need to be more aware of the creatures crossing the road, thank you, and this is our way of helping. It's humorous—"

"And gross," Reeve interjected. "And cruel."

"And they'll remember," Kat finished.

We each snapped a few pictures with our phones, cleaned our hands, got back in the car and hunted the next Get Well Soon victim. I mean, recipient.

I couldn't help comparing myself to the animals. A car crash. A part of me dying.

I prayed I had a better end but had a feeling I was going to have to adjust my to-do list yet again.

DEADLY EYES BETRAY YOU

We dropped Kat off at the school parking lot, where her car waited, and drove home. Another note had been stuck to the bottom of the staircase railing. Sighing, I sailed into Mr. Ankh's office—only to find him in a heated discussion with Mr. Holland.

Interesting.

The moment the men spotted me, they zipped their lips. Mr. Holland had been leaning over the desk, putting himself nose to nose with Mr. Ankh. Now he eased back into his seat, and the two acted as friendly as ever.

Even more interesting.

I couldn't help thinking Mr. Holland was a portrait of Cole in twenty years. Both guys had dark hair and strong, chiseled features. Only difference was, Cole's eyes were that amazing violet and Mr. Holland's were an electric-blue.

"Miss Bell," Mr. Ankh acknowledged.

Did he ever go to work? I settled in the only available chair.

"Good. You're here." Mr. Holland massaged the back of his neck. "The three of us are due to have a discussion."

"Your newest blood work came in," Mr. Ankh said, "and the results have me confused."

I shifted uncomfortably.

"The toxin you and Justin shared, the one that is harmful to the zombies," he continued. "It disappeared in Justin, but it's now stronger in you. Also, your iron is lower than before, and your white blood cell count is higher."

I wasn't sure whether to laugh or cry. My human side was fighting, but my zombie side wasn't backing down. "What about the zombie toxin that is harmful to humans? Did I have any traces of that?"

He frowned. "No."

"Why would you ask that?" Mr. Holland said.

I wanted to tell him, I really did. But he'd killed his own wife when she'd turned zombie. No telling what he'd do to me, his son's unstable ex.

If these men left me alive, Mr. Ankh would for sure toss me out. Where I went, Nana went. I would not allow her to be homeless.

Then, of course, Mr. Holland would tell the others. How would Cole look at me then? He wouldn't worry about feeding me anymore, I knew that much.

"Curiosity," I hedged. In a way, it was the truth.

Mr. Holland sighed and twisted his chair to face mine. "Well, I'm curious about something, too. I know you and my son broke up. What I don't know is why. He won't talk to me."

Instant downer. "And I won't, either," I said hollowly.

He began massaging the back of his neck again, a gesture of irritation or distress he and Cole shared. "He's been sneaking out, talking to people he shouldn't, making bad decisions, and I'm worried about him. Something's going on with him, but I don't know how to help."

"Who's he talking to?" I asked.

Silent, he ran his tongue over his teeth.

He wasn't going to share the information. Got it.

"Will you check on him?" Mr. Holland asked.

"Trina and Mackenzie noticed his odd behavior, too, and asked the same thing. I agreed to talk to him," I said. "I'm meeting him at five."

Mr. Holland pushed out a relieved breath. "Thank you."

I nodded, saying, "By the way, I saw a rabbit cloud today."

The two men shared an uneasy look.

I could guess what they were thinking. The zombies usually rested a week between feedings. Only once before had the creatures come out night after night, and that was to hunt me with the goal of turning me.

Were they focused on someone else now?

"I'll be called into action," I said. And I would find out, one way or another, if the other night had been an anomaly or not. If the zombies would once again ignore me. If I would hear crazed whispers. If I would black out and end up at my old home.

Mr. Holland replied, "I'll put everyone on patrol tonight

and make sure you have a partner who will whisk you to safety if you have another…episode."

"Thanks," I muttered. I left the office and shut myself inside my bedroom. Then I dialed Dr. Bendari. Again, a recording told me the carrier wasn't available. Dang it. Would he ever again activate it?

I thought about the journal, my other source of info. Light chased away darkness. Fire burned away evil. The words snagged me. I just couldn't let them go.

Sighing, I sat in front of the vanity and steeled myself to look in the mirror. I needed a status report, and this was the best way.

My gaze met hers. The smudges had actually spread, stretching from underneath her eyes to her cheeks, even delving down the plane of her neck. Shaking, I whipped my shirt over my head. She did the same…several beats after me. *Annnd* the smudges continued, branching from her neck to her shoulders. The largest smudge rested just over her heart. Once the size of my thumb, it was now the size of a giant's fist. I traced my fingertips over the skin there.

My reflection never moved.

Tick, tock. Tick, tock.

Louder than before.

She was stronger.

Fighting a wave of frustration, I injected myself with antidote, just to be safe, showered and dressed in my all-black fighting clothes. I opened my door to head to Nana's room. I needed a ride to Cole's. Kat caught me off guard, her hand posed as if she meant to knock.

"Everything okay?" I asked.

"Peachy. I came to offer you a ride to Cole's. Frosty texted. He asked me to meet him at the barn at five."

A coincidence? "I accept, thanks."

The barn was packed with slayers, and I realized I'd misunderstood Cole's intentions. We weren't going to talk. He was going to lecture. Not just me, but everyone.

I'd had too many highs and lows lately to let this disappoint me...much.

My gaze landed on Veronica, and I had to fight to keep my lunch. She had two black eyes, a slightly swollen nose and a busted lip, and she was peering up at Gavin, who was saying something to her. I quickly looked away.

"Kitty Kat," Frosty said.

"Jerk Face," she retorted, surprising me.

His eyes frosted over in tribute to his name. "What'd I do this time?"

"Nothing. I thought I'd be mad just to be mad and liven things up. We were getting stale."

In a snap, he lost his air of coldness. He barked out a laugh. "You're too sexy for words, you know that?"

"Actually, I do," she said, and ran to him, throwing herself in his arms.

He caught her, and as he spun her around, a sharp ache tore through my chest. I'd had that once. Would I die before I experienced it again?

Shut up, Downer Ali!

"What's going on?" I asked, hating the tremor in my voice.

Frosty set Kat on her feet but kept her tucked into his side, acting as her shield, her sole support. "Don't know. Cole has something to tell everyone, but he's not here yet."

"Something to tell everyone…even me?" Kat asked, thumping a finger against her chest.

"Even you." He kissed her on the temple. "You're now an important member of our team."

"I am? I mean, of course I am. Duh." She beamed up at him.

He cupped her cheeks, ensuring that she couldn't look away. Tone serious, he said, "You can't go out at night and fight, since you can't see the zombies, so don't even ask. But you *can* patch me up if I come home injured."

"Dr. Kitty Kat," she said with a nod. "I approve."

"I hope you dole out kisses." He leaned down and pressed a soft one into her lips. "They're my medicine."

"Well, that kind of medicine will cost you. Just…don't come home injured. I'll be mad."

"You know I hate when my little kitty is mad. Her claws come out."

"They come out for other reasons, too," she purred.

In seconds, they were going at each other like wild beasts at mating season.

"Break it up before I break you in half, Frost," Bronx called, and he didn't sound like he was joking.

I found him in the crowd and pulled him into a shadowed corner. "Did you find out anything about Ethan?"

He nod was stiff. "Yeah, just not as much as I'd hoped. His name is Ethan Hamilton, he's twenty-one and a business major at Birmingham Southern. He has a fifteen-year-old sister who was diagnosed with leukemia last year."

How sad. "What are you going to do about him?"

Violence gleamed in his eyes. "Besides have a little chat with him?"

I knew that look. The chat would involve fists rather than words. "Are you sure you want to do that? He sounds like a pretty decent guy, and Blood Lines around his house isn't *that* uncommon. And I kind of understood Reeve's point today, about not being able to do the back-and-forth with you anymore. It might be time to let her go."

He peered at me for a long while before saying, "Do you really think you're in a good enough place to be throwing out advice? No, don't bother with a response. We both know the answer. So why don't I live my life, and you live yours?" With that, he stomped away.

Great. I doubted I could have messed that up more.

A chirp from my phone. I pulled the device from my pocket and read Dinner's ready! I made your favorite. Lasagna and garlic bread. I also asked Ankh if we could use his private balcony, and he said yes. I've got everything set and ready, so come out here as soon as you're able.

My heart twisted. *Oh, no.* She didn't know. She—

Another text came in a second later. I'm sorry, dear. I must have missed your text about canceling. Well, no worries. We'll do it another night.

Tears welled in my eyes. Nana had slaved in the kitchen, preparing my favorite meal. She'd probably decorated Mr. Ankh's balcony with twinkling Christmas lights, just because she knew I wasn't the biggest fan of the dark. That was how wonderful she was. And I'd canceled on her. For this.

I was a terrible person.

I moved back into the corner and called her. "Nana, I am so sorry. I'm at Cole's gym. He asked to meet. I thought it would be just the two of us, and I'd be able to find out what's wrong with him, but it's a meeting with all the slayers."

"Ali," she said on a sigh. "It's okay. I understand."

"I'll make it up to you, I swear."

Another sigh. "We'll have leftovers tomorrow, and we can talk then."

"Yes. I would love that."

We disconnected.

"Hey," a voice said from behind me.

Gavin. Every muscle in my body stiffened as I turned and faced him. I made sure to stare at my feet. "Hey."

"I came over to tell you I've got a date with a very hot chick tomorrow, but I'd be willing to do the unthinkable and break it. For you."

Uh, what? "Don't do that. And I thought you were mad at me for what I did to Veronica."

"I was never mad. That would require a range of emotions I never feel. I thought we'd covered that fact about me. So, about our date—"

I shook my head, oddly charmed. And now mad at *myself*. "We're not going out."

"Look at me and say that. Maybe then I'll believe you."

I responded automatically, glancing up. Our gazes locked, and…nothing. No vision.

My shoulders sagged with relief, but Gavin frowned.

Cole stalked out of the locker room, snagging everyone's attention. Conversations ceased.

His gaze snagged on me—no vision—skidded to Gavin and hardened. He climbed into the boxing ring and scanned the now silent, expectant crowd. He looked like he'd gotten in a fight since I'd last seen him. His features were tight with tension, his hair sticking out in spikes, and his clothing ripped.

I quashed my curiosity.

"All right, everyone," he called. "Listen up. We have a new member on our team. You will welcome him with open arms, and you will keep your fists—and weapons—to yourself."

Murmurs of astonishment surfaced.

A new member? Someone we'd want to hurt?

The locker-room door opened, and out stepped Justin Silverstone.

Gasps of shock replaced the murmurs.

Justin nodded stiffly, his puppy-dog eyes guarded. "Before you judge, hear me out. I made a mistake when I left, and I know it, and I'm sorry. What was done to Ali's grandfather... her home... I had no part in that, you have my word."

"Liar!" Trina spat. She pointed a finger at Cole. "He betrayed us once, and it cost us Boots and Ducky, and now you're going to give him the chance to do it again?"

"We need all the help we can get right now," Cole said, and I heard the rigidity in his voice.

Boots and Ducky. Cole bore their names on his chest.

Justin straightened his shoulders. "I'm back, and I'll do whatever it takes to prove my intentions are honorable."

"This is stupid," Lucas snapped. "I'm not working with him."

"You will." Cole eyed the crowd through narrowed lids. "You will or you're off the team."

LET THE DEAD HEADS ROLL

In a daze, I made my way to the back of the barn. The slayers had settled in the chairs, all of them cursing and preparing to push their spirits from their bodies. Justin included.

What a shocking turn of events.

Trina gave me a slitted look, and I knew she was commanding me to speak with Cole ASAP.

Soon, I mouthed.

Had Cole welcomed Justin because he hoped to keep his enemy close? Or did he actually trust Justin? Was he using Justin, pretending to trust him in the hopes of gaining information about Anima?

Was Justin sincere, or was he acting as a double agent?

So many possibilities.

One after the other, the slayers stood in spirit form. Except me. I tried, again and again, but each time I failed.

As I struggled, it felt as if someone was holding on to my spirit, forcing it to stay where it was.

Gavin and Veronica took off, followed by Trina and Collins, then Lucas and Mackenzie, Cruz and Bronx. Although it seemed otherwise, no one but me had a partner tonight—and I hadn't yet been told who that partner was. Everyone was to branch in different directions to cover as much ground as possible. However, no one was to engage until backup arrived.

"What's wrong?" Justin asked me, hanging back.

Was he my partner? No, surely not.

"Nothing. I'm fine. I can do this." I closed my eyes. Drawing on every ounce of my considerable determination, I imagined my spirit rising and felt my body respond. But when I opened my eyes, hard hands clamped around me and jerked me back into the chair. What the heck?

Justin shrugged, muttered, "Good luck," and took off.

Cole crouched in front of me, the only slayer left. *Oh, crap.* He was my partner, wasn't he? He looked at the door, then me. The door, me. Indecision played over his features. "Problem?" he asked.

Why not tell the truth? "Yeah, but I don't know what it is." Unless…was Z.A. now strong enough to hold me in place?

He looked relieved. "Stay here. I was supposed to be your sidekick, so we were going to cover the same area anyway. I'll just do it on my own."

And do it faster, his tone implied.

I scowled at him.

"Tomorrow," he continued, "Ankh can run a few more tests on you."

"That's your answer to everything. Test, test, test. He's run a thousand already, but hasn't found anything. There's nothing else to check."

"So? He'll do the same tests again. The results could be different."

Oh, really? "Do you know the definition of insanity? Doing the same thing over and over and expecting different results."

"Wrong. That's the definition of determination." Cole flattened his hands on my knees. Because he was in spirit form and I was in human, he ghosted through me, somehow leaving a trail of heat behind.

"Just go," I said, shivering. I motioned to the exit.

"Ali."

"Go," I repeated.

His gaze narrowed. "Despite everything, I am your boss, you know. You shouldn't talk to me that way."

Whatever. "You're my boss. My ex. My friend. Sometimes. Maybe. You can't be all of those things at once. You have to pick one."

His gaze narrowed further, until all I saw was the darkness of his pupils. "Today I'm picking boss. Tomorrow I might change my mind."

Frustrating boy. "Go!" Then, to be snotty, I added, "Sir."

He snapped his teeth at me, the same way he'd done when we first met, straightened and strode to the door. He used more force than necessary to push it open, and then he stomped into the night.

I gazed around the barn. Mr. Holland and Kat were locked in a conversation. Anger and frustration mixed, as powerful as a tsunami, and I banged my fist against the arm of my chair. Leaping to my feet, I paced to the end of the row of chairs, turned to pace back…and saw my body in the chair. Wait. I'd done it? But how? Why?

And why were my legs still burning?

Cole's touch… The burn…

Did Z.A. fear him? If so, I'd let him put those hot spirit hands all over me and hopefully scare her to death.

His hands…all over me… I shivered, then scowled.

I raced for the door. Because it was smeared with a Blood Line, I couldn't ghost through. Like Cole, I opened the obstruction and entered the night. I looked, but found no sign of the—

Wait. There was a streak of gold in the center of the yard, as if a tiny lightbulb had been dropped. A Blood Line. I closed the distance, saw flecks of red mixed with the gold and frowned. Or maybe *not* a Blood Line. I found another streak a few feet ahead and followed it, kept following, going deeper and deeper into the forest beyond the barn.

Trees knifed toward the starless sky, and branches clapped in the breeze. An owl hooted. The darkness was so thick it looked like a black blanket had been draped overhead. Cold air battered against me, and goose bumps doubled parked on my arms. Ahead, to my right, a shadow moved—and another smear was left on the ground. I frowned. The smears definitely weren't from Blood Lines, for sure, but from someone's shoes. How? Why?

I quickened my pace, whisking forward. The shadow had

stopped. I did the same. Tall, clearly muscled—a male. Black shirt, black pants, blending into the night. A dark bandanna covered his hair. Was he a slayer?

Frosty had worn a bandanna. So had Bronx. This guy pressed his chest into the base of a tree and leaned to the side.

"—can't believe Cole's doing this to us," I heard Trina say.

"I know," Lucas replied, his voice fading. He must be walking away.

So. The two hadn't left together, but they'd quickly found each other. Interesting.

"Ali better pony up and take care of this, or..."

After that, not even crickets could be heard.

The shadow moved, leaving another smear behind. I claimed the just vacated spot, then bounded forward, finding the shadow several feet ahead. I pressed into another tree.

"Seriously, what are we going to do?" Trina asked, her voice audible once again.

"Be careful. Guard our words and actions. I'm not giving Justin anything to take back to the Hazmats," Lucas replied, unaware of his tail.

The shadow was in spirit form, definitely, and he was... spying on the pair?

Sparks of anger burned through me. This wasn't Frosty or Bronx.

He darted around the tree, and I followed. This time he didn't linger to listen to anymore of Trina and Lucas's conversation. He branched off in another direction. I continued to follow, watching for the smears. The little traitor couldn't hide from me. I'd catch him in the act, and—

Something hard slammed into me, knocking me face-first into the ground. Air exploded from my lungs, and dirt coated my tongue. Stars winked through my vision. I tried to crawl forward, but a heavy weight pinned me down. Fear threatened to overtake me, but I quickly rallied, twisting around and swinging out a fist.

Contact!

Pain cut through my knuckles. Maybe I'd broken one. I'd hit the guy in the jaw—a solid, intractable jaw.

"Let me go!" I demanded, expecting to see red eyes. Paper-thin, rotting skin. Hair, hanging in clumps. Instead, I saw familiar violet eyes…and my blood heated in the most delicious way. I stilled.

"Ali?"

"Cole? What are you doing? I…"

Was underneath him. My thoughts derailed. We'd lain like this before. Every other time, he'd been kissing me. Hands had wandered. My body had come alive. I didn't have my body this time, and yet I felt even more alive, as if I were connected to a generator, my nerve endings buzzing with energy.

His gaze drilled into mine…only to lower to my mouth and linger, everything about his expression softening. His breathing changed, emerging shallow and fast. "Are you okay? I couldn't see it in your body, but your spirit is gaunt. You've lost weight, and there are shadows under your eyes. I wasn't sure if you were a hiker who'd been lost for several days or a zombie."

I stiffened, trying not to panic. "I'm okay."

"Good. That's good." His thumbs traced the rise of my cheeks. "Ali…"

I knew that look, that tone, that touch, and knew where this was headed if I didn't put a stop to it. "Get off me," I said, ashamed of my sudden breathlessness.

He stayed right where he was. "What are you doing to me? How are you making me forget what's best for me... For you?"

"What's best?" Maybe, if he said it, I would finally believe him.

"Me...Ronny. You...Gavin."

No, I still wasn't convinced. "Wrong." I didn't worry about his words coming true later on, either—not in terms of spiritual law. My free will was not on board. I turned my head away, peering up at the sky. "I'm not attracted to Gavin, and you're not attracted to Veronica. Not anymore."

"You're right. I'm not." The perfect answer—until he added, "I don't think."

The addition stung. Pushed me over the edge of calm.

I gripped his jacket, shook him. "Do you really think you'll be happy with her?"

"I don't know."

"Heck, maybe you will be, at least for a little while, but if you're true to habit, it won't last and you won't stay with her."

He glared at me. "I don't have a habit."

Blind! "You seriously don't think you're so afraid of losing the people you care about that you cut them loose before they ever have a chance to get inside your heart?"

He took my hands and pressed them into the ground, over my head, forcing my back to arch and my chest to rub against his. "There are people in my heart," he gritted out.

What he didn't say but I heard anyway: *just not you.*

Have to stop setting myself up for this kind of rejection. "Maybe we're both wrong. Maybe you don't even have a heart."

"Oh, I have one." Eyes narrowing, he reached down with his free hand and parted my legs, giving himself a deeper cradle—a perfect cradle—and foolish, foolish Ali let him. Hardness against softness, male against female. "I just don't want it broken."

"So you go around breaking other people's?"

"I didn't break yours, and you know it," he snapped. "You got over me pretty fast, and I did my best to get over you."

That was all he said, but I knew. In that moment, I knew. "You've already done something with Veronica," I said flatly.

A dark curtain fell over his features. I waited for him to deny it.

He didn't deny it.

He nodded.

Even though I'd guessed, shock hit me with the force of a baseball bat. Shock and betrayal. I had no reason to entertain the betrayal. We'd broken up. But...but...here he was, on top of me, and here I was, loving every sensation, and meanwhile, the memory of messing around with Veronica was new and fresh and burning in the back of his mind.

I pushed him off and jerked upright. "I think I hate you."

"You aren't the only one. I think I hate myself."

I was done with this topic. It didn't matter. It couldn't matter.

What did you do with her? I almost shouted.

Shaking, I said, "Why did you tackle me if you thought I was a hiker?"

He drew in a deep breath, slowly released it. "A hiker sneaking around, as if looking for someone. I didn't want to take any chances." He scrubbed a hand down his face. "Everyone leaves and your ability to spirit walk magically starts working again? You got something to confess to me, Bell?"

I reeled for a moment. "Just what are you accusing me of, *Holland?*"

"Were you spying on me?"

He… Oh… I gasped and sputtered. "I was *not*. I was spying on a spy. Was that you I saw skulking after Trina and Lucas?"

A moment passed, the silence laced with incredulity. Cursing, he settled back on his haunches. "Someone was tailing them?"

"I think so, yes."

"What did he look like?"

"Like you, only not quite as tall. Strong. Wearing a bandanna." Cole wasn't wearing one. "His shoes left little golden smears behind."

Hope filled his eyes, softened his features. "Show me." He stood and helped me do the same.

Having his fingers intertwined with mine…the warmth, the comfort…I liked it, wanted more and hated myself far more than I hated him. The moment I was upright, I released him. My mouth dried as I backtracked, looking for that last smear I'd seen.

"There," I said, pointing. "Do you see it?"

"No."

No matter. He'd never been able to see the Blood Lines, either.

He examined the area. "Is there another one nearby?"

I searched and found another and another, but after a while the smears vanished. Either the guy had left the area or he'd overheard us and had known to take off his shoes.

"Okay. All right," Cole said. He pinched the bridge of his nose. "The spy has been verified, at least. And now I know he's male. That cuts my suspect list down."

"You suspected there was a spy." A statement, not a question. That was why *he'd* been spying.

He leaped into action, closing the distance between us. When he reached me, he grabbed me by the shoulders. "You will not tell a soul, Ali. Promise me."

Had I been a suspect, as well?

Anger returned, white-hot. "Why did you let Justin back in? I know he helped us before, but how do you know beyond any doubt he's not double-crossing you?"

He shook his head. "I'm not talking about this."

"Not with me, you mean. Have you discussed it with Veronica?" *Stop. Just stop.*

His nostrils flared. With anger? With relief? "Do you want to hear what happened with her?" he asked tightly.

Yes! "No." I don't know.

"I'll tell you. I think I actually want to tell you. Then you'll stay away from me, even when I'm stupid enough to come sniffing around. I'll finally stop wanting what I know I can't have."

I glared at him, saying, "You don't have to say another word for that to happen."

"I was at home," he began. "She came over."

I shook my head. "Shut up."

It was an order, but it wasn't his will. He continued. "I had been drinking. I never drink, but I was trying to forget about you."

"Shut up!"

"I had been drinking *a lot*. I kissed her. I thought about never being with you again, and I was angry with you, thinking about you with Gavin, and I kissed her with everything I had. I took off her shirt. I touched her."

"Shut up!" He was throwing the details at me as if they were weapons.

They were.

"She unbuckled my pants. I—"

"Shut up, shut up, shut up!" I was standing in front of him before I realized I'd moved. Both of my arms heated to a nearly unbearable degree, as if I was about to ash a zombie. But when I raised my hand and swiped at Cole's cheek, the flames crackling from my skin weren't white—they were red.

Cole tumbled to the ground as if he'd been hit by a Mack truck. He quickly jumped to his feet, now watching me warily. His cheek was split, but because he was in spirit form, the wound wasn't bleeding. His body would be, though. Back at the barn, I bet crimson streaked his face.

"What's going on with you?" he demanded.

Feed from him.

The words whispered through my mind, and I didn't care who had spoken them. Hunger gnawed at me, relentless. Yes, I would feed from him, would feast on his spirit. Scowling, I stalked forward. The red flames moved to my shoulders. I swung out my arm, but Cole ducked. He could have launched a counterattack, could have kicked my feet out from under me. Instead, he straightened, his hands fisting.

"Don't do this," he said.

Not my will. Do it, I would. I circled him, our gazes locked together.

FEED!

"Go ahead, finish your story," I commanded, doing what he hadn't done and kicking out my leg. His ankles knocked together, and he tumbled to the ground a second time. The bottom of his pants burned away, revealing another gash in his skin. A gash I had caused. My feet were also covered in red flames. "Help me be sure I hate you."

"Is that what it will take?" He stood, saying, "She went down on me. And you know what? I liked it."

With a screech, I lashed out at him.

He dodged.

I would have done it again, but my gaze caught on the fireworks exploding in the sky. One after the other, the other slayers were shooting off their flares. Everyone, it seemed, had spotted a zombie.

Don't care.

A twig snapped.

My gaze whizzed to the left, and I saw red eyes peeking from the brittle wall of foliage.

Still don't care.

Cole moved closer to me, perhaps to protect me from the coming battle. When I scented him, my hunger spun out of control. I growled at him.

He looked at me.

I stepped forward… *When I'm done, there'll be nothing left of him...* The world around me began to darken, until a black sheet enveloped me.

"No," I shouted.

Oh, yes.

I think...Z.A. was trying to take over.

I—she—continued forward in spite of the blindness, tripped.

"Ali," Cole said, concerned.

Time seemed to slow down as I fell, landed. Sound faded from my ears. Except for one.

Tick. Tock.

14

THE SLAUGHTER OF THE WHITE QUEEN

I blinked open my eyes and realized I couldn't catch my breath. Why couldn't I catch my breath?

I took stock. I was standing. My clothes were torn, and I was splattered in black goo from the top of my head to the soles of my feet. I had cuts on my arms and stomach. My entire body was shaking, as if I'd run the treadmill for hours, all uphill.

The forest around me had been torched. The trees were now naked, their leaves burned away, their branches covered with ash. Zombie ash? Or…slayer? The ground was just as bad, black and charred, no grass remaining.

Cole was on the ground, alive. Thank God! There were patches of black all over his skin. He'd been bitten multiple times, and his features were contorted with pain.

"Ali-gator," he gasped out.

I rushed to his side, and he flinched, as if he thought I meant to hurt him.

I frowned. I remembered…throwing a punch at him. Yes, I'd thrown a punch, and he'd ducked. He'd told me about kissing Veronica, about the other stuff they'd done—even now I choked on a well of pain. A need to feed from him had consumed me, and I'd attacked him in earnest. Then… nothing.

"I'm so, so sorry," I said, sliding my hands under the hem of his pant leg. The antidote was strapped to his ankle. I freed the syringe, and though I was trembling uncontrolla- bly, managed to shove the needle into his neck.

He'd done this to me countless times, but I'd never had to do it to him. I remained by his side, watching, waiting. At last, the black began to fade from his skin, and he sagged into the decimated ground.

All of the cuts and gashes remained. At the barn, his body had to be covered in blood.

"What happened?" I asked.

"Do you not remember?"

I chewed on my bottom lip, shook my head. Z.A. had spoken to me—yes, that was right. Oh, good glory. She'd taken over.

Wincing, he sat up. He didn't meet my gaze as he said, "Your eyes went red, Ali, just like the zombies. The crea- tures arrived and ignored you, treating you as if you were one of their own. You burned the trees and—"

I gasped. "*I* burned the trees?"

"You touched them with the red flames, and the leaves instantly withered."

Tears welled in my eyes, and they stung, as if they had been fermenting, ready to spring for weeks, but I hadn't let them. "Did I do anything to you?" Was I responsible for any of the damage?

He fingered the gash in his cheek. "Something's going on with you, Ali," he said, ignoring my question.

I had. I'd hurt him.

"Yes," I whispered. I couldn't keep quiet anymore, whatever the consequences were for speaking out. I'd known I was a danger but hadn't taken enough precautions to protect my friends. "Mr. Ankh told me my blood work was fine, but, Cole, that can't be true. I'm filled with zombie toxin. It's there, inside me, and it's alive. A part of me. A new part. I've seen her—heard her."

I waited for hatred to gleam in his eyes.

I waited for a savage rage to be unleashed.

He had to kill me now. I was the enemy.

"What else?" he asked.

I blinked, confused. "Urges come, dark urges, and I find myself giving in. I never would have believed it unless—"

"What the hell happened?" Gavin demanded, cutting me off with his arrival.

I looked over in time to see him and Veronica stalk past the trees I'd burned. Z.A. might have done it, but she'd used my hands. The realization still flayed me.

The pair was as battle-wounded and dirty as Cole.

Cole reached out, squeezed my wrist. "I don't want you to say another word about this," he whispered.

He didn't plan to tell the others? Why? To protect me? Maybe. What would happen if the slayers learned what I'd done to him? I'd be thrown out, no question. And they'd be smart to do it.

He lumbered to his feet, dragging me with him. "Let's get back to the barn," he said.

"Cole!" Veronica rushed to his side and cradled his battered face, tilting his head from one side to the other to study his injuries. "Sugar, you look like you've been mauled by a bear. Are you okay?"

Sugar.

"I'm fine." Clearly uncomfortable, he set Veronica away from him.

I was too wrung out to feel jealousy just then. Or anguish. Or longing. Yeah. Way too wrung out.

I swiped at the sting in my eyes with the back of my hand.

She tossed me a glare meant to slay me on the spot. "I thought you had special powers or something like that. You should have protected him."

"Yes," I said sadly, "I should have."

Gavin wrapped his arms around my shoulders in a surprising show of support, and I leaned against him. I was getting more and more comfortable with contact with him—and I wouldn't let myself think about what that meant. It wasn't romantic, I told myself, and that was all that mattered. "Catfight round two can wait. Cole's right. We need to get back to the barn."

Cole stepped toward us, the menace I'd expected earlier now radiating from him. His gaze moved from Gavin to me, then to Gavin again. He looked 100 percent capable of murder. Then he stopped himself and spun away.

So badly I wanted to follow him, to catch up to him. It

was utter anguish denying myself—fine, I was feeling it—
but I couldn't risk another fight with him. Besides, I had a
spy to catch.

He led the way through the forest, Veronica staying close
to his heels. Along the way, we met up with Frosty and
Justin, and I did some mental measuring. They were both
about the size of the spy I'd seen. But then, so was Lucas.
And Gavin.

Gavin also wore a bandanna.

The spy had to be someone close to our circle. I mean,
the guy had known the location of Cole's barn and that we
would be on patrol tonight. But…I didn't want to accuse any
of the slayers. I might not be able to trust myself right now,
but I did trust my friends. Even, surprisingly enough, Gavin.

In a lot of ways, he was like Cole. He got in your face with
his with beliefs and opinions. He was fearless, cared nothing about consequences. But he was fierce when it came to
the safety of his friends.

I had a lot to think about.

"What I'm about to say is true, so I'm not simply making it true in your life by speaking it, if you know what I
mean, but she's a terrible enemy to have," Gavin said softly.

"Who? Veronica?"

He nodded.

I shrugged. I'd had enemies before, and I would make
many more, I was sure. "What do guys see in her anyway?
I mean, she's beautiful, but that's all she's got going for her."
I think what I was really asking was—what did Cole see
in her?

Gavin looked straight ahead. "She's actually a very nice

person, but envy has turned you both into raving— Well. Never mind. I want to keep my balls. As I was saying, she's smart, and she's funny, and the best part is, she puts out."

Was sex always on his mind? "Your words are like poetry."

He chuckled, saying, "I admit I'd like to take her to bed, have since the day I met her, and she'd let me, I think, if she weren't so determined to win back Cole, but unlike your Mr. Holland, I've never hooked up with another slayer. I like to keep business separate from pleasure. A cliché, I know, but there are far less complications that way. As I'm sure Cole is learning."

"I'm a slayer," I pointed out, "and yet you keep asking me out."

"You're also not my type. Or you weren't. I'm not sure what my type is anymore. You resist, and it drives me wild."

"That's sad."

"That's life."

I rolled my eyes, a common occurrence in his presence. "You might be the weirdest person I've ever met."

"Thank you."

"I don't think that was a compliment."

"Agree to disagree," he said.

We entered the barn, and my spirit jerked from Gavin's grip, flying forward as if tugged by an invisible cord. I skidded across the room and…boom!

Gasping, I pried open my eyes. I was sitting in the chair, spirit and body joined.

Mr. Ankh knelt in front of Cole, already patching up his injuries. Just as I'd suspected, he was covered in blood.

New to-do list: *Find a way to* disable *the zombie inside me.*
Kill the zombie inside me. Still do whatever proves necessary.

He blinked open his eyes and grimaced.

Mr. Ankh said, "You need stitches, son," and began digging in his bag of supplies.

A lump grew in my throat as Cole's gaze met mine. Violet against blue. A cold mask against sorrow.

I'm sorry, I mouthed.

He nodded, looked away.

Would he cut me from his life now that he knew about Z.A.?

It was better than death, and yet almost as painful.

"Where's Kat?" Frosty demanded. Like Cole, he was covered in blood.

Without looking up from his task, Mr. Ankh replied, "When you started bleeding, she started screaming, and I insisted she go home."

I bet he'd had to threaten to ban her from the building forever to actually get her to go.

Frosty raced out.

"Everyone's been injected with the antidote?" Mr. Holland asked.

I hadn't, but then, I hadn't been bitten. Still, I requested a dose and received it a few minutes later. The cool stream came with a measure of strength, stopping my trembling.

"Zombies were everywhere, man," Gavin said, standing. "We couldn't contain them all."

"Yeah, and they seemed to know exactly where we'd be," Lucas threw at Justin.

Justin shot to his feet. "I didn't tell anyone about tonight.

I didn't know I'd be meeting with everyone until fifteen minutes ago, when Cole came and got me."

"Ever heard of a phone? Texting?"

"Cole watched me the entire time. And do you really think a zombie is capable of taking my calls?"

"You were in the locker room alone for several minutes. You could have gotten a message to someone at Anima," Trina spat. "They could have arranged this."

"You think I'm wearing a wire, too?" He ripped his shirt over his head, revealing a hard, cut physique I hadn't known he had.

A hand penetrated my line of sight, and I glanced up. Gavin stood in front of me, offering me assistance. I twined our fingers, and he tugged me to a stand. I wasn't as strong as I'd thought, because my knees almost buckled. He wound his arm around me and held me up.

A chair skidded. I saw Cole stand, brush Mr. Ankh aside and stalk into the locker room. The door slammed shut with a loud bang.

Of course, Veronica followed him.

I fell asleep thinking about ways to disable Z.A. Cut off my hands? Remove all my teeth? Then I'd live, and she'd have no way of hurting anyone.

Let's make that plan B.

The ring of my cell woke me. From the bed, I blindly reached out, patting my nightstand. "Hello," I rasped when the phone was at my ear. What time was it?

"You missed our appointment, Miss Bell."

Dr. Bendari?

I jolted upright. The fancy wall clock said it was 5:59 a.m. I'd set my alarm for six, and—my phone vibrated, right on cue. I needed to get ready for school.

"Something came up," I said. "I tried to call, but you shut off your phone."

"A necessary precaution."

"And why is that?"

"Do you expect me to believe you don't want your slayer friends to capture me?"

Reverse psychology? Please. "I'm the one with doubts, Dr. Bendari. You could be planning to murder me."

"I guess we're going to have to trust each other. Are you still interested in meeting?"

"I am."

"Good, because I'd like to hear about the trouble you had last night."

Had *he* sent the spy...his source? "How do you know about that?"

I imagined him shrugging as he said, "How else?"

"Well, the only way your source could have heard about last night's activities was if he was at the scene."

A chuckle devoid of humor crackled over the line. "Is that so? Well, you should check the morning news reports."

The news? I scrambled for the TV remote, pressed Power. Colors filled the screen. I switched channels and came to—

"—awoke to find twenty-six people had died from antiputrefactive syndrome," a reporter was saying. She stood on a street, the address of a neighborhood close to Cole's scrolling across the screen.

Antiputrefactive syndrome: when the human body was

infected with zombie toxin. Although civilians had no idea that was the cause.

The reporter continued. "Last year, two local high school boys died of this rare disease, and citizens were told it was not contagious. Just a month ago, an elderly man died. How and why are so many infected? The CDC has arrived, and the houses of the affected have been quarantined."

Dr. Bendari sighed with regret. "People were killed, Miss Bell. People who will rise again. Zombies entered their homes and ate every bit of their humanity, leaving only evil behind."

"Why?" The moisture in my mouth dried. "How?"

"Not every home has a Blood Line."

That would change, I thought, fisting the comforter. Soon.

For once, the C word actually empowered me.

"The zombies are mutating," he explained. "Just like you are mutating. They've become hungrier. They've become stronger. They—"

My door burst open and banged against the wall. Mr. Ankh and Mr. Holland strode inside. Both were scowling with a fury they'd never before directed at me. My heart drummed inside my chest, nearly cracking my ribs.

"What's going on?" I demanded. "What are you doing?"

Dr. Bendari said something, but I couldn't make out the words.

"Come with us, Ali," Mr. Holland said. "Now."

Dr. Bendari went quiet.

Last night, Gavin had dropped me off and I'd showered, dressed in a tank and boxer shorts and fallen into bed. The men weren't seeing anything they shouldn't, but I was still embarrassed. "What's going on?" I repeated. "I'm not going anywhere until you tell me."

Mr. Ankh popped his jaw. "There's something you need to see."

I severed the connection with Dr. Bendari and stood. I was led down the hall, down the stairs, down another flight of stairs and into the basement. The air grew cooler and danker with every step, and I felt a layer of ice glaze my skin—one that matched the layer growing inside me. At the end of a hallway, we paused at the only door. It was closed and locked. Mr. Ankh pressed his hand against a new ID box, and a bright yellow light flashed.

The hinges on the door loosened, the entrance opening under its own steam.

We swept inside the laboratory. The floors were concrete, with drains in several locations. There were multiple curtained stalls, each containing a gurney with wrist and ankle straps.

I gulped.

Mr. Holland motioned to a chair in front of a TV screen. Shaking, I sat. "I've already seen the news."

"That has nothing to do with this moment. Now, I'm going to check your vitals." As he poked and prodded, he asked me one question. Only one. "Are you working for Anima?"

"No! Of course not." I had to tell him the truth, didn't I? Another to-do list: *Talk. Admit everything. Pray for the best.*

So, I did it. I poured out every Z.A. detail I'd been hoarding.

When I finished, Mr. Ankh shook his head. "Impossible. You're still human."

"For now."

He stared at me a long while, silent. Then he grimaced and pressed a button on a remote. Bright green colored the entire TV screen and—the forest! I saw the forest.

"This was taped through a night-vision lens," he said. "I have more cameras out there than any of you realized. I don't always check them, but the gash in Cole's cheek was strange, something I'd never seen before. When I asked him about it, he refused to answer."

I watched as a red line dove at another red line, knocking it to the ground. The two stayed in that position for several minutes, as though…talking. Cole and I, I realized.

"We're spirits. How did the camera pick us up?" I asked, dazed.

"Special camera. Special equipment."

"Did you happen to see the guy I was following?"

"Yes. But like you, he's just a line."

On the screen, Cole sat up. We talked some more. Stood. Walked around. A brighter red consumed my hands and I struck him. He fell. Stood again. We faced off. I came at him. He dodged.

Brighter pricks of red appeared at the tree line. The zombies?

A line—me—crashed into the ground.

That was when I'd fallen and blacked out. When Z.A. had taken over.

I watched myself stand and angle toward Cole. *Oh, no. Please, no.* I walked toward him. He ignored me and ran to the zombies, attacking with a vengeance. I followed him. Rather than helping him, I struck him from behind.

I clutched my stomach, feeling as if I'd swallowed shards of glass. The zombies converged on him, yet still he managed to fight them off, working his way to his feet. I came at him again, obviously intending to hurt him, but he sidestepped me, putting his body between me and the zombies. He could have punched me, knocked me out, or even thrown me to the wolves. I'd left myself wide-open. Instead, he returned his focus to the zombies.

In that moment, I truly hated myself. How could I have attacked Cole in such a way? At such a critical time?

The zombies encircled him, reached for him. I grabbed two of the creatures by the arm, ripping them away from him, my target, and tossing them into the trees.

Wait. Maybe I'd been helping him, after all.

The red flames spread from my arms to the rest of my body, engulfing me. I grabbed two other zombies, repeating the toss. When they recovered, they paid me no heed, keeping their sights on Cole. I closed the distance and flattened one hand against a tree—the leaves turned to ash in an instant—and collared one of the zombies with the other. He didn't turn to ash but flopped around. I leaned down... and bit into his neck.

In the here and now, a scowling Mr. Ankh stepped in front of me. I stuttered around for the right words—found none. The horror of seeing myself do something like that... To know I'd ingested zombie rot...

"Miss Bell, I'm not sure I believe you about being both human and zombie, with the zombie part of you able to manifest outside your body. But I do know I can no longer allow you to live in my home, with my daughter. I want you out within the hour."

YOU HAD
ME at GOODBYE

I went into the bathroom and dressed, then packed up what few belongings I had. A couple of shirts, a couple of pairs of jeans, my daggers and the journal. That was it. Didn't take me long. Ten minutes, maybe. Tears burned at the backs of my eyes, but I blinked them away. No way I'd cry over this. I'd lost a home before, and one I'd loved with all my heart.

This? This was nothing.

Then why does it hurt so much?

I think a part of me had always known this day would come. I anchored the bag's strap over my shoulder and strode out of the room, bypassing the cold-blooded Mr. Ankh and the stone-hearted Mr. Holland.

Nana paced at the front entrance, her bag resting on the floor. Her anxious gaze landed on me as I pounded down the stairs, and she looked as if she'd aged ten years overnight.

Her hair was a mess. Her blouse and slacks were wrinkled. She wore no makeup.

Someone had woken her up and forced her to hurry.

I gnashed my teeth, noticed the second heart pounding ferociously in my chest and forced myself to breathe, to calm before the hunger had time to hit.

"Are you all right?" she asked me.

What had she been told? I forced a small smile. "I'm... stable. You?"

"Oh, I'm fine." Her gaze shifted to Mr. Ankh and narrowed. "What's going on? Why are you doing this to us?"

"I'll allow your granddaughter to explain. But there's no reason for you to fret. I'm not leaving you homeless. I've rented you a place in your old neighborhood. The address has already been programmed into your car's GPS."

I hated that he was paying our way and wanted to refuse. I didn't. Not yet. I'd let him spend his money only as long as it took me to find a new place—our place, one we could afford on our own. One he couldn't ever take away from us.

I picked up Nana's bag. As she struggled to understand what Mr. Ankh *hadn't* said, I ushered her outside. Her sedan was waiting in the driveway, the keys already in the ignition, the engine purring.

I threw the bags in the back of the car and buckled into the passenger seat. Nana claimed the driver's seat, and a few minutes later, we were soaring down the highway.

"Tell me what's going on," she said with a tremor. "Please. Lately I feel a lot like Reeve, desperate for answers but getting none. You're gone all the time, and I'm used to that, but when you're home, you're moody and distant, even violent. And now the men who were supposed to help you with your cause want nothing to do with you."

"Nana, I'll talk to you about this, I promise. Just not in the car." What I had to say would upset her, more than she already was. Cars and emotional drivers were not a good combination.

"Ali."

"Please."

"All right. But the moment we're inside…"

Ten minutes later, we reached the house. She parked in the driveway. It was a two-story in the shape of a C, with red-brick and white shuttered windows. A step up from Nana's home, definitely newer, but colder—and a dump compared to Ankh's. *Keep it together.*

I carted the bags into the living room, surprised to see the place was empty, and surprised by my surprise. What? I'd expected the guy to keep us in style? The walls had been painted in bold, bright colors. Red. Blue. Green. I figured there was a Blood Line around the property, but I wouldn't be relying on a supposition. I'd talk to Nana, then get to work.

"Ali," Nana said, her voice breaking at the edges.

Calm. "I was bitten," I explained. "I was given the anti-dote, and that helped, but it didn't destroy the zombie toxin. I'm doing terrible things. Dangerous things. Becoming what I hate most. Mr. Ankh feared for Reeve. And Nana… I fear for you. I think it would be better if I—"

"No!" she said with a violet shake of her head. She closed the distance between us and grabbed me by the forearms. "You're not staying somewhere else, or whatever you were going to say. You're my granddaughter and I love you. We will stay together and I will help you."

My chin trembled. I so did not deserve this woman.

"Why didn't you tell me sooner?"

"At first, I wasn't sure what was happening to me. Then…" Man, this was difficult to admit. "I was just too scared of what would happen."

"Oh, Ali."

I placed my hands over hers. "If ever I do something to frighten you, or my eyes turn red, or I stare at you too long, run. Run and don't look back."

She gave me a small shake. "You're not going to become a zombie, young lady. I won't let you."

A small laugh escaped me. I wish I had her confidence.

I leaned forward and enfolded her in a hug. "Thank you for loving me. And I really am sorry about dinner. If I'd kept our plans, last night wouldn't have… Well, it doesn't matter now. I'm just so, so sorry."

"Don't think another thing about it, A-diddy. You have responsibilities, and I know that."

A-diddy? I laughed again. Nana used to love to keep up with what she considered popular slang, but she'd stopped after Pops had died. Knowing she was finally picking up the pieces of her shattered life delighted me.

"Nana," I said, hopping on the counter that divided living room from kitchen. "Did you know the journal you gave me is all about zombie slaying?"

Her eyes grew wide. "No. I didn't."

"Has anyone in your family ever… I don't know, talked

about invisible monsters no one else could see? Or been committed to a crazy house, maybe?"

"Well," she said, peering down at her loafers. "My mother was an alcoholic, and she used to babble about creatures of the night desperate to steal her soul. My dad forbade us to discuss her condition with anyone, and as embarrassed as we were, we were more than happy to agree. Of course, when I was dating Pops, he would sneak over and…well…" She cleared her throat. "Never you mind. He witnessed one of her episodes."

Slayers. On my mom's side of the family. How could I not have known?

How many other slayers came from a double lineage?

"It's one of the reasons Pops and I were so adamant about your mother staying away from your father, and oh, Ali, I should have known, should have realized, the two were connected. In my mind, Mother was a drunk, pure and simple. And then, of course, your dad started drinking, and, well, you know the rest."

I did. She and Pops had hated my father, had never welcomed him over. I'd never blamed them, though, and still didn't. There'd been quite a few days I'd hated my father, too.

"How did your great-grandfather die?" I asked.

"He disappeared one day. At least, that's the story I was told when the journal was handed down to me."

Huh. Disappeared. I remembered a passage from the pages of his journal.

Some slayers have inklings of the future. Some can see the Blood Lines and recognize our sanctuaries. Some can destroy the zombies

one by one, then two by two, after being bitten a single time. Some-
thing in their spirit infects the zombies and spreads from one to an-
other like a contagious disease, with no more action on the slayer's
part. Some can do none of that. Some can do all of that. I can do
all. That's how I know about the war that's coming. That's how
I know that not a single slayer—or civilian—will survive unless
something more is done. That's how I know what needs to be done.

I need to die.

Then, a few chapters later, he'd written, *Are you willing to*
give up your own life to save others? Have you realized that dying
is the only way to truly live?

Had he given up his life to save others? Had he died to
truly live?

If so, great. Wonderful. But what did any of that mean?
I hadn't known before, and I certainly didn't know now.

I tweaked my newest to-do list. *Pray for the best. Hope an-*
swers rain down.

Outside, tires squealed. A door slammed.

I frowned and stalked to the window to peer out.

Because of the shape of the house, the driveway was hidden and I couldn't see the car. Or, apparently, the person
who'd abandoned it to stomp to our porch and pound on
the door.

"Ali," a voice called. "I just heard."

My heart nearly leaped into my throat. Cole? He hadn't
cut me from his life?

I rushed to the entrance and opened up. He burst inside,
paused in front of me. He looked me over, and I did the
same to him. His eyes were bloodshot—clearly, he hadn't
slept. His face was battered and bruised, his stitches stark.

His clothes were wrinkled and it was obvious he'd pulled them on hastily.

"I didn't say a word to them," he said.

"I know. They had a video."

One of his brows rose into an arch. "So you got to see what happened?"

I nodded, unable to hide my growing shame.

He cupped my cheeks as if he still had every right to touch me. My chin trembled—*no! no more tears*—and I battled the urge to lean into him, to rest my head on his shoulder and draw from his strength. I pulled away, severing contact.

His expression hardened.

"All right, well." Nana cleared her throat before gathering her purse and keys. "I'm headed to Target to pick up the things we're going to need. You two obviously have a few issues to work out."

"I don't need anything," I assured her.

She kissed me on the cheek, patted Cole on the arm and left us alone.

"I'll talk to Ankh," Cole said, shutting and locking the door.

"No. Don't. I'm furious for what he's done to Nana, but I do understand what he's done to me. I attacked you, Cole. Like, I planned to eat the life out of your spirit."

"I don't care about that."

"Well, I do."

He waved the words away. "You weren't in your right mind."

"What about the other thing? I bit a freaking zombie. No telling what other damage that's caused inside me, or just how tainted I am now. I don't know what to do, or how to fix myself. Not really. I mean, the journal said I needed the fire, but I tried that and nothing happened, and now my fire is red. And did you hear the part about my being tainted?"

"Wait. You tried to fix yourself with your *fire?*"

Uh-oh.

"You actually tried to kill the zombie—you. And we were, what? Just supposed to find your ashes, never wonder what had happened and move on?"

"*You* had already moved on," I countered. "And you would have had answers." Sort of. "I left a note."

His sights narrowed on me as he walked toward me. I backed up. He was so much taller than me, so much wider, he dwarfed me in every possible way. "I am so angry with you right now, I don't even know what to say." He picked me up by the waist, unnerving me enough to swallow my protest, and hefted me onto the counter. Then he nudged my legs apart and edged closer to me, staring into my eyes with unmatched determination.

His heat surrounded me, irresistibly delicious. For the first time since Mr. Holland and Mr. Ankh had burst into my room, I felt warm.

Concentrate. "I thought I was doing the right thing."

"You thought wrong. And you're *not* tainted."

"I am." I flattened my hands on his shoulders. To push him away or draw him closer, I wasn't yet sure. I hadn't forgotten what he'd done with Veronica, and I wasn't sure I could ever forget. "Look. I'm trying to stay away from you. That's what you wanted, and that's what I'd like. You're making it difficult."

Anguish filled his eyes. "I know. But I'm not leaving until I know you're all right, and you understand you're not tainted."

This. This was the boy I'd dated. Concerned. Kind. Willing to fight to stay.

I wanted him back.

I couldn't have him back. Not permanently.

"Sorry, but I don't and won't understand any such thing. My dad was a slayer and apparently my mom was, too, though she didn't know it, and we've all heard the saying about being high and falling hard. With all my abilities…"

"Hey, I'm right there with you. My mom was a slayer, too."

Astonished, I said, "Both of your parents were slayers? Wow. Okay. I wasn't expecting that. Do you think it's why we had the visions?"

"Maybe. Gavin is the only other slayer I know with a double lineage. But then again, he and I never had a vision. Until you."

My breath caught in my throat. "You guys had a vision?"

He nodded stiffly.

My fingernails dug his shirt into his skin. "When? What did you see?"

He set his hands beside my thighs, as if he couldn't trust himself to touch me. "We saw…you. We came through a doorway, and you came running when you spotted us. You smiled and you jumped into his arms. His. Not mine. You chose him, and even kissed the hell out of him right in front of me."

"When did this vision happen?" I insisted.

"The morning I ended things with you. I was so worried about you, on edge, and then he came in the room, and our eyes met, and there it was. The vision." He pressed his forehead against my sternum. "It was terrible, Ali. I reacted the same way I would have if you'd just cheated on me. I wanted to kill Gavin, and I'm not talking figuratively. I wanted to shake you, then kiss you, then force you to make promises I was sure you couldn't keep."

Emotion clogged in my throat. I could imagine the pain and betrayal he must have felt—because I would have felt them, too. "Have you guys had another vision?"

"No."

I thought I'd nixed my wall theory, but…walls could have fallen amid his concern for me, and then gone back up amid his anger. If so, that would mean my walls kept falling, too. At least with Gavin. What did that mean?

"Why didn't you tell me this had happened?" I asked.

"I didn't tell you a lot of things," he replied darkly.

"Like?"

"Like…" He tangled his fingers in his hair, tugged on the strands, as if to rip them free. With a bitter laugh, he said, "Why not? What I've done so far has only made things worse. I'm miserable. You're miserable. Why not try a new path?"

"Cole! Please." My patience was already in tatters.

He closed his eyes, said flatly, "There's a spy among us."

"I know. I saw him—"

"No. In our group." He pinned me with a gaze that failed to hide the torment inside him. "It's one of us. Someone we trust. I've known for a while."

"I know that much, too. So I ask again, why didn't you tell me?"

"Wait. How did you know?"

"Emma."

"I should have guessed." He pushed out a breath. "I didn't tell you because I didn't want to ruin someone's good name before I had proof. And I didn't want to make you suspicious of everyone and ruin your relationship with the slayers who had only just begun to accept you. And what if the spy found out you suspected something? What would happen to you then? You'd be in constant danger, someone desperate to shut you up."

I couldn't argue with his logic. "Why tell me now?"

"Now your relationship with the others is ruined anyway. Ankh and my father will show everyone the video. They'll want the group to know why you're to be avoided."

That was for the best. And yet it still hurt, knowing I would lose so many people I cared about, all in one swoop. "How do you know there's a spy?"

"Justin called me, told me someone was feeding information to Anima Industries. Information only a person on the inside could have. Meeting times. Injuries we'd sustained. Snippets of conversation we'd had."

Justin *had* called him. I wondered what else Puppy Dog Eyes had lied to me about. "I just... I can't imagine any of the slayers doing it."

"Me, either. But someone is, and I have to find out who before this escalates and my friends get hurt."

"What if Justin is playing both sides? What if he told you

all of this, hoping you'd take him back? He could pretend to help and secretly sabotage."

"How would he have already known stuff he shouldn't before I welcomed him back?"

"Spying from the outside before spying from within."

Grim, he said, "I've been watching him, and have even fed him false information. So far, he hasn't taken the bait and moved on anything. And by the way, he mentioned you'd asked him if I'd talked to him and that he'd played dumb because he thought that's what I'd prefer."

A smart move, whether he was the spy or not. It covered all the bases. "Is that why you got so friendly with Veronica? You were spying on her?"

"At first, yes."

My eyes narrowed, even as my heart skipped a beat. "And then you began to believe you belonged with her."

His hands curved around my waist and held me tightly, as if he feared I would run away. "Yes."

Part of me did want to run. But I wouldn't. What he'd done had cut me and left a wound, and it needed to be cauterized. "And then you...made out with her."

He held my gaze unflinchingly, despite the pain now gleaming in those violet depths. "Yes. But I didn't tell you everything—"

"And I don't want you to," I interjected, placing a finger over his lips. His soft, soft lips. I shivered— No! No shivering. "There's no need. We're not together. So what are you still doing here, Cole?"

He pulled my finger away, held it, stared at it as if it

contained the cure for all of his ills. "I don't know." His head dropped, as if he was ashamed, but still he held on to that finger. "I just… I can't seem to stay away. You're like a magnet, and I'm drawn. And what about you? You're supposed to yell at me, scream profanities and tell me to go and never come back. Why aren't you yelling?" he asked almost bitterly.

Because, despite everything, I liked that he was here.

Foolish girl.

"You want me to yell?" I said, and drew in a deep breath, preparing. "I will."

He shook his head, looked up at me through the thick shield of those dark, dark lashes. "It's too late for that. I'm going to kiss you, Ali."

Kiss… Yes… No! "You made your bed."

"I know. But I still want you in it."

Just. Like. That. Every cell in my body woke up, stretching, reaching for him. Desperate for him. I had been thirsty for so long, and he was my water. Had always been my water.

One last time, I thought. Just one more. It would be closure. The end.

The very end.

"It…it won't mean anything," I whispered.

What are you doing?

Common Sense Ali poked out of the mire of my thoughts. In that moment, I hated her. I needed this and wasn't going to argue with her.

"Let's hope," he said, the words nothing more than a low growl.

He meshed his lips against mine, infinitely tender, going

slowly, savoring every moment, as if he could draw out a response—or was willing to do anything necessary to earn one.

That was all it took.

The spark that had always burned between us exploded into a wild inferno. I thrust my tongue against his, and he thrust back. Neither of us was gentle. I clung to him with all of my strength, demanding more, taking more. Taking everything.

It wasn't enough.

I wasn't sure I would ever get enough.

He moved his hands through my hair, fisting the strands at the base of my neck and forcing my head to tilt, allowing him deeper access to my mouth. In that moment, he owned me.

The past ceased to matter. I was the girl who'd been starved, and he was more than the water. He was the honey. I devoured, unable to get enough of him.

"You feel so good," he rasped, "taste so good. I've missed you. Have to have you. Soon. Soon. Don't send me away."

"Stay." My blood fizzed with energy. I tore at his shirt, the force I used causing the fabric to rip. He stumbled backward. Separation. No. I jumped off the counter to follow after him, then pushed him to the floor and straddled his waist.

Our tongues met with even more force. I took more and I gave more, and it was wild, untamed, but it still wasn't enough for me. He tasted of mint and strawberries, my two favorite things—I needed more. He was firm where I was soft, and every point of contact was electric heat—I needed to be burned.

"Touch me," I demanded.

He rolled me over, pinning me to the carpet with his muscled weight, his hands frantic as they moved over me. I licked his neck, inhaled his scent.

Yes. Yes!

He came back down for another kiss, but paused just before contact, and frowned. "Your eyes. They're red."

In an instant, horror doused the flames. Horror and fear, such ugly fear. I wiggled out from under him, then crab-walked backward, widening the distance between us. "St-stay away from me. You have to stay away."

"Ali," he said, reaching for me. "I'm not going to hurt you. I want to help you."

Oh, glory. "Leave," I commanded, barely stopping myself from kicking his hand away. I had attacked him once. I wasn't going to give myself the opportunity to do it again. "Go to school before you get a tardy."

His hands fisted, fell to his sides. "School is closed today. Twenty-six people were found dead in their homes this morning, and three students were among their numbers. They aren't in your grade, so I don't think you ever met them," he added quickly. "Reports claim antiputrefactive syndrome is now contagious and sweeping through Birmingham, and precautions are being taken until it's known how it spreads."

He moved toward me, determined.

"No," I shouted, scrambling back until I hit the wall. Hot tears streamed down my cheeks. Guess I wasn't done crying, after all. "Go! Please!"

A long while passed before he stood. He peered down at

me, different emotions playing over his features. The anguish of before. Anger. Yearning. "I'm so confused right now."

The tears fell harder, faster. "Let me clear things up for you. I thought we could be friends. We can't. I don't want to see you again. Go away and never come back."

WE'RE ALL MAD HERE

The next few weeks passed in a blur. I no longer hung with the slayers, and I wasn't willing to patrol the streets on my own. So, I got a part-time job at the coffeehouse down the street, determined to make as much money as I could before I… Well. I worked Wednesday through Sunday, from five to ten. I walked there and back, and had yet to come across a zombie. My coworkers were nice—at first—but my distant attitude eventually got to them, and they soon stopped trying to be my friend.

Thanksgiving came and went, and I realized I was all out of to-do lists. I was living one minute at a time.

Nana tried to draw me out of my "protective shell," bless her heart, but I was too firmly entrenched. Besides, I hated the holiday. Emma visited for half an hour, but Mom, Dad and Pops didn't, couldn't, and celebrating without them sucked.

School started up just a few days after the "illness" hit. No one else had gotten sick, and doctors were still baffled. I wondered if the slain had turned into zombies. I wondered if the slayers had had to kill people they knew.

I wondered—but I never asked.

Reeve avoided me as if I'd contracted social leprosy, and though it was for the best—what I wanted, needed—it wounded me.

The slayers kept their distance, as well. Frosty especially. He couldn't get over what I'd done to Cole, and now he and Kat were at war because she refused to end our friendship.

For her safety, I confessed my problems to her, explained Frosty was simply concerned for her well-being, and that she would be better off listening to him and staying away from me, and for the first time in our acquaintance, she got mad at me.

"You're my friend," she said. "That means something to me."

"Yes, but *why* do you like me?" I asked. "I'm nothing special."

"Nothing special? Everyone makes fun of love at first sight, but, Ali, that's what I felt for you. Love, not like. You're the sister I never had, but always wanted. The day we met, when I walked into your hospital room, I saw a scared, pale girl with the most haunted eyes. You'd lost everyone, and I understood. I had to bury my mom, *my world,* too. So, why don't you do me a favor and think about why you love *me*—or if you do?"

"I don't have to think. I love your loyalty, your sense of humor, your smile, your courage, your total acceptance of

me, your support, your dedication, your positivity, your...
everything."

She laughed and hugged me, and then she said ten little
words I couldn't get out of my head. "Good. Now, what are
you going to do about Cole?"

Cole...

Oh, that boy. What *was* I going to do with him? He'd
come to my house a few times, and he'd come bearing gifts.
A stuffed alligator. Dinner from my favorite hamburger joint
located nearly an hour away. A protective cover for my great-
great-great-grandfather's journal.

What the heck did he think he was doing?

I doubted even he knew.

Each time, he'd thrust the gifts at me, almost angrily, before stomping away.

Gavin had come over twice, but I hadn't opened the door.
He'd want to talk about our vision, and I wasn't sure what
to say to him.

I'd poured a Blood Line around the new house. I'd also
turned the garage into a gym, using the treadmill and wrestling matt Nana had bought at a thrift store. The stronger
I kept my human side, the longer I'd live. At least, that was
my hope.

I hadn't heard any more whispers, thank God, but I also
hadn't had the courage to look at my reflection. I'd tried to
call Dr. Bendari, using the new number on my caller ID.
Unavailable yet again, I inwardly cursed.

"—paying any attention to me?" Kat asked.

I blinked into focus. She stood on the other side of the
wrestling matt. Today was my day off from the coffee shop,

so, after school, she'd driven me home and we'd decided to work on her self-defense. "Sorry," I mumbled. "I'm easily distracted lately. Maybe it would be better if Frosty took over your lessons."

Exasperated, she spread her arms to encompass the entire room. "Do you hear this?" she said to no one. "Ali, you know I'm not speaking to him ever again, right? Every day he commands me to stay away from you."

"He's just trying to protect you," I reminded her.

"Well, there are better ways." She unwound the tape from her knuckles. "Come on. Let's wash up and head out. I feel like punishing you for your continued negativity."

"And just how are you going to do that?"

"You'll see."

Well, all right, then. As if I could deny her anything—even the right to punish me. I used Nana's shower, and Kat used mine. Nowadays, we worked out so much she always brought a change of clothes with her.

We found Nana in the kitchen.

"You're getting Ali to go somewhere other than school and work?" she said to Kat. "It's a miracle."

I kissed her on the cheek. Her arms wrapped around me, and she held on for a long while, as if she couldn't bear to let go of me... As if she knew I was slipping away. When finally she released me, there were tears in her eyes.

"Nana..." I said, a lump growing in my throat. I hated that I was hurting her.

"Go," she said, waving me off. "Have fun. Be a teenager for once in your life."

Kat and I climbed into her car and headed north. The sky

was gray today, the sun shielded by heavy clouds. I didn't allow myself to search for a rabbit. I didn't want to know.

My phone rang. I checked the screen, but I didn't recognize the number. I chewed on my bottom lip, hopeful.

"Hello," I said, a tremor in my voice.

"Would you like to set up another meeting, Miss Bell?" Dr. Bendari.

I nearly whooped with relief. "Where have you been?"

"Out of the country, if you must know. Do you have an answer for me?"

"Yes. And yes, I would."

"Will you actually make this one?"

"Yes."

"Good. Now that you're away from the surgeon, I can pick you up at midnight."

He always knew my every move. How? His source, whoever it was, couldn't watch me 24/7...right? "Okay," I said. "I'll be ready."

"See you then." *Click.*

"Who was that?" Kat asked.

"Do you remember the SUV that followed us that day with Reeve?"

"The one you threw knives at? Nope. I've totally forgotten."

Har-har. "The old guy... He gave me his card. I called him. He called me back. And so on and so forth. We've now set up a meeting."

Paling, Kat tightened her hands on the steering wheel. "Ali, you don't know this man."

"Yeah, but I know I need answers and he might have them."

"Answers about…the dark side?"

"Yes," I replied softly.

She reached over and patted my knee. "You're going to overcome this. I just know it. You're strong. You've lost so much, and you're going to fight with everything you've got to keep from losing more."

I wanted to believe her, but I was fast losing hope.

She parked in front of—

Collector Park, I realized. It was a Tuesday, close to dinnertime and as cold as ice. No one walked the manicured lawn. The trees were barren, but there were benches, a swing set and monuments. There was also a creepy mausoleum.

"How is this punishment?" I asked as I unbuckled. "You planning to make me strip and streak?"

"You'll see," she said in a singsong tone.

We stepped into the harsh winter winds, and I shivered. Someone had staked Merry Christmas signs along the side of the cobbled path leading from the parking lot to the park.

Another holiday fast approaching. I'd do better with this one, I vowed, and make sure Nana had a fabulous time. Of course, I would need to buy her a present. And one for Kat. And maybe Cole.

No, not Cole.

Kat linked our arms at the elbows and tugged me forward. "Something wrong? Your face got all pinchy."

"Is *pinchy* even a word?"

"If it's not, it should be. And don't think I don't know you avoided my question. I know you're nervous about what I have planned, and you totally should be. Behold." Over the hill, she pointed to—

A moan slipped from me. Reeve sat on a bench, Ethan beside her. The two were talking and laughing, happy to be together.

"You have to face her sometime," Kat said sternly.

"She has no interest in a reunion," I whispered.

"Only because her dad told her you hated living with them and had demanded your own space."

He'd *what?*

Well, that altered things, didn't it? I marched forward, determined.

"—you will love her," she was saying. "Everyone does. Just ask her yourself," she added with an affectionate chuckle.

Ethan glanced up, saw me and stiffened. "Can I help you?"

I ignored him, saying, "Hey, Reeve."

She twisted to look up at me and flinched. "Ali," she said with a reluctant nod. Then, as Kat moved up beside me, "Kat. You were supposed to come alone."

Kat shrugged. "I'm supposed to do a lot of things. That doesn't mean I do them."

Ethan stood. I was five-ten, and he was a few inches taller than me. His hair was disheveled from the breeze, and his features now closed off.

He held out his hand to shake. "I'm Ethan. It's nice to meet you."

His grip was weak, as if he was afraid he'd break me if he squeezed too hard. "You, too. I'm Ali."

He turned to Kat, shook her hand, as well. "Reeve's told me so much about you guys," he said as he sat back down.

Kat claimed the spot next to him, but I remained standing, suspecting Reeve would throw a fit if I encroached. "Look, I'm sorry I moved out without saying goodbye." I hated doing this in front of a guy I didn't know, but I wasn't sure when I'd have another opportunity. "And I didn't move out to get away from you. I loved living with you."

Dark fire snapped to life in her eyes. "Are you calling my father a liar?"

Yes! "I'm saying he was protecting you from the truth."

"And just what, exactly, is the truth?"

Ethan's attention zinged between us.

I remained silent. There were some things I still couldn't share.

"Of course. More secrets," she muttered, the fire in her dark eyes replaced by hurt. She looked at Ethan. "Do you see? This is what I have to deal with every day." She gathered her purse and stood. "Let's go, Ethan."

Stay calm. "Please, don't go."

Ethan reached out and tugged the lapels of Reeve's jacket closer, a total boyfriend move. "She's your friend, sweetheart. I've had to hold you while you've cried about her. Stay and hear her out."

The support surprised me.

"Hey, Eth—you don't mind if I call you Eth, do you?" Kat asked. "Why don't you escort me to the pond? I want to see the ducks, but I'll need someone to throw in their path if they turn violent."

He looked at Reeve, then looked at me. Reeve, me. As if he was considering every possible thing that could go wrong, and wanted to take measures to prevent it. Finally he nodded. "It would be my pleasure," he said and offered his arm.

The two strode away, and Ethan only glanced back twice to check on his girlfriend.

Sighing, I took his seat and removed the bag from around my shoulder and waist. "Look, Reeve. I moved out because...I'm sick. Really, really sick, and I have these violent episodes.... We don't know a lot about what's going on, and your dad wants you safe. *I* want you safe. It's not contagious, or anything like that, but...it's just better this way."

Her features immediately softened, and she eased beside me. "Oh, Ali. I had no idea. I'm so sorry."

"I'm sorry, too."

"I just wish you'd told me. I would have told you not to go," she said, patting the top of my hand. "I don't care about any violent episodes, and I know my dad won't, either, if I talk to him."

"No," I said, shaking my head. "Please, don't talk to him. Don't talk to anyone about this."

"But—"

"Your dad will be mad that I told you this much, and—"

"Why would he be mad?" she interjected. "Unless something else is going on. And there must be. There's a reason Bronx runs so hot and cold. A reason so many of my friends go to bed without any injuries, but wake up covered with them. A reason my dad has a horror dungeon below the house. A reason he tolerates Cole's dad—a man he once hated."

Mr. Ankh and Mr. Holland had once hated each other? "Look, Reeve—"

"No. I'm tired of being in the dark, Ali. So very tired. I need to be enlightened. I crave it. It's become an obsession."

Dark. Light.

Lies. Truth.

"If I tell you, you might long for the days of blissful ignorance, and I think that's what your father fears most." But then, she'd finally know what was out there and would be able to take measures to protect herself. Measures Mr. Ankh would never be able to take from her.

"Please," she said.

"Let me think about it, okay?" I said. "I could get a lot of people in trouble."

That was more than I'd ever offered before, and she nodded gratefully.

"So…Ethan seems nice," I said, taking the conversation in another direction.

I was relieved when she said, "He is, he really is," without pressing me for more.

There was no dreamy sigh from her, no smile. "I sense a *but* coming on."

Her shoulders sagged the slightest bit. "He really likes me. He's sweet, attentive and last year his mother died, and now his little sister is dealing with leukemia, so he's learned to appreciate life and live every day to the fullest, but…I can't get you know who out of my head."

Yeah. "Believe me, I get it. When it comes to Cole, I'm the same way."

Kat cleared her throat. "We're, uh, back. Ethan was missing his girl."

Reeve jumped guiltily, her cheeks flushing.

"You guys make up?" Ethan claimed the seat on the other side of her and snuggled up, offering his warmth. If he'd heard Reeve's words about Bronx, he didn't act like it.

"We did," she replied.

"Thank God," Kat said. "It's about time, and seriously, go me for setting it up."

Ethan nodded, kissed Reeve's temple. "I agree."

It was obvious he cared for her, and I could see why she had chosen him. Despite her feelings for Bronx, they could have something normal. No secrets. No midnight battles with the undead. No suspecting everyone they met of foul play. No worrying if the other would come home every night—or be eaten.

Hungry…so hungry…

As the words whispered through my mind, I jolted to my feet and spun, searching, trying to squash a sudden bead of panic. My emotions had been under control. This shouldn't be happening.

"What's wrong?" Kat asked.

Hungry, hungry, hungry.

HUNGRY.

Hurt. Maim. Kill.

Soon…

"Ali, your eyes," she said.

No! I gasped for breath as I stumbled away from the group. Reeve stood, already reaching for me. Ethan grabbed her by the wrist and jerked her behind him, as if I'd sprouted horns, fangs and a tail. Maybe I had.

HUNGRYHURTMAIMKILLSOON.

The whispers… So loud… Blending together, somehow calling me, drawing me.

Kat withdrew her phone and started typing. Texting Frosty to come help me?

"No. Don't," I said, and tried to turn left. Somehow I'd lost control of my body and turned right. My feet moved one in front of the other without any command from my brain. I drew closer and closer to a creepy mausoleum, the whispers continuing to escalate. Surely my eardrums would burst, unable to withstand the chatter. "Syringe. Purse."

I halted at the double doors.

HUNGRYHURTMAIMKILLSOON!

I leaned forward—until I could go no further and my spirit separated from my body, ripping from me with painful force, as if pushed. Inside the building, cold air nearly flash-froze my skin.

HURTSOON!

HUNGRY!

The small enclosure was dark and dank, but smelled of wildflowers and sunshine. I shifted to the side, and what seemed to be a thousand red eyes opened to track the movement. A gasp of horror escaped me.

I'd just found a zombie nest.

THE ZOMBIES
ARE BACK IN TOWN

The shock must have brought me to my senses. As easily as my body had been dragged forward, it now whisked backward. Spirit and body collided, once again hooking up.

Kat was at my side, tugging at my arm. I tripped over her feet and fell, banging my knees into the cold, hard ground. The scent of rot clung to my nose, the wildflowers and sunshine gone.

"Frosty's on the way," she said. "He'll make everything better."

"Get back. Purse. Syringe. Throw."

"What's wrong with her?" Reeve asked with a tremor. "I know she's sick, but she was just comatose!"

"Sick?" Ethan demanded.

"Gets violent," Reeve said, distracted.

"Violent," he parroted hollowly.

"Back!" I shouted, pushing Kat away from me. If I helped

the zombies... If I hurt my friends... "Go! Please," I croaked. I no longer wanted her to take time to search for the antidote in my purse. *"Please."*

Ethan jerked a protesting Reeve away from me. She worked her way free and raced back to my side, but he quickly caught up with her, hefted her over his shoulder and took off for his car.

Maim. Kill.

Hungry.

Soon.

Cold.

The words played through my mind, a terrible song. I wanted to stand, but my vision was going dark. "Run, Kat," I commanded. "Run and don't look back. It's happening. The worst is happening."

The nearness of the zombies must have provoked Z.A. to rise.

"I'm not leaving you. I'm— Hmph! What are you doing, Ethan? Let me go!"

He was carting her to his car?

He must have. Tires squealed. Gravel sprayed. He had no idea what was going on, but he'd sensed the danger, had understood the truth in Reeve's claim about violence and had reacted accordingly. I'd have to remember to thank him.

I lay on the ground, exactly where I'd fallen. Breath rasped from me, burning my lungs, my throat. Should I stay here and try to calm down?

Are you kidding? Stand up! Fight! Zombies had killed my family, and I had made it my life's mission to return the favor.

What was more, if the zombies emerged and innocents were around…

I pulled my knees into my chest and pushed, unfolding to my full height. I wobbled but managed to stay upright.

I curled stiff fingers around the dagger hilts sticking out of my boots; metal whistled against leather as I freed the blades. The darkness persisted, closing in on me, and I blinked rapidly. Little pricks of color suddenly appeared—all of them red.

The zombies *had* emerged.

Footsteps pounded at my side, and I stiffened. A hard breeze wafted over me, followed by another, and another. Unsure how close the monsters were, I swiped out an arm, encountered only air.

"Ali." Cole's voice registered a split second before I was tackled to the ground.

I lost my grip on the daggers, as well as what remained of my breath. My head thumped against a rock, and a sharp pain tore through my skull.

"Sorry, sorry," Cole rushed out.

I tried to sit up, but he pinned my arms to the ground, making any kind of movement impossible.

"You're staying right here. The others will take care of the zombies."

Around us, grunts and groans erupted. The fight was on, good against evil, light against dark.

I should be helping. I should—hmm, Cole smelled like heaven. The rot had faded, and his scent was crisp and clean, untainted, wonderfully pure, and the more I inhaled, the more I liked it. The more my mouth watered.

So. Hungry.

I could feel the utter emptiness of my stomach, could feel the pangs sharpening into little razor blades. My gaze locked on Cole's pulse. How it glowed and thumped, speaking to me. *Taste. Me. Taste. Me.*

Yes, I thought. I lifted my head, nuzzled my nose against the line of his neck. He was warm, and I was cold. Colder than I'd ever been, surely.

"What are you doing, Ali?" he demanded.

I bared my teeth, with every intension of biting him. *Gonna be so good.*

His strong fingers captured my jaw, keeping my mouth closed. "You don't want to do this. You're better than this."

Better? I wasn't better. I was hungry, and he was preventing me from eating. I wanted to eat! With a growl, I jerked from his grip.

"Ali. You once promised me you would never do this again. Do you remember?"

I stilled. I'd promised him all right, and I hated to lie.

Deep breath in. Out. Mind clearing.

"You can control this. You could control her."

Her. Z.A.

Remembering who—and what—she was gave me the wake-up call I'd needed.

Fight her.

This was a test of wills. Hers and mine. We were separate, and it was time to prove it. I was stronger. I had to be stronger.

"Good girl." He brushed his fingertips over my brow, and I felt a stream of warmth, a total evaporation of the hunger.

How did he do that?

Dark. Light.

The words struck me again.

Suddenly Cole went rigid. "Ow!" he spat, and released a tide of dark curses. I heard the rustle of clothing, the snap of metal hitting bone.

I struggled to sit up, only to realize Cole had left his body on top of me while his spirit slashed at the zombie determined to end him. One of his daggers lodged into the creature's collarbone, and Cole spun, slicing his opponent across the throat with the other.

As the zombie fell, its head detached from its body. Cole held out his hand, flames crackling over his fingers. He flattened his palm against the creature's chest. One second passed, two, three, I don't know how many more, I lost count, and the flames began to spread up and down, until they covered every inch of the zombie.

Boom.

The body exploded and ash rained through the air.

Cole did the same thing to the head, pressing the zombie face-first into the ground to hide the teeth. The creature was still alive, still trying to chomp on him.

Boom.

More ash sprayed.

He straightened, wavering on his feet. The fire had died from his hand. His knees buckled, and he hit the ground. I rallied my strength and bucked the weight of his body off me, then crawled to his spirit. He had no injuries—wait. His pants were ripped at the ankle. I twisted and saw the teeth marks in his flesh, as well as the black goo the zombies always left behind.

I whimpered. He'd been bitten because he'd been distracted. By me.

"I'm so sorry," I said. I'd said those words a lot lately.

"Antidote," he rasped.

Yes, of course. I crawled back to his body, found the syringe in his back pocket and returned to him. Only the needle and my hand ghosted right through him. Why—because he was in spirit form, and I was in natural.

I tried to force my spirit out of my body, but the hard hands from before held on to me, keeping me inside. *Dang it!*

In the back of my mind, I thought I heard gleeful giggles. Z.A. was laughing at me.

Maybe I could start a new to-do list. A small one, with only one task. *HURT HER.*

Scanning the area, I took note of the other slayers. Gavin slashed at two zombies at once. Veronica came in from behind and hobbled the zombies at the ankles. Frosty swooped in and pressed his glowing palm against the zombie's chest, just as Cole had done. Bronx fought every creature trying to reach the stationary Frosty.

I couldn't distract them. This was up to me, and there was only one solution. Back to Cole's body I went. I slid my hands under his shoulders and dragged him, one inch at a time, toward his now writhing spirit. He was so heavy, I stumbled with every step. Eventually I managed to drag him close enough to stretch out his arm and connect natural fingers with spiritual fingers, joining the two together.

Trembling, I rose to my knees and shoved the needle deep into his neck.

He arched, his back bowing off the ground. Then he sagged into place. "Thank you," he said, panting.

I crouched beside him, guarding him from further attack. But I'd taken so long to help him, the battle was over. Gavin straightened, ash from the last creature to die raining around him.

Veronica returned to her body, became one and rushed over to pull Cole up. "Are you okay, sugar?"

Sugar again. I wanted to push her away from him.

I didn't.

"I'm fine." Very gently, he added, "Don't...don't call me that. Okay?"

She blanched. Then she glared at me, spitting out, "You're the worst thing that's ever happened to him. Have you realized that yet?"

I couldn't, *wouldn't,* engage her. And I couldn't exactly refute her, could I?

"If you don't cut him loose, you're going to kill him, and I'm going to... I'll put you... Argh!" Clearly, she'd kept herself on a leash, and the leash had just broken. She launched at me, knocking me to my back and throwing a punch.

I took it, using what little energy I had left to work my legs between us and shove her away. She came back swinging and clipped me in the chin. I rolled with the impact, lumbered to my feet. We circled each other.

"I'm going to—"

"Nothing," Cole said, silencing her as he stood. "You're going to do nothing, Veronica."

Panting, she said, "Please tell me you don't still care about this girl. After everything she's done?" When he failed to reply, she paled and looked to me. "I don't know if you're human or zombie or both, Ali Bell, and I don't care. You're no good for Cole or anyone here, so why don't you do us all a favor and stay away? Or die. My vote is die."

"That's enough," Cole shouted.

I...*wanted* to die. Everything Veronica had said rang true. These people would have been far better off without me. Cole would have been able to fight. He wouldn't have gotten bitten. And what about tomorrow? What would happen then? I was nothing more than a living time bomb. I never knew what I would do next—or whom I would hurt. One day, I could detonate and take out everyone around me.

"The zombies are dead. Where's Kat?" Frosty demanded. He stood a few feet away from me, his clothes torn and splattered with black goo. Just then, his navy eyes did justice to his name—they were coated with ice.

Cole moved beside me and wrapped his arm around me in a shocking show of support. I loved his warmth and his scent and his strength and wanted nothing more than to bask in them, but I forced myself to move away from him.

He might support me in this right now, but it wouldn't last. He'd soon regret it and wish he'd kept me at a distance.

He lifted his chin, every muscle in his body tense.

I pretended to ignore him, marching over to grab my purse and inject myself with antidote.

"Kat," Frosty snapped.

"Ethan," I replied. "She's with Ethan Hamilton."

Frosty went still, a predator who'd just spotted the tasti-est of prey. "Who's Ethan?"

"Reeve's...friend. I know where he lives." Bronx was just as disheveled, just as splattered, just as predatory. "Cole?"

"Go," he said, and the two boys needed no more prompt-ing.

Gavin stepped to my side, saying, "You need a ride, Ali?"

"I'll take her." Cole approached me a second time, but I backpedaled toward Gavin.

"No. He'll take me," I rushed out. Avoiding Gavin had been stupid. He didn't tempt me to do things I shouldn't. I could remain calm with him.

I wouldn't become a menace.

Cole stopped abruptly, looking between us, his eyes nar-rowing. I wasn't sure of Gavin's reaction to this new turn of events, and I didn't care enough to switch my attention. My gaze remained locked with Cole's. My heart cracked.

"It's better this way, remember?" I said softly.

"For who?"

You. "Both of us."

He massaged the back of his neck and turned his now ice-cold focus to the others.

"I'll see you back at the barn," he said.

Trina nodded without looking up. Silent, Lucas flashed a thumbs-up. Veronica approached Cole, but he very gently shook her off and said, "We talked about this, Ronny."

Her features fell.

He stalked away. Twice he glanced back at me, and the crack in my heart widened.

Could *nothing* in my life go right?

TWEEDLEDEE AND
TWEEDLEDUM DUMB

"Don't you need to get back out there?" I asked Gavin as I unlocked my front door. "There could be a flood of zombies tonight." Even though I hadn't noticed a rabbit cloud during the drive home. Yeah, I'd finally broken down and looked.

"It's doubtful. You woke a nest. That's the only reason those zombies came out when they did."

I paused in the open doorway and faced him, my arms spread to block his path. "Well, don't you need to be out there putting Blood Lines around the homes of the inno-cent?"

His lips curled at the corners. "Mr. Ankh and Mr. Hol-land have been taking care of that. Now, aren't you going to invite me in?"

Sure. In…never. "I don't want to be rude, but—"

"Good. Then don't be rude." He picked me up and set

me aside. "I'm spending the rest of the evening with you, then crashing on your couch."

Exasperated, I entered behind him. Did he think I'd leave and go on a killing rampage?

Like you can really blame him.

"Sorry, but we don't have a couch." We'd been buying one piece of furniture at a time, when we found cheap but reliable pieces, and so far had only managed to pick up two beds and a dining room table.

"Uh, are you sure about that?" He sounded amused.

"Maybe not," I said, my tone dry. "I only live here." I shut and locked the door before nailing him with a glare.

"Now, now. Don't look at me like that," he said, chucking me under the chin. "I saw the video, and I know what you're capable of, but I also know you wanted to bite Cole that night—and this one. The look in your eyes, the way you licked your lips… I've seen zombies do that. But the bottom line? You didn't do it. Before, you turned your hunger on the zombies, and today you somehow managed to snap yourself out of it. I respect the kind of strength that took."

He was…right, I realized. Z.A. had controlled me, darkened my mind, yet I'd had the strength to fight her. Hope bloomed brighter than it had in days, as pretty as a flower opening in the sun. Maybe I wasn't such a terrible menace after all.

"If you aren't afraid of what I'll do, why do you want to stay here?" I asked, waving my hand at—

A furnished and decorated living room. I frowned and bustled forward. "Nana," I called.

"Ali, dear. You're home." Dusting her hands together, she

snaked around the hallway corner. "Oh, no. You're injured. What happened?"

"The usual," I said, then motioned to the new furnishings. "How much did all of this cost?"

She fidgeted with the hem of her shirt. "Don't you worry about that. I gave myself a budget and stuck to it."

"Nana," I said.

My expression must have betrayed my thoughts, because she said, "I know you want to save to buy a house of our own, but I don't want us living like paupers while we do it."

Okay. All right. If she wanted this stuff, then I wanted her to have it.

I hugged her tight and kissed her on the temple. "Everything looks amazing, Nana. Seriously."

"I'm so glad you think so. Wait till you see your bedroom," she said with a smile.

Gavin cleared his throat, and Nana peeked around me.

"Oh, I'm so sorry, Gavin. I didn't realize you were here. It's lovely to see you again." Her gaze moved over him, widened. "I'm guessing you ran into the same bit of *usual* trouble my Ali did."

"Yes, ma'am, I sure did."

She gulped. "There were others with you? And everyone…survived?"

"More than. We thrived." He shook off his coat and draped the fabric over his arm. "I don't know about you, but I'm starving. I'd love a chance to cook you dinner to thank you for allowing me to sleep on your couch."

Wait. The he-slut of the great South knew how to cook?

Nana's gaze met mine for a split second, her mouth forming a small O. "You're staying the night?"

"If it's all right with you. I'll behave, you have my word."

"Are you two…"

"No," I rushed out, at the same time Gavin said, "We're debating it."

I glared at him. "We're better off as friends."

"In that case, it'll be nice having a man around," Nana said, once again dusting her hands together. "I bought a bookcase I wasn't looking forward to putting together."

"I'll do it," he said. "I'm always ready for a chance to be a hero."

She giggled like a schoolgirl—a dirty, dirty schoolgirl—and I did a double take. "You already are. The bookcase can wait until after dinner, though. I've got a few more things to arrange in my room."

The moment we were alone, I anchored my hands on my hips. "Will you please stop forgetting you're into brunettes?"

"I realized I can't see hair color in the dark."

Oh, wow. "However will I continue to resist such wondrous flattery?"

Smiling, he swept around me and entered the kitchen. "What can't be manufactured is attitude, and I happen to like yours."

I came in behind him and opened the fridge to grab something to drink. It was now fully stocked with all my favorites. Orange juice, milk, protein shakes, fruits, vegetables and even the chocolate cupcakes I liked to eat cold. I groaned.

"What?" Gavin said.

"She spent too much money on me."

"Most girls wouldn't complain about that."

I selected one of the shakes. "Most girls don't have my Nana. I want to pamper her, not the other way around."

Gavin reached in behind me to snag a juice. Our arms brushed, and I scowled up at him.

"Stop trying to seduce me," I said.

"Why? Is it working?"

"If you like to be stabbed, yes."

"I've let girls do a lot worse to me."

I shook my head, exasperated.

"Look, I don't want to go home. I've been dividing my time between Cole's house, a crappy motel and the homes of the women I'm fu...screwing."

"You can say it. My ears won't melt off."

He snorted. "Cole says we're not to cuss around you. Potty mouth is contagious, I guess. *Anyway.* A guy can only take so much. I'm desperate for a break."

Well, I couldn't exactly kick him out now. I wasn't that cruel.

I nodded my agreement before moving around him.

He grinned at me, his eyes alight with mischief. "You act all proper now, but in the visions, you've definitely got a lady boner for me."

I choked on a laugh. "Lady boner?"

He shrugged. "I kinda like knowing there are two sides to you and I'm the one responsible."

Two sides to me. He had no idea one of those sides was the enemy. "Gavin."

"Nah. You don't need to put me in my place again. Whether you admit it or not, you're softening toward me."

Absolutely, but not in the way he wanted.

A knock sounded at the door, and I stiffened.

"I bet that's Cole," he said with a sigh. "I expected him sooner."

No way. Cole wouldn't come after me. Not after the public rejection I'd just dished. And yet I was trembling as I opened the door. Annnd…sure enough, tall, strong and impossibly beautiful Cole waited on the other side.

Sweet mercy.

"Kat and Reeve are both fine," he said, one arm propped against the wooden frame. "They're with Frosty and Bronx."

"Did the guys hurt Ethan?"

"No. He was pretty freaked out by what he'd seen. They questioned him, nothing more."

I covered my throat with my hand, a protective action. "What did he see?"

"Apparently you looked as if you wanted to eat Kat and Reeve at one point, and not in the good way."

I wasn't going to touch that statement. "Well." I cleared my throat. "Thank you for the update, but it's getting late and you're probably wanted at home."

He shook his head. "Sorry, babe, but I'm not leaving."

What, was this disagree with Ali day? "It's for your own good, Cole."

"Right now I'd rather be bad and deal with the consequences later."

Please be bad. Very, very bad. Downright naughty.

I shivered, and the shiver made me mad. So did my treacherous mind. "You might not survive these particular consequences." I smiled with saccharine sweetness—and tried to shut the door in his face.

He shouldered his way inside. "I'm willing to risk it."

Argh!

"Hey, Cole," Gavin called from the kitchen. "You staying for dinner?"

Cole would have seen his car in the driveway and known Gavin was here, but still his back went iron-bar straight at the sound of the other guy's voice. "Are you the chef?"

"I am."

Cole marched forward and settled into a bar stool as if he owned it. "Good. I'm starved."

This could not be happening.

"We've got the stuff for enchiladas or roast beef sandwiches," Gavin said, glancing at me.

"Enchiladas," Cole replied.

"Sandwiches it is, then," Gavin said.

Cole offered him a chilling smile.

Oh, glory. If they decided to play Animal Planet, I'd… let them, I decided. Both would end up unconscious and I would no longer be trapped in this tug-of-war. Sure, I'd have to clean a pool of blood, but just then that actually seemed like the better choice. We had plenty of baking soda and vinegar.

While Gavin puttered around the kitchen, Cole swiveled in the chair to face me. "How are you feeling?"

"Fine," I said, taking the seat next to him. I could be polite. "How about you?"

"Better." He reached out, pinched a lock of my hair. "I'm not afraid of you, you know."

"You should be." I was. I tugged my hair from his grip. Softly, I added, "But we both know that's not our only problem."

He blanched, and I felt guilty. I shouldn't feel guilty.

"I know what you're thinking, and that's not what I meant," I said and sighed.

"Then what?"

"I'll...have to show you." I motioned to the hall—my bedroom—with a tilt of my chin.

He nodded, something hot and dark in his eyes.

"Once again it's not what you're thinking," I said drily.

I think he...pouted.

What do you know—here was yet another side to Cole.

"Don't you want to show me, too?" Gavin said, his tone a little tight. He chopped the lettuce with more force.

"Not this," I replied, trying to be gentle. "I'm sorry."

"Don't apologize to him," Cole snapped.

O-kay. The ice was back.

"He's my guest," I said, "and I like him, and *he's* acting civil. He deserved an apology from me, so I gave it, and now he deserves one from you. I'm not leaving this spot until he gets it."

Gavin smirked.

Cole gritted out a very mean "Sorry."

"Good. Let's go." As Cole and I stood, another knock sounded at my door. Dang it, who was *that?* Considering my luck, it was probably Veronica. "Just a sec." I stomped to the door. This time, I found Justin waiting on the other side. "You've got to be kidding me."

Cole came up behind me, the intense heat he radiated a caress against my skin. "What are you doing here?"

A bundle of energy, Justin couldn't seem to stand still. "You told me to contact you if I had news. Well, I have news, and besides that, I thought you told Ali what's going on."

Cole glanced over his shoulder, saying, "You should have called."

"No way. This was too big."

"What is?" I asked at the same time Gavin called, "Who is it?"

Justin pressed his lips into a thin line. He backed up, saying, "Sorry. Didn't realize. I'll text you as soon as I get inside my car."

The door shut with a soft click. He'd better hurry. Curiosity was now in the process of eating me alive.

"You were going to show me something," Cole prompted.

I nodded, and led him past the kitchen. Gavin glanced up from the loaf of potato bread he was slicing, frowned. "Seriously? You're abandoning me?"

"Only for a few minutes."

"You don't owe him an explanation, either," Cole said, dragging me away. "And I'm not apologizing again."

I think Gavin flipped him off, but I couldn't be sure. In the hall, I heard Nana humming under her breath.

"We have another guest," I called.

She stuck her head out of the door and brightened. "Cole. It's wonderful to see you."

"You, too."

She arched a brow when she noticed my hand on the knob of my door. "You're going in there...alone?"

"Just for a few minutes," I said.

Her eyes narrowed, but she nodded. "I'll be watching the clock."

I stepped inside—only to gasp. She had decorated my room with everything she knew I'd love. The furnishings were a dark cherrywood and polished to a glossy shine. Wispy white curtains covered my window, and a framed picture of Emma and me hung on the wall. She was in front of me, wrapped in my arms, and we were both smiling our biggest smiles.

There was a note taped to the border.

Angels must have held this photo in their hands, because that's the only way it could have survived the bomb. I had it framed weeks ago, but wanted to wait to give it to you at Christmas. This seemed like a better time.
Love, Nana

Oh, Nana, I thought as tears welled in my eyes.

"You're both adorable," Cole said, stepping up behind me to study the photo. "You look so happy."

"We were. We'd just finished playing hide-and-seek in the house, and of course, she had won. She always won. My legs were too long to fit anywhere. She was gloating in that sweet way she had—*nah, nah, nah, I'm the crown champion again*—so I snatched her up to tickle her. Mom demanded we pose."

He squeezed my shoulder. "I have one of my mom and

me, taken a few weeks before she died. It's more valuable to me than my heart and lungs."

I liked when he shared something from his past. He didn't do it often. I turned, met his gaze.

He hooked a strand of hair behind my ear. I could feel myself getting lost in the moment, in him, so when his phone beeped a few seconds later, I jumped. I also sighed with relief.

"Go ahead," I said. "Check it."

He hesitated a moment before scrolling through the message, his features darkening as he read. "Justin says the spy is someone who was at the park tonight. Information about the fight has already hit Anima."

"So…that rules out Collins and Cruz. And Frosty and Bronx were too busy rescuing Kat and Reeve to hand out any details."

"Not necessarily, but I know them better than I know myself, and they'd never help the enemy. I've never suspected them."

Had he ever suspected me? "You can rule out Lucas and Trina, too. I watched the spy watch them, remember? So that leaves…Veronica."

"You saw a male in the forest."

"Yes, and she could be working with him."

"Maybe." His gaze locked with mine and searched. "There's also Gavin."

My hand fluttered to my throat, rubbed. Gavin… He had to be innocent. And yet he wanted to stay the night here, no matter how uncomfortable he'd be on the couch. Maybe not because he hated the motel, after all, but to keep tabs on me and my dark metamorphosis.

"Anyway, they weren't the only ones there," Cole reminded me.

"Me?" I squeaked.

He rolled his eyes. "I never suspected you. I mean Kat. Reeve."

"Girl. Girl."

"Like you said, a girl could be working with a boy."

"Besides," I continued, "there's no way Kat would betray us, and Reeve doesn't know anything."

"Kat has no filter. She—"

"Isn't responsible," I insisted.

"What about Ethan?"

"Bronx has already looked into him. Found nothing suspicious."

After a short pause, he nodded. "That leaves us with… yeah, Gavin and Veronica. But I've already checked, and they came out clean. As you know, that's the reason I spent so much time with her. I was going through her stuff, checking everything she said. Nothing dubious came up. More than that, the problems started before the pair got here."

"Maybe you didn't dig deep enough. Maybe one or both were working for Anima before they got here and asked to be assigned to your team. Talk to Mr. Ankh and your dad. They'll have ideas about what to—"

"No way. My reasons for staying quiet are still the same. I won't blacken someone's name without at least a little proof."

"Yeah, but once the truth comes to light, whoever you've accused will be vindicated. Or not."

He shook his head, saying, "The problem is, my closest friends will know I didn't trust them. Maybe they'll forgive me, maybe not, but from that moment on, no matter what I do, what I say, they'll always wonder at my motives. That stuff doesn't leave a person."

Had he ever been accused of something he hadn't done?

I must have asked the question aloud because he said, "When Justin started working with Anima, he hung around my team for information, just like the newest spy. I knew something was going on and stupidly blamed Boots and Ducky, members of the team you never got to meet." As he spoke, he rubbed the tattoos of their names. "They were so mad at me, so hurt, they went hunting that night, I guess to prove their loyalty, and they found a nest of zombies. That's the night they were killed. I can't go through something like that again."

"Cole—" I said, but he stopped me with another shake of his head.

"I'll do more digging with Gavin and Veronica. And now let's close this subject and revisit at another date. You said you had something to show me. Was it a kiss?" He backed me into the door, putting his body in front of me, and the hardwood in back of me, effectively caging me. And oh, good glory, had I just used the word *hardwood*? "Lately I haven't been able to think about anything else."

"Cole. No."

"Just one more," he said raggedly. "Then we'll stop. Then maybe the madness will finally end and we'll be able to be friends. I know you said we couldn't be, but I don't like the thought of being without you. I need you in my life, at least in some way."

"Friends don't kiss." Besides, I'd already had my *one more*.

Whimper. "Nana would hear us, we aren't always quiet. She'll come to the door, knock. I'll be hugely embarrassed."

"Okay." He anchored his palms at my temples. "Okay."

I had to stop breathing. He smelled too good, the scent of him invading my senses, making me dizzy with need and want and breaking through whatever new walls I'd managed to build against him. "You're not acting like it's okay."

"When is the madness going to end?" he asked. "I must be obsessed with you, Ali. Addicted. Whatever I feel is definitely unhealthy. Without you, I'm having trouble eating and sleeping. I think about you all the time, wonder what you're doing, and who you're doing it with. Do you know how many times I've been tempted to hunt you down and just carry you away?"

"Cole—"

He wasn't done. "You're smart, fierce, brave. You have a habit of staring off into space, your mind lost to your memories. When you love, you love with your whole heart. And your compassion... When Holly Dumfries went on a date with Chad Stevens, Kerry Goldberg—Chad's ex—dumped a bottle of water on Holly the next day at school. You helped Holly clean up, even switched shirts with her. Yeah. I checked into the shirt thing. Then, when everyone made fun of Aubrey Wilson for getting pregnant, you offered to throw her a baby shower."

My eyes were so wide they had to look like saucers. I'd had no idea he'd known about Holly and Aubrey, and the fact that he did, that he'd kept tabs on me... My knees were threatening to buckle.

"What am I going to do with you?" he asked softly. He

pressed his forehead into mine. "I've thought about sending Gavin back to Georgia, but then I feared something would happen to force you to follow him, and I wouldn't be able to see you."

"Cole—"

"You were right to call me a coward before. I'm afraid of the future, Ali. I can't stand the thought of you with him, so how am I going to survive the reality of it?"

I wanted to wrap my arms around him, which is exactly why I pushed him away. "You don't trust me when I say I'm not interested in him in a romantic way, and that I'm not ever going to be interested in him. You trust the visions more than you trust me and my feelings, and I deserve better."

There was torment in his eyes as he muttered, "You're right."

And like that, something seemed to break inside him.

He fell onto the bed, put his elbows on his knees and his head in his hands. He stayed like that for a long while, simply breathing.

"Are you okay?" I asked softly.

"Not yet, but I will be." He looked up, and I saw determination swimming in his eyes.

Determination to what?

It kind of…scared me.

I turned my back on him. Trembling, I said, "By the way, some of your friends aren't happy with you lately. You've been really mean, apparently." There. A safer topic.

"You want me to be nicer to them?" he asked almost carefully.

"Yes."

He pushed out a breath. "Then I'll be nicer."

That easily? "Thank you." I drew him toward the vanity. I sat down, keeping my gaze downcast. "Now, what I wanted to show you. Take a look at my reflection."

"All right." He remained at my back, his hands steady on my shoulders. "Is there something specific you want me to notice?"

"Watch what happens," I said, and opened my eyes.

Z.A. grinned at me, and there was blood on her teeth.

My blood?

"What do you see?" I asked Cole, trying not to fidget.

He lifted my hair, bent down and placed a soft kiss at the curve of my neck. I stiffened, and his grip hardened, as did his gaze; he straightened. "I see you."

A dangerous shiver stole through me. "No," I said. "What do you see in the mirror?"

In the glass, his gaze met *hers.* He frowned. "I still see you."

My brow furrowed with confusion. "You don't see the black smudges?"

"No," he said.

"Please. Introduce us." She chuckled, the sound low and creepy. "He might prefer me."

"Did you hear that?" I asked, clutching my stomach.

"Hear what?"

"Her."

Comprehension dawned. "The dark presence you mentioned?"

I nodded.

"I didn't."

Dang it. Why? He could see and hear spirits in any form. He could see and hear Emma. Why not Z.A., too?

A hard knock pounded at my door. "Dinner's ready," Gavin called.

Scowling, Cole straightened. I stood, a little relieved.

"We'll continue this later," he said. A promise.

"All right." An evasion.

We were silent as we headed into the kitchen.

GO TO SLEEP, MY DARLINGS

Gavin stayed the night, as promised. But then, so did Cole.

Cole took the couch, and Gavin made a pallet on the floor. I tossed and turned, knowing they were both out there, so close. Gavin, perhaps watching over me; Cole, definitely watching over Gavin. Testosterone charged the air.

I couldn't sneak out to meet Dr. Bendari—even though I'd promised I wouldn't renege on him again. The boys would catch me. All I could do was lie in bed and think.

Was Gavin the spy?

Was Veronica, via someone else?

Were they working together?

I…didn't think so. At least, when I really thought about it, I still believed in Gavin's innocence.

Was I right about him? Could I trust myself with this, when I couldn't trust myself with anything else?

You had better. You scolded Cole for not trusting you.

True.

Okay, so I'd take my own advice, no muss, no fuss. I would believe in Gavin.

That left Veronica. She had to be working with the spy. And, sure, there was a good chance my jealousy was coloring my perception of her. But what if it wasn't?

How were we going to find out the truth? It was too late for me to try and be friends with her and learn more about her. That ship had sailed, and the storm had already beaten us down, left us adrift. I wouldn't be able to fake a change of heart. No matter what I did, she would never believe me.

Cole would have to feel her out—or up. Would he decide to continue his romance with her? Maybe. Just how far would he allow himself to go with her? Exactly what would he have to do to soften her enough to catch her in the act?

A few kisses? A few caresses?

Sex?

I had no right to feel hurt by the thought of Veronica and him getting together again. No matter the reason. I had no right to be upset. And we desperately needed answers. But…

Like every time before, I *was* hurt. I *was* upset.

I forced myself to think about something else. Something less painful. Like Z.A. I snorted. In what world was the creature trying to take over my body a safer topic?

Simple. Mine.

Did she have any weaknesses?

I couldn't think of one.

By the time the sun rose, my nerves were frayed. I lumbered out of bed, showered and dressed in jeans and a T-shirt that read Always Be Yourself Unless You Can Be a Kat Then Always Be a Kat. A housewarming gift from, surprise, surprise, Kat.

In the living room, I discovered the blankets Gavin and Cole had used were folded, and the couch cushions were pushed back into place. Both boys were gone, and neither had left a note.

Had Cole rushed off to see Veronica?

Biting the inside of my cheek, I stomped into the kitchen.

"Good morning," Nana said, having just finished off an egg sandwich.

"Morning."

"I hope you're hungry. Cole did all of this, and he made you a plate before he left." Nana slid a massive pile of scrambled eggs, bacon and biscuits in my direction. "He told me to tell you to eat every crumb or else. Oh, and he also left you a note."

She handed me a folded piece of paper.

Don't give up on me the way I gave up on you. Please. Somehow I'll find a way to make it up to you.
X Cole

Was he saying what I thought he was saying?

Did I *want* him to say what I thought he was saying?

I would have asked him, but he never made it to school. Where was he? What was he doing?

As the day eked by, I thought about calling him, then decided against it. Thought about texting him, then decided against it. I was a mess of uncertainty by the time Kat dropped me off at home.

Nana was gone. I changed into my work clothes and stuffed a few necessities into a backpack. My favorite weapons, a change of clothes, my cell and a little of the money I'd saved. I liked to stay prepared. I donned my coat, hat and gloves and left the house.

The air was bitterly cold, misting in front of my face as I breathed. Frost covered the grass, making me slip a few times. I set off down the street, walking fast. When I cleared the neighborhood, I came to a busy intersection. I passed the light and the convenience store and began to shiver. And yet the exposed skin on my face burned as if I'd crawled inside an oven. I frowned.

Sensitivity to the sun was a zombie trait.

Tires squealed. I palmed a dagger as I searched for the reason. An unfamiliar sedan with dark-tinted windows parked at the curb.

A door in back opened. "Get in," Dr. Bendari commanded.

I stepped toward him, froze. If I did this, I would be late for work, maybe even miss my shift entirely. And if I missed my shift without calling in—would he let me call in or threaten to bail if I tried?—I could lose the job. But could I really pass up this opportunity?

Anticipation, nervousness and dread filled me all at once, propelling me the rest of the way. I jumped into the car, keeping the blade hidden but at the ready. Dr. Bendari moved to the side, giving me space. Even before I'd shut the door, the vehicle was speeding away.

Warm air blew from the vents, enveloping me as I buckled my seat belt.

Dr. Bendari studied me. "Face-to-face at last, Miss Bell."

"I'm sorry I didn't come out last night."

"You had guests. I know." He looked to the driver. "Alert me if there's even a hint of a tail."

"Yes, sir," the driver said.

"How did you know?" I demanded. "How do you always know?"

"I told you," Dr. Bendari said, reaching for something on the floorboard. "My source."

"I'm loaded with weapons," I rushed out, waving the dagger. "Sudden movements aren't an option for you. If you try anything…"

Dr. Bendari straightened without grabbing anything and, looking at me as if I were a wounded animal, gently said, "You need me too much to dispose of me, Miss Bell."

"Yeah? And why is that?"

"I told you. I have the answers you seek."

"If that's so, why would you *want* to help me? Who are you? What's your purpose? Your endgame? Why the veil of secrecy? Who do you work for? Do you have someone spying on my friends? Who is your source, dang it? I want to know!"

He rubbed his temples as if trying to ward off an intense ache. "Are you always this inquisitive?"

"Always."

"It's quite off-putting."

"Well, I'm quite desperate."

He studied me, frowned with a hint of sadness. "I bet you are." Sighing, he very slowly reached for…whatever it was. A pile of folders. He settled them in his lap. "I'm sure you will be less than thrilled to learn this, but I worked for Anima Industries for many years."

Even though I'd suspected, I found my fingers tightening around the hilt of my weapon.

Keeping his eyes on the road, the driver extended an arm, a gun now in his hand, the barrel pointed at my face. "I gave you a chance to put that thing away. You didn't. Now I'm telling you straight-up. If you make a move against my employer, little girl, I'll end you."

"Now, now," Dr. Bendari chided. "Let's calm down, everyone. I said I *worked* with Anima, Miss Bell. In case you missed it, that's past tense. I have since left the company. My source is still working for them, however, and that's where he gets his intel. Whatever I know, they know, too. They are, apparently, watching you closely."

I relaxed, but only slightly, considering what I'd just learned. I set the dagger on my thigh.

The driver lowered his gun.

"I was growing increasingly upset with their...business practices, I guess you could say," Dr. Bendari continued. "Lately, they've been using cancer patients as lab rats, and I couldn't take it anymore. I left the company, but you see, no one with my security clearance leaves Anima alive."

"You seem to be breathing just fine."

"Yes, and I've had to take drastic measures to keep it that way."

Fair enough. "Do you know Justin Silverstone?"

"I know *of* him. I also know he's playing a very dangerous game, and I'm not sure whose side he's on. He reports to Anima, but he also reports to Cole Holland. So he's either betraying both parties or playing one, and it's going to get him killed. It did his twin sister."

"What?" Jaclyn was dead?

He flipped open one of the files. I looked at the page on top—and gagged. It was a photo of Jaclyn sprawled on a bed of grass, her body twisted at an odd angle and splattered with blood. There was a hole the size of a fist in her chest.

I'd never liked her, and she'd never liked me, but seeing her body like that... A well of sympathy bubbled up inside me. "There have been no reports of her body being found."

"I wasn't there. I don't know what happened. But I discovered the pictures and can only suppose someone carted her away and destroyed her. If I know Anima—and I do—there will *never* be a report about her."

Poor Jaclyn. Poor Justin. I had witnessed the deaths of my family, and it had been tragic and terrible, but at least I knew what had happened. "Does Justin have any idea?"

"I'm not sure. The powers that be could have shown him the photos and threatened him with the same fate, hoping to get him to do something they wanted. Or they could have shown him the photos and blamed your group, thinking he'd seek revenge. Or they could be pretending ignorance. They are very good at all three."

I believed him. Justin could be the spy, out to avenge his sister and the part he thought Cole had played in her death.

"I see the wheels in your head spinning. However, my source is not getting his information from Justin's reports. There is someone else spying on your group, Miss Bell, but I don't know the male's identity."

Male, he'd said. Not a girl paying a boy.

Trusting myself, remember. It's not Gavin. "What do you know about me?" I asked. "About my...condition. And how do you know? Or maybe a better question is, how does *your source* know?"

"At first, my source knew only that you had been bitten and begun to act strangely. I deduced the rest. Then you were seen producing a red fire rather than a white one." His expression was sad as he flipped through another folder, showing me photo after photo of people trapped in cages. Human people, not zombies. Only the more photos he showed me, the more zombielike those people became. I was horrified.

"These people are nothing more than guinea pigs," he said. "They were diagnosed with cancer, but without the medical insurance to pay for treatment. They were desperate enough to try anything. They've been experimented on—with my formula." There at the end, shame dripped from his voice. "I first came to work for Anima with the hope of creating a medication to increase life expectancy. A fountain of youth, if you will. Then I learned I was supposed to do it through the zombies."

"You can see them?"

He shook his head. "My staff and I weren't able to see into that other realm like you slayers, and we can't leave our bodies without help, so we can't see or touch the creatures until they are ringed."

Without help? What help? First, I concentrated on the most important thing he'd revealed. "Ringed?"

"Our version of your Blood Line." He showed a picture of a large metal band. "It goes around their necks and sends out electrical pulses that make the creatures tangible, but the pulse does something to the zombies… Eventually works them into a frenzy, and that frenzy makes them stronger. I've had more coworkers have to be killed because they'd been bitten during a frenzy than for any other reason."

"Are you planning to put me down?" I asked with a tremor.

"No. Of course not." He frowned. "Tell me exactly what happened to you, Miss Bell."

I was surprised he didn't already know every stinking detail. "Justin was bitten by a zombie. He then bit me. We were both given the antidote. He recovered, but I got worse. And now I'm slowly turning into a zombie, which sucks more than you probably realize, because my spirit is toxic to zombies—and that means I'm toxic to myself."

He sighed. "I knew you were becoming a zombie, but I hoped I was wrong."

"How did you know?"

"I recognized the signs."

"You also know I'm seeing things. Hearing whispers."

"Yes. As the essence of the zombie takes over your body, you begin to see into both the spiritual and natural realm at the same time."

"I could already see into both realms."

"Not to this degree. One realm will always be more real than the other. Right now you're in transition."

I gulped. "Have you ever saved someone like me? Someone infected with the zombie toxin, after it's too late to be cured by the antidote?"

He played with the wedding ring on his finger. Ignoring my question, he said, "I had no idea you were dealing with the other problem. The allergy. So, all right. Let's break this down piece by piece."

I took that as a no and swallowed my cry of distress.

"I have heard of a few other people having a spirit that is toxic to zombies."

One of them was my great-great-great-grandfather, I would bet.

"Justin reacted as he did because he was bitten by zombies Anima had experimented on and released. Their toxin is stronger, works faster."

"But Justin went back to normal and I didn't."

"Justin isn't allergic to himself." He lifted a small, dark case from the floor and popped open the lid, revealing stacks of prefilled, plastic syringes. "I created different types of the antidote for all the different reactions I had heard about."

"How many different kinds are there?"

"Eight. I took the formulas with me when I left Anima, and I've made several batches of each. Let's give you a dose of the antihistamine antidote now and see what happens."

I should say no. I shouldn't let a strange man inject me with a strange substance.

Common Sense Ali screamed it was foolish. And yet Survivalist Ali shouted it was currently my best chance of winning this.

"Okay," I said and nodded.

He selected a vial from the case. I shrugged my coat off my shoulder and tugged my shirt collar out of the way. He pushed the needle into the upper part of my arm. There was a sting, and a cool river moved through the muscle and spread.

For the first time in weeks, the double heartbeat seemed to vanish. The pressure eased from my chest, and the darkness thinned from my mind.

A burst of relief had me grinning. *Suck it, Common Sense!*

I wasn't out of the game. The new antidote bought me what I needed most. Time.

"I'll send all I've got with you," he said. "Whenever you start to feel zombielike urges, give yourself a dose. It's not a cure, but it's a start. You'll also be safer to be around."

"Thank you."

He removed fifteen of the vials and handed them to me, and I stuffed them in my pack. "I'll make more. But I should warn you… I'm sorry, Miss Bell, but there will come a point when your body will no longer respond to this antidote or any other. The more you use it, the faster you will develop an immunity to it."

Yeah, I knew that. "I was told there actually *is* a cure, that the essence of the zombie is darkness, and that the light chases that darkness away."

He frowned. "The light from a slayer's hand?"

"Exactly." I told him what I'd done, how my spirit had left my body, how I'd summoned the flames and touched my chest, but nothing had happened.

"I'm surprised you didn't kill yourself."

Dying is the only way to truly live.

Maybe that was the point. Maybe I *needed* to die.

Disappointment rose. Before, I might have been willing to risk death. Now I knew I wasn't ready for the end.

"This will require further study and thought," he said.

"Uh, sir. I hate to break up the party," the driver interjected, "but we've got a tail."

Dr. Bendari stiffened, looked back. "Can you lose it?"

"We're on a deserted road. There's nowhere—"

Crunch!

Metal slammed against metal. Our car swerved and then flipped. I screamed, mentally returning to the night my family died. Tires squealed as we hit the ground; metal crumpled as we flipped again, and glass shattered. I was jostled forward and back, forward and back, my brain banging against my skull.

Then everything stopped. Everything but me. *Dizzy…*

"Dr. Bendari." We were hanging upside down. Blood was rushing to my head. "Are you okay?"

He moaned.

I struggled to unlatch my belt. The moment it was free, I dropped, hitting the roof of the car—now the floor—my backpack slapping me in the face. I grunted as a lance of pain tore through me. No time to check for injuries.

"Help," he gurgled. His chest was covered in blood— blood dripping onto his face, filling his mouth. His shirt was ripped, and a jagged edge of his collarbone peeked past his skin.

Can't panic. "I can't release you. You'll drop." As wounded as he was, he might not survive the landing.

As I anchored my backpack in place, trying to decide what to do with the doctor, a pair of leather boots appeared. A shadow moved, and then a man was crouched in front of the shattered window. I was too disoriented to make out his features. "Help us," I pleaded.

"Dr. Bendari," he said, and a sense of self-preservation sent me scrambling as far from him as possible. "I was told to bring you back to Anima—unless you were sharing our secrets with the very people seeking to destroy us. Guess what you were doing?" He pointed a gun, fired a shot.

Pop.

Something warm and wet splattered over me, and Dr. Bendari went lax. His blood…everywhere, all around, all over me. I screamed, too shocked to react any other way.

The shooter grabbed the scattered files, then me, and dragged me out of the vehicle.

BLOOD IS THE NEW BLACK

Dr. Bendari was dead. Shot and killed in front of me.

Pain and panic threatened to overwhelm me as I scanned my surroundings. We were on an abandoned road, just as the doctor's driver had said, thick patches of trees on either side. There was another car behind ours—and the shooter was dragging me toward it.

If I could get to the trees, I could hide.

I was as good as dead if Shooter managed to stuff me inside that car.

Time for a new to-do list: *Get the guy to release me, race to the trees, hide. Use my phone to call Cole.*

I jerked against his hold, adrenaline giving me strength— just not enough to be effective. "Let go!"

"You want to die, sweetness?" he asked casually, making his words that much more frightening. "They've got plans for you, but if you continue to give me problems, you won't arrive in one piece."

They, he'd said. The people at Anima.

I fought that much harder, kicking out my leg, tripping the guy. Down he went, crashing into the gravel road. His hold on me loosened, and the photos he held scattered in the wind.

Shooter reached out to catch one, leaving himself wide open; I sucker punched him in the kidney, a very sensitive area. Grunting, he curled into himself. I grabbed as many files and pictures as I could before jolting to my feet.

I meant to run, I did, but a door slammed, and the driver of Shooter's car raced around the area, trying to gather up the rest of the photos while keeping a gun trained on me.

"Don't even think about it," he growled. He had bright red hair, a shade I'd never before seen. "I'll shoot you in the back without a moment's pause."

He'd shoot me anyway.

I spun and ran, moving in a zigzag to make myself less of a target, my backpack slamming against me again and again. Soon I was huffing and puffing, my lungs burning.

Pop!

I cringed, expecting an explosion of pain. But…I felt nothing and looked back. The driver of Dr. Bendari's car had crawled out from the rubble to shoot Red.

I slowed down and tried to catch my breath.

My only remaining ally faced me, shouting, "Keep running, more will come," before limping forward and pointing his weapon at the first guy, Shooter.

Pop!

Pop!

Dr. Bendari's driver collapsed, and my eyes went wide.

Why… How… Then I watched as Shooter fought to get vertical; despite his obvious pain, his focus was sharp as it landed on me. That was why. That was how. One pop had come from Shooter, and the other had come from Dr. Bendari's driver.

Shooter stumbled forward, taking something small, round and black out of his pocket, biting something off it and throwing it at Dr. Bendari's car. Grenade!

I spun and ran—

Boom!

The world went eerily quiet as a violent gust of white-hot air picked me up and threw me into a tree. I bounced backward, losing what little breath I had, shaking my head to clear the fresh surge of dizziness. Smoke filled the air, choking me, turning my line of sight to a hazy black and white.

A slight ringing erupted in my ears, growing louder, louder still, until it stopped as quickly as it had begun, and the world around me came back into focus.

I stood, almost fell. From the corner of my eye, I could see flames engulfing both cars—and Shooter still standing. Swallowing bile, I rushed into the forest.

Rearrange list: *call Cole, then hide.*

I stuffed the photos into my backpack and grabbed my phone. I was careful to alternate between watching the path ahead of me and looking at the names in my contact list. Around a thick tree trunk. The *C*s. Over a rock. *CO*s. Ragged breath scraped my nose and lungs.

I almost shouted with relief when I found *COLE*.

"Answer," I muttered when I heard the first ring. "Please answer."

"Ali," he said a moment later.

A sob left me. "Cole."

His concern came immediately. "Baby, what's wrong?"

"There was a car crash. They shot him. *Shot him.* He's dead. A bomb. Now they're after me, and I don't know what to do."

I could hear the static over the line, knew he was running as quickly as I was. "Where are you?"

"What's going on?" I heard Veronica ask in the background. "Where are we going?"

He was with *her.*

"I don't know," I said, too numb from the shock of everything that had happened to react. "I didn't watch."

"What's around you?"

"An abandoned road. A forest. I'm in the forest."

"Where were you before? What direction were you headed before the crash?"

"Nana's house." The words left me, barely audible as I panted. "Walked out of neighborhood. South, toward coffee shop. Picked me up. Farther south. Followed. Crash. Smoke. There's so much smoke."

"I'll find you," he vowed. An engine roared to life. Tires squealed.

"Cole," Veronica called.

That was the last thing I heard. I tripped over a limb and hit the ground with all the grace of a china shop bull, my cell skidding out of my grip. Frantic, I threw a glance over my shoulder for Shooter. No sign. Maybe he'd passed out from blood loss. Maybe he'd died. Fingers crossed.

I clambered to my feet, searched, but couldn't find my phone. Decided to leave it behind. My legs stiffened even as

I trudged deeper into the woods, and all too soon, I could barely chug forward an inch at a time. I scanned the area.

Bad news: as naked as the trees were, they wouldn't offer much coverage if I climbed.

Good news: Shooter would have to look up to see me.

Bad news: he could easily look up.

I had no other option. Using pieces of bark as handrails and stepstools, I shimmied my way up the tallest I could find. Every inch was agony. Finally I reached a large enough limb to support my weight and stopped, pressing my back against the trunk. I palmed the two daggers sheathed at my ankles and drew my knees up to my chest, trembling...waiting.

A horde of birds flew overhead, and a gentle wind whistled, hopefully masking the thunderous beat of my heart and the wheeze in my lungs. In a battle to the death, what would I do? I had no problem fighting zombies, ending them. They weren't people. He was.

He wanted to kill me. I should have no problem ending him, too. And there he was, inching from one tree to the other, using the trunks as a shield. He scanned one way, then the other, before moving on. He scanned up, and he scanned down, and—

Our gazes locked.

Instinct kicked in, and I launched a dagger before he could aim his gun. The tip embedded in his shoulder, flinging him backward.

Pop! He'd managed to squeeze off a shot. The bullet hit just above my shoulder, and bark flew in every direction. Some of it landed in my mouth, and I spat it out as I jumped.

Impact banged my teeth together. I tasted old pennies.

Go, go, go. I took several steps, intending to run—then I stopped. If I ran, he would probably find me again. There wasn't anywhere to hide. I could throw another knife and maybe stop him, maybe not. He could just shoot at me again.

It might be better to face him here and now.

Trembling, I turned and approached him. He was lying on the ground, his chest rising and falling in quick succession as he struggled to sit up. His gun had been knocked out of his hand and rested a few feet away.

He dived for it when he spotted me, but then, so did I. I beat him by a fraction of a second, straightening and pointing the barrel at him.

He glared at me. "You wouldn't."

"You're still wearing my dagger like it's this year's must-have accessory. Of course I'll shoot you." My trembling became more pronounced, the weight of the gun almost too much for me to handle.

He replaced the glare with a smug smile, saying sweetly, "You want to go to prison for murder, sweetness?"

"I want to survive, and we both know this would be self-defense." My finger twitched on the trigger. *Come on, Cole.* "Why do you work for Anima?" I asked to stall.

"Why not? The pay is good."

"You don't care that the company isn't interested in destroying the zombies? That they hope to make money off them?"

The look he gave me was pitying. "No need to give me a speech about right and wrong. I'd fight for your side if the price was right." As he spoke, he slowly angled to the side.

He was planning something.

I fired the gun, my arms jerking up with the recoil.

He grunted and pulled his leg into his chest.

"Move again," I said, "and I'll put a hole in the other one."

A mouthful of curses was hurtled at me. "I'm going to make you pay for this, little girl."

Threats? Seriously?

I shot his other leg. Just. Because.

As he writhed in pain, the bushes to my left rustled. Footsteps pounded. I backed away, intending to run. Or hide. Or both.

"Ali!" Cole called.

"Here!" I shouted back, overjoyed.

Cole and Veronica burst into my line of sight.

He'd brought her with him.

Cole seemed to take in the entire scene with only a glance. He dived on top of the man and whaled, throwing punch after punch. The gun fell out of my hand, and my knees gave out.

Now that I was safe, the surge of strength abandoned me completely. As my eyes closed, I saw Veronica watching Cole beat the man senseless. There was no recognition on her face. No remorse over what was happening to Anima's employee.

Maybe she wasn't the spy, either.

WEEP SOME MORE

Boom!

The sound reverberated in my head. Panting, I jolted up-right. Sweat poured from me, every one of my pulse points pounding to the beat of a riotous drum.

"You're all right. I'm here."

Cole's voice. Strong hands urged me back onto the mat-tress.

I blinked to clear my vision, but only darkness greeted me. "Where am I?" I croaked, the words scraping against a throat gone raw.

"Ankh's. He looked you over. Said you'd bruised a few ribs, had a few cuts, but were otherwise fine."

As the surge of panic eased, aches and pangs battled for my attention, and memories surfaced. I'd survived another car crash, but others had died. I'd been hunted, nearly killed. I might have killed another human being. Tears burned the backs of my eyes, and I gave a humiliating sniffle—or six.

Cole linked our fingers and squeezed.

The crack in my heart widened a little more, and warmth seeped through…until I remembered something else. He'd come to the forest with Veronica. I tugged my hand free.

"Ali," he said. A pause. Then, "Can you give us a minute?" he snarled.

Whoa. Where had—

"Tell us what happened, Miss Bell," Mr. Ankh said, and I realized Cole hadn't been talking to me.

I peered beyond his shoulder. Or tried to. The darkness was too thick to penetrate.

"Am I blind?" I shrieked.

"What?" Cole said. "No. Of course not. If you're having trouble seeing, it's because your eyes are a little swollen from the smoke and we put some salve on them. Don't worry. You'll heal."

Okay. Okay, then. "I have to call the coffee shop. Tell them I won't be in."

"Already taken care of," Cole said. "I told them you'd been in an accident."

"Nana—"

"Knows you're alive and well. I've stayed in contact with her and told her I'd try to have you home by eleven."

"What time is it?"

"Eight."

Three more hours; then I'd go home. Could I keep it together?

"Miss Bell," Mr. Ankh prompted.

I still wasn't his biggest fan, but the story poured out of me. I told him about Dr. Bendari. I told him about the photos and what I'd learned about my condition and the antidote. I told him about Justin and his sister. About the shooter, and the two drivers, and the chase through the forest.

I wished I could see his face, judge his expression.

"We found the photos in your pack," he said. "The others must have burned in the fire."

Some were better than none. "Which ones did I grab?"

"One of Justin's sister. Four of an Anima facility, and two of a computer screen with a formula they used for what I'm guessing is an improvement on the antidote."

Not a bad haul.

Mr. Holland cleared his throat, alerting me to his presence. "The shooter Cole brought in escaped his cage in this facility—the dungeon—and we have no idea how. He was weakened from blood loss. We don't think he could have survived for long out on his own without medical attention, but to our knowledge no dead bodies have been found. He could still be out there."

What Mr. Holland was trying to say without panicking me: the guy could still be after me. Just then, in the safety of the room, I didn't care.

"Now I'm going to check your eyes," Mr. Ankh said.

Footsteps. He gently wiped my eyes with a tissue, then flashed a muted light in front of my face. "I don't understand—ah, there we go. You're finally responding." As he continued to shine that light, the darkness began to thin at last.

"It's getting better already," I said.

"Good. We ran some more tests and found your antizombie toxin is significantly lower."

"The new antidote helped, then."

"New?"

"There are vials of it in my pack."

"I'll take one and see if I can replicate it. I'll send the others home with you."

"Thank you."

He stepped back, and Cole stepped forward. Our eyes locked, violet against blue. Need against... I wasn't sure what I was projecting at him. We—

—were standing in my bedroom. His expression was tortured, even sad, as he aimed a crossbow at my chest.

"I'm sorry," he said.

"Cole—"

—We were back inside Mr. Ankh's basement dungeon.

I blinked in surprise. Nothing had distracted us or gotten in our way, the usual reasons for a vision to end. This one had stopped all on its own.

Because he'd shot me and I'd died? Whatever. At least we'd had one. That meant a part of me was back to normal. I *was* better.

How long would it last, though?

Apparently I was going to do something so terrible Cole would feel his only recourse was to kill me. I couldn't even process that.

"I have no plans to aim my crossbow at you," he said tightly. "I won't. Ever."

I nodded. Really, what could I say?

That wasn't good enough for him. "You had to be right before. The visions have to mean something else."

I really, really hoped so.

"I'm not going to hurt you. Trust me. Please."

The very words I'd once—four times?—given him. "Okay," I said, and he exhaled with relief. I just didn't have room for another worry.

"Cole, call Justin and tell him to come by," Mr. Holland said. "I need to tell him about his sister."

I looked and found him standing beside the curtain separating my "room" from the others.

"I'll tell him." My pronouncement was quickly met with inquiring glances. "I know what it's like to lose your family. And I know you guys do, too," I added in a rush. They'd all lost someone in the war. "But with me, the loss is fresh. Jaclyn was his twin, and he loved her more than he loved himself. I felt the same way about Emma."

Mr. Ankh sighed. "Very well."

Cole made the call.

It wasn't long before Mr. Holland was escorting Justin to my bedside. He sat down opposite Cole, his expression closed off. He had no idea why he was here. My chin trembled as I said, "Justin, I met with a man named Dr. Bendari."

He nodded. "You've mentioned him before."

"Yes. He was…he was killed in front of me." Tears streamed down my cheeks, burning, leaving track marks, I was sure.

Justin softened. "I'm sorry."

"Before he died, he told me that your sister—"

With a pained groan, he jumped up, the chair skidding behind him. "I know. Don't say it. Don't you dare say it."

"You know?" Cole asked.

Justin closed his eyes, drew in a shaky breath. But that was it, his only reaction. And yet my heart broke for him. I knew what he was doing, because I'd done the same thing. I'd boxed up my grief and shoved it deep, deep inside.

He would feel better for a little while. Then, one day, someone would come along and say something, or he would see something, and the box would begin to open. All of those negative emotions would come pouring out, and he'd be helpless to stop them. He would break down.

"The leader, Mr. K, showed me pictures."

"Mr. K?" Mr. Holland said. "What does the K stand for?"

"I don't know. It's all anyone ever calls him." He lifted his chin. "Mr. K told me you were responsible, and it was my job to exact revenge. But I couldn't kill you, he said. Just had to spy on you." He offered us a cold smile. "He didn't realize I knew you better than that and knew you'd never hurt my sister—that he was responsible. So I've given him information, but nothing damaging. Just enough to make him think I'm playing his game."

"So you're the spy," Cole gritted out. "And you dared to send me on a wild chase? Why? To distract me?"

"Spy?" Mr. Ankh and Mr. Holland said in unison.

"No." Justin shoved his hands into his pockets. "You've got a traitor in your midst. I never lied about that, I just don't know who it is. Every bit of information I gave you is true. I want Anima taken down, and I want to help you do it."

The fierceness of his expression…the chilling determination in his voice…the hatred oozing off him all combined to scream *I'm telling the truth*.

"Spy," Mr. Holland repeated.

"I'll talk to you about it later." Cole nodded stiffly to Justin, a silent command to continue.

"My parents think Jace ran away. They worry about her, my mom even cries, but I can't bring myself to tell them that she's…that she's… Because I can't prove it, and I can't answer their questions. And now you know everything I know. So we're done here." Justin turned and stalked from the room.

Cole stepped forward, intending to chase, but I grabbed his arm. "Let him go. He needs to be alone right now."

Mr. Ankh and Mr. Holland watched as Cole settled back in his seat.

"Some privacy," Cole said, waving them away.

Mr. Holland rolled his eyes and left. Mr. Ankh opened his mouth, closed it. Then he, too, took off.

"I know you probably have more questions, but I want to talk to you about Veronica first. About what happened with her after our breakup."

"No," I said, anger suddenly rising.

He continued anyway. "I told you she went down on me, and I wasn't lying, but I didn't tell you that I stopped her before…just before. And I don't think you have any idea how difficult that was. With something like that, it doesn't always matter if a guy likes the girl or wants someone else."

"Should I give you a medal?" I snapped. I still hated the image of what they'd done.

"Yes. No." He banged his head against the side of my bed. "I'm screwing this up. Again."

"There's no reason to hash this out—"

He looked up, his gaze beseeching me. "There *is*. When you called me, I was with her." He latched onto my hand, holding tight enough to ensure I couldn't break free. "Nothing was going on, I promise you. I was telling her I wasn't over you, I wouldn't be getting over you and that I would be with no one but you."

My heart dropped into my feet.

I wanted to give in—so bad. *Can't give in.*

I'd warned him.

Take your refusal one step at a time. Otherwise I'd crumble like a cookie.

First step. "Cole," I said, plucking at the sheet covering me. "No. We're not going there. You're a relationship runner, not a sticker, and I can't go through another breakup."

He held me tighter. "Correction. I *was* a runner. I'm now a sticker. I get it now. I was letting fear make my decisions for me. I was so afraid of losing someone else, I was always looking for the expiration date. Not just with you, but with all my girlfriends."

Could a girl dance for joy and sob with despair at the same time?

Second step. "I'm glad you realize that, and that you're determined to move forward, but what happens if you also realize you never got over some of those other girls?"

"That's not possible. I want *you*. And I know you warned me, told me not to even think about crawling back. I know I messed up in the worst possible way, something I can promise you will never happen again. I know, but I'm still coming after you with everything I've got."

I might have sobbed.

Third step, the hardest. "Cole—"

"Shh, baby. Please. Listen to me. You're a part of me, and I'll take whatever you're willing to give me, for however long you're willing to give it." He rushed on, adding, "I've walked away from a lot of girls. Sometimes it hurt. Sometimes it didn't. But I always got over it, and thought I was better for it. I haven't gotten over you, Ali, and I'm definitely not better. I need you. Please," he repeated.

Another attempt at that third step. "No," I whispered. Together, we were a roller coaster. Up and down, up and down. Sometimes you just had to stay off the ride. "My answer is no."

He wasn't deterred. "I gave up too easily, and I'm not making that mistake again. I should have fought for you, just like you said. I realize that now. I didn't trust you. Well, I'm going to trust you now, because I can't live with the results of *not* trusting you."

As he spoke, every word wrapped in longing, he leaned forward, toward me. I absorbed the words, such beautiful, needed words. Soothing words. I wanted so badly to meet him halfway.

Tears filled my eyes, spilled over. Fourth step. The final. "I'm sorry. I can't. I just can't."

"Baby, don't cry. It hurts me to know I've upset you." He wiped the droplets away with his thumb. "Okay, we won't talk about this right now." He drew in a breath, released it. "Let's talk about the spy."

Definitely sobbed. "Yes. Okay."

"I know we suspect Gavin and Veronica—"

"I don't," I said, doing my best to remain calm. "Everything inside me says they're innocent."

He nodded. "Okay. I told you I trust you, and I do. I will. In everything, in every way."

I…didn't know what to say.

I gulped.

"That leaves Kat, Reeve and Ethan," he added, filling the silence.

"Ethan is the only unknown."

"Then we'll start with him."

We, he'd said.

A waft of air hit me, and I shivered with cold.

"May I hold you?" he asked.

I tried to say no, I really did. "Yes." I'd had a last kiss. Now I would have a last embrace.

He climbed into bed with me, gathered me against him.

I'd missed him. I'd missed *this.* His warmth enveloped me, and his strength soothed me.

Meaningless…

Right.

"We found your phone in the woods when we swept the area for more photos. You can text your grandmother." He pulled the device from his pocket.

I accepted gratefully and shot Nana a text to tell her I was okay, I loved her and I would be home by eleven, just as Cole had promised. Her response was immediate. Don't ever worry me like that again.

Me: Will try my best.

"Ask me something," Cole said after I'd set the phone on the cart beside the bed.

"Like what?" I said, confused.

"Anything you want to know. You ask, and I'll answer. I want you to get to know me better. Before, you said we didn't know each other well enough, that the vision brought us together."

Carte blanche? Yes, please. *So sure this is meaningless?* "Who was your first time?" I asked.

He snorted, saying, "Wow, okay. You aren't messing around, are you? And just so you know, I don't usually discuss these kinds of details with anyone. For you, though… I was fifteen, and she was twenty-one, the daughter of one of my mother's friends. I lasted about five seconds."

I tried to swallow my giggles, failed. "Ugh, I shouldn't be laughing at your extremely poor seduction skills. Because, Cole, that pervy woman totally took advantage of your childhood innocence."

He barked out a laugh, the sound rusty but so danged welcome. "You are too adorable for words."

"Why? It's true."

"Maybe."

Not maybe. "If a twenty-one-year-old man had sex with me when I was fifteen, would you be laughing?"

He instantly sobered. "Okay. Point taken."

"Tell me her name. I'm going to track her down and knock her teeth down her throat."

"As hot as that is, no. She's part of a past I'd now like to forget. But…I'm glad you never slept with anyone. I don't like the thought of you with anyone else, probably would have fed the fuc—uh, the *guys* more than teeth."

Must resist this possessive, charming side of him. "Do I get another question?"

"You get as many as you want."

He sounded determined.

I'd probably make him regret that.

"Did you sleep with Veronica?"

He stiffened, but he didn't hesitate to answer. "Yes. But it was over a year ago, when we were dating."

"Mackenzie?"

"Yes. Months ago, for a little while after we'd stopped dating. Then I met you, and that was over."

"Others?"

"Yes. You want the exact number?"

"No," I grumbled. *Yes.* Maybe. "Am I the only girlfriend not to go all the way with you?"

"No," he said. "But I wouldn't change anything about what we've done—and haven't done. I wanted—want—you ready for me, not sleeping with me because it's supposedly expected. I would wait forever for you."

Oh, glory, this totally meant something.

Are you sure you need to resist him? "Yes, well. You might have to." I cleared my throat. "Next, I have an observation rather than a question."

His arms tightened around me. "Go on."

"Sometimes you call Mackenzie and Veronica by cutesy nicknames. Kenz and Ronny. It's hurtful to the girl you're with."

"Do I?" He toyed with the ends of my hair. "I hadn't realized. It's a habit, I guess. We all parted as friends."

"Well, we didn't," I pointed out, now a little hurt by that, too. "I mean, we tried, but it clearly wasn't working."

He pressed his lips together to cut off a...frown? Smile? "A. Dor. A. Bull. Baby, I still wanted you, still considered you mine and didn't want to share you with Gavin. There was no way I could be friendly about it."

Dying here...

He kissed my temple. "Enough chatting. We've got two and a half hours before I have to drive you home, and I want you rested. If you're feeling better by Thursday night, I plan to take you to a party to celebrate the Tigers' winning football season. Since we don't have school on Friday, everyone always kicks off the four-day weekend early."

A chance to act normal. "I'll go to the party, one way or another. And I'm not tired."

He chuckled. "Sure you're not. Your eyelids are already half-closed."

"No, they're..."

I don't remember finishing that sentence.

I woke up in Cole's arms.

The alarm on my phone had gone off. He must have set it before he'd fallen asleep. He never even twitched, his expression relaxed, almost boyish, and I smiled as a deep well of affection spilled over. Looking at him now, no one would ever suspect his violent nightly activities.

Trina sat beside the bed, reading a book. When I stirred, she glanced up and said, "About time," and closed the cover. *Dare You To,* by Katie McGarry. "I want you to know I was upset when I saw the video of you going after Cole so viciously. I still don't understand it, but I'm sorry I never gave you a chance to explain."

"Thank you," I said, and I meant it.

Mackenzie strode into the room. "Heard voices," she said. Then, "Hey."

"Hey," I replied.

"You look better."

"Thanks."

Cole stirred, stretched.

"Okay, time for us to go bye-bye." Trina stood.

"But I just got here," Mackenzie complained.

Trina gave her a push toward the exit. "Ali, do yourself a favor and take a shower before he wakes up. Like, seriously."

Was I that bad?

The two strode from the room. I eased from the bed and nearly toppled to the floor as my knees shook under my weight. There was a bathroom around the corner, and though I was nervous about looking into the mirror, I did it.

Yeah, I was that bad.

There was no hint of Z.A., thank God, but my hair was styled in what could only be dubbed Last Year's Ugliest Rat's Nest. There was a big black bruise on my cheek, a slice in my lip, a knot on my jaw. *So pretty.*

Someone had cut away my blood-splattered clothing and put me in a paper-thin hospital gown. Three possible suspects. Cole, Mr. Ankh and Mr. Holland. There wasn't a front-runner, each equally bad. When Cole first saw me naked, I didn't want it to be like this.

Wait. *When?*

I'd just told him we weren't getting back together.

I'd meant it. Hadn't I?

Now, looking back on the conversation without the fog of anger and pain...and need...I wasn't so sure. What I did know? Staying away from him didn't actually have anything to do with a roller coaster. I'd never actually ridden on one, but I bet they were exciting. They had to be; people kept going back for more.

Was I punishing him for the hurt he'd caused me? Or was I simply afraid of losing him again and doing exactly as he had done?

Pensive, I took a quick shower, dressed in the T-shirt and sweatpants Mr. Ankh kept in the drawers. The first fit just fine. The second barely came to my ankles. Unfortunately Mr. Ankh did not keep a drawer stocked with bras and panties, so I had to go commando—the alternative to slipping back into my dirty underwear. I brushed my teeth twice and then my hair, wincing from the pain. Finally I emerged on a cloud of steam.

Cole hadn't moved from the bed, but now he was sitting up, watching me, his eyelids heavy. His gaze moved over me, lingering in certain places. "Com'ere," he said, his voice low and husky with want.

"We should probably leave," I hedged.

"We will. I want to kiss you first."

"You shouldn't... I shouldn't..."

"I'll make you glad we did," he said softly, almost...shyly.

How could I resist this new side of him?

Yet another one. How many did he have? Would I fall for each of them?

I crawled on top of him.

His big hands tenderly cupped my cheeks, the calluses on his fingers abrading my skin in the most delicious way. Moving slowly, giving me time to stop him, he lifted his head and pressed his lips against mine.

The cut stung a little, but I didn't care. I kissed him with all the pent-up need inside me. The need to taste him. The need to take from him and give to him. The need to brand him, to make him mine. All mine.

As our tongues thrust together, he shifted, rolling me to my side and hooking my leg over his hip. With the new angle, he'd created the perfect cradle and was able to scoot closer to me, practically fusing our bodies...rubbing against me, once, twice.

"You feel good enough for this?" he rasped.

"Stop talking and keep kissing."

He chuckled softly, and I nipped at his bottom lip. "Tell me if I hurt you."

"Still. Talking." I slid my hands under his shirt, tugged the material over his head. He fisted the hem of my mine, and the next thing I knew, the entire thing was being tossed over his shoulder.

Cool air brushed my skin, but the heat radiating from him quickly chased it away, even turned my blood to lava. I wrapped my arms around him, scraped my nails along his back. All the while he continued rubbing against me, back and forth, pressing, easing, pressing again...oh, yes...just... like...*that*.

"Ali," he gasped out.

The most amazing scent wafted from him. Pure, crisp. Familiar.

The urge to bite would follow.

"Ali," he said again.

I licked my lips. "Cole." If I could chew my way past skin, vein and bone, I could get to what I wanted. The heart of him. The—

No! I reared back and tumbled from the bed. "I need the antidote from my pack," I rushed out, crab-walking to the wall, widening the distance. "Now. Please."

He asked no questions. He hopped up, dug through the pack and rushed back to my side. There was a sharp sting in my neck before a cool river washed through my veins. And yet the river couldn't wash away the horror of what I wanted to do.

Cole stayed by my side, and I could still smell him. My gaze snagged on his hammering pulse, and there was a flood of moisture in my mouth.

"More," I said.

"That's too much."

"Just do it."

With a growl, he returned to the pack, found another syringe. He stuck me with more force, and another cool burst cascaded through me. My fascination with his pulse finally ebbed. The delicious smell faded. I sagged into the cold, hard floor, already crying.

"Better?" Cole asked.

"Better."

"Then why the tears?" He traced his fingers over the slope of my nose. "I'll get Ankh. He can—"

"No. No more tests." We already knew what was wrong. "I just want to go home." I'd give Nana a hug. I'd rest some

more, get stronger. By the time Cole picke
party, I'd be as good as new. *Please.*

"All right, but we'll need to put a shirt on you first," he
said, and I heard the thread of humor in his voice.

Oh, spank me. As Kat would say. I was sprawled out, shirtless. Braless.

My cheeks flushed, and I covered my chest with my hands.
"Good idea."

"Not my best," he said drily, "but I think your grandmother would approve."

"I think you're right."

He smiled, and for a moment, I felt as if everything really
would be okay. "Come on. I'll take you home."

CAN'T GO BACK TO YESTERDAY

Nana had waited up for me, and I hugged her as planned. She looked me over and twittered over each of my bruises and abrasions.

"I'm so glad you're okay. When Cole called and told me you'd been in a car accident, my heart almost stopped."

"I'm sorry," I said.

"Ali, I don't know what I'd do if I lost you."

"Nana, I…" Didn't know what to say.

"I know you're fighting for a good cause, but it's hard on me sometimes. Waiting and worrying."

"I'm sorry," I repeated, but I couldn't promise to morph into a normal teenager with normal problems, and we both knew it.

"Yes, well, enough about that for now." As she bustled around the kitchen to make me a sandwich, she changed the subject and said, "Are you and Cole back together? Or are you seeing two hot totties at the same time? Or are you single and just playing the court?"

Hot totties? Playing the court? "No, Cole and I aren't back together, but we *are* going to a party on Thursday. And Gavin… Well, he and I will only ever be friends."

"I think maybe you need to rethink things with Cole. He's good for you. You light up when you see him, and he can actually get you to smile. It's an honor few people receive."

I smiled so rarely? I hadn't noticed.

She slid the sandwich in front of me, and after I'd eaten every crumb, she put the plate in the sink and patted my shoulder. "Ali, bear, I know your mom talked to you about, you know, sex, so there's no need for me to mention STDs and babies."

Someone kill me. "Right. No need," I managed to croak.

"But I'm going to mention them anyway. I read that a lot of teens are too embarrassed to buy condoms, and that's one of the reasons teen pregnancy is so high, so, if you ever want me to, you know, buy you some, please just let me know. Not that I'm condoning sex at your age. I'm not. I really think you should wait until your emotions are as ready as your body."

Seriously. A gun to the head. A knife in the gut. Either would work. "Cole and I haven't had sex."

"But judging by the way you look at him, you've considered it and I'd guess you've come pretty close—"

"Nana. Please."

"Oh, all right. I just don't want to see you get hurt. Sex can be a commitment for a girl, and a mere moment for a boy and—"

"Nana!"

"Okay, okay. Go on to bed," she said, kissing my temple. "You look ready to fall over."

Cheeks burning, I stood and gave her another hug. "Love you."

"Love you, too. I'll see you in the morning before school."

I drifted to sleep the moment I was snuggled in the softness of my covers.

I wasn't sure how many hours passed before I noticed the light streaming through the curtains. A new day. I lumbered out of bed, my body far more sore than it had been last night. A hot, steaming shower helped, but not enough to keep me from wincing as I dressed in a pink T-shirt and jeans and dried my hair, leaving it down.

My door opened, the hinges loud. "Ali?" Nana said. "You awake?"

"Yes, ma'am."

"Good. You've got a visitor."

I frowned. "Who?"

Gavin stepped beside her and grinned. "Me."

Nana arched a brow at me.

I shrugged—I wasn't sure why he was here—then nodded to let her know I'd be okay with him.

For a moment, she wrestled with indecision. And I think if the situation had been any different—if I hadn't been a slayer, used to taking care of myself, if I hadn't been dealing with Z.A., fearing for my life—she would have forced us to go into the living room.

"You have ten minutes," she finally said, and walked away.

Gavin stepped inside and I was grateful he didn't shut the

door. Curious, I motioned for him to sit at the desk, then eased onto the side of the bed, across from him.

He laughed. "Afraid the vision will come true?"

Yes. No. Maybe. "What are you doing here?"

"Thought I'd drive you to school today."

"That's nice of you."

"Well, I'm a nice guy."

"I guess that depends who you ask," I said drily, and he grinned.

"Funny girl." He sobered. "I heard about the crash and explosion and wanted to check on you. You okay?"

"I'm sore and upset a man was killed in front of me, but yeah. I'm dealing."

"I'm sorry."

I nodded to acknowledge the words. My nose wrinkled as I caught a peculiar scent, distracting me. "What is it I'm smelling?"

"My manliness?"

I crossed my arms. "Seriously. What?"

"What do you mean?"

"It's like you couldn't decide on an air freshener, so you decided to use them all."

He gave another exuberant laugh. "Maybe that's exactly what happened."

"Or…you were with another girl or six last night? Oh, my gosh. That's it!"

He shrugged, unabashed.

"How do you get the girls to flock to you like that?"

"Besides this beautiful face?" he said, rubbing his jaw. "I can speak French, and they like it."

I gaped. "You speak French?"

His eyelids dipped to half-mast, as if they were too heavy to hold up. *"Je peux casser trois briques avec ma main."*

Grinning, I fanned myself.

He wiggled his brows. "Sexy, right?"

"Not going to answer that. So, what'd you say?"

"I can break three bricks with my hand."

I couldn't help it. I laughed.

He stood, drawing my gaze to the band of skin revealed as the hem of his shirt lifted from his jeans. Tanned muscles underneath. Beautiful. But I was happy to note I still felt nothing romantic for him.

"We should go." He held out his hand, waved his fingers.

His scent wafted to me once again. This time, hunger pangs followed.

Feed.

I moaned. Not again. Not here, not now. Not with him.

Fight this.

"Ali?" Concerned, he closed the distance.

Even though I told myself not to, I gripped him by the forearms. I rose to my tiptoes and put my nose at his neck, breathing deeply. *So. Good.*

"Ali?" Curiosity this time.

"You should run." Even as I warned him, I swung him around and pushed, sending him to the bed, on his back. As he bounced, I climbed on top of him. "Don't run. I need you," I said, only I wasn't speaking this time. *She* was.

She'd used my voice, putting everything she had into taking me over.

Gavin's brows furrowed with confusion, but he didn't protest as I leaned down…down…and pressed my lips against his neck. One of his hands actually tangled in my hair, holding me close, helping her.

"Let me shut the door," he whispered.

Stop! I inwardly screamed. *Please, stop.*

She laughed with glee. "No." Gripping his chin, she forced his head to the side for better access. He allowed it, his lower body arching into mine. He ran his fingers down my spine, cupped my butt.

She ran my tongue up the length of his throat.

He shuddered. "Yeah. I like that, but one of us really should shut the door."

"Forget the stupid door." She bared my teeth.

Hard bands wrapped around my upper arms and jerked me backward.

She struggled to free my body and get back to Gavin. So close! His eyes were wide. He was panting from exertion, his pulse thumping wildly. He was confused—no, now he was afraid. She'd made him afraid, and she knew the fear would taste so sweet.

"Her eyes are red," he gasped out.

"Ali! Snap out of it."

Cole's voice.

I tried to speak. I gurgled.

He tossed me on the floor and pinned me with his knees. She continued to struggle against him, turning my head in an effort to bite into his inner thigh.

He barked something. I don't know what. Then Gavin was there, placing something in Cole's hand. A needle. A needle Cole jabbed into my neck. A familiar cool stream bathed me.

I sagged into the carpet. Cole glared down at me, violet eyes crackling.

"Ali," he said.

"Yes," I croaked.

He eased off me. "You were trying to feed from him."

I rolled to my side and curled into a ball. "Leave. Please."

"Ali." Gavin this time.

"Get out of here." Cole scooped me up in his arms and carried me toward the bed.

Gavin was trying to lead my Nana away.

"Is she going to be okay?" she whispered.

"Yeah. I've got her now." Cole lay down with me still locked tight in his embrace.

He held me for a long while, whispering to me, smoothing his hands through my hair.

"I hate this," I said.

"I know."

"She took over, Cole. She used my voice, controlled my actions."

"The new antidote stopped her."

"For now. But we both know I can't take the antidote forever."

He kissed my temple.

"Cole."

"Yes?"

"If she takes over and the antidote doesn't work, I need you to—"

"Don't say it," he growled.

"—kill me," I finished anyway. "Please."

"That's not going to happen, Ali."

That wasn't what my instincts said. Maybe it was time to bring back my original to-do list, version two, but with a slight tweak. *Find a way to disable the zombie inside me. Kill the zombie inside me.* Addendum: *even if I have to die, too.*

I made it through the school day without incident. I hadn't wanted to go, but Cole had insisted, citing I couldn't afford another absence. He watched over me, making sure my zombie side didn't try to take over.

He even dropped me off at work, only to return an hour later and remain inside the coffeehouse for the rest of my shift. My coworkers stared at him, the guys frightened, the girls excited. Everyone whispered, speculating about who he was, and why he was there.

I think I blew their minds when I left with him.

"Any zombie sightings tonight?" I asked. The moon was high, full.

"So far, none."

"Shouldn't you be out there searching?"

"I traded nights with Gavin." His voice tightened. "He owed me."

"Don't fight him over me. Over what happened."

"I want to, but I won't," he said tightly. "You aren't mine. Not officially. Technically he didn't do anything wrong."

He dropped me off at home but didn't try to kiss me. I couldn't blame him.

I received a text from him the next day. No party tonight,

I'm sorry & I'm not ditching U this time, promise. My dad is sending me out of town. Will U miss me?

Me: I plead the 5th.

Him: I will definitely miss U.

Sappy girl. My heart soared.

I could have gone to the party with Kat, but after what had happened with Gavin, I wasn't going to risk it. And, to be honest, I was kind of bummed that I wouldn't be seeing Cole.

As the week passed, I received at least one text a day from him.

Friday.

Him: I can't stop thinking about our last kiss. U were topless.

Me (blushing): Thanks 4 the reminder.

Him: If U needed a reminder, I need 2 work on my technique.

Saturday.

Him: Are U eating properly?

Me: Yes, Dad.

Him: I kind of like the sound of that. How about a spanking??

Sunday.

Him: I actually watched the Hallmark channel 2day & thought of U. The main couple went at it like monkeys.

Where was he? Who was he with?

The questions began to plague me, but I never asked. I wanted him to offer the information freely.

Monday.

Him: I hear Z's were out last night in Bama. U being careful? I know U walk home from work—when I get back I'm teaching U how 2 drive, no more excuses from U.

Me: I'm being careful, swear. Are U?

Him: When I've got something precious 2 come home 2? YES.

How did all caps make me feel so warm and fuzzy?

Tuesday.

Him: I'm in a bunkhouse with six other guys, & 3 of them snore. Am considering offering myself 2 the Z's on silver platter just 2 escape.

Me: No girls there 2 soothe UR pains?

What a subtle hint.

Him: Why, Ali B, is that jealousy I detect??

Me: NO!

It was. It so was. Lying? Really? Over this? I kind of sucked.

He didn't respond, and I reeled with guilt.

Wednesday.

Him: There's only 1 girl 4 me.

After that, the texts stopped coming. Another week passed. I couldn't allow myself to worry. The more stressed I was, the weaker my body was, and I needed my body at top strength.

Mr. Ankh had managed to duplicate the antidote, so I had an unlimited supply. And as long as I injected myself three times a day, all signs of Z.A. were kept at bay.

Check off the list: *disabled*.

Side note: *for now*.

How long would the reprieve last? Not much longer, I didn't think.

But I wasn't going to worry about that today. Nana and I stood on Kat's doorstep, a glass partition between us and warmth. Just as Nana raised her hand to ring the bell, an apron-wearing Kat stepped into view. She smiled when she spotted us.

She was pale today. I'd gone to a few of her dialysis appointments and knew she'd had one late last night. She had three a week, sometimes four, and they were grueling on her, but she never complained—more than a dozen times.

"Hurry up before you freeze us all!" she said, waving us in. Flour streaked her cheek, and there was a smear of something red on her chin. "Oh, and Merry Christmas."

This morning, I'd called for Emma, needing her face to be the first I saw on Christmas, just as it had been when she was alive. She'd arrived with a huge smile and hadn't seemed to mind that she was dead (in body) and that our family wasn't together. I was trying not to mind, as well.

Nana had given me a glass heart, with tiny pictures of my mom, dad, grandfather and sister peppered throughout. I would cherish it forever. I'd given Nana a bracelet with a charm to represent every member of our family.

Two guys sat in the living room with Kat's dad, Gary. All three guys stared at the TV, riveted by the football game. *My* attention became riveted on one of the guys and I stumbled to a halt, nearly dropping the pumpkin pie I held.

"Cole," I gasped. He was back. He was here.

He hadn't called or texted me.

Three pairs of eyes swung in my direction.

Gary stood and grinned. "Nice to see you again, Ali."

"You, too," I said with a distracted nod.

My gaze remained locked with Cole's, my heart careening

out of control. I waited for a vision, hoping, praying, but...
no. Not this time. "When did you get back?"

"Three days ago," he admitted through tight lips.

Three days. Why had he stopped texting? Had he met
someone else? I swallowed the questions I clearly had no
right to ask, but couldn't swallow my hurt. "Well, I'm glad
you're okay."

Kat patted me on the butt. "After I explained to Cole the
consequences of not coming, he was more than happy to
show up."

"Threatening people again, Katherine?" Gary tsked.

"Always, Daddy."

"It's one of the things I like best about her," Frosty said.

Gary ignored him and looked to Cole. "I'm sorry about
that, son."

"Don't be." Cole looked me over, seeming to drink me
in, and I shivered. "I wanted to be here."

Then why hadn't he contacted me? Why a renewal of the
hot-and-cold treatment?

Nana swept into the living room, taking a seat between
the two boys. "I've missed you guys, and it hurts my heart
that you never come by anymore. So, now you're going to
make it up to me and tell me what's been going on in your
lives."

"Come on," Kat whispered to me.

I followed her to the kitchen. "What did you threaten
Cole with?" I asked when we were alone.

"I told him I'd set you up with my cousin Rick."

"And that worked?"

"Like magic."

I fit the pie between the giant turkey and the stuffing. The rest of the counter was covered with bowls of broccoli and rice casserole, cranberry sauce, green beans, corn, gravy, mashed potatoes and to my surprise, spaghetti.

"You did all of this?" I asked.

"Everything but the spaghetti."

"Which you have because...?"

"Of my rules. I only eat what I'm craving, and I was craving my dad's spaghetti. He got up earlier and made it for me so he'd be out of my way when I needed the kitchen."

How sweet was that? "Well, what can I do to help?"

"Exactly what you're doing. Stand there and look pretty. The rolls are baking, and as soon as they're done, we'll be ready to consume like the manimals we are."

Cole stalked into the room. He didn't say a word, but grabbed my hand and led me away, much like he'd done Halloween night. I glanced back at Kat. Just as she had at the club, she gave me a thumbs-up.

He didn't stop until we were on the front porch, the cold surrounding us.

"You have to stop doing that," I said.

"What?"

"Tugging me around without a word."

"And give you a chance to refuse?"

Good point.

"How are you?" he asked, peering deep into my eyes, searching for...what?

"I'm good." I licked my lips. "How have you been?"

"Busy. My dad was upset that I didn't tell him about the spy sooner."

"Is that why he sent you away?"

"One of the reasons. By the way, he's been following Ethan and so far hasn't found anything suspicious."

Were we on the wrong track? "What's another reason?"

He sighed. "He thought I needed to take a break from… Well, it doesn't matter."

From me, then. I did my best to mask my wounded feelings.

"Don't," Cole said, brushing his fingertips over my cheek. "He thought I needed some perspective, so he sent me to Georgia to help Gavin and Veronica's usual crew."

"They went with you?" I shrieked. Then I cringed.

He actually smiled. "No. They stayed here." He tugged at the hem of my shirt, causing me to stumble into him. "So…I got you a Christmas present."

My eyes widened. "But I didn't get you anything. I mean, I thought about it, but I didn't—"

"That's okay," he said, his grin widening. "I can't give yours to you now. I have to wait till you come over to my house. Having you there is all the gift I need."

What could he have gotten me?

His expression suddenly darkened, surprising me, reminding me of a storm about to break. "About Gavin, and what happened with him."

Guilt pierced me, and my gaze dropped to my feet. That was right, we hadn't talked about it. Not really. "I'm sorry. He came over. We were in the middle of a conversation, an innocent conversation, and the hunger hit."

"Don't be sorry. I came over, too, hoping to drive you to school. Your grandmother mentioned Gavin was there, so

I sprinted back to your room. I was planning to clean the floor with his face. Then I saw you on the bed with him, and I admit, it looked bad. But then it hit me. I know you. You wouldn't kiss me one day, and another guy the next, and you wouldn't kiss a guy with the door open while your grandmother was in the other room. The truth hit me a second later, and I grabbed you before you could bite him."

"You trusted me," I said, shocked to my soul, "despite what you saw." That was absolutely, utterly *huge*.

"Yes," he said. He fit his hands against my jaw. "I told you I did. I'm in this thing, Ali. All the way."

"But…why did you stop texting me?"

I saw the ice frost over his eyes, and I shuddered. "My dad was monitoring my phone feed."

Oh. The ice wasn't for me, but for his father.

I looked away from him, trying to give myself time to think, and caught a glance of my reflection in the glass. I stumbled backward.

Zombie Ali was back.

Flickers of red burned in her eyes, and the black smudges on her cheeks were thicker. She smiled at me, waved—and then, through the reflection, I watched her step out of my body, away from the glass.

THE RAIN OF BROKEN GLASS

With the tick of a clock loud in my ears, I watched Z.A. glide off the porch and into the driveway. She paused to look back at me and crook her finger, a silent command for me to follow. A need to know her purpose consumed me, and I stepped off after her.

Uncheck from list: *disabled*.

"Ali," Cole called.

"Tell Nana I'll be back as soon as possible. And don't come after me." Who knew where she was leading me?

Z.A. continued moving forward, across the street, into someone else's yard. The sun was hidden behind thick gray clouds, creating a dreary backdrop. Any moment, I expected fat raindrops to fall, soaking and freezing me. I wondered how she would react—if the water would even touch her.

"Food's ready," Kat called. She must have stuck her head outside the door.

I never heard Cole's reply.

Z.A. ghosted through a fence, and I was forced to climb it. Thankfully, no one was in the backyard to accuse me of trespassing. We repeated this process three more times before coming to a creek with tall, brittle grass.

She glanced back at me and giggled.

"What are you doing?" I demanded.

"You'll see," came the singsong reply. She continued on.

I stayed in place, debating the wisdom of my actions. But then, the farther away she moved, the more I felt pulled toward her. Compelled. My feet kicked into gear without any prompting.

She reached another front yard, another fence. Again she ghosted through. Again I climbed. We exited the backyard, came to a street, and she stopped to once again crook her finger at me. I closed the distance, putting us nose to nose.

"How are you doing this?" I snapped.

She reached up, traced her fingers over my cheek. I couldn't feel the pressure of her touch, but I could feel the coldness of her skin—a cold far worse than the air around us.

I shuddered.

"So pretty," she said.

I jerked away from her reach. "I can't return the compliment."

Her lips curled in a slow smile. She leaned forward and whispered, "If I can't have your body, I'll have to get rid of it and free myself from our connection."

In the distance, I heard the honk of a car. A second later, something hard slammed into me, throwing me a good distance. I landed, lost my breath and then the "something" slammed on top of me, pushing out any air that had managed to remain in my lungs. As pain tore through me, the sound of squealing tires registered.

"Are you trying to kill yourself?" Cole shouted.

I glanced up. A car zoomed past the place I'd just been standing, swerving, finally managing to straighten out. I looked across the road, my gaze colliding with Z.A.'s.

I saw fury.

"You disappeared for a moment," Cole said. "I couldn't see you. I don't think the driver could see you. Then you reappeared and the car honked, but you just stood there."

"I…" Wasn't sure what to say. Z.A. had just tried to kill me.

"That's it. I'm officially signing on as your keeper." He stood, hefted me over his shoulder as if I were a bag of potatoes and carried me toward Kat's house.

"Let me go, Cole. I'm going to *murder* her!" I beat at his back, not to hurt him but to gain his attention. He never slowed.

Z.A. watched us warily as we closed in on her.

"Murder who?" he asked casually.

"Her! My tormentor." I would force my own spirit out of my body, and I would summon the fire and burn her to ash—whether the fire was white or red. If she could survive without me, I could survive without her. Surely.

He turned a corner, and she stretched out her arm. He had no idea. I, however, felt her as she was sucked back inside me.

Argh! "Why can't you see her? You can see other spirits."

"I don't know. Maybe, like you, she has special abilities. Maybe she can cloak herself."

That…made sense. Terrible, scary sense.

"Tell me everything that just happened, Ali. Give me the long version, but make it short. I want the full story before we reach Kat's."

"She left my body, and she tried to kill me, and now she's back inside me, and she'll be more careful, because she's smart and she knows I can't get to her until she leaves me again." Frustration overwhelmed me, and I banged my fists into his back with more force. "I hate this. I hate her!" I accidentally kneed him in the stomach, but he held firm.

"Ali, calm down."

No. I was done with calm. I twisted my upper body, sliding off his shoulder. He couldn't stop me, but he made sure to catch me before I hit the ground. I came up fast, trying to avoid him, intending to run. The moment I was alone, I was going to freaking *kill the zombie inside me!*

He grabbed my wrist and kept me in place. "Calm down," he repeated. "I mean it."

Calm? Calm! I. Utterly. Exploded.

I launched myself at him, throwing a left, right, left. He ducked, then arched, then swung in the other direction, but I never managed to land a blow and that angered me all the more.

"What's wrong with you?" he demanded.

"My life is changing again, and just when I think I'm on the right road, something else happens to prove me wrong, and I'm so tired of being wrong and I think I'm mad at you because you stayed away an extra three days, and now you're back but I know it would be best if I stayed away from you and everyone else because I could hurt you, seriously hurt you, and I just don't know how much more I can take!"

I swung at him. Again he ducked.

"You think it was easy to stay away from you?"

"Yes."

"My dad told me he'd keep his nose out of my relationship with you if I'd keep away from you for ten days. Just ten. No contact. I think he hoped the craving would fade. Do you know what day this is, Ali? Nine. I couldn't make it one more damn night."

I stilled, panting. I didn't know what to say to that.

He stared over at me. "I love you, Ali. Do you understand? I love you."

Wait. What? "You love me?"

"I've never said those words to another girl." He lifted his chin, squared his shoulders and braced his legs apart, as if preparing for a real battle. "You're stubborn, too curious for your own good and you've become a wild card, but yes, I love you."

He.

Loved.

Me.

"And that's how you tell me?" Snarling, I kicked out my leg and knocked his ankles together. He fell backward, and I followed him down, throwing more punches—but these lacked any heat. My heart was too busy doing somersaults.

He rolled me to my back and pinned my arms over my head. I bucked, but he weighed more than me, and I couldn't dislodge him. Our gazes met, and tension smoldered between us, hot and strong and undeniable.

"Let me go," I rasped.

"Never again," he replied.

I was breathing so heavily my chest rubbed against his. Our legs were tangled, and I could feel every inch of him. I ran my tongue over the seam of my mouth, anger giving way to need.

"Tell me how you feel about me," he croaked.

"No," I said, shaking my head. I couldn't. I wouldn't. If I said the words—*I love you, Cole, love you so much I ache*—he would keep his word to never let me go, and he had to let me go. "I told you. I'm no good for you right now. That's the only thing that hasn't changed, and I'm not going to risk—"

"So you're not ready. Okay. I get it. We'll revisit this subject later." He lowered his head, until his nose brushed mine.

I breathed him in. "No. Not later."

"Fine. We'll finish it now. I want you, and you want me. For now, that'll have to be enough." He smashed his mouth against mine, his tongue thrusting deep, and I moaned at the perfection of it. His taste, his heat, his strength, his... everything. This was what I'd missed. This was what I'd craved. Us...together. Not out of anger or hurt. Just need.

I wrapped my legs around his waist and arched up, unable to help myself. He released my hands, and I immediately tangled my fingers in his hair.

"This doesn't mean we're back together," I said.

"Whatever you say, Ali-gator."

The pressure escalated, almost unbearable, yet not enough—*not enough, must have more*—as his hands roamed over me, kneading my breasts, doing things to the centers...such thrilling things. With all the different emotions still rampaging through me, my skin became more sensitive, my blood all the hotter; my nerve endings hummed. I loved it. I hated it.

I loved him. Had to tell him. Couldn't tell him. I had to stop this, but I wanted more. So much more. Desperate for as much skin-to-skin contact as I could get, I slid my hands under his shirt and scoured my nails over the ridges of his spine. He hissed in a breath.

"I love it when you touch me," he said.

I did it again, and the kiss spun out of control, until we were nipping at each other, and he was pulling at my clothes, and I was pulling at his, and oh, this was going to happen, wasn't it? Here and now, outside, in the cold. I wasn't sure how much time I had left, so nothing would stop me from stealing this moment.

"O-kay. I should have guessed this was why you both took off so unexpectedly."

Nothing except Frosty.

Dang it! I was so sick of interruptions!

Cole sprang away from me, assuming a battle-ready position.

Frosty rolled his shoulders, hard and intractable, and just as ready. "Don't bother trying to get rid of me. I'm not leaving without Ali. Nana is worried."

"Fine. But you will turn around," Cole snapped.

Though he looked as if he wanted to protest, Frosty obeyed.

My cheeks burned, and my heart pounded as I sat up. Cole helped me right my disheveled clothing before righting his own. Our gazes locked for a long, strained moment, and we both knew there were a million things we needed to say, but couldn't. Not now.

Later, he mouthed, hooking a strand of hair behind my ear.

I should tell him no again, that this was it, the end. I might be dangerous to his health, but he was dangerous to my self-control. Instead, I found myself nodding.

Cole kept his arm around me while we walked back to the house.

"So, listen, Ali," Frosty said. "I know I haven't been your biggest fan lately, and I'm sorry. I like you, I do, and I know you're going through something tough right now, but I saw what you did to Cole and I imagined you doing it to Kat. I can't let you do it to Kat," he said raggedly. "She isn't strong enough to survive."

"I understand," I replied. "I've been so careful around her. If ever I feel even the slightest urge come upon me, I leave her and dose up on the antidote. I don't want to see her hurt, either."

His nod was stiff, but it was a start.

"Ali, honey."

Nana's voice pulled me from a deep sleep.

"I'm headed to the grocery. Is there anything you need?"

"What time is it?" I asked on a moan.

"Eight."

Too early. It was the day after Christmas and I didn't have anywhere to be until five. I would have liked to sleep till four. I'd stayed up late, trying to taunt Z.A. into leaving my body and fighting me. She'd ignored me, and I'd finally fallen into bed. Now I was tired. So very tired.

"I'm good. Thanks, though."

"All right, then. I'll be back in an hour or so."

I put a pillow over my head. Heard footsteps. The whine of my door as it shut.

I wasn't sure how much time actually passed before I heard cabinet doors banging shut, then silence, then the slam of the front door, as if Nana had left again.

I wanted to get up and investigate, but I just didn't have the energy.

The doorbell rang.

I rolled out of bed, pulled a robe over my tank and shorts and stalked into the living room. Expecting Kat and a thousand questions about what had happened with Cole, since we hadn't had a moment alone to talk, I opened the door. Gavin leaned against the frame, a formidable sight with his pale hair spiked back from his face and his eyes glinting ice.

He'd come over several others times, but I'd reverted to ignoring him.

"You need to stop avoiding me, and we need to talk about what happened the last time I was here," he said.

"Okay," I said, and moved aside. I could be brave. "Fine."

He stomped his way inside, and I shut the door.

"Just…give me a few minutes first. I just got out of bed." I raced into my room, brushed my teeth and hair, then threw on a T-shirt and jeans. I glanced at the mirror as I raced back out and gritted my teeth when I saw Z.A. grinning smugly at me.

I scowled at her. "Soon," I told her. "We're going to have a showdown."

She smirked.

"You hungry?" I asked Gavin when I reached the living room. "You want some breakfast?"

He eyed me suspiciously, but said, "Sure."

I put biscuits in the oven, fried bacon and whisked up some gravy. He watched me, but didn't speak (or try to help). I didn't push him. When everything was ready, I slid a plate in his direction.

"No eggs?" he asked.

"Wow. Your gratitude is humbling."

A smile teased the corners of his mouth. "What? I like eggs."

My lips twitched, as well. I hadn't liked seeing him so formal. I sat beside him, and we dug into the food.

Finally he said, "I've been thinking about things, and I'm sorry I didn't realize what was going on with you sooner... sorry I put my hands on you and tried for more than a few licks. I've gotten to know you over the past few months, and I should have realized you never would have made a move on me while your grandmother was a few feet away. And you *did* try to warn me."

Wait. *He* was apologizing to *me?* Not what I'd expected. "Well, I'm sorry I tried to eat you."

His lips stretched in a full-blown smile this time. "From anyone else, those words would be a turn-on. You, not so much."

I laughed. "I have to admit, I'm a little surprised you didn't kill me the moment you realized what was happening."

"I won't lie. I thought about it. I mean, I know you had pulled out of similar crazes before, but this was the first time one had been directed at me. Problem was, I would have had to go through Cole to get to you, and I would have had to kill him to get through him, because he wouldn't have stopped shielding you any other way. That boy really loves you."

I turned away to hide the elation surely shining in my eyes; someone else had noticed his feelings for me—and came face-to-face with Zombie Ali.

She stood beside me, and she was still grinning.

Looked like our showdown was today.

Heart slamming against my ribs, I pushed my spirit out of my body without any hindrance; chilly air enveloped me. As I shivered, I reached for her, but she giggled and darted behind the couch.

"You're gonna get it now," I said.

"Ali?" Gavin said.

"Do you see her?" I pointed.

"See who?"

Cole thought she could shield herself, and maybe she could. "Stay here. You can't see or hear the zombie in the room. She cloaks herself, and I don't want her to hurt you."

"Can't catch me," she sang.

"I can't wait to prove you wrong." I dived for her, and slammed into the top of the couch. Had we not doused all of our furniture with the Blood Lines, I would have ghosted through. But we had, and now everything was as solid to my spirit was it was to my body. Couldn't forget again.

As I threw my legs over the edge of the couch, I summoned the fire. Small red flames began to crackle at the ends of my fingers. Red? Why red? Z.A. was no longer inside my body.

Maybe her toxin was still there. Maybe—

The cushions beneath my palms burned to ash. What the heck?

Z.A. zoomed past me, and I reached for her. I missed, popped to my feet and gave chase. In the kitchen, she circled the granite-topped island. I threw myself on top, sliding…falling…the entire structure crashed into the floor, taking me with it.

"Stop," Gavin shouted. "Ali, you have to stop this."

Laughing, Z.A. raced down the hall, into Nana's bedroom. She jumped on the bed. Again I dived for her. When I hit the pillows, the bed disintegrated, and I toppled to the floor.

Dang her!

She slipped out of Nana's room and into mine. I was right behind her. She knocked a chair into my path. I picked it up and threw it across the room, aiming for her head.

The chair burned midway, ash drifting through the air.

Can't blow this chance.

"Nah, nah, nah, nah, you can't catch me."

"—happening?" I heard Nana say. "How? Her body is in the kitchen. She can't be doing this! No one can! There's no one in here."

Her voice penetrated the dark determination urging me on. I blinked, forcing myself to focus on the natural world. Nana stood in the doorway, pale and trembling, gazing around the room I'd destroyed. Gavin and Cole stood beside her.

I took a step toward her.

The boys moved in front of her, blocking her from my path.

"Get her grandmother out of here," Cole said to Gavin.

Gavin took Nana by the arm and drew her back. I reached for her again, realized my hands were still ablaze with the red flames and froze with horror.

Had contact been made, I would have reached past flesh and burned her spirit—and what happened in the spirit always manifested in the flesh. She would have died.

I would have killed her.

Exactly what Z.A. must have wanted. She'd failed to kill me, so she'd gone after my loved one *through* me. And I'd let her. I hadn't stopped to think about the wisdom of my actions.

"You're worse, Ali," Cole said, holding out his hands in the most nonthreatening gesture he could manage, approaching me. "I'm afraid we won't be able to control you if something like this happens again."

"Cole."

"Don't agree with me," he interjected. "Don't say anything. Just think about what you're doing right now, all right?"

But I had to tell him—no, I couldn't. He was right. If I believed it, I would receive whatever I said.

I looked behind me, unsure what to do about Z.A.

She wasn't there.

My gaze darted to the mirror. There. She was there.

Back inside me. Scowling.

"Put the fire out for me, okay?" Cole said gently.

I tried, I really did, but the flames only grew hotter, only spread faster.

"I'm sorry, Ali," Cole said, and reached for the minicrossbow he kept stashed at his ankle. Rather than load it with an arrow, he loaded it with a syringe. Then he stepped out of his body, so that we were spirit to spirit.

He paused, then said, "I thought about the vision, and stopped carrying arrows. Realized I might need antidote instead." A second later, a sharp pain hit my neck.

In a blink, he had another syringe loaded and flying at me. I experienced another sharp sting. Warmth rushed through me, and yet the flames began to wane…finally vanished.

He loaded a third. "This is a sedative."

I felt a third sting, and whatever the sedative was, it worked quickly. Darkness fell over me, and my knees collapsed. I knew nothing more.

My head pounded as I blinked open my eyes. I lay on… my bed? No, the mattress beneath me was too narrow to be mine. Gingerly I sat up. Dizziness struck me, and I moaned.

"Hey, Ali-gator."

Cole's voice. I breathed deep in an effort to clear my head, saw the haunting beauty of his face. I hated to look away, but curiosity got to me. We…were in a small bedroom I didn't recognize, with log walls and planked floors.

"You're in a secluded home Ankh owns. It's twenty miles from my house," he said, "but they aren't highway miles, so it takes me forty minutes to get here."

I'd been banished.

My expression must have fallen to reflect my dismay, even though I knew this was for the best, because he added, "You're too dangerous to be around others right now, sweetheart."

Acid eroded my throat, and I choked. "I know, and I probably should have been sent here weeks ago. But, um, how long will I be allowed to stay?"

"As long as it takes."

To heal…or to die, whichever came first. "Cole…"

"You have to quit your job, I'm sorry. Your grandmother is going to call your boss. And when school starts back up, she plans on speaking to the principal about allowing us to set up a computer so that you can remotely attend your classes. If they won't let you, you'll have to quit the district for a home school program."

"Cole," I said, trying again. What did I want to say to him? I wasn't sure.

He shook his head, dark hair falling and hanging in his eyes. "I took your journal," he continued. "I'll go through every page, every passage. Emma told me the key to saving you is in there."

"When did you talk to her?"

"This morning. She came to see me, and I think I freaked out my dad. He wanted to know why I was talking to air."

I smiled.

Cole pushed out a breath. "Better."

"What?"

He cupped my cheek. I reached up, wrapped my fingers around his wrists. "I hate that you've been hurt by all of this, I *needed* to see you smile."

No wonder I was drawn to this boy. "How can you still like me after everything I've done?"

His thumb brushed away a tear that had seeped from the corner of my eye. "It isn't that I like you, Ali, it's that I can't *stop* liking you. And I don't want to stop. Besides, you were trying to end a zombie. That's admirable."

"You saw her?"

"I did. Her shield slipped for just a second when Gavin and I stepped in front of your grandmother. She was so angry her eyes glowed bright red. When I met her gaze I think it scared her, because she raced back into you."

"We haven't seen the end of her." I could still feel her, a presence in the back of my mind. A heartbeat I had failed to stop.

"We'll find a way to beat her," he said, and I nodded despite my fears.

Emma had said the same.

Nana had said the same.

Heck, I had said the same.

Now…I wasn't so sure.

"You know," Cole said, "my mom once told me a boy would know he'd become a man when he stopped putting himself first. She said a girl would come along and I wouldn't be able to get her out of my mind. She said this girl would frustrate me, confuse me and challenge me, but she would also make me do whatever was necessary to be a better man—the man she needed. With you, I want to be better. I want to be what you need. Tell me what you need."

I need…you, I thought.

Mackenzie had told me she hoped Cole would meet a girl he couldn't live without. In that moment, I was pretty certain I was that girl. And it was odd to me. So much had happened. So much had yet to happen. But this…thing between us *hadn't* changed.

"Will you get on the bed with me?" I asked.

His smile was wry. "I will give you anything but that. I know us, and I know what happens when we kiss and if I get up there, we're going to kiss. And I'm good with that, crave it, but there's no one here to stop us."

"You think Zombie Ali will take over again?"

"Maybe she will, maybe she won't, but it's not that."

"Good. Because I don't think I'll want you to stop," I admitted softly.

He brought my hand to his mouth, kissed my knuckles. "And you don't know how happy that makes me. But I don't have a condom and I refuse to risk you, even by pulling out. I don't have a disease or anything like that," he added in a rush. "I've never been with a girl without a condom, but getting you pregnant is a very real concern."

For once I wasn't embarrassed to talk about this with him. "Oh. Well, that sucks."

"Believe me. I know." He stood and looked down at me. "I stocked the fridge with all the food I know you like. I expect you to eat it."

"I will."

"I'll come back tomorrow. And every day after."

"I'll miss you," I said.

He reached for me. Balled his hand just before contact. And then he walked away.

This time, he looked back more times than I could count.

I'M LATE FOR A
KILLER DATE

I felt sorry for lab rats. Like, really sorry. Every morning, Mr. Ankh came to the small house in the woods and drew my blood, checked my vitals. I'd been poked and prodded so much I had to look like a junkie.

I'd told him all the testing was unnecessary.

I was going to die here, and I knew it. All I could do now was enjoy the time I had left.

And I was. Because of Cole. But deep down, I admitted this wasn't the way I wanted to go out. I wanted to die fighting, taking as many zombies as possible with me.

I sighed. Cole visited me every afternoon, and he always brought Nana. I could tell she'd asked him for a ride and he'd been unable to tell her no, because there was always a gleam of frustration in his eyes. But even though he wanted to be alone with me, he never complained.

Once, he pulled me aside and said, "Your grandmother is the toughest coc—uh, sex block I've ever come across."

I'd giggled.

On New Year's, the three of us sat on the couch, watching a movie Nana had brought. I was too distracted by Cole's heat and scent and general deliciousness to care what it was. I occupied the middle, he had my right, with my head on his shoulder, and Nana had my left.

When the credits finally rolled, I said, "I really am sorry about the new furniture you bought, Nana." I'd said the same words every day. Guilt hadn't left me.

"I told you. Furniture is replaceable. You aren't."

"But the money—"

"Ali Bell," she said, wagging a finger at me, the charms on her bracelet slapping together. "If I hear one more word about money, I'm going to scream. I mean it."

"Good luck with that," Cole said. "Ali is the most stubborn person I've ever met."

"Hey," I said.

"It's not an insult if it's true." He kissed my temple. "I wish we could stay longer, but my dad is expecting me back."

And he probably had some zombie hunting to do.

Nana kissed my cheek.

Cole gave me a long, searching look that told me he would be on me if we were alone. Then the two of them were in his Jeep, driving away. I watched from the window, trying not to cry.

Needing a distraction, I walked through the home, my bare feet thumping against the wooden floors. All of the mirrors had been removed. There were hundreds of books—

romances, mysteries, science fiction and fantasy, nonfiction, a Bible—plus a TV and a fully stocked refrigerator. Cole had made sure I had my own clothes, an iPod loaded with Thousand Foot Krutch and Krystal Meyers, two new favorites, and the picture of Emma and me that Nana had found.

A chirp sounded from my phone. I check the screen, and smiled widely as I read Cole's text.

I'm coming back after I check in w/my Dad. If U could B naked by the time I get there, U would really save me some time.

He was coming back.

To-do list: *kiss him. Touch him. Own him.*

Hinges creaked, jerking me out of my dreamy elation.

I frowned. I knew the sound well. Someone had just opened the front door, but it couldn't have been Cole. I grabbed a knife from the kitchen counter and pressed my back against the wall. Slowly moving forward, I peeked around the corner. My heart hammered erratically.

Footsteps closed in.

Squeezing the weapon's handle, I jumped out, prepared to attack.

A girl screamed. Her hand flattened over her heart as she scrambled backward, away from me.

"Kat?" I asked, lowering my arm.

"Don't you dare stab me, Ali Bell." She stepped from the shadows, moonlight washing in from the window and spilling over her. She anchored her hands on her hips, becoming the very picture of ire, despite the paleness of her skin and the bruises under her eyes. She wasn't well. "You have some explaining to do. We finally figure out where you are and come to your rescue, and you almost murder me before we can complete the job."

We?

Shock barreled through me at an alarming rate. "I have missed you so, so much, Mad Dog, but you shouldn't have come."

"Like I could really leave you out here once I learned Ankh had you deported to Siberia."

"I'm only twenty miles away, and he did me a favor. I like it here. And how did you learn about it?"

She ignored my question, saying, "Of course you don't like it here. There are bars on the doors and window."

Those bars were meant to protect people *from* me. "I don't want to leave."

Her eyes narrowed. "Are you suffering from Stockholm or something? Because I know my Ali, and she would never move away without saying goodbye, and she would never choose to live here."

I wasn't going to get through to her, was I? "Seriously, how did you find me? And who is *we?*"

"I can answer that." Ethan moved to her side, watching me warily.

Ethan? The potential spy?

Great. Wonderful. This couldn't get any worse. "Fill me in before I have a panic attack."

"Well, for starters," said another female, "I found out about the zombies."

Reeve stepped up to Kat's other side.

Okay. It was officially worse.

"My dad doesn't know that I know," Reeve said.

"When you disappeared, Reeve did some investigating, and told me what she learned," Ethan said, "and that's when we discovered the zombies, and your whereabouts, and decided to bring Kat in to help us save you. You're welcome, by the way. Do you have any idea what we had to do to hack into Mr. Ankh's computer and get the coordinates to this place?"

I hoped that was rhetorical.

"In other astonishing news," Kat said before I could process everything I'd been told, "Frosty and I broke up—of course. He wouldn't tell me where you were being held."

"I doubt he knows."

She waved away my words, and I noted her hand was trembling. "Semantics."

"You have to stop pushing that boy away every time you're feeling vulnerable," I said. "One day he's going to stop coming back."

Her mouth opened, closed.

"Enough chatting," Ethan said. "Let's get out of here."

"Wait." The three of them weren't safe with me, not without a trained slayer nearby, but if there were zombies out there tonight, they wouldn't be safe without me. I'd have to escort them to their car, wherever it was. "Give me a minute."

I stalked to my bedroom, dressed in a black shirt, camo pants and combat boots. Then I strapped blades to my ankles and wrists, sheathed a larger revolver at my waist and stuffed two smaller ones in my pockets.

I phoned Cole but immediately went to voice mail. Either his phone was now turned off or it was in use. Probably in use. "Ethan, Kat and Reeve just showed up at the cabin. I'm going to walk them back to their car. I'll also try to do a little detective work on Ethan. Call me."

When I returned, Kat wouldn't meet my gaze. Dang it. I shouldn't have stepped into her business. I thought I'd learned my lesson in the butt-in department.

"I'm sorry," I said, and squeezed her hand.

She nodded, the action stiff.

I read the fine print: not forgiven. I sighed. "Follow me." When we reached the front door, I drew in a deep breath for strength. My hand trembled as I twisted the knob, and my knees knocked as I walked outside. Cold air enveloped me, hugging me with unwelcoming arms of ice.

A forest loomed around me. A dusting of snow had fallen, leaving the slightest glaze of white. It was pretty. I stiffened, searched the darkness…but saw nothing out of the ordinary.

"Where's your car?" I asked.

"On the road outside the forest," Ethan replied. "We didn't want your captors to hear us coming."

I'd talked to Cole about the area, and knew we had a two-mile hike.

"I'll take the lead," I said. "You guys will do what I say, when I say, without any argument. I'm serious. I love you girls with all my heart, but if you question me out here, I'll knock out your teeth, I swear I will."

Kat finally cracked a grin. "Look at you, all forceful."

Ethan stepped in front of Reeve, protecting her from my supposed wrath. Did he understand I'd do what I'd threatened—and so much worse—to him?

"Stay behind me." I entered the forest, listening. Footsteps crunched behind me. No sound in front of me. Good. We maneuvered around trees, going downhill, minute after minute ticking past.

"So, Ethan," I said, "have you ever heard of Blood Lines?"

"No."

"Then why do you have them around your house?"

"Your friends asked me the same question, and I'll tell you what I told them. I don't know."

He was lying. He had to be lying.

"How did you and Reeve meet?"

"Can we not do this now?" he asked tightly.

"You're right. We'll wait till we get to the car. We'll put the girls inside, and then you and I will walk away for a little chat." Afterward, there was a chance only one of us would be walking back.

"Ali?" Reeve said. "What's going on?"

He nodded readily. Too readily? "The car."

"I'll let Ethan explain it later." We reached a small, round clearing, the sky no longer shielded by the tops of the trees. A big white cloud shaped like a rabbit appeared to be… pulsing. There. Gone. There. Gone. There.

I stopped, stiffened. Smelled nothing I shouldn't.

Hungry, a voice whispered. *So hungry.*

Hmm. Smells so good.

Must have.

Want.

Mine. Mine, mine, mine.

The zombies *were* out, and they were nearby.

"What is it?" Ethan whispered, his voice trembling.

"Kat, Reeve, climb the trees behind you," I demanded, palming a dagger and a gun. "Now!" I scanned the line of trees in front of us. At the far right, a bush shook, snow dancing to the ground.

A second later, Emma burst through, even though I hadn't summoned her.

Panic bathed her expression as she ran, her tiny arms pumping quickly at her sides. "They're coming!" she screamed. "Leave! Alice, leave now! It's a trap!"

A trap? I couldn't leave *and* protect my friends. What was more, I wasn't going anywhere without my sister. I launched into motion. As I raced, I tried to push my spirit from my body, but Z.A. wrapped her hands around me and anchored me inside.

"Let go," I screamed at her.

She laughed.

Behind Emma, zombies broke through the thicket.

They were chasing her?

Oh, heck no. She was a spirit. They were spirits.

They would be able to touch her.

Not on my watch.

The closer we drew together, the faster we both pushed ourselves. Then she darted *through* me, the contact shoving my spirit out of my body, making Z.A. shriek in pain.

I stumbled backward, my body remaining in front of me. The cold should have thickened. Instead, I felt embraced by warmth. I looked back. Emma had finally stopped—in front of Ethan. She swung her fists at him, but no contact was made. He stood beside a tree, his hand resting on the bark. He was unaware of what was happening around him, watching me, his expression grim. The girls were nowhere to be seen. They must have obeyed me and climbed.

I turned back to the zombies, aimed the gun and squeezed the trigger. *Boom, boom, boom! Boom, boom, boom!*

Bodies fell…only to crawl back up. I threw down the gun, the clip empty, and grabbed a second dagger. The creatures came closer and closer, moving faster than ever before. Almost within reach… For the first time in weeks, those red, evil eyes were utterly focused on me. Eager for a go at me? Oh, yeah. Whatever the reason—had Emma done more than freak out Z.A.?—I was once again a target. I pounced.

My daggers slashed through one throat, two, six, then severed a spine, two, eight, rotted arms continually reaching for me. Blackened teeth chomped at me. At least no other whispers bombarded me. I arched backward, forward, avoiding being grabbed. I turned, stabbed. Turned, stabbed, staying in constant motion, knowing a single moment of hesitation would lose the battle for me.

I swung a zombie in front of me, using him as a shield as I spun around and stabbed his partner in the side. Black goo sprayed in every direction. Then I decapitated my shield.

No one else made a play for me, and I realized a wall of writing bodies had formed, blocking the others.

I climbed out, on alert, and my new targets stalked around me as if pondering the best course of action.

Some were mindless. These were not. And they weren't just stalking around me, but were inching closer and closer, closing in. I exploded into motion—*crap, I'd lost my daggers.* I slammed the heel of one hand into the jaw of the zombie on my left, and the heel of the other into the throat of the zombie on my right.

As multiple other arms stretched out, I rolled to the ground, knocking several of the creatures off their feet. Coming up with two new guns, I aimed, fired, aimed, fired, taking no more than a second for each action, but always swinging my arms to ensure that I got the zombies closest to me.

I shot a zombie in the face, and both guns clicked. Out of bullets.

As a new horde approached me, I pressed the button on the side of the handles, causing blades to extend from under the barrel of the guns. Gnarled arms reached for me. I crossed the weapons in front of me and hit two creatures in the temple, twisted, hit two more, twisted, hit two more—

A hard fist slammed into my jaw.

Stupid stars, winking at me. Still I managed to duck, missing a second blow and forcing the zombie behind me to take the brunt of the impact. I straightened, grabbing another zombie, intending to use him as a shield, but his arm detached. I stumbled to the side, my momentum jacked. One of the creatures shackled my wrist and tugged me to the ground. Jerking free, but losing my hold on the weapons, I rolled, once again knocking down several of the zombies.

"Light up!" I shouted.

The smallest of flames flickered across my knuckles, and it was white. Relief speared me.

Footsteps behind me.

I twisted, reached out to brush my fingertips against the

zombie closest to me. He didn't ash, but he did hiss and stumble away from me.

He came back for more, the fool, and I did it again. This time, he batted my hand away, determined. Someone stepped up behind him, stopping him, attaching a metal collar to his neck. He sagged to the ground, motionless.

I looked around, confused.

Hazmats surrounded me, and they were snapping collars on the rest of the zombies.

Realization sent me backpedaling, but I ran into something solid. I turned, already swinging, and nailed a Hazmat in the chin. He stumbled to the side and would have given me a clear shot to my friends, but three other Hazmats took his place.

Before I realized what was happening, a collar was being snapped around *my* neck, sharp electrical pulses shooting through me. Suddenly I couldn't move, could barely breathe. Panic filled me, joining the adrenaline rushing through me, and my body wasn't sure how to react. Keep fighting, or shut down.

"What are you doing?" I heard Kat scream. "Let her go!"

She could see me? The collar, maybe...

Keep fighting. Definitely keep fighting. I tried to stand, but my legs refused to cooperate.

"You want me docile? Leave the girls out of this," I tried to shout, but only gurgles escaped.

"Ethan?" Reeve gasped. "Help us!"

"You told me you wouldn't hurt Reeve," Ethan shouted.

Instant comprehension. He knew the Hazmats, because he was one of them.

He was the spy—no doubts about that now—and he had gotten some of his information from Reeve. When I'd lived with her, she'd known my schedule. The rest he must have gotten by watching me.

He'd covered his tracks very well. I still felt stupid. I should have known.

Someone crouched in front of me and removed the clear panel from his mask. He had to be in his fifties, with salt-and-pepper hair and thick lines around gunmetal-gray eyes.

He offered me a sad smile. "I hate that matters have come to this, Miss Bell, I really do, but my daughter is sick, and I suspect you're going to be her cure."

WHO STOLE THE POISONED TARTS?

My spirit was dragged to my body, the collar removed by one Hazmat while several others forced the two halves of me to join. At the moment of connection, I jolted into motion, determined to fight these people with everything I had. Some of the Hazmats were not in spirit form, however, and one of them managed to slam a hard fist into my temple.

Dizzy…

Slowing…

Still I fought.

I heard a whoosh of air, felt a sharp stab of pain in my arm. I patted blindly at the spot and dislodged a small dart.

The dizziness spun out of control, helped along by…a drug? I swayed, bones liquefying, knees buckling. When I hit the ground, I was roughly hauled to my feet, my hands tied behind my back, and there was nothing I could do about it. A black hood was draped over my head, and I was stuffed into a vehicle, driven I don't know how many miles. Time ceased to exist. There was only here, now. Darkness, rising panic. Where was Kat? Reeve?

I listened for movement—or whimpers—but heard only the wet slosh of tires, the zoom of passing cars and the soft hum of the radio.

Stay calm.

Easy to think, so difficult to do. Tremors racked me, and sweat beaded over my skin. The blood in my veins was somehow a dangerous mix of too hot and too cold.

After we parked, I was towed outside with the *kind* aid of two guards. We ascended a flight of steps and entered a pool of warmth. A heated building? I heard footsteps. A *ding*. We stopped, and the world around me jostled. We were in an…elevator?

Another *ding*. Again I was towed forward. We stopped several more times, and I imagined my surrounding went far beyond grim. A dungeon, like Mr. Ankh's. A torture chamber, with wall after wall of deadly weapons once found in the Middle Ages.

We entered a room with a deluge of new sounds. Moans, groans, rattling metal.

Other prisoners?

Can't stay here. Act! Gathering every ounce of strength I possessed, I struggled for freedom. I managed to head-butt one of my captors and trip another, and we all tumbled to the floor. Before I could run, someone fisted the back of my shirt and lifted me to my feet. The ties were cut from my wrists, and I was thrust forward. As I tripped to my hands and knees, I thought I heard Kat and Reeve gasp. Hinges groaned, and a door slammed. Trembling, I ripped off the hood and blinked as the bright light in the room stung my eyes.

We were in a laboratory. There were computers, strange equipment I didn't recognize and a handful of humans wearing lab coats. There were also cages, with collared, frenzied zombies locked inside.

Locked inside—like me.

And in the cage next door to ours was a girl I'd thought dead. Jaclyn Silverstone.

She was dirty, her hair in tangles, her far-too-thin body stretched out on a cot. But she was alive, and in that moment, she stopped being my enemy and became my best ally.

"They're not allowed to talk to or look at us," she said weakly. "Mr. K is too afraid they'll start feeling guilty and set us free."

The horror of the situation struck me, followed by rage, and I lumbered to my feet. I had to know if she was right, and threw myself into the bars, shaking the entire cage. "Let us out!"

As Jaclyn had promised, everyone ignored me.

"Hey!" Kat called, stepping up to my side. There was a tremor in her voice. "She's talking to you. You better listen or you're gonna regret it."

Again we were ignored.

Soft sobs echoed behind me. I turned to see Reeve standing in the center of the cell, her arms wrapped around her middle. Tears streamed down her cheeks, little pink track marks left behind.

"He betrayed me," she said with a sniffle. "I caused this.

I talked to him, told him everything I discovered. I just…
I never suspected he already knew what was going on, that
he was pushing me to find out more for him, that he was
using me. *Using me*."

Kat raced to her side.

I threw one last look at the lab coats—no one met my
gaze—before striding to my friends. Reeve verged on the
edge of a breakdown; I recognized the signs.

"You couldn't have known his plan," I said, doing my best
to sound calm, rational. But when my words registered, I
realized I'd lied. She *could* have known—if I'd told her what
was going on when she'd first expressed interest. "Your dad
has cameras everywhere. He will have seen what happened
in that forest. He'll find us."

He had better find us.

Kat nibbled on her bottom lip. "I'm so sorry, Ali, but
Ethan helped us disable all the cameras. He said he didn't
want anyone to be able to see or stop us from rescuing you."

The brightest hope I'd had died a quick death, and I
pinched the bridge of my nose. This was bad. Really, really bad.

But I had three small hopes left. The first, Emma. She
could warn Cole. The second, the message I'd left him. The
third, Justin. He might know the truth about what had happened to us. But…was he truly on our side?

I did my best to keep my expression neutral as I urged the
girls to the back of the cage and onto the cold, concrete floor.

"What are we going to do?" Reeve whispered.

"Yeah, Ali, what?" Kat asked, her usual bravado gone.

"Right now we're going to rest," I said with a small smile. I glanced over at Jaclyn. "I'll think of something. Promise."

Hour after hour ticked by with agonizing slowness. I summoned Emma, but she didn't appear. I studied my surroundings, taking in every detail. The same glow I'd seen in the forest, when I'd tracked the spy, streaked the floor and walls in here. Zombie toxin, maybe?

There was a camera posted at the top right corner of our cage, recording our every move and word.

There were no beds for us, no blankets and the toilet was out in the open. The number of lab coats thinned out in an unhurried but continuous stream, until only two people remained. The others would be back, though. I knew they would.

I stepped up to the bars blocking me from Jaclyn. Up close, I could see the gauntness of her cheeks.

"How long have you been here?" I asked.

"A little over a month, I think. I lost track of time."

"We thought you were dead."

"Only in my favorite dreams." She shrugged, the action weak. "Mr. K wanted a way to control Justin, to force him back to Cole...to you. Rather than tell him I was a prisoner, and risk him spending his time searching for me, he told my brother Cole killed me."

Mr. K. The guy running this show. Ms. Wright's replacement. The man whose daughter was sick—the girl I was somehow supposed to help.

"I've tried to escape," she said. "I think that's why they keep me undernourished now. So I stay pathetic and feeble."

Good plan. Fatigue had added weight to each of my limbs, and my eyelids felt as if they'd been replaced by sandpaper. Blinking was a terrible chore. *Can't allow myself to fall asleep.* An opportunity to do something, *anything,* might present itself.

"People come in, but they never walk out," she continued. "Mr. K likes to experiment on cancer patients. I think maybe he's trying to cure them, because he's always upset when they die, but he's sucked it up worse than a Hoover. The patients are now the zombies that you see here."

He'd made an army of zombies out of cancer patients? The man was seriously unbalanced.

"What kind of security does he have?" I asked.

"There are always guards outside the room, monitoring us. I don't know how many. And they've got their version of the Blood Lines all over the place, even the bars, so our spirits can't leave and alert another slayer."

No wonder Emma hadn't shown.

Another hope withered.

At 7:58 a.m. the doors at the far end of the room slid open, and the grinning man from the forest entered. Two tall, armed men flanked his sides, and the group approached my cage. Kat and Reeve were huddled together, leaning on each other, their eyes closed and their breathing even. Their adrenaline had crashed, I think, and when sleep had finally come, they'd been unable to resist.

"You're coming with us, Miss Bell."

Jaclyn reached through the bars and squeezed my wrists. "It's going to hurt. I'm sorry."

Metal rattled against metal as the cage door was unlocked.

The armed men pounded inside, and my heart beat in tune with their angry steps. I wouldn't leave my friends easily and threw a punch. My knuckles connected with the nose of the guy on the left. Blood spurted, and he howled with pain. Before I could do the same to the other guy, he grabbed my arm and twisted it behind my back, pain exploding through my shoulder.

Cuffs were slapped on me and I was shoved out of the cage. That. Easily.

"Hey! What are you doing? Let her go!" Kat called, the commotion having roused her.

The zombies erupted into a flurry of motion and sound. Grunts, groans, shuffling footsteps.

Hungry...

Feed...

Soon...

Now...

As the whispers reached my conscious, making me tremble, I was led into another room. There was a chair; something usually found in a dentist's office. Beside it was a padded stool, a table with different-sized blades and syringes strewn across the surface and some kind of machine that looked like a car engine.

As I was strapped to the chair, I fought for freedom.

"Calm down, Miss Bell," Forest Guy said. "We're going to talk, you and I."

"Screw you."

He ignored me. "I'm Kelly Hamilton. I don't usually share my name—I prefer the anonymity of Mr. K—but you and

I are going to be closer than most. You, my dear, may call me Kelly."

Hamilton. Like Ethan Hamilton. Kelly had to be his father.

More of a betrayal than I'd realized.

And oh, glory, I wasn't meant to leave this laboratory, was I? That was why he felt so comfortable sharing his full name, his link to Ethan. It had nothing to do with closeness.

He sat on the stool and tugged on a pair of latex gloves. "I must admit, you have been a difficult girl to find. Just when I decided you could help me, you disappeared."

"For good reason."

"And what would that be?"

"I'm dangerous." *You better believe it, jerk.*

"Yes. I was told you'd developed a few zombielike tendencies. The fact that you're still alive, your body healthy and whole, intrigues me."

I snapped my teeth at him. "If you aren't careful, I'll show you those tendencies firsthand."

He gave my shoulder a comforting pat. "I know you're scared, and I'm sorry for that, but you can rest assured that what happens in here is for a very worthy cause. My daughter is dying, Miss Bell, and I must find a cure."

Ethan's sister. Leukemia. "Exactly how do you think I can help?"

"Unless you slayers use your fire to ash, the zombies possess the ability to live forever. It is my hope to harness that ability for humans."

"That's ridiculous. The zombies live, in their way, but they never stop rotting."

"And even that, in itself, is a miracle, Miss Bell. Think about the possibilities. If we can figure out how, and why, the rotting occurs, then we can figure out how to eliminate it as a side effect and save human beings from death."

"Zombies *are* death, in every sense of the word. Those tendencies you mentioned make me want to kill people."

"A small price to pay for eternal life." He held up an empty syringe and waved the needle in front of my face, making sure he had my attention. "Just think. Your actions in this laboratory will help save countless lives."

Maybe. One day. But what about the countless lives lost in the meantime?

He wanted to save his daughter. I got that. I did. I'd want to help Nana, Cole, Kat and all of my friends if the situation were reversed. I'd be desperate to help, actually—I already was. Watching Kat's decline was a true horror. But this wasn't the right way.

"You love your daughter," I said, "and I'm betting she loves you. Would she want you to do this? To hurt people in order to help her?"

His lips compressed into a thin line. "This is going to sting, but I'll be as gentle as I can." Leaning over me, he wound a tourniquet around my upper arm and stuck the needle in the soft tissue of my inner elbow.

I cringed, watching as crimson filled the belly of the tube.

"We're going to figure out what caused your body to embrace the zombie toxin, and yet not actually kill you or even cause you to rot." He removed the tourniquet and bandaged the puncture wound.

He's too determined. You're not going to talk any sense into him.

Gotta work with what you've got. "You don't need the girls for this. Let them go. They have nothing to do with our war."

"Your concern is admirable, but we actually do need the girls. We want to keep you malleable, and they are our insurance card."

I knew that wasn't all Kat and Reeve were to him. They were witnesses.

I had to get them out of here.

"I'll promise malleability if you let them go."

"You'll give it anyway. Now, are you light-headed?" he asked. "I've got a cookie with your name on it if so."

I would have preferred evil straight-up, with no dash of kindness.

"Very well. We'll move on. What comes next is going to be far more painful for you, and I'm sorry for that, but I need to know what your body can take...and what it can't. Your strengths and your weaknesses, if you will. I also need to know what happens to the zombie toxin when your body is placed under tremendous stress." He held up another syringe; this one had a thick green liquid swirling inside the tube.

My bonds stretched taut as I tried to scramble away. "What's that?" I demanded, unable to mask my tremble.

"An isotope of adrenaline and other goodies meant to speed your body into a fight-or-flight response, to put you under that tremendous stress I mentioned. My hope is that you'll recover swiftly, and the toxin won't be able to overtake you and harm you."

I had nowhere to go, no way to twist, as he jabbed the needle in my arm and injected me with fire. Molten lava spread through me, burning me up, melting all of my organs.

Sweat suddenly poured from me. Maybe blood. I couldn't tell—my vision hazed. Muscles I hadn't known I possessed jerked painfully, and both of my hearts kicked into a dangerously swift rhythm. *Boom, boom, boom, boom,* no pausing, no slowing, just pound after pound against my ribs. I bit my tongue to keep from screaming.

"Stop it," I gasped out, my lungs squeezing tight. "Stop it right now."

"Don't worry. It won't last long. Just a few minutes." He smoothed a hand over my brow. "I'm not a terrible person, and I don't like to see you worked up. But I'm also a determined person. I have to save my daughter, Miss Bell, and if that means destroying the world and everyone in it to do so, I will."

"Criminal," I managed. "Deserve…prison."

"That's the pain talking. I take no offense." He stood and taped electrodes to my temples, neck, wrists, belly and ankles. "We're going to keep track of what happens to your spirit, too."

He grabbed another syringe of green liquid. Before I could protest, he'd injected me a second time. Another stream of lava blazed through me.

My back bowed of its own accord. This time, my heart thumped with so much force I expected to hear my ribs crack. I couldn't stop my screams. They came, one after the other, scraping along my throat, until fists seemed to wrap around my neck and squeeze.

"Interesting," Kelly said, pressing his fingers into my carotid. "Your body and spirit are weakening at a rapid rate, and yet there's something inside you that's strengthening."

My eyesight blurred, but I think I saw Zombie Ali standing in the corner of the room, watching me.

"Why won't you die?" she snapped.

Yes. She was here. Was she the thing that was strengthening?

One step, two, she approached me. Floated, really. Pale hair tangled around a face now completely smudged. She grinned, revealing teeth still stained with blood. "It's just a matter of time now."

I closed my eyes to block her image.

"There, there," Kelly said. "That's enough. We'll take a break."

I felt another sharp sting in my neck, though this one was accompanied by ice rather than fire. My heartbeat slowed, and I sagged into the chair, a wet, soggy mess.

"I must admit," Kelly said, as he made a notation in a notebook, "I was hoping to see the red fire. I was told it hurt the slayers *and* the zombies, yet not you. And that makes me wonder...what did it do to you?"

Z.A. stood just behind him, and I was careful not to meet her gaze.

"What would you have done if you'd seen it, huh?" I panted. "I would have burned the chair and, fingers crossed, you."

"There's an extinguisher in the ceiling, directly above you." He motioned to it with the tip of his pen. "With the press of a button, I would have you doused."

"Maybe."

"Definitely." He tapped the pen against his chin. "I know. We'll see if the red fire makes an appearance when I introduce more zombie toxin to your system." He set the note-book aside and held up another syringe, this one filled with black goo.

What? "No!" I struggled against the leather straps. They tore into my wrists and ankles—held steady. Blood dripped onto the chair, the floor.

Z.A. clapped. "You'll never be able to stop me now!"

"You'll kill me," I said, snubbing her, "and you won't learn anything new. Won't help your daughter."

Kelly shook his head. "I've done this to others, Miss Bell. I know what I can give, and what I can't, and still keep a person alive."

He didn't understand. The words rushed from me, desperate. "I'm different. Don't do this. Please, don't do this."

"Calm down. This is an engineered version of the toxin, made not to infect you permanently but to burn through you in about half an hour. You won't even need the antidote to improve."

"No, you don't understand. I—"

He stuck me with the needle.

ALL THE MONSTERS
WANT TO PLAY

Many times, as a little girl, I'd looked at the home my father had built and considered it a prison. Only twice had I
fought my forced incarceration, screaming and yelling at my
parents about the unfairness of it all. Not just for me, but for
Emma. She had no life, no friends.

And maybe that was why the two of us had been so close.
We'd only ever had each other. We understood each other,
because we'd been trapped in the same boat, in the middle
of the same storm.

Then my dad had begun to train me in the art of self-
defense, and I'd discovered I had a talent for it. It had given
me something to do, something to think about, something
to look forward to. But when it had come to the zombies,
he hadn't known many tricks.

Those I'd learned from Cole. Under his tutelage, I'd

begun to feel confident, maybe, at times even undefeatable. But none of that training helped me now.

Though I struggled with all my might against the hold of the guards, they managed to drag me back to the cage.

HUNGRY!

NEED!

SOON!

MINE!

No longer whispering, the zombie thoughts now shouted through my mind—an echo of my own thoughts. I could smell the sweetest, purest perfume in the air…wafting from the guards, from Kat and Reeve, from Jaclyn.

Mmm…so good…

Z.A. had stepped back inside me, and I could feel her hunger. Why she hadn't attacked Kelly while she was out of my body, I didn't know. Unless she couldn't. She hadn't gone after Cole or Gavin, either. Maybe, as long as she was tethered to me, she was bound somewhat to my will.

"Stand at the back wall," one of the guards yelled. Kat and Reeve had rushed to the bars upon spotting me. "Now!"

The girls obeyed, probably desperate and willing to do anything to get to me, and the door was opened. I was thrust inside, the door slammed behind me. Strength had long since abandoned me, and I fell to my hands and knees.

The girls rushed to my side, the sweetness of their scents so strong I had to be drooling.

"Get away," I croaked. "You have to get away."

"Do what she says," I heard Jaclyn demand. "It's for your own good."

What would one taste hurt?

"What did they do to you?" Kat demanded.

"Oh, Ali," Reeve breathed.

"Now!" I crawled away from the girls and huddled in the far corner of the cell. I wrapped my arms around my middle, my entire body trembling from residual pain. From cold and weakness and fear and dread and hunger...oh, the hunger...

I banged my head into the brick. *Can't think about the girls. Can't think about how easy it would be to overpower them, to hold them down and work my teeth past skin and muscle and into—*

No! Can't think.

I banged harder, faster. So much harder. Black spots appeared behind my eyelids, and I smiled with my first wave of relief. The end of my torment was coming, sneaking in... would soon arrive... I sighed happily as I sank into blissful unconsciousness.

When I woke up, the world was, strangely enough, a much brighter place. I hadn't hurt my friends. I'd been at my worst, hunger-ravaged and desperate, but I'd kept to myself.

Some part of me—my love for Kat and Reeve, maybe— was stronger than Z.A.

I could do this, win this. I could fight and overcome.

This time, I actually believed it.

I put together a new to-do list. *Do whatever's necessary to escape with Kat, Reeve and Jaclyn. Come back with Cole and the other slayers. Destroy Anima—start with Kelly.*

To escape, I needed strength.

For strength, I needed food.

We were each given a small, dry sandwich and told to

make it last—it was supposed to be our breakfast, lunch and dinner.

Amendment. *First convince someone to feed us.*

A little while later, I was escorted to Kelly's chamber of horrors and strapped to the chair, electrodes taped all over me.

Kelly sat beside me. "See. I told you the toxin wouldn't kill you." Grinning proudly, he patted my hand like Pops used to do. "Now, let's talk before we begin today's testing."

"Let's not. I'm too hungry."

He ignored me, saying, "We know where each of your friends lives, but what we don't know is if they possess any unusual abilities, like you. More specifically, I'd like to know if any of them are able to heal supernaturally fast."

"I'll trade answers for food." False answers.

His expression hardened. "I admire your spirit, Miss Bell, but it's going to get you into trouble. I told you I would do whatever was necessary to help my daughter and I meant it."

"Cheeseburger. Fries. Chocolate shake."

He stickered me with more electrodes, these attached to the funny-looking machine, and flipped a switch. Volts of electricity shot through me, sharp and hot and carnivorous. I opened my mouth to scream.

The pain stopped as swiftly as it had begun.

Desperately trying to suck oxygen into deflated lungs, I glared up at my tormentor.

"Now, I'm sorry I had to do that, but you brought it on yourself. Thankfully for you, I'm willing to try again. Do any of your friends possess the ability to heal supernaturally fast?"

"Pizza," I rasped.

Frowning, Kelly flipped the switch.

The pain lasted longer this time, my heart actually stopping in my chest before restarting on its own.

On and on we continued. He would ask a question about the slayers and their abilities, and I would name a food—if I could speak. I was pretty sure my brain had turned into a cherry Slushie.

"Pay attention, Miss Bell."

My head rolled in Kelly's direction. He thought to break me, and with my body, he was succeeding, but he was only strengthening my resolve.

"If you don't want to talk about the slayers right now, we won't, but we're not quite done with today's session. You see, I sent a man to capture you. He shot Halim Bendari, and someone else shot his driver. I haven't seen or heard from him since. Do you happen to know where he is?"

"Try looking...up your butt."

He popped his jaw—and flipped the switch.

The chair shook with the force of my shudders, the pain acute, gut-wrenching and soul-zapping. Kelly was going to kill me. How could he not? After a while, even my skin began to vibrate, and it didn't stop when he turned off the machine. My bones felt brittle, as if they would break at any second. My lungs had to be filled with glass rather than air. Every breath was agony.

I...came to as Kelly tapped my cheek. I must have passed out.

"That's enough for today," he said with a sigh. "We'll pick

this up again tomorrow. I hope you'll be in a more agreeable mood."

I think he'd pushed me harder than he'd intended.

"Lasagna. Spaghetti. Garlic bread."

He scowled. "I don't want to do it, but I'll strap your friend Kat to the table. I'll make you watch as I infect her. Will you talk before I inject the first needle?"

Monster! I bared my teeth at him, wishing so badly I could do more.

He smoothed the soaked hair from my forehead, knowing he'd reached me on a level the machine hadn't. "Tomorrow we'll have another chat. If you fail me as you've done today, I'll use the already sick Katherine Parker."

He knew. He knew she was sick, and he was still going to use her.

I was unable to support a single pound of my own weight and had to be carted back to the cage. I wanted to assure Kat and Reeve I was okay, but the moment the guards dumped me on the floor, darkness swallowed me.

"—so sorry," a male was saying. I recognized his voice. It made me angry. Angry enough to force myself out of my deep sleep, the only thing preventing me from feeling the pain still lingering in my body.

I blinked, looked through eyes glassy from the strain they'd endured. Ethan stood at the bars of our cage, pleading with Reeve to forgive him for the part he'd played in our capture.

The anger magnified, giving me strength. Snarling like the very animal I might be becoming, I launched myself at the bars. I reached for Ethan, intending to choke the life out of him—and laugh while doing it.

He reared backward, out of reach.

Two of the lab coats rushed toward him, to protect and shield him, most likely, but he held up his hand and they stopped, quickly returning to their stations. He tugged at the collar of his sweater, keeping enough distance between us to prevent a repeat of what had just happened.

"You did this," I shouted, surprised at the sound of my voice. I'd shouted, but only a whisper could be heard. "I'll kill you. I'll kill you so dead."

"Let me explain," he said, expression as tormented as his tone. "Please."

"Save your words. There's no explanation good enough."

His gaze slid to Reeve for a second, as if seeking some kind of softness. "The man who runs this place is my father. He's worked for Anima for two decades and was finally promoted to one of the top positions."

A family legacy. How sweet. "I'm going to cut out your eyes, stop you from ever doing this again! You were the one in the forest that night, spying on Trina and Lucas."

Ethan's head dropped. With shame? He nodded. "My dad and I can't afford failure, not if my sister is going to survive. So we wanted all the bases covered. That's why he sent me to Reeve and why I agreed. That's why he sent Justin to the slayers."

"You used me," Reeve said quietly. "And you expect me to forgive and forget?"

Reminded of her presence, I turned to her. I waited for the scent of her to hit me, to unnerve and obsess me, but encountered only a soft waft of the expensive perfume probably embedded in her skin. The darker urges were at bay.

I squeezed her hand in reassurance, and she offered me a small smile of thanks.

"I didn't use you," Ethan said with a shake of his head. "I mean, at first, yes, I did, but even then I was attracted to you. The more time I spent with you, the harder I fell. You were never supposed to get hurt."

"With your dad, everyone is expendable," I said hotly. "You should have known that."

Ethan popped his jaw. Ignoring me, he said, "I love you, Reeve. I never lied about that."

She raised her chin, and I knew her stubborn side was about to kick in. "I never said those three little words back to you because I never felt the same. I still don't."

He closed his eyes, released a heavy breath. "I don't care. I think I love you enough for both of us. I won't let them do anything else to you."

"Like you'll be able to stop them. They're already starving us. And one day, when I've outgrown my use—" or died "—your dad will kill her and you know it." I knew I was scaring her, but I considered the results worth it. If Ethan feared for her life, he might aid in our escape. And with his aid, food was of little consequence. "She knows too much, has seen too much."

"No," he said, again shaking his head.

"Oh, yes."

"I'll talk to my father."

"And you'll believe whatever he says? You'll believe the

man who's already betrayed you and locked up the girl you love?"

Ethan's mouth opened and closed, and I knew he was searching for a response. When he found none, he turned on his heel and marched out of the laboratory.

"Good riddance," Kat muttered.

I turned and found her in the spot she'd occupied for the past several hours. Her skin was pale—too pale—and her body shaky. Her eyes were glazed, as if she were in tremendous pain.

"Kat," Reeve said, concerned.

"I look terrible, I know. I got myself a set of bad kidneys. Sorry I never told you."

"What?" Reeve rushed to her side.

"What can I do?" I asked.

"I'm okay," she assured me. "Really. I'm just so hungry I'm considering having Paula Deen tattooed on my stomach when this is all over. She makes these scallop sliders I'd stab my dad to have."

She needed dialysis, like, now, and I knew it. From this point on, she was only going to get worse. And with kidneys, there was no recovering from the damage. I'd checked.

"This is my fault," Reeve said with a trembling chin. "I never should have trusted Ethan."

"We all made mistakes," Kat said, and with a confident smile added, "But Frosty will come. He'll save the day. He won't let anything happen to me. Or us. Mostly me."

Reeve played along, saying, "Maybe he'll bring Bronx and I can beg for his forgiveness."

"Beg while naked," Kat suggested. "He'll agree to anything then."

I patted Kat's hand. It was limp, cold. I couldn't wait for Ethan to grow a conscience or a pair of balls. Couldn't wait for the boys to find us, or food to strengthen me. I had to act now.

How?

I moved to Jaclyn's side of the cage and studied the lab, searching for things I might have missed. Anyone coming or going had to flash an ID badge over the box on the door. There was a glass case on the far wall with several tranq guns inside. I'd seen the lab coats use those weapons on the collared zombies.

The guards had the keys to the cells. Maybe the lab coats did, maybe they didn't, but I couldn't see evidence either way. The guards were the sure thing.

I needed to steal a key the next time they came for me.

"What are you thinking?" Jaclyn asked.

"Probably the same thing you are."

"Yeah. Blueberry pancakes would be awesome."

I almost grinned. "No. I'm thinking it's time to go."

We both looked at Kat. She yawned and rested her head on Reeve's shoulder.

"She shouldn't be this bad this quickly," Jaclyn whispered, unable to mask her worry.

"It's the stress of the situation," I replied. "It's making everything worse."

"I can hear you, you know," Kat said. Then, "What are we going to do?"

"Let me worry about that." I held Jaclyn's stare until she nodded.

"I wish there was something I could do," she said, "but they don't even open my cage anymore. I could try, but they're used to me, expect my tricks and just ignore me, whatever I say."

I motioned Reeve over.

She eased Kat's head to the floor and closed the distance. I put my mouth to her ear and whispered, "When the guards come for me, and they will, I want you to attack one. He might hit you, and I'm sorry for that, because it's going to hurt, but I need him out of the way for just a few seconds. Can you do it? Can you remember what Veronica taught you?"

She gave a determined nod.

"Enough of that, you two," a hard voice snapped. A stick was rubbed against the bars.

I looked over. One of the guards stood at the door of our cage.

"We're hungry and thirsty," I spat at him. "Why don't you reduce the number of crimes you've committed against us and fix that?"

He looked us over, lingering a bit too long on Reeve, before pivoting on his booted heel. "Get them something to eat and drink," he commanded one of the lab coats. "Now."

We were each given a bag of peanut butter crackers and a bottle of water, even Jaclyn.

As hungry as I was, it was like a four-star meal. How sad was that?

"Protein isn't good for me right now," Kat mumbled. "Makes my kidneys have to work too hard."

"We'll scrape off the peanut better and you can eat the crackers," I replied, "because you're eating *something*." Words Cole had once spoken to me. I got it now.

Kat and Reeve fell asleep soon after they'd eaten, and I paced the cell, watching the clock. As the day wore on, the labs coats thinned out, just as before. By 2:00 a.m., there were only two people left in the lab. Again, just as before. By six, the others returned. Hello, pattern.

I'd have a four-hour window to act.

I wondered how many guards were stationed at the monitors at 2:00 a.m. One or two I could take. Any more than that, and I'd have big-time problems.

I'd have to risk it. Tonight.

Tomorrow, Kelly would try to use Kat against me.

The guards returned for me at 10:00 a.m.

"You two," said the one who—pressed his thumb into a keypad. *Crap!* No actual key to steal. "Get against the back wall." His attention moved to me. "You, stand in the middle."

"Forget my plan," I whispered to Reeve, and she blinked with surprise.

Her eyes were wide, her body quivering as I was cuffed and led out of the cell. I knew she wanted to help me in some way, any way, but I couldn't cut off the guy's thumb, so there wasn't anything to do.

I was escorted into the torture chamber. Kelly was already there, sitting, waiting for me.

"How are you feeling?" he asked.

"Gotta admit I've had better days." As I looked him over, another plan took shape. It was dangerous. It was stupid. But there was no other way.

"I'm sure you have," he said, and nodded to the guards.

Have to act now. The moment I was uncuffed, I lunged for Kelly, purposely slamming my body into the cart of syringes and scalpels along the way.

We hit the floor, and I grabbed the first thing my fingers found and shoved it into his neck. As the guards scrambled to catch me, I grabbed the second thing my fingers found and shoved it into my pocket.

Everything happened in two, maybe three seconds.

A hard fist slammed into my temple, throwing my body to the side. Stars. Pain. A heavy weight crashed into me, forcing me to my stomach. My arms were roughly twisted behind my back and the cuffs reapplied.

"Get her...out of here..." Kelly gasped.

As I was hauled to my feet, I watched him sit up and pull a syringe out of his neck. Only a syringe. Too bad.

The guard shoved me forward, and I tripped my way back to the cage. Once inside, I did the same thing I'd done yesterday. I threw myself into the far corner, hiding my face—and my actions. As stealthily as possible, I reached into my pocket. Felt...a scalpel.

Perfect.

Whatever's necessary.

Reeve approached, placed a soft hand on my shoulder. "Are you okay? Your hand is bleeding."

I looked down and realized the scalpel had sliced through my palm. My adrenaline must be riding high, because I didn't feel it. "I'll take care of it." My shirt was already torn and easy to rip with my teeth. I tied a strip of material around the wound, applying pressure.

"Get some rest," I told her. For what came next, she was going to need it.

As I paced the cage, watching the clock yet again, waiting, waiting, I felt as if my sanity…my emotions…my *everything* hung at the end of a horribly frayed rope. Any second the threads would snap, and I would fall, crack open and all the darkness inside me would spill out.

Death and destruction would ensue.

No one would be safe.

I just… I had to hold it together for Kat, Reeve and Jaclyn.

Fatigue rode me harder than ever, but I forced myself to look past the burning eyes, the quivering limbs and the aches and pangs. I could sleep when the girls were safe.

Finally 2:00 a.m. arrived. The moment of truth.

All but one lab coat had left. The straggler was a heavyset man around forty years old. I could take him in a fight, no problem. The only unknown was how many guards were monitoring the camera feeds.

Actually, no, that wasn't true. I also didn't know how many people were in the building. Or how many security clearances I'd have to go through to reach the front doors.

That wasn't going to stop me. *Whatever's necessary.*

I glanced back at the girls. Kat was asleep, though not at rest. Her eyes rolled behind her lids, and violent shivers racked her body.

Though Reeve was awake and watching me, she lay behind Kat, arms curled around her, offering warmth.

Jaclyn sat at the edge of her cot.

Now, I mouthed, then faced Lab Coat.

"Let us out," I shrieked, the sound startling the guy enough that he actually glanced over at me. I rattled the bars with every bit of my strength. "My friend needs help. Where's your heart? How can you leave us like this? To starve? To face torture?"

The shrillness of my voice awakened the zombies. Moans and groans erupted all around me.

Hungry.

Eat. Must eat.

Lab Coat pushed to his feet and stomped from the room. If he failed to bring back a guard...

The side door opened, and Lab Coat stalked inside with a tired-looking guard at his side.

I did my best to hide my relief.

Frowning, the guard pointed a finger at me. "Be quiet," he barked.

Smells so good.

Him. Want him.

Must eat...drain...empty...

Zombie thoughts...or Z.A.'s?

"I'm through being quiet," I shouted. *Bang, bang, bang.* I punched at the bars, unconcerned by the sting in my already sore hands. "I'll never be quiet again. You'll have to make me."

Reeve rushed to my side, her voice harmonizing with mine. "We want out. Let us out. Let us out."

I laughed, but it wasn't a nice sound. "So brave out there, aren't you?" I taunted the guard. "Doubt you'd be so confident in here. I could take you down in seconds."

"This is your last chance to be quiet," he snarled, hand curling around the stick hanging at his waist. Then his gaze landed on Reeve and narrowed. He licked his lips. "But please, do me a favor and refuse it. I'll come in there and show you just how brave I can be."

"Let us out. Let us out." Reeve.

"Coward!" Me.

Grinning a terrible grin, he pressed his thumb against the lock. When he pulled the door open, I shoved Reeve behind me and backed her toward Kat, who had woken up and now leaned against the far wall. All the while, I gripped the scalpel I'd stolen, the blade hidden by my arm.

He stomped toward us, his eagerness to get his hands on Reeve making him stupid. He grabbed me, probably intending to toss me to the side, but I struck without hesitation, stabbing him in the neck.

Howling, eyes going wide, he stumbled away from me. His knees buckled before he could exit the cage, and he went down. Blood gushed from the wound, leaking through his knuckles as he applied pressure.

Whatever's necessary, remember?

"Scalpel," Jaclyn shouted, jerking me out of the daze.

I tossed it to her, wondering why she needed it, then rushed out of the cage, closing in on Lab Coat. He remained on his feet, as if frozen.

"Don't hurt me," he pleaded.

"Like you didn't hurt me?" I punched him in the throat

with a blood-covered hand, and he, too, went down. I tore the badge from around his neck before stalking to the glass case where the tranq guns were stored.

In the hallway, an alarm erupted, screeching through the airways. *Dang it.* There was at least one more guard.

"Get Kat and get out of here," I instructed Reeve, and pounded my fist into the glass. "I'll get Jaclyn."

Shards rained to the floor; my knuckles stung and bled. I grabbed the gun as the side door burst open, a single guard rushing through. Just before he reached me, I managed to turn and squeeze the trigger. He fell—right on top of me.

Struggling to breathe, I wiggled out from under him and turned to finish off Lab Coat, only to realize he'd already regained his bearings, found another badge to use on the door and rushed out of the room.

"Ali." In the cage, Reeve was struggling to hold up Kat. I pocketed as many tranq darts as I could hold and rushed over to help, passing Jaclyn along the way.

She'd freed herself.

I looked around and computed how. The guard's arm had been close enough for her to reach through the bars, and she had removed his thumb with the scalpel. *We think alike.* Then she'd used what she'd taken to unlock the door.

The guard had stopped writhing, was motionless in a pool of his own blood. Unblinking eyes stared off in the distance.

I'd taken a life.

WHATEVER'S NECESSARY.

A sob escaped me, a testament to the still-fraying rope holding back my emotions. It wouldn't last much longer now.

Shaking, I removed his badge and handed it to Reeve, just in case we were separated.

"Got another tranq gun." Jaclyn came up beside me and gently removed Kat from my hold, wrapping her arm around the girl's waist to remove half the burden from Reeve.

"You're strongest. You lead the way."

"I'm just going to slow you guys down," Kat panted. "Leave me here and come back for me later."

"Don't be ridiculous," I said. "I'd rather stay here than leave without you."

"Seriously, Ally Kat," Jaclyn said. "Shut it."

"Now follow me."

I used Lab Coat's badge to open the door to the hallway. We entered a long, narrow passage I was relieved to find empty. Maybe I'd disabled the only guards. *Please, please.*

"Where should we go?" Reeve asked, her voice strained.

I ripped the emergency exit map from the wall, considered the corridors and said, "This way."

Down the hall. Around a corner. Another hall, another corner. In the stairwell, our breathing and footsteps echoed off the walls. But those were the only sounds. No one was following us. Others would be here soon, though. I was certain the alarm had already been reported to Kelly, wherever he was.

Kat's head lolled to the side as the girls carried her down, down, down the steps. As fatigued as I was, as undernourished, as wounded, my trembling seemed to magnify with every new inch of ground I gained.

Finally we reached the end of the well, and I used the key card to open the door.

"—remote camera show they entered the stairwell." Kelly's voice rose above a symphony of pounding footsteps.

Dang it! How had he gotten here so quickly?

Jaclyn and I shared a look of absolute, utter panic.

"I want you six to comb every inch of it. And I want a man posted on every floor. We're dealing with four half-starved teenage girls. You should have no trouble finding and subduing them."

As yet unnoticed, we dragged Kat to the side of the now-abandoned security desk.

Perfect timing. A group of men whisked past us. Six entered the door we'd just left, and one muttered, "We aren't paid enough for this." Some entered the elevators. They were all dressed haphazardly, as if they'd been roused from sleep and had had to hurry. There must be a facility close by. Like army barracks, maybe. We'd have to be careful to avoid it.

I gazed longingly at the wall of glass doors leading outside.

"You two," Kelly said as he entered the elevator, "wait here." There was a white bandage wrapped around his neck. He was pale, almost as shaky as I was. "Call me if they make it this far."

The doors closed on him.

The two men he'd left behind assumed their positions, forcing us to inch our way around the desk to continue to hide our presence. I sat for a moment, trying to decide on our next move.

There was only one thing to do, really.

"Wait here," I whispered, and crawled to the end of the desk. I peeked around the edge, noting the exact positions of the guards. Then I set a dart beside my thigh, readied my gun, aimed.

Deep breath in…hold…ouuut…I squeezed the trigger.

There was a gasp, a rustle of clothing—then a heavy thump. The first guard had just gone down.

Yes!

"What's wrong?" the other asked, racing to his side.

He saw the dart in the man's thigh, frowned and glanced up.

Before I could finish loading the gun for round two, he was placing a walkie-talkie at his mouth.

"Mr. K, I found—"

I fired.

His knees buckled, and he went silent.

"Found what?" Kelly demanded over the walkie-talkie.

So close! "Come on," I said, and Jaclyn and Reeve tugged Kat to her feet.

Together, we rushed forward. We stepped on the guards, too tired to leap over them, and shoved our way past the glass doors. Frigid air enveloped us, worse because we were without coats, hats and gloves. We wore only T-shirts and jeans.

Since our captivity, the snow had continued to fall, and there were now several inches covering the sidewalk and parking lot. Kat wouldn't last long. "Hang on," I said, going back inside the building, meaning to take a coat from one of the guards. But pulling the garment off a deadweight proved to be too much for me. *Failure!*

Plop.

A cell phone had just fallen out of one of the pockets. *Silver lining.* I picked it up and rushed outside. With Kat tucked between us, Reeve and I angled away from the lamps in the parking lot and toward the darkness of the landscape.

A treacherous-looking hill loomed ahead. It was covered in ice, but there were also trees. We could hide there. Maybe we'd freeze to death. Maybe we wouldn't. I didn't care anymore, as long as we were out of Kelly's clutches.

As we ran, I dialed Cole's number. Or rather, I tried to. The motion—on top of my trembling—caused me to misdial. *Come on, come on. You can do this.* I tried again, succeeded.

He answered on the third ring, demanding harshly, "Who is this?"

"Cole," I panted.

"Ali!"

"That's Ali?" I heard Frosty say in the background. "Ask her about Kat."

"Ask her about Reeve," Bronx rushed out.

"Help us," I interjected. "Have to…help us."

"We are, sweetheart," Cole said, and I heard the worry in his voice. "We are. We finally tracked your location, and we're almost there. Hang on just a little longer."

"Escaped building…headed for…hill. Kat, medical attention. Kelly…after us. Cold. Jaclyn…alive."

"Faster," he commanded whoever was driving. "We're two minutes away, baby. Just hang on," he repeated.

"Miss Bell," Kelly suddenly called out, and in my panic, I dropped the phone. "I know you're out here."

Reeve gasped.

Jaclyn growled.

Forget the phone. I picked up the pace, soon bypassing the first line of trees. Wind gusted, and, I thought, sliced at my skin. Two minutes. I could outwit my enemy for two minutes. Actually, one minute, forty-five seconds now.

We settled Kat against the tree trunk.

I whispered, "Guard them," to Jaclyn. To Reeve, "Keep Kat warm."

"Where are you going?" Reeve wrapped herself around Kat, offering what heat she could. "What are you going to do?" Terror glazed her moon-darkened features.

"Let her do what needs doing, and ask questions later," Jaclyn said, already in position, gaze scanning. She would shoot anyone who approached, without hesitation.

I squeezed Reeve's hand and tiptoed away without another word. When I reached the edge of the forest, I pressed against another trunk, peering out at the building. Lights spilled from the windows, illuminating the area around it. Kelly stood just outside the doors, his hands on his hips, his breath misting in front of his face every time he exhaled.

Just how far would the tranq gun shoot?

Just how good was my aim?

While staying at the cabin, I'd continued my training. Nowadays, I hit more than I missed, as proven by the guards in the lobby. But just then, I was shaking so badly I couldn't hold the gun steady.

Gotta try. I set the scalpel in front of me on a rock, just in case, and stretched out flat on my belly, my elbow beside the blade. No matter what I tried, however, my hand couldn't be steadied.

A crunch of snow at my left. Instinct kicked in, and I had the scalpel palmed and thrown in the next second. A man fell to the ground, gasping for breath, the blade sticking out of his throat.

How many other guards were already out here?

In the distance, I heard a crash. Metal against metal. A second later, a Jeep skidded into the lot, the tires locked. The moment it stopped, Cole, Justin, Frosty and Bronx hopped out.

A second vehicle arrived, and out came Trina, Gavin, Veronica and Lucas.

A third vehicle pulled in, and out came Mr. Ankh, Mr. Holland and the rest of the slayers.

I wanted to… Was about to have… *Hold it together. Just a little longer.* They were here. They were here, and the girls would be saved, and all of the pain and suffering would have been worth it, and oh, glory, I was crying, the tears hazing my eyesight and freezing on my cheeks.

"Where are they?" Mr. Holland demanded.

Every slayer unsheathed a gun and aimed at Kelly.

Every guard around him unsheathed a gun and aimed at the slayers.

Kelly's hands fisted. "I don't know what you're talking about. I do, however, know that this is private property and you were not invited. Leave, before I'm forced to take measures you won't appreciate."

"We know they're here," Cole growled. "Ali!"

"You're surrounded," Kelly gritted out. "Are you sure you want to go this route?"

"Are you sure that you do?" Mr. Ankh said, as calm as ever. "I'm sure a dozen dead bodies in your parking lot would be too difficult for even you to explain away or hide."

"We want the girls," Cole spat. "Now."

"Here," I called. "We're here."

Kelly stiffened.

Frosty and Bronx followed the echo of my voice. They reached me in seconds.

"Where's Kat?" Frosty demanded.

"Back here," Reeve called, and I knew she was doing her best to sound brave and unaffected.

"Jaclyn, lower the weapon," I said.

"*Jaclyn?*" Justin took off in a run.

Frosty and Bronx, too. It wasn't long before Frosty was carrying Kat, Bronx was carrying Reeve and Justin was carrying Jaclyn. I think every one of them was crying. I forced myself to stand, to inch forward, toward the slayers.

Cole kept his gun trained on Kelly, his finger twitching over the trigger. He wanted to kill the man. Like, bad. I saw it in the posture of his body. Felt it in the rage radiating from him.

"I know you hate the man and want him dead for taking Ali, but you need to go get your girl," Gavin said, wrapping his fingers around the barrel of the gun. "Or I will."

Cole cursed under his breath but relinquished the weapon without tapping the trigger; he rushed to my side. His gaze swept over me, and his expression hardened. He swept me up in his arms, and I could only rest my head on his shoulder.

"I've got you, sweetheart," he whispered, "and I'm not ever letting you go again."

My chin trembled, a fresh round of tears threatening to fall.

"Go ahead, take them," Kelly said, his body trembling

with rage of his own. "You'll find no evidence that they were ever here. In fact, I should call the authorities and let them know four teenage girls were sneaking around the premises."

"Shoot him," I said, my voice weak, strained.

Of course, no one obeyed. They'd begun to back up, heading for the cars. Well, sorry, but I couldn't let Kelly walk away unscathed, no matter how noble he considered his cause. I had to do something. Now, while I had the chance.

With Cole's body heat surrounding me, some of my tremors waned. So, with my last burst of energy, I lifted the tranq gun and squeezed the trigger.

A dart sank into Kelly's cheek.

I'd aimed for his eye. Oh, well.

His knees buckled and he went down.

Some of the guards rushed to him. The others cocked their weapons, ready to retaliate. I was shoved into a car as shots rang out, Cole using his body as a shelter.

"Sorry," I mumbled. "Couldn't resist."

"Don't be sorry. Ali, I don't know what I would have done… I couldn't stand…" His arms tightened around me, squeezing me. "You have to tell me what happened in there."

"Not now," I said, even the thought threatening to immobilize me. "Please."

"Okay. All right. But soon."

"Soon," I promised.

The first two days back at Mr. Ankh's, I slept, my body doing its best to recover from the abuse it had suffered—but its best wasn't quite good enough. My strength continued to diminish. I was vaguely aware of Nana coming to see me and clutching my hand, Emma pacing beside my bed and Mr. Ankh checking my vitals.

Where was Cole?

It wasn't until the third day that I discovered he'd been sleeping in a chair in the corner of my room the entire time. I woke up crying and couldn't stop. I cried until my tear ducts dried from overuse, and he rushed over, gathering me in his arms, whispering the sweetest words into my ear.

I missed you so much.

I tore the world apart looking for you. I wasn't going to stop until I had you back.

You are so special to me. I need you.

I clung to him as if he were my only lifeline.

Just then, he was.

He told me Kat and Reeve were on the mend. That he knew Reeve had been the unwitting spy, and because of her, Ethan. He'd told the slayers everything that had been going on; they were eager to see me, he said.

"How is Jaclyn?" I asked.

"She's at home with Justin, and he says she's healing physically but not mentally. She refuses to leave the house."

"They were terrible to her," I said with a shudder.

"The were terrible to you, too. To all of you. Will you tell me now?"

"Tomorrow," I whispered, not wanting the taint of dark memories to intrude upon this moment.

Then tomorrow came. My fourth day back. Mr. Ankh and Mr. Holland strode into the room, asked for details, and I told them everything I'd learned...and suffered. Cole

held me then, too, and I was glad. Though he stiffened
and cursed, he remained tender with me, sifting his fingers through my hair, whispering how brave I was when I
thought I'd have another breakdown, telling me how sorry
he was.

The adults were pale by the time I finished.

"Well," Mr. Ankh said, then cleared his throat. Were his
eyes gleaming with tears? "I'm sorry for everything you endured, Miss Bell."

I nodded to let him know I'd heard him.

"But I'm afraid you're not in the clear yet," he added. "The
antizombie toxin in your blood is higher than ever. We gave
you more antidote, and it helped…for a while. You burned
through it so quickly I believe you're already developing an
immunity to it. You'll be able to use it another few weeks,
is my guess, but not much more than that."

So little time.

I gulped.

When the adults left the room, Cole parted my hair and
held on to the pigtails he'd created, peering into my eyes.
"Kelly isn't going to get away with this. You have my word."

He was so beautiful. So fierce. "Cole."

"No, don't say anything. You're still recovering, and I
want you focused on that. I just… I want to show you something." He rolled to his back, leaving me on my side, and
lifted the hem of his T-shirt to reveal the entire expanse of
his muscled chest.

His tattoos were—*oh, glory.*

In big, bold letters, my name had been added among his
plethora of tattoos.

ALI BELL arched from one nipple to the other, the pierced one, taking up far more real estate than any other.

"Cole," I repeated with a tremor.

"I wanted to give you more than words. I wanted to *show* you that you're it for me, that there is no one else, that there will never be anyone else. I don't care what happens. I don't care what the visions tell us. I just want you."

No boy had ever made such a finite gesture for me. No boy had ever looked at me like this one did, as if I were the most important part of his life. As if he couldn't *not* look at me. "I love you," I whispered, my heavy eyelids drifting closed and my mind falling into a pool of black.

I think I was smiling.

My fifth day back, Cole moved me into Reeve's suite. With both Mr. Ankh's and Mr. Parker's permission, Kat had moved in as well, and the two girls had been asking for me—needing me. An unbreakable bond had formed inside that cell, one that would last as long as we lived.

The men in our lives weren't willing to upset us, so, re-gardless of the danger I still presented, three twin beds now dominated the sleeping area.

But…

On the sixth day, I began to feel Z.A. stirring. She was angry. Hungry. Determined. I fought her with all that I was, doing my best to keep her on a tight leash, and it cost me. What little strength I'd won, I lost again, confining me to the bed.

Reeve recovered from the trauma first, and that was when her father pounced.

He strode into the room, sat at her bedside and held her

hand. Uncaring about his audience, he said, "I'm going to talk, and you're going to listen without saying a word until I'm done." He waited for her to nod before he continued. "I want to send you abroad. I never wanted you to know what was going on here, didn't want you to live your life in fear and danger—"

"I'm not going anywhere," she interjected. "And are you trying to tell me the zombie problem is isolated to this area?"

"No, it's not," he gritted out. "But I don't want you around the people who fight in the war. They're targets. Magnets. If you're here, you'll cave and hang out with them. Then, as you see the injuries they receive, you'll start to fear and stop living your life."

"I've seen the injuries, and I'm not afraid. I'm ready and willing to help. Those guys carry a huge burden, and I need to step up and take on my share."

I lay on my side, and Kat, who had the middle bed, lay on hers. We peered at each other, remaining quiet, listening to the conversation over the beeps and hums of medical equipment.

"What can you do?" Mr. Ankh demanded. "You can't see the monsters."

"Neither can you, and yet you manage just fine."

"I'm a doctor."

"And I'm a healthy girl with two arms and two legs, capable of taking orders to assist the doctor tending to the slayers."

He shook his head. "The zombies could bite you."

"And I could be given the antidote," she sniped. "Look, Dad. I'm going to help the cause whether I do it here or somewhere else. That's not something you can stop. I caused the mess we're currently in. Me. And I want to make amends. I *need* to make amends."

"No, you—"

"Dad," she insisted. "We both know the truth. I've been spying on everyone, trying to figure out what's going on and why the people I love, the people who profess to love me, kept lying to me. In my quest for answers, Ethan was able to encourage me and teach me how to be a better spy. I told him everything I learned. *I caused this.*"

His shoulders drooped, and he scrubbed a hand down his face.

I yawned, my eyelids growing heavy.

"If you want to stay, stay," he said softly. "If you want to help, help. But you will not go near that boy." There at the end, his tone had hardened. "Do you understand me?"

Reeve scowled at him. "He has a name."

"Bronx," the doctor gritted. "You'll not go near him."

"Why? Why do you hate him so much?"

"I don't hate him. I just hate the thought of you with him. He's too…rough for you, honey. You haven't read his file, and you don't know his past or the trouble he's been in, the things he's done or the things he'll do."

Her smile was sad. "And I don't care. I know the boy he is now, and that's all that matters to me."

"Reeve—"

"No! I'm not Mom. I didn't understand her breakdowns before, or what they did to you, but I do now. I get it. But you don't get to control this part of my life. And if you try to punish him and the slayers because I want to be with him, then you will lose me. I will move out. And who do you think will be there to take me in?"

I gave another yawn, this one nearly cracking my jaw. My eyelids drifted closed, and the rest of the conversation faded from my awareness.

Not over… Will try again… You're not going to win… Z.A.'s voice filled my head, oozing past the barriers I'd managed to build.

I wanted to reply, but there was a strange fog in my head, muddying up my words.

"—still sleeping," Kat said.

"Yes," Cole said. "She sleeps all the time."

I tried to open my eyes but couldn't quite manage it.

"I'm worried about her." Kat said. "I've never seen her look so…fragile."

Were they talking about me?

"She'll recover," Nana said. "I'm not going to lose her."

Nana was here, too?

If Cole replied, I missed it.

I wasn't sure how much time passed before I felt warm fingers brush through my hair. At last the fog dissipated. I pried open my eyes as sparks of energy bloomed. Nana was gone, I realized. Kat and Reeve were asleep. Cole was next to me, his eyes closed. He absently stroked my scalp.

I smiled. I needed more of this, more of him.

I thought about the journal. The answer. Light. Fire. Clearly, he was a light to me. Just as clear, I burned for him. But there was more, something I was missing.

To-do: *figure it out, and fast.* Time was running out.

"—I've always known," Frosty was saying to Kat.

My eyelids fluttered open, and I realized two things at

once. I'd fallen asleep while Cole stroked me, and morning had arrived.

Frosty sat beside Kat's bed, holding her hand. Her other had tubes sticking out of it—tubes attached to a dialysis machine.

Her eyes widened with shock. "You have?"

"Well, yeah. Kitty Kat, I'm, like, a master black ops agent man, and not just when it comes to Call of Duty. To hang around you, and to let you hang around my friends, I had to know all about you. I never said anything about your illness because I wanted you to trust me enough to admit the truth on your own."

Oh, wow. He'd always known.

"Well, that didn't stop you from asking a bazillion questions about what I was doing each day," she grumbled.

"I was giving you the opportunity to come clean," he said with an unrepentant grin.

"It was entrapment, you turd, plain and simple. I should be furious with you."

He arched a brow. "Should?"

She sighed. "For some reason, I've never found you sexier. And you know I have trouble staying mad at anything sexy."

He barked out a laugh, but sobered only a few seconds later. His gaze pierced her, intense and demanding. "I want you healed, Kat. I want you around, tormenting me, forever."

"I want that, too," she whispered. "More than anything. And I'm sorry I've broken up with you so much. I just didn't want you to see me while I was sick. I didn't want your sympathy or pity, or worse, you staying with me because you felt obligated."

"You have nothing to be sorry for. You made me chase you, and I loved it. And I stayed with you because I love you, no other reason."

My heart constricted. I shouldn't be listening to this. It was private. A moment of vulnerability and longing I wasn't meant to share. I rolled to my other side, giving the pair as much privacy as possible, and came face-to-face with Cole.

He was watching me.

"You look better," he said.

"You're still here," I replied. I wasn't sure why I was surprised.

"Of course I am. There's nowhere I'd rather be."

My heart leaped into my threat. "Cole," I breathed. "Thank you for coming to find me. Thank you for everything."

He nodded, but a hard gleam appeared in his eyes. "I dropped your grandmother off, checked in with my dad and went back to the cabin. You weren't there, but your tracks were outside. Then I got your message. I think I was an hour and a half behind you, and by then it was too late. And *I'm* sorry for that. No," he added when I opened my mouth to respond. "You don't get to tell me I have no reason to feel guilty. I love you, and I'll feel guilty if I want."

He'd once told me he was coming after me with everything he had. This. This was all I needed.

Though I tried, I couldn't find the strength to lift my arms and hug him. All I could do was lean forward and press my forehead against his chest. His heart beat fast but steady.

"How did you track us?" I asked.

"Justin had the address for several Anima facilities in the area. I nearly shouted my house down trying to get your sister's attention. She showed up, I gave her the addresses and she was better than a camera."

"But she couldn't get into the building to see us. There was a block."

"Yeah, but she could see and hear everyone who entered and left. You were mentioned."

Oh. Thank you, sweet sister.

He kissed my temple. "Will you tell me what I want to hear now? Without falling asleep on me while you're doing it?"

"Totally. But what do you want to hear?"

Two of his fingers gently pinched my chin and lifted my head until my gaze locked on his. He searched me for a long while, silent, before grinning wryly. "Never mind. I'll wait."

"For what?"

"You." He tucked my head against his chest—against the final *L* in my last name—breaking eye contact. Toying with the ends of my hair, he said, "I know you like to ask a thousand questions. Is there anything you're dying to know about what's been happening around here?"

I was confused by the exchange—seriously, what did he want me to say?—yet caught up in the seduction of him. Everything about him lulled me into a deep sense of relaxation. "Do you know where Nana is?"

"Earlier she was walking by, heard you talking in your sleep and decided to spend the rest of the night by your side, just in case you needed her. I came in a few hours ago. I'd left to shower, and sent her to her old room to rest. She refused to go until I promised to call her when you woke up."

Darling Nana. She'd seen so much death lately. "I want to kill Zombie Ali *so* bad."

"Urges?"

I knew what he was asking. "I can feel them, the desires to attack and feed, waiting at the edges of my conscious. I need more light."

"Yes. That's what the journal says."

Surprised, I said, "You were you able to read it?"

"I was. I sat with that thing for hours, getting nowhere, thinking about the numbers and the symbols, about what they could mean, rolling them around in my head, and finally, all of a sudden, the words began to clear. I was so startled I looked around to make sure I wasn't dreaming and caught a glimpse of my reflection. My eyes were silver."

"Silver?"

"Yeah. Like mirrors."

Mirrors. Interesting. "If eyes are the windows to the soul, I guess they can be mirrors, too." I paused. "What was the catalyst, do you think?"

"Maybe my utter absorption with it. We are what we eat, right? My brain was definitely eating that journal."

"What were you able to read?"

"A passage about some slayers having gifts others do not, like the visions, and your ability to see the Blood Lines."

Yes, I'd read that part, too.

"Then there was a section about dying to really live, and the fact that you need fire to burn the toxin out of you." He arms tightened around me. "I know you tried that on yourself, but I'm thinking your fire was already compromised. Either that or Zombie Ali is as immune to your fire and toxin as you're becoming to the antidote."

That one, I thought. That second one. That was the answer. "I wonder what will happen if you use *your* fire on me."

"I've thought about that, and I'm not willing to risk it. What if it kills you? Ashes you? I would never forgive myself."

What if Z.A. died, and I lived? "Just...don't take it off the table, okay?"

He sighed. "All right, but it'll be a last resort. It's risky, and I'm not happy with the idea of risking you."

"Great risk comes with great reward."

"Yo, Muhammad *Ali,*" a female voice said before he could reply.

I peeked up from my position against Cole's chest and watched as Trina, Mackenzie and Lucas approached the side of my bed.

Trina said, "You got yourself and three wimps out of Anima. I'm not sure I've ever been prouder of you."

"Hey," Kat huffed.

"Yeah! Who are you calling a wimp?" Reeve demanded.

"I believe she was talking about you," Bronx said.

He was here? I looked over and found him seated beside Reeve's bed, and the two were...oh, glory...the two were holding hands. Openly. Unashamedly.

Happily.

Mr. Ankh must have relented.

"Ali Bell doesn't play hide-and-seek," Lucas said. "She plays hide-and-pray-I-don't-find-you."

Mackenzie smiled. "When Ali Bell gives you the finger, she's telling you how many seconds you have to live."

Cole chuckled, saying, "Fear of spiders is arachnophobia, and fear of tight spaces is claustrophobia, but fear of Ali Bell is just called logic."

"Oh, oh." Kat clapped excitedly. "There used to be a street named after Ali Bell, but it was changed because nobody crosses Ali Bell and lives. True story."

I snorted.

"I heard Ali Bell once got bitten by a rattlesnake," Lucas said, deadpan, "but after three days of pain and agony, the rattlesnake died."

"Well, I heard that when Ali Bell wants to laugh," Reeve exclaimed, "she reads the *Guinness Book of World Records*."

Giggles spilled out of me, but they quickly turned to coughs. I wasn't sure how many minutes passed before the hacking stopped. I only knew I'd spewed blood all over my hands. *Awkward*.

"Ankh told me this might happen," Cole said. "The zombie toxin and the antizombie toxin you produce are going head-to-head."

Trina tossed me a rag.

"Thanks." As Cole cleaned me up, he kicked her, Mackenzie and Lucas out of the room. "You, too," he said to Frosty and Bronx.

"Sorry, bro," Frosty replied, sounding anything but apologetic. "I'm not leaving Kat."

Bronx gave him the finger. "And yes, I'm telling you how long you've got to live if you try and make me go."

Cole opened his mouth to protest. I knew he wanted to

limit the scope of my embarrassment, and I fell a little deeper under his spell.

"They can stay," I said. How could I deprive my friends of their boyfriends? I'd hate anyone who tried to take mine away.

Cole rested his chin on the top of my head, petted my hair. "Okay. For you."

Bronx leaned forward in his seat and buried his face in his hands. "I don't think I'll ever leave your side again. You were so close to death, Reeve, and there was nothing I would have been able to do to stop it from happening."

Reeve traced her fingers over the shell of his ear. "I survived. We all survived."

The way he looked up and stared at her caused the air in the room to crackle with awareness.

It was the same stare Cole often gave me. Needy. Confused. Resolute. A little savage.

"We have to bring Anima down," Cole said, determined and cold. "We can't allow such a threat to remain."

"What are we going to do?" I asked.

A pause as the three boys shared a look fraught with promise.

"Go to war," Cole said.

BLOOD BATH AND BEYOND

The boys lived up to their promise.

A few days later, after I'd gotten caught up on my school-work, a grinning Cole strode into the bedroom. It was Tuesday afternoon, and Kat and Reeve were in class. Nana was downstairs making cookies.

She hadn't wanted to leave my side, but she'd started to cry every time she'd looked at me, and her worry had pricked at the darkness writhing and frothing at the back of my mind, banging at the barely standing barriers.

I'd told her I had a craving for something sweet.

Cole leaned down and kissed my forehead, his lips soft and perfect. I wished I'd had the energy to fix my hair and slap on a thousand pounds of makeup.

Maybe it was a good thing all the mirrors had been re-moved from the room.

"You should be at school," I said.

His grin only widened. "School shmool. I've got a surprise for you." He swept me into his arms and carried me through the house…then down the stairs and into the basement.

I sniffed, expecting to smell rot. There was a good chance he had a zombie down here. But no. I smelled copper. Dried blood. I frowned. Then I heard the rattle of bars.

Frosty, Gavin and Bronx formed a wall of menace in front of one of the cages, and Cole shouldered his way past them to give me a front-row look at—

Ethan.

If I had been standing, I would have fallen from the shock.

One of his eyes was swollen, and there were several cuts on his bottom lip. Someone—or four someones—had beaten the crap out of him.

Gavin winked at me. "We did good, yeah?"

Frosty cracked his battered knuckles. "Hunting him down was easy. Taking him captive was easier. Still. You're welcome, world. Now, who wants to watch me get a little information out of this douche purse?"

I would never live that down.

"You didn't capture me," Ethan spat. "I gave myself up."

"Sure you did," Bronx said. "After we pounded your face into the dirt."

Ethan shook his head. "Just listen. The same way my father got the zombies to enter people's homes, he's sending the zombies to Cole Holland's barn tonight." He drew in a breath. "My father captures and collars the creatures, and lets some of them go. The collars have GPS, and he's able to monitor their whereabouts. Then, through electrical impulses, he's able to lead the zombies to where he wants them to go."

Remote control zombies. Nice.

"If that's true, why haven't the zombies entered any other houses?" Cole demanded.

"The night they entered the houses was a test to see if it would work. Tonight isn't a test. My father wants Ali back. He thinks she's the key to saving my sister. Izzy only has a few more months to live—if she's lucky."

"Which gives you motive to pretend to help us," Cole said.

Ethan shook his head, sad. "Believe me. I learned my lesson. I can't save someone I love by hurting someone else I love."

Like Cole, I remained suspicious.

Cole returned me to the bedroom and tucked me back into bed.

"What are we going to do about the supposed zombie attack?" I asked.

His knuckles ghosted along the curve of my cheek. "I'll plan my own attack. Meanwhile, you'll rest and regain your strength."

Translation: I wasn't to be involved.

"I have to go," he said. "But I'll come back after… I'll come back."

Then he was gone. And I was alone.

I didn't worry about the outcome of the coming battle.

I drafted a new to-do list.

Only one item: *don't let my friends go into the danger zone without me.*

When I was at my best, I was an asset. I could be at my best again, if only for a little while. So, when Nana came in with cookies and milk, I thanked her and kissed her and sent her on another errand. I told her Mr. Ankh was at work (finally), and his PMS—personal male secretary—wasn't here to guard the office, then asked if she would grab the bag filled with vials of antidote.

He wouldn't mind, I assured her. And I needed it.

She didn't understand I was developing an immunity to it, and the more antidote I used, the faster that immunity would build, so she found nothing suspicious about the request. To her, it was medicine, and I was entitled to medicine.

"Found it," Nana said as she strolled inside the room. She lifted the black medical bag for my perusal before setting it beside me on the bed. She was smiling, always smiling. Until she looked at me.

Nowadays, no one but Cole smiled when they looked at me.

"You're the best, Nana."

"Of course I am. I'm partly responsible for your creation." Tapping a fingertip against my wrist, she said, "Ali, darling, when were you going to tell me about your tattoos?"

Uh-oh. "Are you mad?" I asked softly.

"No, but you're a minor and I would have liked to be a part of the decision."

"Well." If I survived the coming events, and I would… *confidence matters*…I might as well warn her about tattoos three and four. "I would like to get two more."

"What? And why?"

I explained about the slayers, and the memorials they had

etched on their bodies, and her expression softened. I told her how badly I wanted to honor Pops, but left the details of the fourth tattoo vague. It had to do with Cole…

"All right," she said with a sigh. "I give my permission. But next time, I'm going with you. Now, should I inject you with the medicine? I've never used a needle before, but I've watched a lot of TV, so I'm just sure I'll do it right."

"Sure, just—" My gaze had locked on her neck…on her pulse, glowing so prettily, beating so softly, wafting the sweetest scent to my nose.

Shuddering, I closed my eyes. When it came to the protection of the people I loved, I was stronger than I'd ever realized. But right now I wasn't going to take any chances.

"Are you all right, dear?" she asked, flattening her hand over my brow. "You do feel warm."

I hissed at the moment of contact.

Bite her, Z.A. whispered.

"I'll be fine, don't worry. Just… Nana, I love you so much, but I need to be alone right now. I'm going to inject myself, okay?"

"I love you, too," she said, but I heard the hurt in her tone. "And I'll give you your privacy, but please don't shut me out." She kissed my cheek before striding from the room.

My hand shook as I dug through the bag, withdrawing one, three, six specially marked syringes. The ones with the antiallergy antidote. I stuck myself in the arm, again and again, and felt the familiar warm tide. Z.A. screeched, then quieted. The urge to bite and feed left me. And, with the massive amount of the dose, Z.A. was no longer able to feed off *me,* and energy returned to my body. The trembling faded from my limbs.

Testing my range of motion, I threw my legs over the side of the bed and stood. I remained steady, my knees rock-solid. I stretched my arms over my head, then twisted from the left to the right. No pain. No weakness.

It had worked.

For the past few days, I'd had to suffer through the humiliation of Nana's sponge baths. Once, when I had been whining about my desire for a shower, Cole had picked me up and carried me into the stall. He'd gotten in with me, holding me up, and we'd washed with our undergarments on.

All I could say about that: if I'd been well, I wouldn't be a virgin.

Today, though, I showered on my own. After drying off, I dressed in my fighting clothes. Long-sleeve black top, camo pants and combat boots. My weapons had been moved into Reeve's room with me, more for my peace of mind than anything, and I loaded up with daggers and throwing stars.

There was a mirror in the hall, and I meant to bypass it, I did, but I found myself stopping and peering into the glass. I saw…me. Just me. My face a little too thin for my liking, and there were bruises under my eyes, cracks in my lips, but my color was good, rosy, all health and no sickness.

I found Nana in the kitchen, cleaning up the mess she'd made while baking the cookies.

"Ali!" she exclaimed, running over and throwing her arms around me. "You look… Wow! The medicine worked."

"Thank you." I took a moment to absorb her love and

warmth, basking in the sense of home. "Now, I need to borrow your car."

She pulled back, frowned. "My car?"

"I'll be careful with it, I promise."

"I know you will, but you've never shown an interest in driving before. And I know you've had a few lessons, but you still only have your permit, and—"

I cupped her cheeks. "Trust me, Nana. I need to do this." It was time. A girl on her way to war had no room for fear. I wasn't going to tolerate this one anymore.

"I can drive you anywhere—"

"Please, Nana. Please. I'm not shutting you out. I just want to prove to myself that I can do this." I needed to start this new journey with a victory.

"All right." She nodded. "I'll get the keys."

Perspiration dotted my brow, and I struggled to draw air past the lump growing in my throat. On the wheel, my knuckles were bleached of color. Cars zoomed past me, and horns blared.

Someone gave me the finger.

What was the problem? I was only going ten miles an hour under the speed limit. If ten was the new word for twenty. And twenty was the new word for thirty. Whatever. I was motoring forward, and that should be good enough.

I managed to double the usual fifteen-minute drive before reaching Cole's barn—and miracle of miracles, I didn't crash. Several other vehicles were parked in the gravel driveway, so I knew a handful of slayers were already here, preparing for the night's activities.

As I stalked to the door, I glanced at the sky and found a rabbit-shaped cloud directly overhead.

Emma was still looking out for me.

I smiled as I entered the building. Cole, Frosty, Gavin and Veronica were bent over a table, talking, probably planning as they looked over a stack of papers.

I took a moment to enjoy the utter normalcy of the moment. The savage beauty of Cole. The bond between the four. The determination they radiated.

Anima should run and hide.

"Ali," Veronica gasped out.

All eyes lasered straight to me. I cared only about Cole, and—

—he had me draped over his shoulder. Blood dripped from both of us, and I couldn't tell if it belonged to us or someone else. I was panting, struggling to free myself from his hold.

"Let me go," I demanded.

"Never again."

"You keep saying that. What do you want with me—"

—as quickly as the vision had appeared, it vanished.

I blinked, shook my head. I'd asked Cole Holland...*what do you want with me?* As if he were a stranger?

Why?

"What'd you see?" Gavin asked, and I looked to him—

—we stood in the middle of a night-darkened road. Zombie ash was piled at our feet, twirling into the air, dancing away, and Hazmats surrounded us.

Kelly raised his mask. He was scowling. "Where is he? What have you done with him—"

"—this again," I heard Veronica say, jerking me back into the present.

Gavin scowled at her. "Next time, shut your mouth and let the vision finish. We saw tonight's battle. At least, what I think is going to be tonight's battle, and it wasn't pretty."

She sputtered for a response.

Cole closed the distance between us. "How?"

I knew what he was asking and I wanted to lie. "Antidote." No lies. I jutted my chin. "What we saw—"

"I don't know what it means, and I'm not going to try to guess. I've never been right before. What matters—you were told not to use the antidote unless absolutely necessary. Today, it wasn't necessary." His eyes narrowed, and he took my hand, tugging me into the locker room. I expected him to turn and lecture me the moment the door closed, shutting us inside, alone.

He did turn.

But he didn't lecture.

He meshed his lips onto mine, feeding me a bone-melting kiss I'd never forget. I responded immediately, wrapping myself around him, drawing him closer, drinking him in.

Backing me up, he pinned me against the wall and caged me in. His body enveloped me, pressing, rubbing, seeking. All the while his hands roamed, stopping to knead here and there and oh…glory. I shivered with the force of the pleasure.

"You feel so good," he rasped. "Taste so good. You're ready for me, right? You told me you were ready."

"So ready."

"We have to stop, though. We can't do this here."

Whimper. "I know."

Panting, we broke apart.

A hard knock sounded at the door. "Cole," Frosty called. "Your dad just walked in."

Cole pressed his forehead into mine. "We'll be out in a sec."

Murmuring. Fading footsteps.

"One day," he said to me, "we're taking off, just the two of us."

One day. I wanted that—wanted a future.

Cole's eyes narrowed. "What you did was stupid, Ali."

"Sometimes the wisest decision seems like the most foolish."

"I should spank you."

"Try. Please."

He chuckled. "You thinking you'll end up spanking *me?*"

"Knowing it."

Before I realized what was happening, he was spinning me around and smacking me on the butt. "Come on. You can help us figure out the best course of action for tonight. In the morning, we'll talk about our latest vision…and what you did with the antidote. And more about you being ready for me."

I heard the husky promise in his voice. "Cole," I began.

He shook his head. "Later."

Yeah. That was probably for the best. I nodded.

GAME...SET...DEATH MATCH

The rest of the slayers arrived at different times throughout the day, and all of them had the same reaction upon spotting me. Absolute, utter shock. I was hugged. I was patted on top of the head. I was met with sad little smiles because everyone knew the situation wouldn't last.

Took us a few hours, but we all finally agreed on a plan of attack.

I kinda felt sorry for the Hazmats.

When the sun began to set, Cole gave me a quick kiss and took his place among the chairs lining the far wall. "You see a zombie," he said, "you light up and start ashing. Don't waste your energy trying to fight. That's what we're here to do."

"Sir, yes, sir." I eased beside him.

"If your flames are red—"

"I know. Inject myself with the antidote, then run far, far away."

He tweaked the end of my nose, a gesture of affection. "When it's over, I'll come find you. You better not have a single injury."

"Same to you."

Veronica walked toward us, and I watched her purse her lips as she noticed our easy banter.

You should see his chest, Ronny dear.

She sat across from me. The rest of the slayers joined us, and one by one we forced our spirits out of our bodies. The antidote continued to do its job, and I was able to stand with only the slightest resistance from Z.A.

The chill in the air was more pronounced than usual. Cole wrapped me in his arms, sharing his warmth, before leading the way out of the barn.

Night was in full swing, the sun completely gone, the moon in its place, and the halogens Mr. Holland kept around the property glowing brightly, illuminating our way. My eyes burned and watered against the glare.

We passed the gate at the property line, each of us on alert.

In the sky, Emma's rabbit cloud pulsed, as though agitated.

I remembered the last time that had happened and gulped. "They're close," I said.

"No." Cole's expression was menacing. "The zombies are already here."

They sure were. I looked, and saw multiple sets of red eyes glowing in the distance. Moans resounded, and the scent of rot drifted. I hadn't expected things to kick off so fast, but that didn't stop anticipation from firing me up.

Ethan had told the truth.

"Go, go, go," Cole commanded.

As one cohesive mass we rushed forward. Cole fired his crossbow, the arrow sprouting four points at the end and slicing through a zombie's throat. Trina picked up speed, surging ahead, already swinging her ax. Frosty and Bronx tag-teamed two zombies, whipping around the creatures and binding the pair with rope before slicing here, slicing there. The creatures could only endure the violence—before their legs were removed and they toppled to the ground.

Gavin stayed close to Veronica. She was in the process of shoving a row of zombies into the swing of his sword. Lucas, Derek and Cruz hacked through the second and third line of monsters. I stopped in the thick of it and spread my arms. A zombie tried to grab me, but Cole was there, swinging a short sword and removing the limb just before contact.

Another zombie made a play for me, but this time I was ready, filled with power—I could do this. Fire leaped from the tips of my fingers. It was white and tipped with gold, thank God, and in an instant it spread to my shoulders. I could have whooped with joy.

The zombie touched me and burst into ash.

I was grinning as the fire continued to spread to my head, then down my chest, to my waist, down my legs and over my ankles and feet. I gave myself up to the heat, basking in it, empowered by it, and marched forward, ghosting my fingertips over the spine of the zombie chomping at Cole.

Ash.

I moved to the next and the next. Ash. Ash. One touch, that was all that was needed. Soon there were no creatures left standing. The slayers were panting, watching me with rapt fascination.

"Dibs on being Ali's partner," Gavin said with a fist pump to the sky. "For, like, infinity."

Veronica jabbed him in the stomach.

"What?" he said, frowning. "I believe it. I say it. I receive it. Right? That's a spiritual law."

"Not if you violate my free will." I stuck my tongue out at him. "Was anyone bitten?"

"No," echoed a welcome chorus.

"Good." Cole nodded with satisfaction. "All right. It's time to split up." He looked to me. "You still good?"

My pores seemed to open up and suck the flames inside, but the heat stayed just under the surface, ready and eager for more. "I am. You?"

"Yeah."

We held hands for a moment, only a moment, offering silent assurances, before I moved to Gavin's side. The two of us parted from the group, heading for the road we'd seen in our vision, maintaining a normal, natural pace.

"You and Veronica seem awfully close," I said to him. "Closer than usual."

"Makes sense. We hooked up last night."

"You did not."

"It was good, but not great." Amusement dripped from his tone. "Practically a pity fu—screw."

"Ugh. You shouldn't be telling me this."

"Why not?"

"Telling people who you've banged is so low class."

He shrugged. "Lucas walked in on us. It's not like it's some big secret."

Still.

"You jealous?" he asked.

I rolled my eyes and made sure he noticed. "Gavin, I suddenly find you repulsive."

"Funny. That's what she said after I told her sex is sex, and I'd be willing to make myself available to her anytime she wanted it, but not to expect anything more. And you know what? She still jumped me."

"Some girls have no taste."

"In this case, you're the one without it."

That earned him another eye roll. "While she's making herself available to you, you're going to be seeing other women, aren't you?"

"I thought I'd made that clear. Was that not clear?"

"The fact that I've had my tongue on your body…" I shuddered.

His grin was slow but full-wattage. "So we can joke about that now?"

"Why not?" I said, mocking him. It felt good to tease him, to act like the girl I used to be. "As terrible as it was, I don't think there's anything else we can do about it."

"Terrible?"

"You practically checked my tonsils for infection, Gavin."

He barked out a laugh. "Ha! If you were lucky enough to be kissed by me, you'd still be screaming with pleasure."

"You say pleasure, I say—" I spotted the telltale red eyes in the distance. Inhaling sharply, I smelled the putrid stink of rot. My ears twitched, and I heard the grunts and groans of a hunger never to be satisfied. "They're here."

He got serious in a snap, and we picked up the pace.

Seconds before I reached the creatures, I summoned the fire, and just like that, my entire body erupted with flames. Then contact, contact, contact. Ash, ash, ash. The fight wasn't even fair anymore, I thought with a surge of satisfaction.

The zombies had no defense.

But then, they weren't the ones we were after tonight.

The remaining monsters branched off, half surrounding me, half surrounding Gavin. The air was so fetid it clogged my nose and tickled my throat. I gagged, felt the flames begin to sputter and practically danced through the ranks to fell as many monsters as possible before it was too late.

I focused on Gavin and realized he hadn't had the same level of success. Around twenty of the mutated zombies still encompassed him as he sliced and hacked with his blades. I moved toward him, but not fast enough. One managed to crawl up behind him and bite into his calf. Howling with pain, Gavin dropped to the knees.

I dived for the creature, and at the moment of contact my flames licked over him. *Buh-bye now.*

"Others," Gavin rasped, the toxin already working through his bloodstream.

I destroyed the remaining zombies and crouched at Gavin's side, whipping the antidote from my pocket and sticking him in the neck. The white-gold flames hadn't dissipated, I realized too late. They licked over his throat and face, and he howled, his entire body bowing.

"I'm sorry!" I hadn't meant… Might have… Crap! What if I'd just signed his death warrant?

He screamed as the flames disappeared under his skin. I fell backward, panting, praying, trying not to panic, and then, babbling, "Thank you, thank you, thank you," as he quieted and sagged against the brittle grass, still breathing.

He would live.

As the flames at last left me, I looked around and realized piles of ash surrounded us.

Piles I'd seen in our vision.

Excited, and trying not to give way to a rise of dread, I reached out and slapped Gavin across the cheek. "Wake up!"

"I am. Jeez, woman! That hurt."

There was enough derision in his voice to scare the bravest of men, but I could only laugh.

"What just happened?" he demanded.

"I think the flames burned through the toxin." Chased away the darkness, like the journal had promised. "Is the toxin still active?"

He thought for a moment, blinked. A sense of amazement radiated from him. "No. It's gone."

Would his flames have the same affect on me? Or, because I was part zombie, would his flames destroy me? Either way, I now knew without a doubt this was the solution I'd been hoping for; there just wasn't time to explore it.

I climbed to my feet and helped him do the same. "Stay aware."

"Sir, yes, sir," he said, mocking me as I'd mocked Cole.

Footsteps suddenly beat into my awareness. I spun, my

heart drumming swiftly. Hazmats. Coming at us from every angle, soon surrounding us. Guns aimed at our heads.

Because they weren't slayers, but could see us, I knew they were in spirit form. They must have used the mechanical device Dr. Bendari mentioned.

Gavin and I pressed back to back.

"Where is he?" Kelly demanded as he removed his mask. "What have you done with him?"

The vision.

"Who? Your precious son?" I grinned. *Payback sucks, doesn't it?* "I think I'll keep that information to myself."

A cock of a gun. "Actually, why don't I show you where he is?" Cole said from behind him.

Kelly paled.

The slayers were still in spirit form, and they had come out of the darkness to circle the Hazmats.

Our hope was that they would be so intimidated by having our weapons trained on them, they would submit to us. We would lock them up in Mr. Ankh's basement until we figured out our next move. But that best-case scenario wasn't what we'd planned for—and I was glad.

Without further ado, the Hazmats exploded into action, and the battle was on.

Some of the slayers' guns were knocked away. Some weren't, and the sound of gunfire filled the night, reminiscent of firecrackers. *Pop. Pop. Pop.*

Two suited bodies fell.

Punches were thrown. Grunts abounded. Bones cracked. Screams joined the chorus. For several heartbeats, I stood there, pinned by uncertainty—I was supposed to step back, wait. Forget being benched. I marched toward Kelly as he watched the madness.

From the corner of my eye I saw Cole knock the mask off one of the Hazmats. Trina took a punch to the chin, but quickly recovered, swung her ax and hit her mark. Another suited body fell. This one didn't get back up. Frosty played with his prey, grinning as he sliced through his opponent's suit. Bronx whaled on two men at the same time, punching one and kicking the other.

Justin backhanded the guy in front of him. Mackenzie vaulted on a man's shoulders, wrapped her thighs around his neck and arched back, forcing him to his back. Somehow she maintained her hold when they hit, choking him until he passed out. Veronica blocked a punch to the head only to take one to the side from another Hazmat. Impact stunned her, but she recovered quickly, and oh, was she angry! Growling, she threw herself into the culprit, and the two hurtled to the ground in a tangle of limbs. Two of the suits had Lucas's arms trapped behind him while another suit tried to fit a metal collar around his neck.

In front of Kelly, I punched him in the cheek. He stumbled, caught himself and glared, fury blazing in his eyes.

"You won't stop us," he said. "I won't let my daughter die."

"We *will* stop you—and you'll have no one but yourself to blame."

He made to flee. I kicked out my leg and knocked his ankles together. As he fell, flailing for an anchor, I dived on him. We hit the ground, and he lost his mask.

He swung at me, but I shifted out of the way. Then I

broke his nose. Cracked his eye socket. Split his lip. His teeth shredded the skin on my knuckles, but I didn't care.

He wiggled his legs between us, flattened his feet on my belly and pushed. I sailed backward, and he jumped to his feet, stumbling away from me. As I stood, I searched the crowd for him, but one white suit bled into another, hiding him.

Someone grabbed me by the hair and flung me in the opposite direction. I recovered, rolling and kicking my legs into the culprit's stomach. I straightened as he tripped over one of his fallen comrades.

I heard the whistle of metal against air and turned to see a man swinging a blade at me. I arched out of the way, but not quickly enough. Impact—

Never came. Gavin had swooped in and removed the guy's wrist, saving me.

"Thank you!" I called over the screams.

"Anytime, cupcake."

Movement at my other side. I turned.

Another Hazmat came at Gavin, gun already aimed. I grabbed hold of his arm, his momentum strong enough to pull me to my feet. The moment I was balanced I used all of my strength to twist the guy's arm behind his back. The gun dropped as bone snapped. He unleashed a wail of agony as his knees buckled.

I caught sight of Trina a few feet away, a collar now clasped firmly around her neck. It was the same collar these people had once used on me, the same collar they used on the zombies to send electrical impulses through their bodies. At least Lucas had escaped the same fate. He savagely fought anyone who dared approach the girl.

I tried to pry the metal from her neck, but the clamp held steady. She peered up at me with hazel eyes now dark with pain. Her lips parted, but no sound emerged.

Anger rose. "Hold on. I'll find a way to help you."

"Yes, help her," Lucas gritted, ducking to avoid a punch.

I looked around the field, found what I needed. I stalked to a motionless suit and dragged the guy to Trina's side. After cutting away his glove, I pressed his thumb into the small ID pad that acted as a key. Nothing happened.

Maybe Kelly had learned from his mistakes. Maybe his print was the only one that would work.

I searched one more time. Still no sign. Coward that he was, he'd probably left the battle. But he wouldn't have gone far. He would want to watch, to see whether his men succeeded or failed.

I panned the darkness, watching for movement rather than a silhouette. There! A bush swayed. Kelly? Only one way to find out.

"I have a plan." Needing a boost, I dosed up on antidote before racing off, staying in the heart of the shadows, heading for the line of trees. The moment I broke the first, I changed direction, heading for the trembling bush.

I kept my steps as light as possible, but a twig snapped. Though I tensed, I didn't allow myself to stop or slow. I palmed two daggers, and just before I reached the bush, I raised them. Ready.

But he wasn't there.

A few feet away, another bush danced, and I figured he'd

heard me and moved on. I picked up the pace, charging after him.

I smelled the rot before I passed the wall of brittle foliage. The moment I stood in the small clearing, I saw the zombies surrounding him. Six creatures, reaching for him, snapping teeth at him.

What happened next happened quickly. Within three seconds, at the most. I could only watch.

One of the creatures bit into his arm. The suit protected his skin, but he felt the pressure of the action and grunted. He swung with his other arm, hitting the zombie in the head. The creature bit down with more vigor, like a bulldog with a bone, refusing to give up the prize. Another zombie latched onto his other arm, jerking to the ground.

"Let go," he commanded. "Stop. Stop!"

Another creature fell upon him, sinking teeth into his unprotected cheek. Kelly released a high-pierced shriek.

I launched into action, willing the fire to come as I moved. White-gold flames spread. They weren't as wild and consuming as before, nor as weak as they'd been with Gavin, but they would do. I reached the zombies and got to work. Contact. Ash. Contact. Ash. Contact. Ash.

Victorious, I peered down at the writhing Kelly.

"Antidote," he rasped. "Please. In my pocket."

Strapped to a chair… Injected with poison… Electric shocks tearing through me… "I'll help you, but then you're going to help my friend." I slid my hand into the pocket of his suit. Placed the needle at his neck.

Just like with Gavin, my flames licked over him, and his back bowed.

"Don't worry. It'll fade in—"

Kelly burst into ash.

Shocked, I fell to my butt, my flames dying. Like Kelly. I stared down at the pile of blackened dust he'd left behind, wide-eyed. I had…I had just…

Hard hands dug into my shoulders and jerked me backward. I hit my head on a rock, and dizziness took advantage, consuming me. Two collared zombies circled me, peering down at me with abject hunger. Their red eyes were bright, no more than a blur to me.

What were they doing? Why hadn't they attacked?

The collars?

I tried to sit up and fight, but my body had thrown in the towel. I should…oh, pretty…stars swirled overhead, spinning round and round, hypnotizing me. *Think. Concentrate.* "Emma." Yes. She would help. "Get…Cole." He could see her. She could tell him where I was.

I thought I saw a wall of clouds part and my little sister float down to me. Worry contorted her features, and she opened her mouth to speak, but I couldn't hear the words.

Zombie Ali rose from my body and grabbed her by the arm. The two faced off.

"Don't…touch…her," I tried to shout.

The zombies bared black-stained teeth.

The zombies!

How could I have forgotten?

Done waiting, the pair fell on me, biting into me. The pain was intense, white-hot yet freezing cold. I needed to summon the flames…flames…*flames*…but they remained at bay, out of reach.

All of a sudden, the zombies sprang away from me, sickened by the antitoxin, seizing, clutching at their throats.

Emma raced out of the area, and I tried to call her back, to tell her never mind, it wasn't safe, she needed to leave.

Where was Z.A.? Back inside me?

Flames…flames…still nothing. All I could do was lie there, a bone-deep hunger growing inside me.

I wasn't sure how much time passed before I felt a warm caress against my cheek. My eyelids fluttered open. Cole loomed over me, his features bathed in red. Red…from my eyes? He was speaking, but just like with Emma, I couldn't hear him. He stuck me with a syringe, then another, and another.

How many doses had I had today?

I felt a rushing river of strength, and some of the pain faded. The cold and heat evened out.

Careful of my injuries, I sat up. How much trauma could I endure? "I broke your rules," I said. "Got bitten."

"Don't care." Cole kissed me hard and fast. "You're okay now. That's what matters."

"I'm okay," I agreed. "You? Everyone?"

"I'm fine. Some of the guys are cut up pretty bad, and Trina…"

"I know. She's collared. I think Kelly's print would have opened the metal, but I…I killed him. Cole, I killed him with my fire. He was full of zombie toxin, and I touched him, and just like the zombies, he ashed."

He traced his thumbs over my cheeks. "Baby, he needed to die. As for Trina, we'll find another way. Come on."

As he helped me to my feet, I said, "How did you find me?"

"Emma. She said she had to fight Zombie Alice to get to me."

That was right. Z.A. had tried to hurt my little sister.

No one hurt my little sister and lived to tell about it.

We left the clearing, hand in hand. When I tried to hurry him, he shook his head.

"It's over." He grinned, violet eyes glowing with triumph. "We won."

We decided to leave the Hazmats in the forest, both surviving and dead, rather than taking the time to cart them to the dungeon. Our main concern was Trina, and our own injured. We hooked up with our bodies and rushed to Mr. Ankh's basement. There, Ethan was able to remove Trina's collar with his thumbprint.

After everyone had been bandaged up, Mr. Holland, Cole, Frosty and Gavin shoved Ethan into the back of a car and drove off...somewhere. They planned to release him into the wild. With his father gone, Ethan was the only one left to take care of his sister, Isabelle. I hoped the girl recovered, I really did. Just not at our expense.

Despite our ragged condition, the rest of us ended up congregating in Mr. Ankh's game room. Some played pool. Some Ping-Pong. Some darts. Anima wasn't out for the count, we knew that, but the entire company had been severely crippled tonight, and we were flooded with the intoxicating taste of victory.

Reeve and Kat heard the commotion and hurried down the stairs. They looked for Frosty and Bronx, and when they didn't see them, raced to me and H-bombed me with a thousand questions about what had happened. I explained as best I could, and they relaxed.

"You should have seen our girl, the Ali-nator," Justin said, coming up to my side and putting his arm around my shoulders. "I've never seen anything like it."

I smiled at him. "You weren't so bad yourself."

"Probably the second best out there," he said with a nod.

"Please. Your skills aren't even close to mine, Justin," Lucas called. He had his front pressed against Trina's back as she lined up a shot at the pool table, and she didn't seem to mind.

Were they a couple?

"You looked like a beginner compared to me," Justin said.

Lucas flipped him off, and Trina laughed, her stick digging into the table.

"Concentrate on the game, Rina," Collins commanded. "Seriously, my mom plays better than you. And she's blind!"

"Maybe Trina's just that poor of a player," Justin said as if sticking up for her. "Ever think of that?"

Trina blew him a raspberry.

I liked that the group was so relaxed around Justin now. He'd proved himself. He was one of us.

"See you girls around. I'm going to dominate that pool table," he called, moving off.

Reeve's gaze continually darted to the entrance. "The second Bronx gets here, I'm going to corner him and we're going to talk. We haven't discussed anything that's happened, haven't dared broach the subject of a future together. We've just hung out without fighting—which is a first for us, yes, but it's not enough."

"Good for you," Kat said. "If he doesn't tell you everything you want to hear, I'll have Frosty beat him up."

"But…" Reeve shifted from one bare foot to the other. "What if he doesn't want me? What if he liked having an excuse to stay away from me?"

"Please tell me I don't get silly ideas like this," I said to Kat.

"Well, do you want me to lie?" she replied.

I fought a grin. "He wants you," I said to Reeve. "There's no question about that. I mean, you weren't there the night we discovered you sneaking out to meet Ethan. Wait. You *were* there, you just didn't know *we* were. He freaked out. Like, hard-core."

"Really?" she asked hopefully.

"Really."

"Ali-Kat Bell," Kat said, putting her hands on her hips. "You caught Reeve sneaking out and you never thought to share the information with me?"

"Or me," Mr. Ankh said from behind us, and we all stiffened. "I brought up a tray of snacks. Ali, why don't you and Kat go eat and give me a few moments alone with Miss Prison Break?"

I mouthed an apology and headed to the table, Kat at my side.

I smacked into Veronica.

We both ricocheted a few steps back. "Sorry," I mumbled.

"Yeah," she replied. Neither of us moved away.

Kat hadn't noticed the interruption and rooted around the tray Mr. Ankh had brought.

"I'm not sure what Cole sees in you," Veronica said softly.

Cole and I hadn't made anything official yet, but he *was* committed to me. I could tell her to stay away from him, but I didn't want to be that girl. If I couldn't trust him with Veronica, even if she came sniffing around, I shouldn't be with him.

"It's safe to say he sees something he likes." I tried to step around her, but she moved with me. "Do you really want to do this here, now, and ruin everyone's night?"

"You're right," she said, and I could tell she was fighting tears. "I've finally accepted that's not going to change. I guess I'm sorry I made a play for him."

I…wasn't sure how to respond. *Gee, thanks* seemed like a mistake.

"Cole and I wouldn't have lasted long anyway."

Was this a trick? This had to be a trick? "Why do you say that?"

"Other than his massive obsession with you?" she said, and my heart fluttered. "I've never argued with him. I've always acquiesced. But you…you beat him up and call him names, and he can't stop panting for more. I want no part of that kind of relationship."

Poor girl had no idea what she was missing.

"Well, I hope you find what you do want," I said, and that was about as gracious as I could manage considering the circumstances.

She closed her eyes for a moment. When she refocused, her vulnerability was replaced by anger. "Just don't hurt him, or I'll do more than make another play for him. I'll reveal my ace and bury you." With that, she was gone.

Her ace? What was her ace?

Why did I even care? He'd tattooed my name on his chest. He was mine, period.

I joined Kat at the snack tray and nearly moaned at the bounty spread out before me. Crab cakes, mini egg rolls, some kind of cream puffs. Slices of chocolate cake, apple and cinnamon scones.

Only the Ankhs could create such a feast on such short notice.

For once, I was going to let myself sponge. I ate my fill, and as my stomach rejoiced, a sense of fatigue began to plague me. I yawned, and maybe even swayed as my head lolled forward.

"Come on," Kat said, leading me toward the couch. "You look dead on your feet."

I sprawled out, and Reeve appeared to cover me with a blanket.

"How'd the conversation with your dad go?" I asked after another yawn.

"He's decided not to ground me for the rest of my life."

"Oh...good...." After that, I dozed on and off, the rest of the gang continuing to celebrate around me.

"Finally! They're here," Kat said minutes...hours...days... later, clapping with excitement.

I sat up with a jolt, and as I peered through the window, I saw Cole, Frosty and Gavin exit Mr. Holland's dark SUV and enter the night. Morning hadn't yet come. When they reached the porch, I lost sight of them.

Heart beating wildly, I eased to my feet. My knees held steady. Good. The fatigue had left me, too. I waited. And waited. And then Gavin strode through the game-room door, tall and strong, a commanding presence that drew the eye. But his clothes were dirtier than when he'd left, and he had a scrape on his cheek he hadn't had before.

I'd find out why. First, I owed him a big, fat thank-you. He'd saved my life tonight.

I raced over and threw my arms around him, hugging him and planting a grateful kiss right smack on his mouth. "You," I said. For some reason, that was all I could manage.

Knowing what I meant, he hugged me back, kissed my cheek. "My pleasure, Blondie."

I found my wits and added, "You're a better man than I ever gave you credit for." I frowned, the words familiar to me somehow.

"I know."

"And you're *so* modest."

He chuckled.

"You…went to him first," Cole said, an odd note in his voice as he stepped up beside us.

Seeing him, I grinned and threw myself at him. "You're back."

"You went to him first," he repeated.

I pulled back and blinked, a little unsure now. "I didn't see you."

"I came in right behind him."

"Cole?" I asked, a *lot* unsure now.

"The vision," he said, and I noticed he, too, had a few extra scrapes.

Like me, Gavin blinked. "Yeah. That was it. The one we had. Part of it anyway."

And there'd been nothing romantic about it. "He saved my life. I owed him. I was just saying thank you."

"I know. Now." Cole massaged the back of his neck. "I broke up with you for nothing," he said softly.

"That wasn't the only reason. You were afraid I'd—"

"Don't make excuses for me. I'm sorry. I'm so sorry." He grabbed me up and meshed his lips onto mine.

Cheers quickly abounded, soon joined by whistles. I didn't care. I took and gave and took some more. All that he was. All that I was. The past, the present and the future.

When he lifted his head, I could only sag into him.

"I missed you," he said, rubbing his nose against mine.

"I missed you, too."

"How are you feeling?"

"Better now."

He chuckled softly, but the spurt of humor didn't last long. "I'm sorry for everything, Ali."

"Hey. It's done. It's over. We're here now. But why are you and Gavin sporting new injuries?"

"The guy who shot and bombed your Dr. Bendari showed up and tried to take Ethan away from us. He must not have realized we were letting the guy go. Anyway, he was back on his feet, and stronger than he should have been, so there was a fight. We won, but he got away again."

The cheers seeped back into my awareness, and I looked around.

"Sweet fancy," Nana said, fanning herself. When had she gotten here? "The hormones in this room."

Frosty and Kat were engaged in a similar kiss. Bronx and

Reeve had claimed the couch and were talking softly. Everyone else watched us unabashedly and grinned.

"Give me five minutes to check on everyone," Cole whispered to me, "and then I want some time alone with you."

I nodded, already counting down the seconds.

He gave me another kiss before joining his friends at the Ping-Pong table, and they each clasped palms before punching each other in the shoulder. It was like a secret handshake or something.

Nana ruffled my hair, saying, "Oh, to be young again."

"You're still young enough to go on the prowl," I said, then immediately wished I could snatch back the words.

She smiled, and suddenly she looked ten years younger. "Speaker's remorse?" she asked with a laugh. "No worries. I might enjoy looking, but I'm not interested in taming one." Rising on her tiptoes, she kissed my cheek. "I'm headed back to bed. I just came down to find out what was going on. Have fun...but not too much."

"Love you, Nana."

"Love you, too." She flittered away.

I munched on a crab cake and watched as Cole went from friend to friend, talking and laughing. He epitomized beauty, everything right in the world...in *my* world. He moved to Veronica's side, and said something that made her frown. There wasn't a single spark of jealousy inside me. *Good Ali.*

"By the way, I want you to know I'm done coming on to you, Ali Bell," Gavin said as he approached me. "You've never looked at me the way you look at Cole, and I'm starting to think that's a look I'd like to receive."

"Aw. This means my little boy is growing up. I'll even help you out with rock-solid tip to get you started."

"And that is?"

"Give up your ho-bag ways."

Grinning, he bumped my shoulder with his own. "Has anyone ever told you that you're a brat?"

"I'm just certain Cole has mentioned it a time or twelve."

"Smart boy." He enfolded me in his arms, giving me another hug.

I hugged him back.

"Are you happy with the way things worked out?" he asked.

I cupped his cheeks, and the action reminded me of the vision. I looked at Cole, still with Veronica. The tension he'd worn like a second skin had fallen away. "I am. But what about you?"

"Never better. Veronica and I have decided to move here. I don't know her reasons, but mine are simple. Alabama is an ocean of untapped, horny fish and daddy likes his seafood."

I laughed. "I'm glad you're staying. I would have missed you." My gaze returned to Cole. He was watching me now. There was no suspicion in his eyes, no anger. He still trusted me, the same way I trusted him.

He closed the distance between us.

"I'm more certain by the second that the visions don't always mean what we think they do. And now your five minutes are up," he said, taking my hand. "It's time for our talk."

"Talk? That's what we're calling it these days?" Gavin said with a laugh.

We passed Mr. Ankh, and then Mr. Holland, and my cheeks heated.

"Where are you going?" Mr. Holland demanded.

"Ali's old room."

"You have ten minutes. And then I come up to get you."

From the corner of my eye, I think I saw Cole flip off his dad.

"Fine, fifteen minutes," Mr. Holland grumbled.

"You give them fifteen. I'm giving them five," Mr. Ankh said. "Her grandmother has a temper and I don't want to face it again."

Nana had a temper?

The moment we entered my old room and shut the door, I turned to him and wrapped my arms around him. We were kissing in the next instant, and it was electric, consuming, the force of it so great I felt as if I became a part of him.

"Ali," he said, when he finally came up for air. "People are always throwing the word *love* around, but before you, I never did. And I'd never needed to hear it, either. Then, the other night, you uttered those words to me, and it's okay if you don't remember, but I heard them, and it affected me, and now I want to hear the words for real because I love you so much it hurts. I *need* to hear the words. If you're ready to give them."

Huge step. The one that would send me over the cliff.

He took my hand and shoved it under his shirt, placing my palm on his skin, just over his heart, where the last part of my name was etched. "You're a part of me, and you'll always be a part of me, and if you need more time, that's all right, too."

"Cole…"

He shook his head. "Don't say anything. Not yet. I want to get the rest of this out."

My eyes widened. There was more?

"I think I've told you how stubborn you are, how curious and now, even jealous, and you're also quick tempered, and you've got the meanest right cross of all time."

"Hey," I said, losing a little of my happy buzz.

"But I get more joy from your smiles than anything else," he continued. "I look at you, and I want you. Actually, I have only to think about you to want you. There's a sweetness to you, a vulnerability you allow so few people to see, but I'm one of the lucky ones and I'll be forever grateful."

Oh.

Who was I kidding? I'd already leaped off the cliff.

"You're mine, Ali Bell."

Silence.

"Can I talk now?" I asked.

He nodded stiffly.

Did he fear what I had to say? "Breaking up with you was the toughest thing I've ever gone through. At least I thought so at the time. Staying away from you proved tougher. From the moment our eyes first met, I've been drawn to you. Not just because you're the hottest guy I've ever met, but also because you have a core of courage and honor and when I'm with you, I feel safe and protected, and even cherished. I might be yours, but you are certainly mine, and I'm never letting you go. I love you, too, Cole Holland."

"Thank God." His hold on me tightened.

Now for the bad news. "When I'm no longer able to use the antidote," I said softly, "I want to use the flames on me."

"No."

"Yes," I said. "You must."

"I can't lose you."

"Maybe you won't." To-do: *survive*.

"Maybe I will."

"Faith," I said. "Have faith in me, in this. The last time you didn't, we fell apart."

"Ali—"

"Light will chase away the darkness," I interjected.

"Ali," he repeated again.

"I know. I know it's hard." I kissed him and said nothing more. But I didn't change my mind.

I never would.

END AT A NEW BEGINNING

For the next week, I floated on clouds of bliss. I stayed dosed
up on the antidote, so I stayed somewhat strong, though I
had moments of utter weakness and moments of depraved
hunger.

Z.A. was fighting.

Cole rarely left my side. He showed me the Christmas
present he'd gotten for me—a drawer in his bedroom. I'd
jumped into his arms, wound my legs around his waist and
whooped like a madwoman. He'd broken up with Mackenzie when she moved in, citing things were getting too
serious. For me, he said, things couldn't get serious enough.

Afterward, he'd taken me to visit Jaclyn. Poor girl. Since
our rescue, she had turned away every visitor. Me, she'd let
inside her bedroom, and she'd hugged me and sobbed until
she'd passed out from exhaustion.

I was now determined to draw her back into the world.

Wren and Poppy had been there, hanging out with Justin. They knew he and Cole were friends once again, so I was a little surprised to learn Wren and Justin were still dating. I was also surprised when the girls talked to me, as if we were still on decent terms, and promised to call.

Change. No matter where we were, it always showed up.

Right now all of the slayers and those in the know were in Cole's barn, gathered around a huge TV screen, watching a video of five-year-old Cole being trained by his father to fight zombies.

He was beyond adorable—Cole, not his father—with a mop of black hair and big violet eyes. He got a little over-eager with the nunchaku and nailed his dad between the legs. The crowd burst into laughter.

I was perched on his lap. He grinned at me, saying, "Yeah. I'm just that good."

I loved this playful side of him.

Who was I kidding? I loved every side of him.

Kat, who sat beside us, shouted, "Rewind that!" and threw popcorn at the screen. "Mr. Holland's expression was all, like, oh, no, I'm going to need my balls reattached, and Cole's was all, you're about to lose something else, sucka."

She and Frosty had not broken up once since she'd confessed her illness. And Reeve's talk with Bronx had gone better than she'd dreamed—and exactly as Kat and I had expected. He was fully committed to her and demanded exclusivity.

Everyone was so happy. Even Veronica seemed to be at peace. (I wondered if she'd made use of Gavin again.)

I rested my head on Cole's shoulder, and he hugged me

tight. We still hadn't had sex. As much time as he'd spent with me, Nana had spent with me. And if not Nana, Mr. Holland or Mr. Ankh. Or Kat and Reeve. We were never left alone, and I got it, I did. Everyone knew Cole's kisses sometimes overwhelmed me, allowing Z.A. to take over my body.

Sometimes not even a kiss was necessary. And oh, glory, now was one of those times. I was rubbing my nose against the length of his neck, I realized, barely even conscious of it, getting caught up in the sweetness of his scent. My mouth watered.

Hungry, I thought.

No. Oh, no.

Smell so good.

No! Never.

Must feed!

No.

Shaking, I held my breath and stood. "I…have to go," I said.

"Something wrong?" he asked, looking up at me and frowning. He held on to my waist, keeping me in place.

"I need another dose."

The frown intensified. "But you had one only half an hour ago."

"I know." A sickening heat swept over me, causing me to both sweat and shiver. A sensation I knew well. Only this one was far more intense. A strange buzz replaced the noise in the room. "I…I…" I backed away from him, shaking my head. "It's worse this time."

"Ali?" Kat reached out to grab me, only to shriek in pain and jerk back.

Frosty jumped up and threw her behind him.

Cole jumped to his feet, as well. I glanced down. The red flames had returned, crackling over my hands. My *human* hands. The fire was so strong it had breached my spirit and seeped out of my flesh. As I fought to douse it, the blaze spread.

Everyone but Cole scrambled away from me. "Ali," he said, approaching.

"Don't touch me," I croaked. "I'm going to walk out of here, and give myself a final dose. Then someone is going to use their flames on me. Please."

He violently shook his head. "They'd have to get through me, and that's not happening."

Z.A. whispered inside my head. *You think you could have lasted this long if I hadn't let you? I've been waiting for this moment, when the antidote would no longer help you. So go ahead. Dose yourself again. See what happens.*

I watched in horror as the flames spread even farther, to my elbows. And it hurt. Oh, it hurt. Pain shot through me, undeniable, agony in its purest form. "Have to…go," I panted. "Go. Everyone."

Not heeding my command, Cole picked me up. I was careful to keep my hands pressed against my middle, away from him, and my ankles straight out. He stopped at the table piled with food and drinks and anchored me against his chest to sweep everything to the floor. Then he gently laid me down.

I heard the gurgle of spilling liquid as he peered at me.

"Fight it," he commanded.

The flames spread to my shoulders. "Trying."

"Try harder."

The rest of the slayers surrounded me. I saw pity. I saw fear. I saw dread.

They hadn't left. They needed to leave.

You're going to die, and I'm going to rise.

"Don't let her live," I said. "Kill her. Kill her through me."

Impossible now, she gloated. *I'm going to feast on him. Empty him.*

"No," he said, his voice breaking at the end. "Anything but that."

"Cole, have to…kill her…*please*." She wouldn't stop with him. She would destroy *everyone*. "She's here… Wants you."

"No," he insisted. "There has to be another way."

Tears fell down my cheeks, and even those burned. "Please," I begged. "Hurt. I hurt. The pain. Too much." And like the flames, it was only growing stronger.

"You'll just have to bear it, because I can't bear to lose you. If you die, I'll go with you."

"No," I shouted, and I think the other slayers did the same.

"Fight, then," he demanded. "With everything you've got, fight."

Didn't he understand? That was what I'd been doing.

I tried to scoot away from him, my gaze scanning the faces of those around me. "Help."

"I survived it," Gavin rushed out. "She accidentally touched me with her flames, and I survived. The zombies had bitten me, and she had to give me the antidote, and she burned me. Afterward, I felt stronger than ever before."

I'd already told him.

He shook his head, giving Gavin the same denial he'd given me. "You didn't have a full-grown zombie living inside you."

"True, but if you do nothing, she dies anyway and we'll have to battle her evil twin. A twin with powers of her own."

Cole scrubbed a hand down his face, clearly torn. "Ali touched Kelly with her flames, and he burst into ash."

"She isn't like Kelly."

"Did you not hear me? There's a *zombie* inside her. Right now she's more like Kelly than like you."

"I heard. Now hear me," Gavin said, reaching out. "I'm going to do this for her whether you like it or not. I'm not just going to watch her die."

"Wait." Cole grabbed his wrist, stopping him. "Let me think."

"You've been thinking. The time for action has come." That said, Gavin used his free hand to punch him in the face.

Cole stumbled backward, and Gavin moved closer to me, his spirit arm rising from his physical arm. A second later, he flattened firelit hands on my chest.

I screamed as I realized *this* was pain, not what I'd felt before.

Thankfully it didn't last long. The red flames burned him, and he hissed and jerked away.

Cole shoved him. "You better pray she doesn't—" His gaze landed on me and he jolted. "Ali, your color is better." He reacted instantly. His spirit stepped out of his body. Eyes narrowed, he held out his hands, and white-gold flames lit over both, glowing brightly. He was shaking as he pressed his palm over my chest—inside my chest.

I released another scream.

No! Z.A. shouted.

The red intensified, and though Cole hissed from the pain of it, he didn't back off.

Lucas left his body, too, and jerked him away from me, shouting, "She might not mean to, but she'll kill you, my man."

Cole fought him, throwing the boy backward. I sagged against the table, the red flames spreading faster, as if to compensate for what Cole had tried to do. Then Cole was once again beside me, once again touching me.

The pain magnified a thousand degrees, shooting through me, eating at me, consuming me, and another scream burst free. My back arched, coming up off the table, all of my weight settling in my shoulders and toes. I'd shatter. Any second, I would shatter.

What if Cole died because of this?

"S-stop," I managed. "Stop."

He snarled, but never severed contact.

"Cole!" Frosty yelled. "Stop this. We won't let you do this."

"Help me pull him away," Bronx gritted.

My skin felt as if it were snapping and popping and ripping away. The agony... Nothing compared to this. Now it was too much, too much, far too much. I *wanted* to die.

"The red is fading now," I heard Gavin shout. "She's healing. Help Cole. Light up and put your hands on her."

I wasn't sure how many seconds—minutes?—passed before

everyone obeyed. I couldn't see past the pain, but I eventually felt pressure on my ankles, knees, thighs, belly, arms and shoulders. A terrible heat filled me up and split me apart.

No! Zombie Ali shrieked. *No, make them stop, make them stop!*

No longer on…my to-do…list, I tried to tell her.

Her voice grew quiet, quieter…until it evaporated altogether.

And then the pain was…leaving?

Yes, I realized a few seconds later. It was. The heat was becoming bearable, almost pleasant. I sagged against the table, finally able to breathe.

My eyesight cleared, and I could see flames dancing all over me; they were no longer red, but gold, like they were supposed to be.

The slayers had saved me.

Their hands fell away from me. Someone held a mirror in front of my face, and I looked, seeing no sign of Z.A. Then the mirror was gone, and I was staring at Cole, marveling that I experienced only a desire to hug and kiss him, not to bite.

Excitement, relief and undiluted joy filled me, and I found the strength to lift my arms and encircle his neck. "Cole," I sobbed.

His hands shook as he brushed the hair from my face. "You're still here. You're still here!"

I was, and he was, though there were blisters all the way up his arm—blisters I had caused. "I'm so sorry I hurt you."

"Don't be. I'm not."

"Well, don't ever do anything like that again, do you hear me?"

"Don't ever scare me like that again."

"Don't worry."

He pressed a swift kiss into my mouth. "The light chased away the darkness."

Yes. I'd finally died to the evil and lived to the light.

"But your father. Your grandfather. Kelly. They ashed when you touched them with the flames."

True. I'd put my glowing hands on all three men, and they'd ashed. "My dad and grandfather were fully zombie, with no humanity left. And Kelly had destroyed his own humanity with his actions. I was still fighting." A thought occurred to me. "Have you ever put your hands on another slayer like that?"

"No. Never. We were too afraid we'd burn each other."

I sat up, surprised to find there was no ensuing dizziness, no weakness. Just pure, unadulterated strength. Actually, I'd never felt better.

Check off list: *kill Z.A., survive.*

I flexed my fingers, popped the bones in my neck. "There isn't a trace of the zombie toxin," I said, marveling. "I don't need the antidote. I don't need anything. I'm one hundred percent racer ready."

His violet gaze studied my face. "You look it. The bruises have fled. The chapped lips are gone. The gauntness has even left you."

We'd had the power to do this all along; we just hadn't known it. Now I suspected none of us would ever need the antidote again. We wouldn't have to worry about developing an immunity to it. We wouldn't ever have to stop fighting the zombies. We could help each other. Strengthen each other.

Someone would have to get bitten, and we would have to try this again to be sure, but deep down I knew I was right. Even Mr. Holland would be able to fight the zombies again.

Kat shoved her way through the crowd, shoved Cole aside and threw her arms around me. "You're healed!"

I hugged her back.

And there was Reeve, wrapping her arms around me, and then the three of us were jumping up and laughing. I wanted this for Kat, couldn't stand the thought of losing her to kidney disease. What would the fire do to her, though? Would we kill her if we touched her, a nonslayer, with the flames?

What I knew: she was going to die if we didn't.

I bet I could read the journal now. The answer might be inside it.

"Okay. My turn." Cole pried me out of the girls' arms and pulled me into the locker room. He faced me.

Before he could speak, I stood on my tiptoes and pressed my mouth into his.

His hands wrapped around my waist and lifted me, even as he pressed my back into the wall. I wound my legs around him and drew him ever closer. The kiss deepened, our tongues rolling together, sure and confident, driving me crazy with heat and sweetness and sensation.

His strength surrounded me. He was all that I knew, all that I wanted to know. We were the only two people alive. And we were together. Now, always.

"You need to sleep in your old bedroom tonight," he said. "I'm sending everyone home and sneaking in."

"Don't want Kat and Reeve to hear your best moves?"

"Don't want Kat and Reeve to hear the way you respond to my best moves."

Oh, my.

"Are we officially back together?" I asked.

"I should spank you for even saying that. We've been together this whole time. You were just being stubborn." He kissed his way down my neck. "I've never been so scared in my life, Ali. I've been trying to hold it together, but watching you spiral, then watching you fade and not knowing what to do…" He shuddered.

"I told you to have faith." I nibbled on the lobe of his ear. "We survived and we learned. We're stronger than ever now."

He moaned, tilting his head to allow me better access. "Against the zombies, yes. But what about Anima? They're still out there, and they have to be stopped for good."

"We'll figure it out," I said. "Right now you're going to kiss me until I have a permanent impression of your lips on mine. Then you're going to send everyone home. Then you're going to sneak into my room, as promised. *Then* you're going to show me just how much you love me."

"Consider it done. But if someone interrupts us tonight, I'm going to… I'm not sure there's an action violent enough."

I laughed.

He softened. "I love when you laugh. It's the perfect birthday present."

My eyes widened. "Today's your birthday?"

"No. January ninth."

A few days ago. I'd missed it, I realized, and frowned. "Cole—"

"No. You were sick, and I wasn't going to celebrate without you."

"Well, you're eighteen. Legal. You're getting a party," I said. "A surprise party."

He was the one to laugh this time. "Then why are you telling me about it?"

"Oh, just shut up and kiss me."

★ ★ ★ ★ ★

A NOTE FROM COLE

I'd rather not write this. You want to know how I feel. You want to know, in minute detail, why I did what I did, what happened behind the scenes, what I think of my mistakes, the outcome and what I plan to do next. You want me to describe the things I'm desperate to do with Ali.

Why don't you just take my sac, instead? The result will be the same.

I'm not a bare-your-heart-to-strangers kind of guy, and that's not going to change, so I'm not going to give you what you want. No, I'm not sorry.

I know this proves everything you've heard whispered about me. I'm too hard-core. I'm only nice to a select few. I'm mean, bossy. I'm not an easy guy to like. Some people can take me, but most would rather leave me.

I don't really care.

I am what life has made me.

Besides, you're wrong about all of it—I'm worse.

Here's what I *will* tell you: I've seen and done things that would make you vomit. I spend the majority of my time in the shadows, and sometimes darkness clings. Sometimes it's hard to shake off. But most important, I will die to protect what's mine—better yet, I will kill.

Ali is mine.

If you're out there, Anima—and I know that you are—if you're planning to make another move against my girl, you had better be prepared to battle the beast you'll wake. I will hunt you, and I will not stop. I will take you out one by one, until the last of you is gone.

You may look at me and see a teenager. An afterthought. I will look at you and see a target. A dead one.

I'm very good at hitting my targets.

So, think long and hard before you decide to take me on. There is nothing I won't do—*nothing*—to ensure the health and wellness of those I love. If you're smart, you'll run and hide before it comes to that.

This is the only warning you will receive.

Cole Holland

DEDICATION

To the two best kids any mother could ever have—my kids. R and V. I'm blessed to have you, blessed to have raised you and blessed to know you. May your lives be everything you dream. Mommy loves you.

To a wonderful husband who, after almost twenty years of marriage, still makes me feel pretty...even though I wear the same sweatpants almost every day of the week. Washed smoshed.

To my best friend Jill Monroe, who still takes my calls, even at the most inopportune times. What a treasure you are! One of my favorite divine connections.

To my "totes amazeballs" editor Natashya Wilson, who goes above and beyond for me every time. Your support means more to me than I can possibly say. And I don't think I can ever thank you enough for your notes on this book. Talk about nailing it! Woman, you make me smile.

To my mother, who, when I called crying, picked me up, dusted me off and helped me stand back on my feet.

To my agent, Deidre Knight, who supports me every step of the way. I'm excited to march into the future with you!

To Alyshea Rains. I'm blessed to know you!

And to God, because at one of the lowest points in my life, I looked up and there You were with Isaiah 43:1-2.

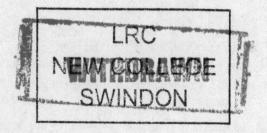

SHE WON'T REST UNTIL SHE'S SENT EVERY WALKING CORPSE BACK TO ITS GRAVE. FOREVER.

Had anyone told Alice Bell that her entire life would change course between one heartbeat and the next, she would have laughed. But that's all it took. One heartbeat, and everything she knew and loved was gone.

Her father was right. The monsters are real.

To survive, Ali must learn to fight the undead and trust the baddest of the bad boys, Cole Holland. But Cole has secrets of his own and those secrets might just prove to be more dangerous than the zombies.

www.miraink.co.uk

M290_AIZ

WE'LL EITHER DESTROY THEM FOR GOOD, OR THEY'LL DESTROY US

Alice 'Ali' Bell thinks the worst is behind her.
She's ready to take the next step with boyfriend
Cole Holland, the leader of the zombie slayers…
until Anima Industries, the agency controlling the
zombies, launches a sneak attack, killing four of her
friends. It's then she realises that humans can be
more dangerous than monsters…and the
worst has only begun.

www.miraink.co.uk

M380_TQOZH